THE MANSION

MICHAEL J. MILFORD

An Authors OnLine Book

Text Copyright © Michael J. Milford 2011

Cover design by Siobhan Smith ©

British Library Cataloguing Publication Data.
A catalogue record for this book is available from the British Library

ISBN 978-0-7552-0695-7

Authors OnLine Ltd
19 The Cinques
Gamlingay, Sandy
Bedfordshire SG19 3NU
England

This book is also available in e-book format, details of which are available at www.authorsonline.co.uk

About the Author

Michael J. Milford was born in Guernsey in 1938. During the war he lived in Halifax in England. He returned to Guernsey in 1945. He served in the British Army and the Merchant Navy between 1954 and 1965. He also lived in Australia for a few years.

He has written numerous poems and articles for the local newspaper. He is married to Joan and lives in Guernsey. This is his third novel; his other two were The Ernie Prettle Story and The Hypnotist.

To BRENDA,

Thanks, and all the Best.

Michael J milford. X.

14ᵗʰ sep.
2015.

Acknowledgements

I want to thank my wife, Joan, for helping with the typing and spelling, for her continual support in my endeavours, and for her patience when I insisted on her hearing the latest chapter.

Thanks also to my friends Tony and Jan Attwood, Beryl Turner, and Sandy McClean, for their help and faith in me.

To all my readers who said they enjoyed my first book, and gave me the inspiration to continue writing.

I would also like to thank my niece Claudette and grandniece Kira, for their help in computerizing the manuscript.

A special thanks to my publishing company for the work they put in in producing this book.

Contents

Chapter 1

THE BRIARS

History teacher Nigel Maythorn was at his desk in his classroom, it was just an ordinary day in school. In his lunch break he had visited his doctor for a check up, and was passed A1 His students were busy writing and for the moment all was peaceful. He looked up from his book and saw a pretty woman pass the window in the corridor that passed all the classrooms. She smiled and blew a kiss. He smiled back, but just gave her a wave. He had been going out with her for two years, ever since they had met when he had joined the school. It had been love at first sight. Jane was two years older than him at twenty five, and she taught English. Recently they had decided to get married within the next year, but first they had to find a nice house to live in. He had seen a few houses, but they had been too small for the big family that they were intending to have.

"O.K. put your books down, stop writing. Just a little revision, Jarvis. Tell me what you know about the TITANIC."

"A big liner that sank in the North Sea in nineteen hundred and twelve. It was said to be unsinkable, but it sank, sir."

"Did everyone go down with her? Did everyone drown?"

"No sir, over seven hundred were saved, and I read a book that said that some people got off the ship in Queenstown, before she sailed for the last time. Some people missed the ship, they were the lucky ones. And some were advised not to sail by some people who had had dreams. One man in particular, who was sure the ship would founder."

"Well done, Jarvis. James, the First World War, tell the class what I have taught you!"

"Yes, sir. The war started in 1914 and lasted for four years. Millions were killed, it was a terrible war. The worst battle was the Battle of the Somme in 1916. The bloodshed at that time was beyond belief. As the soldiers went over the top they were mowed down with machine gun fire. I wouldn't have wanted to be there, sir. No-one knew what it was like if they didn't experience it, it must have been hell!"

"Once again, well done James, it's very obvious to me that you lot are taking in everything I teach you. Now, let me ask you this; if you had been on the Titanic, or at the battle of the Somme, and know what you know now, how would you have gone about trying to tell those people on the ship that they were in grave danger? Or the soldiers in the trenches not to go over the top? Just say, if it was possible to go back in time, so to speak?"

"Don't know, sir," said Jarvis.

"It's impossible to go back in
time anyhow," said James, "so there's no point in discussing it, is there, sir?"

"Yes, you're right James, but let's have a little imagination here. Just suppose it was possible to go back in time, and you could change history, how would you go about it?" He looked at his class, smiling.

"Gentlemen, that is your weekend project, time travel, and how you would go about it, to save some lives!"

"Do you believe in time travelling? Is it possible to go back, or even into the future?" asked Jenkins.

"No," replied Nigel, "but I wish it was possible. I would have done my best to stop the Titanic from sailing, for a start!")

There was a bit of laughter in class as the bell rang for the end of class.

"At least a thousand words, gentlemen," Nigel said as his

students made their way to the door. "See you all on Monday morning."

He picked up a few papers, and put them in his briefcase. It was 3-30p.m. The calendar on the desk showed it was Friday 6th April 2007. Nigel locked his classroom door, and made his way to the teachers' day-room for his routine cup of coffee, before heading home.

"Had a good day darling?" Jane asked, smiling fondly at him.

"Normal day really, but it will get more interesting on Monday, because I've set my class a weekend homework project."

"And may I ask what project?"

"Time travel, you know, the possibility of going back to the past."

"What rubbish," she remarked. "That's impossible, and it will never happen."

"Maybe not, but it will open their minds, and make them think, I hope."

She shook her head in disbelief. "Surely you could have given them something more worthwhile to do."

"Like what?"

"How to live well now, in the present time, without dwelling on the past. It's today that counts, not what happened yesterday. Too many people live in the past!"

Nigel wasn't in the mood for an argument so said, "It's history that made us what we are today. Anyhow love, let's not argue about it."

"It's not an argument," she replied, "just talking my sweetheart."

"O.K, let's change the subject to present time, like our new home, when we find one. I would like to live in the country, as you already know, near Bakefield somewhere," Nigel said, with conviction in his voice.

"Oh, that reminds me, I was speaking to Jean earlier on, about our search for a home, and she told me that she was speaking to Alice, her sister, on Wednesday, who said there's a house going up for sale in Moreland Road. I know the area well, nice and quiet."

3

Nigel said, "But I believe the houses are small, only three bedrooms and little gardens."

"Well, what do you want Nigel, to live in a mansion?"

"That was a good guess my darling. I only want the best for my loved one, you know. "

"Can we go and see it, at least have a look? It might go at a good price. The people are going to live in Canada, and, I understand, want a quick sale."

"O.K, we'll go and see it, if that's what you want," he said, as he washed his cup, dried it, then placed it on the table top.

"I'll see you at seven tomorrow evening, might have a few drinks and a meal to celebrate the forthcoming viewing of our first home. I've got a lot of work to do, papers to mark." He kissed her gently, smiled, then left her to finish her coffee.

He went out to his car, and drove towards the home he shared with his mother and father, and younger brother. He had always been happy to live with his parents, but now he knew he was ready to take the plunge, and get married, with a home of his own. He had been looking at houses for the last six months, but none had made an impression on him, or her, come to think of it. Some had been too small, or overpriced. They had decided that it was time to tie the knot, but somehow hadn't yet decided on a date. They had been engaged for a year, and he loved her with a passion, she was the girl for him.

His mind was on such things as he drove on that Friday afternoon, through the lanes that took him home. The sign was hidden by tree branches, but Nigel caught a glimpse of it, as he slowed his car down to let a farm tractor go by in the narrow lane. He got out of the car, and walked back to where he could see the sign better, and noted the phone number and the agent's name. The big gates were beginning to show signs of rust, and the road leading up to the house was covered with leaves and branches, fallen during the winter storms. Even the sign looked like it had been up there for a while, the 'f' had fallen off, and it read 'OR SALE!' He returned to his car, got a note pad, and wrote down the number, then continued on his journey.

As soon as he got home, he phoned the agent, and made an appointment to see the property in the morning of the next day. He had decided that he would see this place on his own, then if it was suitable in his eyes, he would show Jane what he had come up with. He didn't relish the idea of living in the small house on Moreland Road, so he might give his wife-to-be a pleasant surprise, if the big house was at all acceptable. He liked the idea of living in a big house on the hill, like a Lord!

After a bath and a meal, he got down to marking some papers, then went to bed early. His appointment was at nine o'clock, when he was to meet the agent at the house. He didn't know as he drifted off to sleep that he was on the verge of a fantastic adventure!

Saturday morning was overcast, the rain holding off for the moment, but a storm was on its way. Nigel had his breakfast, and left the house for his appointment with Mike the estate agent at 9-00a.m. He was waiting in front of the iron gates, with the rusting lock in his hands.

"Good morning," said the agent, "not the best of days, a storm is on the way, so the forecast said."

"Yes, I believe that's true," Nigel answered, looking up at the grey sky.

"We'll leave the cars here, too many branches in the drive up to the house. But it's only a five minute walk; you can see the mansion from here."

Nigel liked the word 'mansion' it had a nice ring. 'Fancy living in a mansion,' he thought. On the way up to the house, the agent explained that the house on the hill had been on the market for a year. Why it hadn't sold, he had no idea.

"A lovely property like this would have been snapped up a few years ago, but the people who have viewed it didn't want it for various reasons, and of course, there have been the time-wasters," he had said.

He could see with a little effort the property could be restored to its former glory. It had been beautiful years ago, and had a history, having been the Headquarters of the British Army during both wars. Now it needed attention, it needed loving care.

"The overgrown garden," he said, "could soon be brought back to its original state, where flowers once bloomed, and the grass of the lawns was neat and tidy. Yes, a bit of loving care is needed."

They had reached the solid oak front door set between two columns. There was a round driveway, and a dried up fountain in the middle of an empty flowerbed.

"Ten acres of land," Mike said, as he unlocked the front door that led into a long corridor, with a bathroom on the left and a big room on the right and a staircase on the left side of the hallway. At the end of the hallway was a door that led into the large room with a gigantic fireplace. Bits of furniture had been covered over with white sheets that now looked a bit grubby with dust. There were pictures on the walls and one caught Nigel's eye; a man with a golden helmet on his head, a Spanish painting.

The rooms were very spacious. Mike showed Nigel the bedrooms and told him the potential of the property. But the agent had no need to sell this house because Nigel had already 'bought' it, he loved the place! He knew he wanted it, 'a dream come true,' he thought. Now, all he had to do was to get Jane to love it as well! The Easter holidays were coming up, and he could see himself getting the gardens in order. The house needed nothing doing to it, it was in good repair.

"What do you think?" Mike asked. "Nice place, there's plenty of scope to make it into a nice home."

"I will have to bring my fiancée to see it first, before I make a commitment. How much is the asking price anyhow?"

"You won't believe the price, it's £300,000 but you know, with some negotiations we may get the vendors to bring it down. They are going to America to live; they're living in a hotel at the moment, and are keen to sell. Here's my card, let me know if you are still interested, and we'll go from there."

"So, can I make another appointment with you, when I bring my girlfriend? I have to see what she thinks; you know what women are like. Anyhow, that's the only way to do things, is that not the case?"

"Look Mr.Maythorn, I'11 tell you what I'll do, I'll leave the keys with you, then at your own pace you can show your wife-to-be the whole property. There's a wonderful view of the River Test that goes up to Southampton, you can see the big ships pass by from the bedroom window. There's a little wood and a stream on the side of the house, and some sheds and out-houses where you could keep a pony, or even a pig!" Nigel laughed.

"Just a thought," said Mike, handing over the keys to the gate and the front door."Feel free to come here when you want to, and when you have made your decision, bring back the keys and, who knows, you could own a mansion!"

"Sounds good," said Nigel. The men shook hands on the deal and both men left the house; it had just started to rain. They walked down the drive to their cars.

"More branches down tonight I expect," said Nigel.

"Yes, I guess so. Now I have to show somebody another house in Moreland road this morning. I'm hoping to get this afternoon off and get home by the fire. Hope to see you soon, take care," Mike said, as he got in his car, and drove away.

Nigel got into his car and was just about to drive off when he had second thoughts. Why was he going home? It was only 9-50a.m. He had nothing to do at home, so he opened the gates again, shut them behind him, and went back to the house. He spent the next hour looking in every room and closets. He made some notes and did some measuring in each room. He had a feeling at one time that he knew the house well, a feeling of déjà vu came over him, a strange sensation! What a stroke of luck he had had; if he hadn't pulled over for that tractor yesterday, he wouldn't have ever been in his mansion now, he thought. Now all he had to do was to get Jane here to see his dream. He looked at the big fire-place once more, and walked down the hallway to the door, locked it, and walked around the place before he set off home; it had been a fruitful morning.

His father was happy to hear of his dream house, as Nigel enthused about the size of the place.

"I know that house," his father said, "I remember going up there a few years ago, back when you were still at school, if I recall.

Me and your mother went there for a party. The Mays had it then, they lived there for years. Wonderful people, Mrs. May was on the church council, that's where she met your mother, good friends they were. Then we heard that they left without telling anyone, and left everything behind, all the furniture, all their clothes. It's still a mystery, they were never heard of again, they were nice people. Yes, I remember the house on Eastern hill, big beautiful rooms, nice gardens, all prim and proper you could say. There was a big fireplace in the dining room, is it still there?" he enquired.

"Yes Dad, it's still there, a little dirty, but it's certainly the centre piece. But a little bit of elbow grease, I'll have it gleaming again in no time," Nigel said.

"How much is it going for?"

"I don't know yet, we will have to see, but I may get it for a lot less than the asking price, the vendors are keen to sell. They're going to America. Come to think of it, I heard today that another couple are going to Canada, is everyone leaving this country?" Nigel said shaking his head.

"Has Jane said 'yes' to it then?"

"No Dad, she hasn't seen it yet, I hope to take her to see it tonight when I pick her up. We're going for a drink and a meal down at the pub, the Fox and Hounds Inn."

"Well, at least the house isn't too far away from here, not too far for us to visit. To think of my son living in a mansion on the hill!" Both men smiled.

"I'll phone Jane and tell her the news. I can't wait until tonight."

"Good idea, son. Do you want a cup of tea?"

"Yes, that's a good idea, Dad, thanks."

Nigel went into the other room to use the phone.

"I've found our dream home darling," Nigel said with enthusiasm in his voice.

"So have I, in Moreland Road," she replied.

"Never mind Moreland Road, wait till you hear my news, you'll be over the moon!"

"And where is this wonderful house you've found?"

"It's the mansion on Eastern hill, it's got acres of land, a stream, a wood, big rooms, and it will be a bargain once we negotiate."

"Hold on, Nigel, don't I get a say in this? I haven't even seen the house yet, I may not like it."

"Oh yes, you will like it, you will love it. I can tell you now, it's a dream come true. I looked at it this morning, and it's just great. There's a bit of work to do to the gardens, but I'll soon sort them out!"

"Since when have you been into gardening, Nigel?" she said, sounding a bit sarcastic.

"I'll soon learn, my brother will help me, and I'm sure my father will also lend a hand. Anyhow dear, don't put up barriers, it's my dream, and I hope it will be yours once you have seen the place."

"And when will that be?" she asked.

"Tonight, when I pick you up at seven o'clock. We can look it over before we go for our meal, how does that sound darling?"

"O.K. I'm looking forward to this, Nigel, but I will look at the house in Moreland Road as well, before I make a decision. You understand we have to get it right, no mistakes. How much is it? you haven't said."

"It's £300,000."

"What?" she replied in shocked response. "We haven't got that kind of money. Don't forget we are only teachers you know, the pay's not that great."

"Don't worry yourself, my father will help us out, plus a bank loan and the money we have saved. Also, we may get it cheaper, the people are very eager to sell, they want to go and live in America," Nigel said with conviction.

"OK, we will have a look at the place tonight. I have to go and have my bath now, I want to smell nice for you darling."

"OK, see you later, love you."

"Love you too." He felt he had got his message over to her, she would love the place, he felt sure. He spent the rest of the afternoon drawing sketches of where he would put the furniture. Then he had a bath and got ready to meet his Jane.

"That's nice for you son, if that's what you want," his mother said, as he slipped on his coat. "Your dad was telling me of your house find, I'm happy for you." She didn't like to see her son leave home, although she knew that it was bound to happen one day. "It sounds like a nice place."

"It is Mum, it's just what I want, there's a sense of history about the place."

"That's true," his father said. "For years it was a general headquarters for the army, all the top army people used to work and live there during both wars, the First World War and the Second, but they sold it after a while. It has been reported that strange things have happened up there."

"You've never told me that before, Dad."

"I didn't know you were interested, that's why I'm saying it now, because you are interested in the property. I know it was built in 1900, and it was owned by some very rich people. It would be on the deeds who owned it, the estate agent would know." He went back to reading his newspaper.

"I'll ask when I see him again, I would like to know the house's history," said Nigel, finishing his cup of tea.

"We went there once, to a party, Mavis Mays invited me and your father. It was a nice house, if I remember, but we didn't get to see much of the grounds."

"I know Mum, Dad told me." He kissed his mother and left to pick Jane up.

He felt excited at the prospect of owning such a prestigious house, if he could get the price down from what the vendors were asking.

Jane was waiting outside her parents' home. As they drove, Nigel explained that the gardens needed a lot of work, but he was prepared to do the job. He hoped she wouldn't be put off by the unkempt gardens, the place hadn't been lived in for awhile.

"We are just going to have our first look, then if we want to go ahead and buy it, the estate agent will show us around in detail. He even gave me the keys so we can spend as long as we like there," Nigel pointed out.

"Sounds good to me," said Jane.

The drive took them half an hour through the countryside. The storm raged, and lightning zigzagged across the black sky.

Are the water and electricity still on?" Jane asked.

"I don't know, I didn't ask."

"But you were there this morning, didn't you switch on any lights, or use the toilet?"

"No, I just took some measurements and checked out how many rooms there are. I just didn't think of lights," Nigel said, shaking his head. "We'll find out when we get there. If the electricity has been cut off, we'll have to abandon our visit until tomorrow. It's too dark tonight with this bloody weather."

The rain was beating down as they got to the big iron gates. From there the house on the hill could be seen because the lightning lit it up.

"Do you know Nigel, this reminds me of a film I once saw, called

'PSYCHO', remember Bates Motel, and the lightning lit up the place?"

"Well, that's a great start, you thinking our new home looks like a horrible house of horrors you once saw at the movies!" said Nigel, looking disappointed.

"It looks spooky to me," Jane said.

"Hell Jane, how can you say that, we haven't even got out of the car yet, we're not even on the property! And the view's not that great from here, with this rain, and you say it's 'spooky'."

At that moment a thunderclap made them both jump, and the lightning flashed across the house, once again, making it look ghostly.

"Nigel, I'm not getting out of the car in this rain, we'll get soaked before we get to the front door! And if the lights are off, we have no way of looking at it properly. Let's come back tomorrow in the daylight?"

"You're right darling; it would be pointless trying to view it in this weather. I'll get more information on the house from the agent. Shall we abandon it for tonight, and go for a meal at the

Fox and Hounds pub? We can celebrate the fact that we have seen our first home, at least from the road, for you."

"Now you are talking sense my darling. I knew you would see it my way," she said with a smile.

"I always see it your way, you have a way of making me," Nigel said with a laugh.

The car pulled away from the gates, and in a short drive they were outside the public house called the Fox and Hounds. The pub was snugly warm, with a roaring fire, an oasis for people who wanted to get out of the stormy night. They parked the car as close as was possible to the pub's entrance and made a dash for the door. They held hands and laughed at the way they ran into the pub. They took off their coats and hung them on the rack near the entrance, then went to the bar. There weren't many customers in the pub, and the storm kept regulars away, apart from one or two die-hard drinkers.

Nigel and Jane had been there before, but only on nights when a band was playing, so they were known by the old landlord, Brian Small.

"Hello Nigel, what are you doing here on a night like this? There's no music on tonight," said Brian.

"We're celebrating! You know my fiancée Jane?" Nigel said, looking at his wife-to-be with a smile.

"Of course I do, how can I forget a beautiful woman like her?"

"I bet you say that to all the girls, Brian. I know you have a way with the ladies," she joked.

"Me?" he said, smiling. "What can I get you lovely people?"

"I'll have a pint of beer, if Jane will drive home?"

"Of course I will, you don't have to ask," she said, sitting on the bar stool.

"OK, a pint of beer, and a small glass of wine, one will be ok."

"One won't hurt you," Brian said, pouring the pint. "What's the celebration then?"

"We're buying a house near here..."

Jane stopped Nigel talking by saying, "Who said we are buying anything yet? Let's see it first, love."

"Sorry, I mean we are looking, maybe to buy it. It's the house on the hill, Eastern Hill, do you know the place?"

Brian's face changed to one of concern. "The Briars, at Eastern Hill?" he enquired.

"That's the place," Nigel said with pride in his voice. Brian then went into the other bar to serve a customer.

"He doesn't seem to like the place, did you see the expression on his face?" Jane said.

"I didn't notice," Nigel lied. "What are we eating? I'll get the menus from the dining area." He left her at the bar.

"Got the menus Brian?"

"There, over on that table," he said, pointing to a table near the window.

"What's wrong with the house? I saw your face in there?"

"I didn't want to say anything in front of your girlfriend, but my advice to you, my boy, is leave well alone, that place has a curse on it. I can tell you I've heard stories of heartache, tragedy, bad luck! Every family who's ever lived there has had great suffering since the time it was built. My grandmother told me the story when I was a boy. She remembered when it was built in the nineteen hundreds you know."

"I don't know anything about the house really, except that I intend to buy it."

"You're making the biggest mistake of your life. Look, I'llexplain it to you after you have eaten, I don't want to spoil your meal," Brian said, walking away to do more bar work.

Nigel took the menu back to Jane. They ordered, had a nice meal, then returned to the bar.

"Nice meal Brian, give my regards to the chef," Nigel said.

"Not likely, she's too big-headed already, I don't give her any compliments. She knows she's good anyhow, after all that's why I married her thirty five years ago," Brian laughed.

The evening wore on, the storm was still in its fury, with the rain beating a rhythm on the window panes. It was cosy in the bar, and no-one wanted the evening to end.

Jane excused herself, and said she had to go to the ladies' room.

Brian took his cue. "This I can say, the first people to live there went to America in nineteen hundred and twelve, for a holiday. What a tragedy!"

"What, the holiday?" Nigel said.

"They never had a holiday, they went over to America on the Titanic, and never came back. The next family had three brothers who went into the army and were all killed at the battle of the Somme in nineteen sixteen! Then again in nineteen twenty nine the family lost all their money on the stock market, and the gentleman of the house was found hanged in one of the bedrooms!"

"Jane mustn't be told any of that; she is not the kind of woman who would live in a house where someone had committed suicide."

"I didn't say it was suicide did I? It was reported that his family strung the old feller up, when they found out that they were skint. Apparently he had been warned that the stock market crash would happen, but he didn't heed the warning. I'll tell you, my friend, don't put your hard-earned money in a place like that. It will only bring you bad luck, like it has done to many people who have lived there, it's got a bad 'feel' about it."

Nigel didn't say a word, just sat there listening to the old landlord, slowly dismantling his dream.

"Maybe all those things didn't really happen that way. Maybe there was a rational explanation, or maybe they are just rumours! I'm not superstitious and I believe what has gone has gone, and what's been done is done, and it can't be changed."

"Things can be changed, if only people would listen to advice," Brian said, "like I'm telling you that you shouldn't buy the house, because I believe that there is a bad omen or curse on the place. They weren't rumours; believe me, on what my grandmother told me. Do you know I was never allowed to play in the woods near the house when I was a child? My mother forbade me to go around there. Two children died in the pond on the property, for example, that was another family tragedy. And that was true, because it was in the papers. But after all I say to you, you won't take my advice, will you? You will go ahead and buy it?" said Brian, wiping a glass and putting it on the shelf.

"We are going to see it tomorrow, and I will take on board what you have said. But I saw some potential there today, and we are desperately looking for a house before we get married this year."

At that moment Jane came back. "What are you two talking about, you seem to be in deep conversation?"

"About our forthcoming wedding this year," said Nigel, holding her hand, and smiling. "And we've been talking about the house on the hill. It's called The Briars, by the way love."

"I thought it was called Bates Motel when I saw it lit up tonight by the lightning," she said, laughing.

"I understand what you mean," Brian chipped in. Nigel gave him a certain look, as if to say, 'Please say no more'.

"One for the road, then we must head home, this storm doesn't seem to be going away. A beer and a pineapple juice please, Brian."

"Coming up," he said, reaching for the glasses.

Half an hour passed, Nigel called to Brian, "I'll see you again, and maybe you can tell me more history about what we were talking about? I'm very interested in history. Did you know I teach it at the school?"

"I knew you were a school teacher," Brian said, "but I didn't know it was History you taught."

"Yes, I'm fascinated by the subject," Nigel said, as he finished his drink and went to put his coat on. Jane was by the window, looking out on a very wet, dark night. Nigel joined her.

"We have to make another dash for the car darling. I was hoping this would pass before we left here, but it's not to be."

At that moment, the whole sky lit up as a gigantic lightning bolt streaked across the dark night, and hit the ground with a thud.

"Hell, I felt that," Nigel said. "I'm glad I wasn't under that one, it would destroy a house! I'm glad I'm in here and not where that one hit."

"Same here," Jane said looking concerned.

Nigel gave her a hug. "Let's get home, it doesn't seem to be easing."

They said 'goodnight' to Brian.

"Pop in any time you want, I can give you the full history if you want it," Brian said, looking stern.

"I might take you up on that, goodnight," Nigel said, going out of the pub door.

"What history was he on about?" Jane enquired.

"Oh, the history of the pub and the area."

"How boring," she replied, as they set off for home.

The bolt had indeed hit a house. It had hit the chimney of The Briars, and a panel had been dislodged in the gigantic fireplace which had been in place for years! It was very important that the panel would have to be fixed, and fast! But at that moment Nigel was ignorant of its importance.

Chapter 2

THE GATEWAY

The estate agent was optimistic as he entered the Portland Hotel lobby. He had an appointment with Mr. and Mrs. Cladmore to up-date them on the sale of their house, The Briars. Mike didn't normally work on a Sunday but after the phone call from Mr. Cladmore, he said he would pop in to bring them up to date, on his way to his mother's house.

Mrs. Cladmore was an American citizen and wanted to go back home, as she called the U.S.A., even though she had lived in England for years. She had come to England with her English husband who she had met in New York in nineteen seventy seven. They had made many trips to the Big Apple over the years, and now wanted to live there permanently. The Briars had been bought by them in nineteen ninety eight, but she had never been happy there, and was keen to sell. They were comfortably off, but the thought of living in a hotel indefinitely was not to both their likings. She had had a hard battle to get her husband to agree to sell, but at last he had relented, to save their marriage.

She hated the house for several reasons, and was convinced that the place was haunted! She had seen ghosts on many occasions, strange noises in the night, and had seen complete strangers walk through the house, then just disappear! One day in two thousand and one, in August, a complete stranger had come to the house. She had thought at first that he had come to be a house-sitter (a person who lives in the house while the owners are on holiday). She had even started to interview him! But it turned out he wasn't a house-sitter after all. He told her he had something very important to tell her, a warning, and she had thought he was mad! He had said to get her son out of the work he was doing in New York, and warned her not to visit him at his place of work, which they had intended to do. She had told her husband to come in and hear the man tell his story, and he had related it again, that they should not visit the place where her son worked, but most of all, get him to give up his job. 'Preposterous', she had thought at the time, and they went to America just the same. The plane was delayed luckily. But their son had died in the North Tower, on the eleventh of September two thousand and one.

Then there was another time when another stranger in the house was mistaken for one of the guests when they were having a fancy dress party. He told them that the house was going to be hit by a bolt of lightning, and they would die as the house burned down, if they didn't put a conductor on the chimney! They did, after the insurance company insisted that it was a 'must' so reluctantly they put the conductor in place. The strange goings-on had taken their toll and Mrs. Cladmore decided to sell. They had moved out six months ago and were waiting to see the agent.

Mike, the agent, went to the reception desk. "Will you tell Mr. and Mrs. Cladmore that Mike from the estate agency is here for the appointment we have at ten o'clock?"

"Sure thing, sir," said the man behind a highly polished desk. He picked up the phone and after the briefest of calls, said that the Cladmores would be down right away, and would meet Mike in the bar.

"Thanks," Mike said, as he walked toward the bar area. It was empty at that time of the morning. He chose a table near a window, sat down to wait and the Cladmores arrived within five minutes.

"Good news," he said, before any 'good mornings' were exchanged. "Good news Mr.Cladmore," he repeated with a smile. "I had a man interested in your property yesterday, he seemed to be keen. He is showing the place to his wife-to-be, as I talk I would think. I let him have the keys, I put no 'hard sell' on him, so we might be lucky this time. We have had no-one come forward to buy the house, since you left. As you may know, there's a stigma attached to the place, people in the area think it's haunted, but we know that's rubbish, don't we?"

Mrs. Cladmore looked at her husband, but didn't say anything.

"One of those people is sitting right opposite you, Mike," said Bob Cladmore.

"You think it's haunted do you?" Mike asked her.

"I know it is," she said with conviction. "I was happy when we first moved in, for a while. Then strange things started to happen, and in 2001 we were warned by this complete stranger, who came to the house, to not go to New York to see our son who worked in the Twin Towers. He warned us that there was going to be a tragedy, but we didn't believe him. We lost our son, and if our plane hadn't been delayed we would have been there as well! If only we had heeded the warning, we may have saved our only son." She looked down, although nearly six years had passed, the memory was still crystal clear. "If only we could go back in time, how things would have been different. I may have been a grandmother now!"

"Don't, love," Bob said, holding his wife, sharing her sorrow.

Bob took up the story, "We also had this stranger who appeared from nowhere, who gave us a warning, he told us to get out of the house because it was going to burn to the ground! Naturally we asked him how he knew that, and he just said that he came from the future! How preposterous, we both thought, didn't we dear?"

Alice Cladmore nodded, remembering the incident. "He said we had to put a conductor in the chimney, because a bolt of lightning would hit the house, and without a conductor installed, the house would burn to the ground. We checked with our insurance company, and they insisted we get the job done, otherwise they wouldn't give us house insurance, so we thought it was prudent to get the job done. It cost us £8,000! Do you know,

Mike, we even thought of having a priest come in, to do whatever they do, to get rid of evil spirits, but we never did. Of course, we can't tell any prospective buyer this story, because nobody will ever buy it, I think it's best if we keep this quiet!"

"I will try my best to sell it; maybe we'll be lucky with this guy! I'll keep in touch with you. By the way, this man from the future you mentioned, do you remember if he said when the house would burn down?" Mike asked.

"Yes," said Bob, "he said, if I remember right, he said it would be 2007, this year! That's one of the reasons we got out, my wife is very superstitious." He looked at Alice, and smiled.

"He didn't tell you the exact date, did he?"

"No, he said that a bolt of lightning would strike the house. That's all." Bob said.

"That's very strange," said Mike, frowning.

"Why is that?" Alice remarked.

"Well, we were informed this morning that in last night's storm, the house was hit by a lightning bolt, and the chimney was badly damaged, and if it hadn't had a lightning conductor, it would have been a lot worse!"

"You mean the house could have been burned down?"

"Yes," said Mike, "it could have burned down."

"It's a pity it didn't," Alice said, "we would have got paid out by the insurance company!"

"Yes, but my dear, we may have still been living there, have you thought of that?"

"No, but I am now," she replied.

"I'll let you know if this man buys the house, we are as keen as you are to get the place off our books, I'll be in touch." Mike got up, shook hands with the couple, and left the hotel. 'A stranger from the future,' he thought, 'what a load of rubbish!' He shook his head in disbelief. How could people tell such stories, it was unbelievable! But then, he had met many strange people in his years of selling houses, but this was the strangest so far!

Nigel was up early and raring to go, this was the day that a big decision would be made. It turned out to be a lovely summer's day, and the big storm had gone. Nigel was a happy man as he drove to pick Jane up. As he passed the pub, he decided to go in for an early morning drink, but mainly to see Brian about what he had said the night before, concerning the history of The Briars house. At ten thirty he pulled into the car-park, the pub had just opened, and there were no drinkers yet, at this early hour.

"Morning Brian," he said, as he walked into the empty bar.

"Hello there, Nigel, I knew you would be back soon."

"How did you know that?"

"I saw it in your face last night," he said, as he drew a small beer for himself.

"Just an orange juice please," Nigel said as he sat on the same bar stool he had sat on the night before.

"What do you want to know?"

"History," Nigel said, "I want to know what you know about the house."

"As I have told you, I knew you would be back, so I've made up a list of people who lived there over the years. You may wonder why I take such an interest in the place, and I'll answer that as well." He pulled up a stool behind the bar, and had a sip of his beer."I'll start with the time the house was built. First off, as the story goes, the builders were set with problems from the beginning. I didn't tell you everything last night, because your lady was here, and I didn't want to frighten her."

"She's very fragile," Nigel pointed out.

"One day, so the story goes, my mother told me that her mother told her, that there was a gang of men, four of them, started on the footings in 1899,and the foreman set them working, then returned to his hut to make the tea. After just half an hour, he returned to the site, and there was nobody around. Tools had been left about, but there was no sign of the men, they had disappeared!"

"Maybe they had downed tools, and came here to the pub?" Nigel said, laughing.

"It wasn't funny at the time, the men just disappeared, and they were never seen again! Imagine the heartbreak of the wives and girlfriends, the children without their fathers? It was a tragedy! The police investigated, they were about for years, but the men were never ever seen again."

"Strange," Nigel said, shaking his head.

Brian continued, "There were markings in the footprints where the concrete had been disturbed, it was rock hard. But the building took shape, and it was finished in 1900. The first people who lived there were a Mr. and Mrs. Anderson and their daughter, lovely people it was said. They lived there for many years, and Mr. Anderson did a lot for the local people, with charity events held at the house. Tragedy struck them in nineteen hundred and twelve. They went for a holiday to America, and never came back, they left Southampton on the Titanic."

"That's a sad story in itself," said Nigel, sipping his juice.

"Yes, it was sad. In nineteen thirteen a family lived there for two and a half years, the Giles family. The army took the place over after that, it was the Headquarters throughout the rest of the war. A lot of the war's decisions were made there.

In nineteen nineteen a new couple bought the house, and in nineteen twenty nine he was found hanged, they were Mr. Charles Bloomberg and his wife. A Jewish couple lived there until nineteen thirty eight, a Mr. and Mrs. Bactram, then they went back to Poland, Warsaw. They ended their lives in Auschwitz concentration camp. Then the army took over through the Second World War, and they left in nineteen forty seven."

Nigel listened intently. "Brian, you're very good with dates. How and why have you taken such an interest in that house, and all the people who lived there?"

"I was once going to buy the place myself, with ideas to change it into an hotel, but the cost would have been too high, so I never went ahead with it. It was at that time that I went into the history of the place, and with what I was told and what I found out on my own accord, I'm glad I didn't go ahead. Do you know whenever there is a thunder storm, that place always gets struck with lightning? I've heard that it was struck again last night, it seems like someone up there has something against the place." He pointed skyward. "It's a wonder the place is still standing! Do you want me to continue? I don't mean to put you off your dream, maybe I should stop now?" Brian said, arms akimbo.

"No, carry on Brian, you're not putting me off at all. I'm not the one who's superstitious, that's Jane's department. I haven't been put off, I can still see a lot of potential in the house."

Brian nodded and continued. "The house was empty for a while, nobody seemed to want to buy it. Then in nineteen fifty, it was bought by a family who lived there for forty eight years, until nineteen ninety eight, nine years ago. And the bad luck on the house seemed to have ended, because the years I've been in this pub, there has been no incidents at all, the bad luck my mother told me about, seemed to end. But then it came back in two thousand and one. The people who lived there lost a son in America, the Twin Towers tragedy in New York. The house has been empty for the last six months. The people who owned it went to America, then came back, to sell it I believe. They now live in an hotel, and have been in here on occasion, Mr. and Mrs. Cladmore. And that, my friend, is all I know. I wouldn't live there, but then I'm like your fiancée, superstitious of things. There you go, now I've spoilt your dream!" He tossed the list of dates under the counter.

"No, you haven't, it's been very interesting to hear the history. And I'm grateful to you Brian; at least I've been warned!" he laughed.

"I'm just a bringer of bad tidings!" They both laughed.

Nigel looked at his watch, "it's time I went, I'm meeting the wife, and then we will be exposing ourselves to the 'unknown'".

He pretended to shudder, and smiled as he left the pub, then went to pick Jane up.

She was waiting outside the house. "Have you been waiting long darling?"

"No, I've just got back from looking at the house that Jean told me about. It's lovely, and it's within what we can afford," she said, full of enthusiasm.

"I'm sure when you see the house you called 'Bates Motel' you'll love it."

"Well, I'm keeping an open mind at the moment, but the house I've just seen would suit us down to the ground."

"Let's wait and see," Nigel said. They drove the twenty minutes to the house on the hill. The gates needed oil, they were hard to open, but at last they arrived at the front door. The gravel drive had weeds and grass growing in clumps, and everything in the garden had overgrown.

"Plenty of gardening for you love," she said, in a mild, slightly sarcastic way. He just looked at her and said nothing. They walked to the front door, it was five past eleven in the morning, Sunday the 8th of April. The door creaked open, and they found themselves in the hallway, with a staircase on the left. He tried the light switch, but the electricity had been turned off.

"It's a good job we didn't come up here last night, we would have seen nothing. You could have asked the agent if there was light," she said.

"I can't think of everything! I just assumed the lights were on," Nigel retorted. "Anyhow let's have a good look around this beautiful place." She gave him that certain look, as if to say, 'Who are you trying to kid?' She didn't like the place, as soon as she walked through the door!

They looked at the upstairs rooms, and Nigel pointed out the beautiful view of the river. They briefly looked in the kitchen, and at a big room that was used as a dining room. Then they came to the room where the gigantic fireplace stood. It was a big room and one could imagine that it may have been used in the past for conferences or board meetings. There was the picture of the man with the golden helmet on a wall, and a chest-of-drawers. Jane went over to the dresser, opened a drawer and looked in, with her back to the fireplace. Nigel went to admire the art work and carvings, and he took a step towards the recess inside the fireplace. But somehow he felt a strange 'force' stop him entering the space. 'How strange,' he thought. He walked to the other side of the recess, inside on the very edge and stepped into the space at the bottom of the chimney Breast. He was in a small alcove. The light from the chimney gave him enough light to see. He walked out again, back into the big room.

"I found a little recess in the fireplace, so when you turn around and can't see me, I know you'll wonder where the hell I got to, but I will only be in here, o.k.?" She didn't turn around at that moment. "Did you hear me Jane?"

Jane turned around from the drawers and walked the ten paces towards him, and said, "I hear you, but don't be long, we haven't got all day," and she turned on her heels, and returned to the drawer.

He entered the chimney space and saw some numbers like dates on the wall. As he turned around in the small space, he couldn't see the room that Jane was in, although he was now facing that way! He touched the number on the far side, just above his head, and a force like a magnet pulled him towards the panel-like partition, a flash of light flashed through his head. He fought the 'pull' at first, but as the 'force' grew stronger, he succumbed. It pulled him through the wall, and into the room he had just come out of.

The first thing he noticed was that Jane had gone, but so had the dresser, and the picture on the wall of the man with the golden helmet was also gone! There was furniture that he hadn't noticed before, there was a settee suite, a table and chairs, there were five pictures on the walls and the dust sheets had gone! He stood there for a few minutes, just amazed at it all. Then he heard voices coming from the hallway, so he walked across the room, it must be Jane talking to herself, she had done on occasions he thought.

He opened the door slightly and saw a lady looking at some labels on some luggage that, once again, he hadn't noticed when he had walked through the hallway a few minutes before!

"That's the labels done dear," he heard her shout out. She was dressed in old-fashioned clothes, he noticed the long dress she wore, and she was very pretty. A man also funnily dressed, came out of a room, and had a quick look at the labels, then they both went into the first room down the hall on the left of the front door. He wondered how the hell they had got in the house, he had the keys in his pocket! Then it dawned on him, the agent had given another couple another set of keys, and they were viewing the house as well. He stepped into the hall, closed the door quietly behind him, and went to the front door. Maybe Jane had gone back to the car. He knew she wasn't really interested in buying this house, he had sensed it. He opened the door and looked out, but there was no sign of her. He was just about to go back into the house, when the lady he had seen came out of the room.

"Oh, hello," she said with a smile, "have you come to see to the chimney? Are you the sweep?"

Nigel was taken aback, and then he noticed that his hands had some soot on them.

"No ma'am," he said, feeling a bit foolish, at being mistaken for a chimney sweep, "I've come to view the house."

"And why would you be doing that?" she asked demurely. "Because it's for sale, are you looking over it yourself?"

"Of course not, we own it."

"Oh, I thought you were in a hotel while it was being sold!"

"I think you're mistaken, this house is not for sale. Would you like to come and have a word with my husband, he's in the study?" she asked.

"Thank you," Nigel replied. She was a lovely well spoken lady, a bit old fashioned in her dress, but very nice, with a big smile.

At that moment a car pulled up in the drive. Nigel noticed that the weeds and grass growing out of the gravel had gone! The gardens were well kept, and the car was a very very old vintage type, with big wheels and an open top. The driver was dressed in old-fashioned clothes as well!

A little girl got out and ran to embrace her mother. "Who's the funny man ma?" she enquired.

"Now don't be rude, this gentleman's come to see Papa."

She turned to Nigel, "Sorry about that, you must know what children are like, they find everything and everyone funny, oh to be a child again."

"I understand. Can I ask you a question?" he said. "Are you going to a fancy-dress party?"

"Of course not, we haven't got the time for that, we are too

26

busy packing, we're going on holiday this coming week. Come and have a word with my husband." She led him into the study, and introduced him to her husband.

"This young man was at the front door dear, he said that he has come here today to look at our house. He believes, for some unknown reason, that it's for sale. Naturally I've told him it's not, unless you are selling it behind my back?" she smiled sweetly. He laughed out loud, "Goodness gracious, I would never do that, dear. Good afternoon sir, how do you do?" he asked.

"Very well sir, thank you." They shook hands.

"Would you like a cup of tea?" the woman asked.

"Thank you, but could I possibly have decaf coffee?"

"We have coffee, but I'm sorry I've never heard of decamp coffee, is that a brand?"

"Decaf, you've never heard of decaf?"

"No sorry," she replied, "will ordinary coffee do?"

"No, tea will be fine," he smiled, and turned back to the man, who had sat down.

"Take a seat," the man offered.

"Thank you," Nigel said, sitting down.

The lady of the house disappeared into the kitchen, with the little girl.

"Would you like to wash your hands? And you have a black smudge on your face?"

"Oh," said Nigel, looking at his hands, "I don't know how I got my hands so dirty. Thanks for the offer."

"The bathroom is in the hallway on the left."

"Thanks again, you are very kind,. He got up and left the room.

The bathroom was very old-fashioned, with hot and cold written on the taps. He switched on the light by habit, the light came on.

'That's funny,' he thought, 'there was no light a while ago, when I came into the house.' He washed his hands and face, and returned to the study.

"That's better, sir." He sat down. "So this house is not on the market, it's not for sale then?"

"No, it's certainly not for sale. How can anyone make that mistake? We will never leave here, I built the house twelve years ago, and we love it here."

At that moment the lady came back with the tea and a plate full of cakes. "You're welcome to a bite to eat Mr. eh…"

"Maythorn, Nigel."

"And where do you come from?"

"I live in Stockton, in Claymore Street, with my parents at the moment, but I'm to be married soon, that's the reason I'm here, I'm looking for a home, and I was led to believe that this house is for sale."

"And what do you do for a living young man?"

"I'm a school teacher, I teach History."

"What a fascinating subject," said the gentleman.

"Yes, I enjoy it very much." He drank his tea and ate two cakes. 'What lovely people,' Nigel thought.

"Well, if you will excuse me, Mr.Maythorn," said the lady, "I have to finish the packing, we're going on holiday you know."

"Oh of course, going somewhere nice?"

"Yes, we are going to New York."

"That's nice, what time's your flight?"

"Flight, what do you mean, flight?" she said with a frowned expression.

"Flight, you know, aeroplane type flight!"

"Never heard of such a thing," she remarked.

The gentleman looked at Nigel, also not understanding what he meant.

"No, we are going by ship," he volunteered. "From Southampton, sailing on the tenth this week.

"That's why we are leaving soon, to catch the train to Southampton, we're staying in a hotel until we leave. Goodbye Mr.Maythorn, it's been nice meeting you. Don't keep the young man from his business for too long, darling."

"Of course I won't," he replied. She left the room, her smile lingered on in Nigel's mind. "She's a lovely lady, if you don't mind me saying so sir?"

"No, I don't mind, she's the salt of the earth," replied the gentleman. The little girl came in at that moment. "Papa, I've got your morning paper."

"Thank you darling," he said, and placed it on the table in front of Nigel.

"What's that thing you have in your shirt pocket?" she asked Nigel.

"Darling, don't be so nosey, go and help Mama, she's packing upstairs."

"No, I don't mind at all," said Nigel. "It's only a mobile." He showed it to her.

"What's it for?" she asked. The man leaned forward in his chair to look closer.

"It's for getting in contact with people, haven't you got one?" Nigel enquired.

"No. How does it work? What do you mean, getting in contact with people?"

Nigel just smiled, they were playing a prank on him, he was sure.

"Millions of people all over the world have these things now, couldn't be without them, or the telly."

"Telly, what's a telly?" said the man.

"Oh, come off it, this is a joke, you're playing a joke on me, sir?"

"No joke, I've never heard of the things you talk about, and I surely don't know anyone with one of those mobells!"

"Mobiles, sir."

The man took the phone from Nigel, and looked it over. "It looks like something, but I've never seen one. Excuse me a minute, I'm just going to the toilet, then I must bid you goodbye, I have things to do, time is passing by." He got up from his chair and went out of the room. "We are going on a big boat to America," the little girl volunteered.

"Oh yes," said Nigel, "and what's the name of the big boat that you are going on?"

"It's the biggest in the world, and it's new, it's only been built last year. It's going to be smashing; I've never been on a boat before, this is my first time."

"I think it's called the, the, oh, I've forgotten, but it's a big one," she smiled, and stuck her finger in her mouth.

"How old are you?"

"Six," she replied.

"That's old," Nigel said. She smiled.

The door opened. "Papa, what's the name of the boat we're going to America on? I forgot the name, and this man here wants to know the name." She pointed her finger at Nigel.

"Go and see your mother and get ready now my little darling, now do as Papa asked, be a good girl."

"Yes Papa," she said, and went to the door. "Goodbye sir, it's nice to have met you." She had heard her mother say the same thing, and copied her.

"Goodbye," said Nigel, "enjoy your holiday on the big boat."

"Thank you, what was the name Papa?" she asked, as she went out of the door.

"The big ship you talk about is called the Titanic," he replied.

It was a good job that Nigel was sitting down, otherwise he would have fallen over, his face had 'shock' written all over it!

"The Titanic?" he said. "The Titanic?" he repeated.

"Are you alright my young fellow? You seem to be sick, you have gone white, was it those cakes you ate?"

"What date is it today, sir?"

"It's the seventh of April. Sunday seventh of April."

"Yes, but what year?"

"Nineteen twelve, are you alright?"

"Nineteen twelve! You must be joking! You are playing a practical joke on me! Has my girlfriend had anything to do with this? Is this one of those games, like 'candid camera' or 'Gotcha' kind of show! Where's the cameras?" He stood up and looked around the room. "I know this must be a joke! OK, it's been funny! Jane, Jane, OK, you win, I get the joke," he laughed.

The man sat in his chair, and looked on in amazement, not

understanding what Nigel was on about. "I'm sorry young man, but I must ask you to leave."

The door opened, Nigel went towards it, thinking it was a camera crew, and Jane would appear with the lady and the little girl, saying that they were actors. "Jane," he said. Then the lady came in.

"What's all the shouting about dear?" she asked, concern on her face.

"I think this young man is sick, he's been talking about things that I'm afraid I cannot understand."

"What's the name of the ship that you are going to America on?" asked Nigel.

"It's called the Titanic," she replied.

"What date is it today? Don't you know the date?"

"No, I don't, well it's on the paper. Where is that newspaper?" "Here," the gentleman said, and picked it up and gave it to her; she passed it on to Nigel. The date on the newspaper was seventh of April nineteen hundred and twelve.

He looked at it, and said, "Is there a shipping page in here?"

"Yes, on page thirteen."

He opened it to page thirteen, and there in big print was a picture of the Titanic, with an advert; THE SHIP OF DREAMS.

"This is unreal, can I see your luggage labels please? "he asked.

"Certainly," she said.

He walked into the hallway, and looked at the labels; RMS TITANIC, NEW YORK, it said on each label.

"Can I ask you another question please?"

"Most certainly," the gentleman said.

"What's your names?"

"Well, I'm Gerald Anderson, and this is my wife Alice Anderson, and our daughter is called Bertha. Why all these questions? Please sit down, you look ill, can we get you some water, or maybe a shot of whiskey?"

"Thank you sir, I apologise for my behaviour, but I'm trying to sort out what has happened to me. I came here to look at a house, and find myself in nineteen hundred and twelve! Do you know I come from-" Nigel stopped, would they believe him?

"Excuse me sir and madam, but would you bear with me for fifteen minutes more, because there's something more I want to ask you?" he said in a pleading way.

"Is that alright dear? Have we the time?" Mr. Anderson asked his wife.

"Yes, if you want to dear, shall I leave you alone?"

"No," Nigel interrupted, "I want you to stay as well, it's very important for you, and for me, I can assure you."

"Alright, I'11 just go and get your drinks, and I think I'll have one myself, I won't be a minute." She left the room.

"Look Gerald, can I call you that, do you mind?"

"Not at all," Gerald said.

"You have to convince me of something, so I will ask you some questions, is that alright?"

"Yes, alright," he said, looking somewhat surprised.

The lady came in, and put the drinks in front of the men, and sat down. "Now Mr. Maythorn, please tell us what this is all about. Did you really come here to buy the house, or have you got another motive? We have been very nice to you, so if you mean to rob us, then we cannot do much about it. I have some money, and some jewellery, if you want it just take it and go." She looked a little frightened for a moment.

"Please believe me, it's nothing like that, I'll try and explain the best I can."

The clock on the mantelpiece struck one o'clock, for that moment he thought how the time was going so fast. He took a sip of his whisky, and felt its worth go into his body.

"Can I ask you a few questions before I explain myself?"

"Yes of course," said the gentleman.

"How many wars have we had this century?"

"That's an easy one, the Boer War that ended ten years ago, in nineteen hundred and two. Two years after I built this house."

"What kind of lighting is there in the streets of the town?"

"Gas lamps you mean?"

32

"Have you got a telephone?"

"I don't know what you mean!"

"Have you heard of a biro, or toaster?" Nigel got no reply. "Can I just look in your kitchen?" he jumped up.

"It's through there," he pointed.

He went through, and looked at a nineteen twelve kitchen; no washing machine or coffee percolator or fridge, he came back within a minute."Have you a hi-fi, or a C.D. player, or D.V.D.?"

The Andersons looked bemused, and didn't understand what he was talking about!

"Alright, I don't know what's happened, but I must tell you this; don't go on this trip to America on the Titanic."

They both looked at him, and now knew that he was mad! They had let a madman into their house, they believed.

"Don't go on that ship, it's going to sink, it's going to sink on the fifteenth of April, off Newfoundland. It will be a tragedy, and you will lose your lives if you go!"

"How can you say that this 'unsinkable' ship will sink? What proof have you?" she said.

"I was taught about the sinking at school, and I've read many books about it."

"How can you read a book about a sinking, when the ship hasn't even sailed yet? Now Nigel, you are playing a joke on us, are you not?" he said.

"It's deadly serious, I must explain. I already know it will be hard to believe, and I can't fully explain it, but I will try. I live in the future, I live in the year two thousand and seven, and I'm a History teacher, I've told you that. Now today is the 8th of April two thousand and seven. I came to this house to look at it with my fiancée Jane, with the intention of trying to buy it. We were in the room down the hallway, the room with the big fireplace, when I went into a little room in the chimney breast, and the next thing is my fiancée has disappeared, and I meet you lovely people! Now, I believe I have travelled back in time! Please don't ask me how, I can't answer that. But it seems I'm here, how I'm going to travel back I haven't the faintest idea! I will have to work on that later.

In the meantime, I feel it's my duty, now this has happened, to try to help you people. Do you know that I have read about you in a book and you went down with the ship! Now, I want you to cancel your trip, and don't go on that ship. Leave your trip for a month or so, what do you think?"

"Sir, your story is preposterous! It's impossible to come from the future! I have never heard the likes, and we will not cancel our trip on your say-so! We would be the laughing stock if we cancelled, and told our colleagues and family in America, that a man from the future told us so! I'm sorry, we have heard enough, we must carry on with our business, and sir, you must carry on with yours."

"Look, the ship hasn't got enough lifeboats for everyone on board, and fifteen hundred people will perish! I'm telling you, you must change your mind, I plead with you, think of your little girl's life?"

"I'm sorry Nigel, if that's your real name? We must ask you to leave, we are leaving at two o'clock, and it's now one-thirty, so please leave," said the gentleman.

"I've done my best to convince you, but I guess you can't change history. You will go, won't you?" Nigel said, with a sad look of disappointment.

"We certainly will, we have been looking forward to going on this ship, and our family in New York are looking forward to seeing us."

The Andersons stood up and went to the door and held it open, indicating that they wanted Nigel to leave.

"There's nothing more I can do for you. But can I just tell you this, on the night of the fourteenth of April, towards midnight, the liner will hit an iceberg, and in the morning of the fifteenth of April, it will sink. Be aware of what I have told you, and get yourself into a lifeboat as quick as you can. You sir, will find it more difficult, as it will be women and children first, but try your best, I wish you luck." Nigel already knew that they wouldn't survive. How could history be changed? It was a question he had no answer to. He shook hands with both of them, went to the door, and out into the garden. The door was shut behind him. He wandered down the road, thinking how he would get back to two thousand and seven. As he walked towards the gates, he saw that his car was gone, but he didn't expect it to be there. In the distance he saw a house that looked like the public house, The Fox and Hounds. He walked down the lane that he had driven up that very day. The pub looked different, no car park, the pub sign was hanging in a different place than where he had remembered.

As he walked into the entrance, and through the door, he realised that this must be another pub. The bar was in the same place, but the decor was drab and old-fashioned. There were a few customers in the bar, who all looked up as he walked up to the counter.

A woman behind the counter had a baby in her arms, who was about two years old. She sat him in a high-chair to try to get him to eat his dinner, when she saw Nigel.

"Hello, what can I get you?" she said with a smile.

"Coke please," Nigel said, standing at the bar and looking around.

The other customers were sitting at a long table, with tin tankers, and smoking profusely. Smoke hung in clouds throughout the bar.

"Sorry?" the woman said.

"Have you any Coke?"

"Sorry, I've never heard of it, we only sell beer and spirits here. Do you mean coke as from coal?"

"No, never mind, I'll have a pint of beer please."

"Bitter?" she asked.

"Yes, that will do, thank you."

She poured the beer into a tankard, and placed it in front of Nigel."Three pence please."

"Three pence!" he said to her in surprise. He put his hand in his pocket and pulled out a pound coin, he held it out for her.

"Sorry sir, we can't take foreign coins."

Nigel realised at that moment that he didn't have any old shillings and pence.

"I'm sorry, but I haven't got any of your money, you see."

"Then you can't have the pint," she interrupted.

"Look, can I explain? I have come here without any money, but this is worth a lot more than three pence."

She looked at the coin, and showed it to a customer nearby. They talked for a few minutes, and she came back to Nigel.

"I'm sorry, there's a Queen's head on it that we have never heard of, and the date is two thousand and five. It's a forged coin, Bill has told me." She pointed to her customer, who came over to join Nigel.

"Where did you get this coin from sir? I'm a police officer, off duty at the moment, but never the less, a police officer."

"The coin belongs to me. Look, I'll leave you an I.O.U. if you Like." He took out a 'biro' pen, and wrote down an I.O.U.

"What kind of pen is that?" Bill the policeman enquired.

"Oh, it's a throw-away pen, that's all."

"I've never seen such a nice pen, and you say you are going to throw it away?"

"Yes, when the ink runs out."

"Well, I've never seen that before."

"You can have it if you like."

"Thank you sir, that's nice of you."

Nigel had put his mobile on the counter; it was a habit, and he noticed the little boy playing with it, so did the mother.

"Brian, you naughty boy, give the gentleman back his thing," and when she took it off the boy, he started crying.

"It's alright, let him play with it, it won't hurt," said Nigel.

"What is it?" asked Bill.

"It's a mobile phone."

"What's it for?"

"It's to talk to people, when you are away from home."

Bill looked puzzled, "How does it work?"

"I'll show you." He took the mobile off the baby, who started crying again, and demonstrated. He decided that he would ring Jane up to explain what had happened to him. More people joined Bill at the bar. He punched in Jane's number, and there was no response, the phone was dead.

"Don't work very well," said Bill.

"Normally it works perfectly, everybody has one, they're all over the world," said Nigel, trying again.

"Not in these parts, I don't know anyone with one, do you Fanny?" he said to the barmaid.

"No, I haven't seen such a machine ever," she replied, trying to pacify the crying baby.

Nigel gave up on the phone. "Here," he said to the woman, "let the baby have it, he can keep it, seems it's the only one of its kind around here."

"Thank you," she said. "Look, you seem to be a nice man, so you can have that pint of bitter on the house." She was happy that the baby had stopped crying. "You're a happy little boy now, ain't you my little cherub, being a happy little boy for Mummy," she said in baby talk. He looked up and gave a big smile, as he played around with his new toy, a silver mobile phone.

"Where do you come from?" another customer, who had gathered around this funnily dressed man, asked.

"I've just come from the house on the hill, I thought it was for sale, but it seems I was wrong, it's not for sale."

"Oh, that's the Andersons' place," said the man who had asked the question, "they are very rich people. They are going to America on holiday, the other side of the world. Further than Australia, America is you know! It's a long way, they are going on that 'unsinkable' ship called The Titanic I think, someone told me, I can't read you see, I didn't go to a proper school."

"Alright Ben, the gentleman doesn't want to know your history," said Fanny, looking at Nigel, indicating with her finger to her temple, that there was something wrong with him.

"I don't mind, really," said Nigel as he took his first sip of beer, it tasted really bitter!

Bill was looking at his attire. "Those trousers you've got on, I've never seen any like them before. What kind of material are they made of?"

"They are called jeans, this is called a tee-shirt, and my shoes are called trainers."

"You look smart," said Fanny.

"Thank you," Nigel replied, starting to enjoy being the centre of attention, although he was always the centre of attraction at school. But this was different, he was having fun.

"Can you tell me what your name is?" he asked the barmaid.

"It's Fanny Small and this little one is Brian."

Nigel smiled at the little boy, who smiled back. Nigel worked it out fast. 'This little boy was Brian Smalls, the grandfather of the Landlord of the Fox and Hounds!

Time was going by; there were at least ten people around Nigel, and Bill had bought him his second pint, it was very strong, and he decided that he wouldn't drink any more. He would have to be leaving soon. They were all fascinated with his stories of what was going to happen in the future. He didn't say that that was where he came from, because he knew that they wouldn't believe him. The Andersons hadn't, and they were going to their doom!

They all laughed at him, as he tried to explain about talking pictures, and T.V. in the homes. How people would one day be able to talk to one another across the world, with a little receiver held in the hand! They laughed louder when he told them that they would never see Mr. or Mrs. Anderson again, that they would go down on that 'unsinkable' ship, the Titanic'. And that millions of young men would die in the nineteen fourteen-eighteen war. Then there would be another war with the Germans in nineteen thirty nine! The 'flying' story was the most funny to his audience, when he tried to explain how people would get into a 'cigar' shaped object, and it would take to the sky, and on the same day you would be somewhere else, hundreds of miles away, it was too much for them to understand!

He looked at his watch; it had stopped at twelve o four.

"Fanny," he said, by now he was on first names with his new-found friends, "can you give me some paper? I want to write something for you to pass down to little Brian, and you must promise to look after it, until Brian is old enough to pass it down to his son, and so on. And the same thing with this machine," he picked up the mobile."This now belongs to little Brian, don't lose it, and hand it down also. And Bill, when your pen runs out, give it to Fanny, and she will hand that down to Brian. That way, you will never forget me, and I will live on throughout your lives."

Fanny agreed, and just for the sake of it, gave Nigel some paper. On it he wrote with the pen he had given Bill; 'Nigel Maythorn came here on the seventh of April nineteen hundred and twelve, and had a drink in the Fox and Hounds, and met Fanny and little Brian, who is two years old, and Bill. God look after you people.' Then Nigel signed it, and handed it to Fanny, who put it under the counter.

"I have to go now," he said to his friend. "Have another pint," said Bill.

"Sorry Bill, but I must go. I have a long way to travel to get home, and at this minute, I don't know how long it will take." Fanny handed him his pound coin, which had remained on the counter throughout.

"Keep it as a souvenir," he said as he made for the door. "Goodbye my friend, two things to tell you before I go, don't join the army, and don't smoke because it causes cancer!" They all laughed, as he went out of the door and headed up towards the house.

Nigel walked through the gates and up the long path to the front door. He knocked on the door, but there was no answer. Then he realised that the Andersons had left to go on their 'fateful' trip. He put the key in the lock, but it didn't fit, the locks were different ones to the ones he had opened three and a quarter hours ago! Of course they were not the same locks, Nigel thought to himself, but he had to get into the house somehow. He came here through the fireplace, and he presumed that was the way back, if there was a way back! He felt a feeling of apprehension for the first time since he had had the experience of time travel.

He walked around the back of the house and tried a door, and that was locked. He would have to break in, he saw a window on the upper floor, and shinned up a drainpipe and climbed on to a ledge. He looked in; it was one of the bedrooms. He climbed down again and looked around for a stone; he picked one up, and went up the drainpipe for the second time. On the ledge he hit the window just near a latch. It was a small latch, so he tapped the window and a small piece of glass came out. Just enough room for him to put his hand in, the latch sprang back, he pushed the window up, and within a minute he was in, and standing in the bedroom. He picked up the broken glass, threw it out of the window, and closed it. The glass landed near a wall in the undergrowth. He walked through the bedroom and into the corridor that ran to the top of the stairs. He went down the stairs, and passed the place where he had seen the luggage, and back into the big room with the fireplace. He walked towards it, he felt the 'force' push him back, so he moved to another spot, and once again the 'force' got stronger the more he pushed himself! He tried all along the fireplace, even the part that he had first entered, but to no avail. He went to the other side of the room, and ran at the panel, the force didn't hurt him, but he just bounced back into the room. After fifteen minutes of running and bouncing, he gave up, he now realised he was stuck in the year nineteen hundred and twelve, with no way of going home!

The sweat was pouring off him, so he went out of the room, and to the room where he had talked to the Andersons. Then into the kitchen, he looked to see if there was anything to drink, and got himself a cup of cold water. He sat at the kitchen table, his head in his hands, and thinking that he was stuck in time!

Chapter 3

A NEW LIFE

Pangs of hunger told him that he needed a meal; there was nothing he could find to eat in this strange quiet house, so he decided to go to the pub again, to see if he could find something. He left the house the way he had got in, and walked the now familiar road that took him to the pub. Most of the customers he had met that very afternoon were still there, and he was given a real welcome, which made him happy for a moment.

"No sign of a World War yet," one of the men shouted, everyone laughed.

"Don't you worry yourself my friend, it will come, I hope you are marking my words!" Nigel retorted.

"Are you going to tell us any more of your stories?" another man asked.

"Only if you get me food and drink," Nigel said in a joking way.

"You're on, we'll all chip in and get you some bread and cheese, and a good pint of beer." The men threw pennies on the table, and a grand total of one shilling and two pence was collected. They made room at the table, and Nigel made himself at home with his new-found friends.

"How is it that you have no money? Are you a vagrant, you know, of no fixed abode?" one man asked.

"It's true, I have no money at the moment, because of the circumstances I find myself in, but I will remember you all for your kindness to me, as soon as it's possible," he replied, eating his bread and cheese that Fanny had made. All eyes were on this strange man with funny stories, and unfamiliar clothes. "Where do you live?" one of the men asked.

"Now that's a good question," Nigel said, "I suppose I might say that at this moment in time, I have nowhere to live. In a way, I'm lost between two worlds."

"Where do you come from, you don't sound like a Southampton man?"

"I am from around here."

"Hey Bert, less of the questions," Bill, the policeman who had made friends that very afternoon with Nigel, pointed out. "Let him eat his meal in peace."

Nigel looked up, and with a smile and a nod, thanked Bill for intervening. He was feeling under pressure, who would believe his story if he told them the truth? That he had travelled through time, that he really did live in the future? He would have to make up a few things and develop a new identity, otherwise he was sure he would be locked up in some mental institution! His mind went into overdrive, as he ate his meal.

As the day crept towards the evening, and the sun said goodbye to another day, the pub got crowded with men who had finished work for the day.

Nigel was given more drinks, as he entertained people at his table.

"So, you think that the Titanic will go down on its maiden voyage, do you?" said an Irish sounding man who had been standing at the bar and talking to a man who had been in the bar all afternoon, and heard what Nigel had told them all.

"Yes, I'm afraid to say, the ship will go down on this trip."

"How do you know that? I think you are a trouble-maker, a prophet of doom, scare-monger! You said that there is going to be a World War as well, why all these things? I'm a crew-man on that ship the Titanic, and I'm sailing on her on Wednesday, so if I believe you, are you telling me I should not go?"

"Yes my friend, please don't ask me how I know, because I can't explain, but I can tell you that the ship will go down on Monday the fifteenth of April," Nigel said, to laughter from everyone within earshot.

"Why will she sink, tell me dat?" the Irishman said.

"Iceberg, she will hit an iceberg, as she heads for New York, so yes my friend, sign off."

"You're bloody mad, I've been at sea for years, and been to New York, I've never seen an iceberg, someone should take you away!"

"Now John, no trouble," said Bill, standing in between the Irishman and Nigel.

"No trouble," said John the Irishman, as he retreated back to the bar.

"Who was that?" Nigel asked.

"Oh, that was John Coffey, he's normally OK, he's always in here when his ships are in port. Nice fella really, maybe he's got a point, you might upset people with your future predictions."

"It might be a good idea to keep your thoughts to yourself," said one of the men at the table.

"Look my friend, I'm sorry if I have told you things you don't like to hear, but believe me, all these things will come true, and by next week, you may start to believe me, if I'm still around here."

"Why, where are you thinking of going? Not to America on the Titanic, that's a certainty!" Loud laughter once again.

"Alright, have your laughs, I understand, but I will not shut up, if I can save just one person from drowning, and going on that ship, I will try. It's my destiny, I must try." Nigel could feel the strong ale taking effect, he wasn't used to heavy drinking, and the beers kept on being put in front of him.

"If only I could have saved the Andersons, I would have, but it's too late now, they have already gone," Nigel said.

"No they haven't gone; I saw them outside the gates, going in as I passed by. In fact I talked to Gerald and wished him a good trip. He told me they had taken their luggage to a depot, for the delivery in two days' time. Maybe you could have another talk with them," said Bill, who seemed to be the only man who didn't laugh like the rest of them when Nigel made one of his predictions.

"I thought they had gone. Thanks for that information Bill, I might have another talk with them. It would be a shame to let them go to their deaths, I'll give it another try tomorrow."

As the evening came to an end, Nigel felt like he had been hit by a truck! His mind slowly gave up, and he blacked out at the table.

'What a dream,' Nigel thought, as he came back to life the next morning. He heard voices downstairs, and visualized his mother making breakfast for him, before he went to work at the school.

His head was throbbing, and he opened his eyes. The strangeness of the room he found himself in made him realize that he hadn't been dreaming! The room was small and old-fashioned. The small dresser with a bowl and jug of water caught his eye. The single bed he was in was warm and comfortable, and he was reluctant to face the day! How did he get in this strange bed? Where was he? Questions, but no answers, came as he lay there, contemplating his position. What had happened to him? Why? A tap on the door brought him back to reality.

"How do you feel?" Fanny the barmaid enquired.

"Not too well, where am I?" Nigel asked, sitting up in bed.

"Last night you had a bad turn, and we couldn't bring you around, you were dead to the world, too much mead, if you ask me," she said with a smile. "I've brought you some tea, and when you get up, I will make you something to put you right, a nice breakfast should do the trick." She put the cup on the bedside table, and made for the door.

"Thanks for your kindness, I'll get up now." She left with a smile.

Nigel got up; he was fully dressed, apart from his shoes. He looked out of the window onto the sign that told him he was still in the pub! Looking at his watch he realized he had slept all morning, it said twelve-o-four. Sprinkling cold water on his face from the jug, he made his way down the steep stairway to meet the day.

"You drank a lot last night, and we thought that the best thing was for you to stay here for the night. So some of your friends helped to get you up the stairs to bed," she said, as she made a breakfast for him.

"Why are you doing all this for me? I can't pay, you know that, I've no money at all, I've never seen so much kindness," Nigel said, as he sat down at the kitchen table.

"Don't worry about that, your friends had another whip around for your bed. They must like your story telling. In fact six of my customers have popped in this morning, on their way to work, to find out how you are, I told them that you were sleeping soundly."

She placed a plate of egg and bacon with bread, on the table. "Eat that," she said, "it will make you feel better."

"Thank you so much, I will pay you back as soon as I can get some money, I promise."

"I have a few jobs around the pub that need doing, maybe you could help out? I pay well, fourpence an hour."

Nigel nearly choked on his breakfast."Sure, I'll do what I can, but I've no experience in the pub game."

"Don't worry, I will show you how to serve a pint, it's easy," she said, putting a cup of tea in front of him. "Can you start this morning, after you've finished your breakfast?" she enquired. "Hardly, the morning has gone," he said.

"What do you mean? It's only nine thirty."

Nigel looked at his watch; it said twelve-o-four! It had stopped the moment he'd left the future! He tried to set the watch right, but to no avail, it had seized up completely!

Slowly, he started to feel better, as the morning went by. He did various jobs, sweeping the outside of the pub, learned how to serve a pint, and getting to know the prices of things, in this 'new' money, pound, shillings and pence. Fanny asked Nigel a lot of questions throughout the morning; where he lived, why he was not working, how funny he looked in his clothes, if he had a wife? And numerous other things. Nigel tried his best to answer each one with white lies; he had decided to tell the whole truth was not an option. He accepted the job at the pub, but emphasized that it would be on a part-time basis. He also accepted the room at the pub, and the wages. But his main thought was to try to go back to the house to try to get back home.

After finishing his first day's work, he set off for the house. On arriving at the gates, he noticed how new they looked, the roadway towards the house was bedecked with border flowers, the trees had new leaves, all spick and span.

The little girl answered his knocking. "Hello sir, it's very nice to see you again," she said. "Do you want to see my papa, or will Mama do? Please do come in." It was obvious she was at the age where she copied the things her beloved mother said! She was a delightful little girl, thought Nigel.

"Papa, that nice man is here to see you again," she informed her father. He came out of the side room, slippers on, and smoking a pipe.

"I'm sorry to bother you, sir, but I believe I left my phone here yesterday, and as I was passing I thought I would pop in and pay you a visit. I thought you had left to go on your holiday, but I was told that you were still here."

"Yes, it's nice to see you again, Nigel isn't it?" he enquired.

"Yes, Nigel sir."

"Do come in, and I'll find your phone, I believe you left it on the table in the front room, that's where I last saw it," he said, leading the way into the room.

"Would you like a drink while you're here?"

"That would be lovely," said Nigel, his hangover now gone.

"Sit down, let's have a talk," said Gerald, "how do you feel today? You were in a bad way yesterday, I thought at one time, that you had gone off your head, if you don't mind me saying so. You went white, you looked bad, and with all that rambling, well, what was I to think? I thought you were a mad-man! Oh, please excuse my forthright way, my wife is always telling me off about

46

my tactlessness, but I don't mean to be that way," Gerald said, as he poured wine into two glasses.

"I don't blame you for thinking that way of me, I know it's hard, because you have never met me before. I would act the same way if a stranger told me of something that might happen to me. Like you, I wouldn't believe it. Anyhow sir, I wish you would consider what I told you yesterday, and not go on that ship!"

"Oh please Nigel, let's not go into that again. We're going, and we leave on Wednesday morning at nine o'clock."

"Oh I thought you were staying in a hotel, or so you said," Nigel said, sipping his wine.

"We have changed our minds about the hotel, it was just something I said when booking the holiday. But with second thoughts, we can get into Southampton within the hour from here, and we sail at mid-day. A friend is picking us up at nine o'clock in his car. Our luggage went to a collecting depot yesterday, so we are all looking forward to going on that wonderful ship!"

Nigel shook his head, and felt sadness come over him. Gerald seemed such a nice man, his little girl was so pretty, and his wife so lady-like, it was unbearable to believe they were all going to die! If only he could prove that what he had told him was going to happen, but there was no way that he could do that.

"Another glass Nigel?"

"Thanks sir, it's good wine."

"The very best, my wife tells me that I drink too much of it, but that's women for you."

'Some things never change,' thought Nigel.

"Do you still believe you come from the future?" Gerald said smiling. "You were saying strange things you know. At first, my wife mistook you for the chimney sweep so she told me, then she thought you may be here to rob us, but I didn't think anything of the kind. I'm a good judge of men, I fought in the Boer War, I was a Major, and that's how I got to know men, yes I'm a very good judge. And funnily enough, if you don't mind me saying, I can tell you are a nice fellow. After all, you said you are a teacher didn't you?"

47

"Well thank you sir, I am a teacher, and like you, sometimes I have judged my students and their abilities. You have a lovely family and in a strange way it seems like I have known you for some time, yet we only met a day ago. I enjoy your company very much."

"So do you still say that you come from the future, or was that a joke? Gerald said, pouring another glass of wine.

'There is no point in pursuing that any longer,' Nigel thought. "I said a few things, I don't remember everything I said, I must have been confused, and this feeling of the future is difficult to explain."

The men were interrupted by Mrs. Anderson coming into the room. "Hello, how do you feel today, better I hope? Bertha told me you had come back to see us. I've just finished writing a letter to my friend in New York."

"I'm fine thank you," Nigel said.

She went to the cabinet and got herself a glass, and presented it to her husband, who filled it without a word. "So what do we owe the pleasure of you coming to see us again?" she said, sitting down.

Gerald answered the question. "Nigel was just passing, and he remembered that he must have left his silver machine phone here, have you seen it dear?"

"No I haven't seen it, maybe Bertha has it in her room? I'll ask her, she's playing with her dolls at the moment upstairs. Shall I ask her down Gerald?"

"In a moment dear, Nigel and I were having a discussion on how we are both good judges of men, a very interesting conversation. It's been a while since I had any male company, I miss a good old talk."

"Do you want me to leave dear?" she asked.

"Good gracious, no. Women are good conversationists as well. I didn't mean any disrespect dear," he said, looking at Nigel then back to his wife.

Nigel just smiled, but felt slightly uncomfortable. "I will have to go soon, but may I ask you a favour? I noticed you have some wonderful paintings, and I wanted just a few minutes to see them, I'm an art lover."

"Most certainly," Gerald said with some pride, "I have some nice ones in the big dining room at the back of the house. You can see them, go there, it's just at the end of the passage. It's the door in front of you, next to the bathroom, go along, I'll join you shortly."

"Thank you sir, I appreciate that very much." Nigel got up and walked down the passage and into the big room. He had made up the excuse to see the paintings to get access to the fireplace. He had to try once again to get back where he belonged. The 'force' was still the same, he pushed and pushed, trying every angle, but to no avail. After a few more tries, he gave up as he heard the door open.

"This is a nice one, the Countryside in spring, cost me a pretty penny I can tell you," Gerald said, pointing.

"Yes sir, they are beautiful."

After pretending to look at a few more, Nigel made an excuse to leave. "I must go now, I'm on duty tonight at the pub. I forgot to tell you I have a job there, started today, and I also have accommodation."

"Oh, I thought you said you were a school teacher!"

"I am really, but I just wanted a change, I hope to go back to teaching soon, this is only temporary, a kind of a holiday from school really." Nigel hated lying, but couldn't think of any other explanation at that moment.

The men walked towards the door.

"Bertha hasn't seen that phone 'thing', I have just asked her," Mrs. Anderson said from the top of the stairs.

"Don't worry about it; I'll pop around before you leave, maybe it will turn up. Goodbye for now, and thank you for your wonderful hospitality, you're lovely people."

"Thanks for your kind words Nigel," Gerald said, as he opened the door, "I enjoyed our talk."

"And the wine," said Nigel as he walked away, back to the pub.

"Yes, and the wine," said Gerald with a smile.

Nigel felt sad as he made his way down the drive to the gates. He had tried once again to save the new-found friends from their fate, but to no avail. And he had tried to get back home, the ploy to get back into the house had worked, he already knew that little Brian was the 'owner' of his mobile phone.

He wondered how Jane was taking his disappearance! Were the police involved in searching for him? And his mother, father and brother must be in turmoil by now! He had failed to turn up for school! What a mess he had got himself into. And what if he did get back? Who would believe him when he told them that he had been transported back to the past? Nobody! He would end up in a mental hospital! Meanwhile he said good bye to a world he once knew and loved, a life with Jane now gone, he would never see any of them again! Tears fell to the ground, everyone he loved had all gone out of his life, what was he to do now? He had no idea.

On arriving at the pub, he went to see Fanny to ask her for the day off the coming day. He had had an idea, he would go into Southampton to see the Titanic, maybe he might be able to persuade somebody not to sail on her! He told Fanny he would do the bar work that evening, so she could have the night off, and she readily agreed, but how he would get to the docks he didn't know.

The customers were very happy to see their new-found friend working behind the bar, a lot of laughter ensued, and for a while Nigel forgot his troubles as the evening wore on. He enjoyed the bar work, totally different to what he was used to. The teaching profession could be hard at times, but there behind the bar, he found it very pleasant indeed!

Fanny came to see him, and watched him serving customers with a certain flair. 'He took to the work like a duck to water' she had thought. He would look at her and smile and she found herself smiling back at him with ease.

"Time gentlemen, please," she shouted, and almost all the men were gone within the time allowed, with no problems. Nigel swept up (and collected the tankards. She locked the door, and poured a tankard of beer, and a small drink that looked like gin, indicating that a nightcap was in order, so they went into the kitchen of the pub and sat down at the table.

"How did you like it then, the bar work? You seemed to get on well?" she asked.

"Yes, I did enjoy it; you've got a good lot of customers."

"They are a good crowd, when they don't drink too much and end up under the table," she laughed. They talked for the next hour or so, she made him supper of bread and cheese, and asked him questions that he found hard to answer and he tried to change the subject by asking her other things.

He found out that her husband was away at sea, but she hoped that he would give up that way of life soon. He had opened the pub, but after working behind the bar for a few years, had decided to go back to sea. Fanny had decided to keep the pub, with the help of a barman, but the barman had gone into the army. That was why she was pleased that Nigel had accepted the job as barman-come-handyman. She had had a hard time trying to look after her baby and the bar as well, so she considered Nigel a Godsend!

Nigel had to lie when she had asked him how he had arrived, it seemed, from nowhere, in strange clothing with no money! He told her he had lost his money. He felt really bad in having to tell these blatant lies, but he couldn't tell her the truth.

"You're a strange one," she said as she cleared the table.

"So I've been told," he laughed, getting up from the table. "I wonder if you have some trousers and a shirt, a coat maybe, until I earn some money to buy some?" he asked.

"I think I could find something for you, my old man won't be wearing them, and I'm sure this will help you out, you can owe it to me." She handed him one pound in coins.

"You're very kind Fanny, I won't let you down, and I'll pay you back, I promise you. Look, take my watch as a token of my goodwill. It's a good watch, worth a lot more than a pound," he slipped it off his wrist.

She looked at it. "Yes, it is a nice one; it's a pity it's not working, it's stopped at twelve-o-four," she exclaimed.

"I will get it going again when I get it back from you, after I've paid you back. Goodnight Fanny, and thank you, I'm off to bed now, got a busy day tomorrow. I'm going into Southampton to see the Titanic. How will I get there, transport I mean?"

"You can take my bicycle, it's in the back room, but the brakes are not too good, so you be careful. I don't want my new helper having an accident, now do I?" She smiled as she took off her apron.

"Goodnight, and thank you," Nigel said as he made his way up the stairs to his little room. 'She's a lovely woman,' he thought as he undressed and got into bed. At least he had some money now, although how far a pound would go, he had no idea!

He had been in bed only five minutes, when there was a light tap on his door. "Yes?" he said.

"Are you decent, can I come in?" she called.

"Yes, I'm in bed."

She opened the door, and in her arms she had a bundle of clothes.

"I hope these will do you for now?" she said, as she placed them on a chair. She turned around to face him, then with a smile said, "Goodnight Nigel, sleep well," and left the room.

He blew out the candle, and within a few minutes was fast asleep.

Chapter 4

THE SHIP OF DREAMS

It stood there in the docks, looking magnificent, the picture that Nigel had seen only in photographs, now he could see it with his own eyes! He walked alongside, and looked up at this 'wonder'. He had, like most people, learned about the ship at school, and here he was, actually there, he was in awe! He walked towards the crew's gangway, and made his way up. There was only one young looking sailor on gangway duty.

"Got a message from headquarters, for Mr. Ismay," Nigel said with authority in his voice.

"Who's Mr. Ismay, sir?" said the sailor.

"You mean to tell me you don't know who owns this ship, your boss? How long have you worked for this company?" Nigel said in a school masterly tone.

"I'm only standby sir; the main crew comes along later in the day."

"Do you know Fred Fleet, or who the captain is?" Nigel enquired. "No sir, never heard of them, and as I've already told you, I'm new here. I may not even sail tomorrow, I'm only on standby." "Well, take my advice, don't sign on, sail on the sister ship. I have to go and find Mr. Ismay, don't worry, I have plenty of time, I'll find him. Keep up the good work sailor." With that, Nigel walked onto the ship, and up the first staircase he found.

He couldn't believe his luck; here he was, on the Titanic, he was living history! It had been very easy to get aboard; the security was almost nil, compared to what it had become in two thousand and seven! Nobody said a word to him as he found his way to the restaurants and public rooms. He picked up a menu-type folder, and with pen in hand whenever anyone was in the vicinity, he pretended to write something down, until the coast was clear again.

He spent an hour wandering around the ship, from the gym to the smoking rooms, to the famous staircase, the Café Parisien, where Colonel Archibald Gracie and his friends would soon be frequenting. But now his ideas of trying to save someone came to the fore.

He already knew that most of the passengers would not be arriving until the next morning, but he could at least try to save some of the crew, and crew members tend to frequent pubs. So now he knew that what he had to do was find a Southampton crew pub.

He went up to the upper deck, towards the Bridge and for the first time since he had been aboard, he was approached by an officer.

"Can I help you, sir?"

"Yes," said Nigel. "Mr. Ismay, I have a message for him, from headquarters."

"He's not aboard sir, I understand he is staying at the Southwestern Hotel here in Southampton, he will be coming aboard tomorrow. That's where you'll find him, at the hotel."

Nigel thought he recognised the officer from photos he had seen but wasn't sure.

"Thank you, I'll go there, the message is important."

"Very well, sir. Will you be sailing with us?" the officer asked, as he made his way to the bridge.

"No, I'm only a messenger that's all, thank you once again for the information, goodbye." Nigel made his way towards where he had come aboard, and after getting lost a few times, got back to the gangway.

"Did you find him, sir?" said the sailor.

"Yes," said Nigel, "I know where he is, thank you. Oh by the way, good luck if you sail, but her sister ship is a better one as far as I can see. So try on that one if you don't get on here. I don't like maiden voyages, you never know what can go wrong and this ship has that feeling for me, I wouldn't sail on her. Goodbye my friend."

The sailor said nothing as he watched Nigel walk down the gangway. He picked up his bike he had left just inside the gate, had one last look at the liner, and headed into the town. The old trams and buses fascinated him. He saw places he knew, the Bargate area, the old mediaeval gate where now in his world there were coffee shops and multi-storeys, it all now looked drab!

He made his way to a pub near the docks and went in. It was soon established that this pub was indeed a place where sea-men drank. Nigel soon got talking to a man who was going to sail the next day on the Titanic. He told the sea-man that he believed the liner was doomed, but once again he was not believed. As more men got involved in the talks and the beer went down, an argument ensued, as to why Nigel was against the White Star Line. A lot of men were grateful for their jobs during these hard times and had nothing bad to say about the company. Some wanted to know what his motive was in wanting men not to sail on the most beautiful ship that had ever been built!

Nigel, who hadn't been drinking a lot, could plainly see that his plans and warnings were not being heeded, but gave it one last try. "Please gentlemen, that ship will founder within a few days of sailing! In fact it will go down on Monday next! So I beg of you, you men who are sailing, sign off! Otherwise it will leave your wives as widows!"

Nigel looked at the now angry men, some who grabbed hold of him and boldly threw him out of the pub, with angry shouts of not to ever set foot in their pub again!

Nigel picked himself up and made off, just missing a tram that happened to be passing by!

Fanny had been right; the brakes on the bike were not

in good order. He made his way to the Southwestern Hotel, where he hoped he might meet Mr. Bruce Ismay, Managing Director of the White Star Line. But Nigel was out of luck, he was informed that Mr. Ismay had not yet arrived, and the receptionist didn't know when he would arrive, maybe later in the day? he suggested.

Nigel could see he was having little success in his endeavours to warn people of a coming tragic event, nobody believed a word of his warnings! It was impossible to save anyone, he thought, what a waste of life, and he was useless in trying to prevent it happening. It would happen, he knew that, but the frustration of trying to avert it, was impossible. History can't be changed, that was a certainty, he thought. He was drawn to the docks again, and found a little café and went in for a bite to eat. Mashed potatoes, sausage and peas at two pence, was a bargain, with a mug of tea for an extra penny! 'That one pound will go a long way,' he thought. He sat in the window watching the world go by; trams ran past the café every few minutes it seemed. Men who were working making pavements just opposite came in from time to time for a mug of tea.

Two days had passed since he had arrived at this place, but it seemed in a strange way, that he didn't feel too unhappy with his lot. He had a job of sorts, a place to lay his head and, it seemed, lots of friends. If he was to be stuck here in this time, he would make the most of it, it was in his nature, on the other hand, he had no option! He had tried twice to get back, but it seemed he was meant to be here in nineteen hundred and twelve. With his knowledge, he would do his best to alleviate the suffering that he knew the future would bring. A world war was only two years away.

"Mind if I join you?" said Bill. Nigel looked up, and there he was standing there with a mug of tea in his hand.

"Sure thing Bill, sit down. What are you doing in this neck of the woods?"

"Neck of the woods?"

"Oh, just a saying," Nigel replied.

"Just keeping an eye out for you," Bill said.

"How did you know I was here?"

"Fanny told me you were coming down here to see the Titanic, have you seen her?"

"Yes, I've been on her this morning. Had a good look around, it's a beautiful ship, really is, it's a pity..." there Nigel stopped.

"Nobody believes you do they?" Bill said. "I was in the pub when the trouble started, luckily you came to no harm, but you had better watch out, these sea-men can get rough at times."

"I know, they set on me and threw me out, did you see that?" Nigel retorted.

"Yes, I was there, I've just told you, but if it had got that bad, you'd've been in for a hiding. I would have backed you up, that's a certainty. Like I said, I'm keeping an eye out for you."

"That's nice of you, Bill." Nigel felt that at least he had a good friend in Bill.

The woman who had served him came to the table with Bill's Meal. "You gentlemen sailing on the Titanic?" she enquired.

"No," Bill said abruptly.

"She's a beautiful ship; my Ronny is in the engine room on her. He says it's the biggest and best ship he's been on," she said matter-of-factly. Nigel looked up at her, she was a nice looking woman, but had a tired look in her face.

"Well, tell your Ronny not to go on her, she's a doomed ship, she is going to sink, and will never get to New York."

Bill shook his head, "Don't Nigel, don't," he whispered.

"What do you mean, sink? That ship's unsinkable, so Ronny told me, it will never sink," she said.

"Believe me, most of the crew will go down on her, they will drown! So, beg your man, on bended knees if need be, or you will lose him!" Nigel was talking now in a determined way.

"Why are you saying this?" she enquired, hands on her hips. "How do you know what is going to happen? Why are you frightening me like this?"

"I do know, let's leave it at that, and you will find out in a week's time. But if you don't keep your man with you at home, you will lose him. Tell him to have a week off, and sail on another ship next week, but not on the Titanic!"

"Look, you finish up your meal and leave. I will not listen to any more of this; you are making me worried, please leave!" With that, she disappeared behind the counter.

"Nigel, give up this business of trying to warn people, you're wasting your time. Nobody will believe you, as I have already said. Who could comprehend such a tragedy as the sinking of the world's biggest liner? You are only getting yourself into deep trouble!"

"Bill, you don't understand, it's my duty, my destiny, I have to try to save as many people as I can, who, if I don't, will surely die!"

"So, you think it's your destiny to save the world, do you?"

"Bill, if only you knew what I know, I can't explain at the moment. I feel so inadequate, but I'm not mad, if that's what you're thinking. "

At that moment a burly man approached the table.

"Which one of you has been upsetting my missus?" he said in a menacing manner.

"I didn't mean to upset her," Nigel said apologetically. "I only warned her of a tragedy that will happen in her life, if her man sails on the Titanic. The Titanic is a doomed ship!"

"Well, I'm her man, and she's crying out back, and now I'm in trouble because she doesn't want me to go to sea anymore, she's in a hell of a state. Now, explain yourself before I throw you out. Why are you trying to ruin our lives?"

"I'm sorry," said Nigel standing up from the table, "I'll go now. I don't want any trouble, but I had a dream about that ship, and when she told me that Ronny was sailing on her, I felt I had to warn her, that's all."

Ronny stood there, fists clenched, about to explode, when Bill stood up. "Listen here Ron, I'm a policeman, not on duty at the moment, but I'm a witness to what was said. He didn't mean to upset your wife, so let's leave it at that, shall we? I wouldn't want to make any arrests on my day off, now would I?" Bill looked hard into the face of Ron, who got the message.

"Alright, there will be no trouble this time, but don't come in here again," he said to Nigel. He went to the door and opened it.

As the two men went out Nigel said as a parting shot, "Ronny, don't go on that ship, take a week off, you will remember me, I'll see you next week then?"

"Oh no you won't," Ronny shouted, as he slammed the door of the café!

The two men walked down the dock road, towards the gates that the crew used to get to their ships.

"I've forgotten my bike, I left it outside the café," Nigel said. "I'll have to go back for it."

"No," Bill said, "I'll go, you wait for me here. Ronny may think you are going to upset his wife, no, you wait here." In the ten minutes that Bill was away, Nigel warned at least ten sea-men returning to the ships, not to sail on the Titanic! Most laughed at him, but Nigel continued, until a policeman told him to go away. Reluctantly Nigel left the area, when Bill came back with his bike. Nigel noticed a photographer had taken a picture of the ship.

"Thanks Bill, you're a real friend, I'm going home now, but I've got a plan for tomorrow. Got to give it one more go, maybe someone will believe me. What are you going to do now?" he asked.

"Don't worry about me, I have things to do in town. I'll see you in the pub later tonight," Bill said as he walked towards the town centre.

Nigel rode home slowly, thinking of the poor brakes, but also thinking about his warnings, and the fact that nobody believed a word of it! He had been aboard the 'ship of dreams', and it was as it said in the books he had read, a beautiful ship! But nobody would ever believe him when he got back to his 'real' home, it would have to remain his secret for ever.

"Had a nice day Nigel?" asked Fanny, who was behind the bar.

"Yes, I went on the Titanic," he said. "I'll take over now."

She smiled as she went out the back to make some supper.

The banter that night at the pub was the same as the night

before. Once again Nigel enjoyed his work; he didn't stay too long in the kitchen, and made an excuse to go to bed early, once the pub had closed.

"I'll get the brakes fixed on your bike as soon as I have the time," he told Fanny. Then after a drink and a bite to eat, he went up to his room. He had a plan for the next day, and he wanted to be up at first light.

Chapter 5

THE GAME

After a good sleep, Nigel was up before seven o'clock. He dressed quickly, and very quietly left the pub. The day was dry and crisp as he walked swiftly towards the house, through the gates and up the avenue of trees towards the front door. His knock was answered by Mrs. Anderson, who looked surprised to see him this early in the morning. "Nigel, what are you doing here at this time of the day? We are just having breakfast," she said.

"I said I would see you before you set off, and I was up early, so here I am."

"Do come in and have some coffee then," she said. "We don't have to leave until nine o'clock. Bertie is taking us in his car."

"Thank you," he said, as he slipped off his cap and followed her in.

"Look who's here again, your friend Nigel."

"Hello Nigel, you're a man of your word, you said you would visit again before we left. Sit down and join us for our last breakfast before we go on our fantastic trip to New York," Gerald said, smiling broadly.

He sat down with the Anderson family for breakfast of eggs and bacon, coffee and bread. "You're very kind to me," Nigel said.

"Well, we are friends now aren't we? We are drinking partners," Gerald laughed out loud.

For the next hour they sat and talked, while Mrs. Anderson did the last minute chores before their departure time. The little girl asked her mother if she could wear her pretty bonnet, and her mother told her to go upstairs to find it in one of the bedrooms. This was the cue for Nigel to ask to use the bathroom in the hallway. Quietly he went into the hallway and up the stairs. He looked in each room and found the little girl looking in a wardrobe. He noticed a key in the door.

"Found your bonnet yet?" he said.

"Oh Nigel, you made me jump," she laughed. "What are you doing up here?"

"I've come to help you," he said, taking hold of her hand. "Now, I want you to call your mother to come up here to help you to find your bonnet, because I want to speak to her without your father there. It's all a secret, just between me and you. Our secret, a game, so call her now. For fun, just say you have hurt yourself, we will have a bit of fun, yes?"

"But Mummy may be angry with me," she said in an enquiring way.

"No she won't, she will join in the fun, call her."

"Alright Nigel," she said demurely. "Mummy, come up please, I've hurt my leg, I can't move," she shouted down the stairs.

"Go and see to her, I have to just check the back windows,"

Gerald said, not concerned, it seemed, to his daughter's call.

Mrs. Anderson made her way up the stairs, and entered the room. The shock on her face was acute, as she saw Nigel sitting on the bed holding her baby, and in his hand was a knife.

"Be quiet, I don't want your daughter to lose her life, and I'm sure you don't either, do you?" he said.

"Nigel, what are you doing up here? Let my daughter go, I beg of you!"

"Listen to me," Nigel said with mock menace in his voice, "call your husband up here, and do it now. Don't tell him I'm here, understand?"

"Yes, Nigel please don't hurt her."

"If you value your daughter's life, call him now!"

"Gerald, please come up here will you? Straight away?" she shouted from the top of the stairs. "Alright dear, I'm coming, what's wrong?"

"Oh, just come up and see for yourself," she shouted.

"What's going on?" he said as he entered the room.

"Sit on the bed over there," Nigel ordered. "Now, I'm not joking, I'm deadly serious, your daughter will not be in any danger if you do as I tell you! I have taken command, now do as I say and no harm will come to any of you. I will be back in five minutes, and I'm going to lock you in. I'm taking Bertha with me, only five minutes, understand?"

"Yes Nigel, please don't hurt her, we'll do anything you ask, but please--"

"Don't worry, time is short, I have to do something, just five minutes!" He picked the little girl up, left the room and locked the door. He went downstairs and out of the back of the house, to a shed he had noticed.

"Are we still playing the game?" she asked.

"Yes, it's only a game, help me to find some rope or wire." He picked up a hammer and nails, and some cord, then taking the little girl by the hand, went back to the upstairs room.

Mrs. Anderson was crying in her husband's arms, as Nigel went back into the room. The little girl became alarmed to see her mother's tears, and went to go towards her to comfort her, but Nigel held her to him.

"Don't cry Mummy, it's just a game, isn't it Nigel?" she said, looking up at him.

"Don't worry, Mrs. Anderson, as I have said, you will come to no harm if you do what I tell you. All will be explained very soon. Now, I am going to tie you up, just for a while, so please bear with me."

"Look Nigel, I have money," Gerald said at last, in a pleading way. "It's yours, all of it; we wish to continue our lives in peace.

"There's no time for talk now, I'm sorry, I have to tie you up first, then we can talk. So go to the end of the room in the corner, and face the wall, sir, please do it now!"

Gerald kissed his wife on the forehead and went to the corner of the room.

"Thank you, sir, now Mrs. Anderson, place that chair and sit down facing the window, and put your hands behind the chair."

She obliged him, Nigel then took out his knife and cut a length of cord, and tied her hands behind the chair, then tied her legs together. The little girl ran over to her father and hugged his leg. With that, her father picked her up, then turned around, seeing the knife in Nigel's hand pleaded, "Don't hurt her please?"

"Put the girl down and sit on this chair!" he ordered.

Within a few minutes both were tied up. He took Gerald's pocket watch and the time was eight forty five a.m.

"I am doing this for your own good; you are not going to sail on the Titanic today, or any other day. So, for your own good I'm stopping you from going on that ship!"

"That's preposterous!" Gerald said.

"I'm not going to argue with you, sir. I will have to leave you for a short while, now I was going to gag you, but I think you will be very quiet. Remember, if you shout out you will be in serious trouble, remember I have the girl, you must think of her welfare." Nigel went to the window and hammered a nail to secure it from opening. He caught hold of the girl, went out and locked the door.

"I don't like this game any more, Nigel, it made my mummy cry, and Father is furious, I can tell." She looked up at him sadly.

"The game will end very soon, but you must play your part, you must go into your room, and don't say a word for fifteen minutes, just for that short time you must be quiet. I'll give you your papa's pocket watch, and when the big hand is on the three, the game will be over. Then we will make your mummy and papa happy again with a big surprise. Now, can you do that Bertha, be quiet for fifteen minutes?"

"Easy," she said with a smile. He took her to her bedroom, and with a finger to his lips, he left her sitting on her bed looking at the pocket watch. He told her he would be back at nine-fifteen on the dot. Locking her door quietly, he walked down the stairs, and got himself a cup of water. He was just drinking it, when he heard the light knock on the door. A car was parked in the driveway, and a distinguished looking gentleman was standing, back to the door admiring the landscape.

"You've got a lovely garden, Gerald, well tended, if I say so myself." Then he turned around and said, "Sorry, I thought you were Gerald, I'm here to pick the lucky blighters up, his ship is waiting for him you know."

"I'm sorry sir, but they left about half an hour ago."

"But we had an arrangement, I was supposed to take them to the docks! That's strange, why didn't he tell me that he had made some other arrangement?"

"I'm sorry sir, I can't help you there, he didn't mention to me that he was meant to be given a ride by you. I believe they were going by train." Nigel lied.

"And who, may I ask, are you, sir?" The gentleman asked.

"I'm Nigel, Mr. Anderson's personal assistant, house-keeper in a way."

"Strange, Gerald never told me he had a man-servant, and I was with him last week, he never mentioned you at all, the dark horse!"

"You may catch up with the family if you go down to the docks, the ship doesn't sail until mid-day. You must excuse me now sir, I have my duties to attend to, good day to you," Nigel said as he closed the door.

"Very strange," he heard the gentleman mutter as he went to the car.

His duty was done, he had saved their lives, so at least some good had come out of this. He then went into the big room, and went to the fireplace, for the third time he tried to get into the back of the chimney, but the force held him back. He went up the stairs and into Bertha's bedroom. She was still sitting on the bed, pocket watch in her hand.

"Well done, you did it, you have been a good girl, the game is now over," he said. She looked up at him, and shook her head from side to side, without speaking, pointing at the watch. He approached her and looked at the watch, it said nine thirteen! She held up two fingers. He smiled, "Two minutes to go, you really are good at the game, aren't you?" She nodded.

Nigel had done it, it had been a success, he had altered history! He had saved three lives, it made him feel good. In a few hours the ship would sail, but the Andersons wouldn't. By next week, he would be a hero, their 'best friend'!

It was now time to tell them the truth about himself, they may not believe him now, but they soon would.

"Time up, you're such a good girl, you played the game well."

"Can I talk now?" she asked demurely.

"You certainly can, you can laugh, live, love and live a full life. There is one thing I have to tell you before we see your mummy and papa. Your holiday has been put off for a week, because that ship you were going on was a bad ship. So, don't be disappointed, a week isn't a long time, it will pass in a flash!"

"In a flash," she repeated.

"Yes, in a flash." Nigel took the watch off her and slipped it in his pocket."I'm going to see your parents now, play with your dollies. Then we will have a drink to end this game.

"It was a good game wasn't it Nigel?"

"Yes, it was a good game," he said as he left her with her dolls and went to the other room. He unlocked the door, apprehension showed on their faces.

"What have you done to Bertha?" Mrs. Anderson asked. It was obvious she had been crying, "You haven't hurt her, have you?"

"No, I haven't hurt her, we have been playing a game, she is perfectly happy," Nigel said with conviction.

"Where is she?"

"She's playing with her dolls in her bedroom. I don't know what you take me for; I am saving her, and you both. So, why in heaven should I want to hurt her? Or you for that matter?"

"Well, in that case, and you mean us no harm, release us, and let us carry on with our business. Bertie will be here soon, to pick us up in his car. We have to check in this morning, and we still have things to do, so I implore you, Nigel, before someone gets hurt." Gerald said.

"Nobody is getting hurt, on the contrary, you're being saved from any harm. And your friend Bertie has been and gone, so you have no way of going on that ship now. She is going to sink, and you would have drowned! Your wife and daughter may have had a chance, but once again, 'may have' is not good enough for me. I have saved you, I just couldn't stand by and watch you go to your deaths. You have been too good to me. You have got a wonderful little girl, and a beautiful wife, and you were about to lose it all and I wasn't going to allow that to happen! I will release your hands now." He went behind the chairs and cut the cord, also their legs that were bound. He slipped the knife into his pocket, and suggested that Mrs. Anderson might make some coffee. They both looked surprised at this request.

"Maybe something stronger, dear?" Gerald said, looking at Nigel.

"Of course, anything you want, you are now free to do as you please. You will miss the ship, and that's all I wanted. The only thing is, you cannot leave the house for the next two hours, but you are free to do anything else you like, I will not harm you, as I have always said."

"Get me a scotch and water will you dear?"

"If I must," she said unhappily. "Bertha, where are you?" she called as she went out of the door.

"Here Mummy," Bertha said. "Did you like the game Nigel played on you?"

"Hardly a game darling, I was worried sick, I didn't like it one bit. We won't be going on our holiday now, we have missed our ship."

"But Nigel said we can go next week, so that won't be too bad Mummy, will it?"

"Well, I suppose not," Mrs. Anderson said, realising that if Nigel had said that to the child, there was no danger to them.

In the meantime, Nigel said that it might be in order to go downstairs to have their drinks. But first of all, he took the hammer, and with the claw end removed the nail from the window, and the nail fell to the floor and fell between a crack in the floorboards. He tried to get it out, but it was no good, it was well and truly lodged there. Downstairs, they sat at the table, and their drinks were delivered.

"First off, I must say I'm truly sorry to have put you through this, in a way I had no alternative," Nigel started. "You will be able to go to New York any time you want to, but as I have said, not on that ship the Titanic. Before I go, I have to tell you something you won't believe, but I must tell you anyhow, I have to get it off my chest. If anyone is to be pitied in this whole affair, it's me, not you. Although at this moment I can understand your dislike for me, and you can't understand my behaviour. But you will understand. My name is Nigel Maythorn, I am a history teacher, I was born in eighty four, that makes me twenty three years old."

"That makes you twenty eight years," Gerald interrupted, "eighteen eighty four to now is twenty eight years.

"No, twenty three sir, because I was born in nineteen eighty four, seventy two years from now. And the year I live in is two thousand and seven, that's where I come from, the future! I can already see by your faces, disbelief, but please hear me out? My fiancée and I came to this house in that year, because it is up for sale. We were looking over the house, and I went into the big room, and was looking at the fireplace, when all of a sudden a strange force pulled me out into the room, I found myself in this time, nineteen hundred and twelve! When you saw me at the door that first time, you thought that I was the chimney sweep, I had just arrived, via the fireplace, hence the soot on my hands! You don't realise the shock I was in, I was as surprised to see you here as much as you were surprised to see me. When we were viewing the house, it was empty, so I assumed you were looking over the house like me. Then when I found out you were going to sail on the Titanic, I couldn't believe it! I was in shock, how could I come back in time? It was, and still is, beyond my comprehension!"

Gerald and his wife listened intently, and realised that this man called Nigel was indeed a mental case, so were still wary, and in Mrs. Anderson's case, frightened of him! She hoped that he would soon go, and she knew he would never be invited to her house again!

"I've tried to get back, but the force won't let me. It seems I'm lost in time! So while I'm in this position, it's my duty to try to save as many people as I can. I know it's very hard, because nobody believes me! Most think I'm an 'escaped mental case' but I'm not! I haven't told anyone at the pub about who I really am, you are the first to know. I'm not sure I'm making much sense. I lost everything,   my mother and father, I also have a brother, my wife-to-be, my fiancée Jane, all gone, my job as a teacher, everything! And here I am, with no way of getting home! My friends;at school, we were taught about the sinking of the Titanic, she will go down on the fifteenth of April, after hitting an iceberg. Fifteen hundred plus people will be lost. Captain Smith will drown, but Bruce Ismay, the Managing Director, will survive, seven hundred will survive. She hasn't got enough life boats to save all the passengers. But at least I have saved you, and that's the best I can do. I was on the ship yesterday, I warned people, but to no avail, nobody will listen to me! And to conclude, things will not get any better in the next seventy years, in just two years' time we will be in a world war with Germany, and millions of the young men will be slaughtered in the battlefields of France and Belgium. In the battle of the Somme alone, on July the first, nineteen hundred and sixteen, thousands will die on the first day! And in nineteen hundred and thirty nine we will be at war again, and it will last for six years, and I can't do a thing to stop it, if only I could! I'm sorry to be a bearer of all this bad news of coming years. Why me? I ask myself. Why was I put in this position? If only I could go back home now, I would give anything just to see my Jane again! This, to me, is hell!"

"Another drink darling," Gerald instructed his wife, and she promptly went to get one.

"You must show me the place in the fireplace you talk about Nigel, the force you mention. I have never noticed it, and I've cleaned out that area many times."

"I'll show you after our drink, I need one, come to think of it. In my world I don't drink very much, yet since I've been here I've drank every day! The way I'm going, I'm going to get myself in more trouble, I've never been in so much trouble in my whole life! I could tell you a lot more things about what's going to happen in the coming years, but that's enough for now, and I don't expect you to believe me anyhow, so for now, we'll leave it at that. I'm pleased at least I saved your family. I'm sorry if you were frightened, I would never have hurt any of you. I realise you will be annoyed at me for stopping you going, but wait until next week before you make another booking on a ship to New York. I'm going to leave you in peace now."

He drank his drink, and they went into the big room. The fireplace looked no different as Gerald went towards it.

"Show me where this force is?" he said.

"It's there in front of you, go forward into the back of the fireplace."

Gerald walked towards the entrance, and walked right in, then came out again. "I can't feel any force," Gerald said, looking puzzled.

Nigel went forward and walked into the access, he felt no force at all. "It was here I tell you, it was here," he walked in again. "Let me go back," he shouted, "let me go back to my life."

Nothing happened, he felt a little foolish as he faced the Andersons.

"There was a force, there was," he said with conviction. Then Nigel broke down and cried like a baby.

"Gerald, the man's ill," Alice said.

"I know," Gerald whispered, "Nigel, go home now and have a sleep, or go and see a doctor, my poor man, you need some help."

He put his arm around him and led him to the door.

"Is this still a game Nigel?" said Bertha.

"No my love, the game is now well and truly over." He said 'sorry' once again, and made his way down the avenue towards his destiny and the pub.

The Titanic gangway was being pulled in and the Titanic was set to sail on her maiden voyage.

Chapter 6

TOUGH TIMES

Nigel was in a daze as he made his way down the country lane that took him to the pub. The force had gone, he could see that he hadn't been believed, nobody believed anything he said. At least he felt some satisfaction in the fact that he had changed history. He had saved the Anderson family from certain death. He was slowly coming to terms with the fact that he was lost in time, and would never see his loved ones again. He was at a loss as to what to do to get back, he had tried. What kind of life was in store for him now, he just didn't know. Although his mind wanted an answer, none came. He got to the pub at last, where Fanny was working behind the bar, and pulled up a stool. "Where have you been all morning?" she asked.

"Trying to change history," Nigel replied. "And I may have pulled it off; in fact I know I did." He looked around the bar; there were not many customers at this time of the day. But he knew they would be coming in soon because of the sing-song arranged for the evening. A piano player was going to play, they were always popular evenings, so he had been told.

"Do you want a tankard?" she enquired.

"Yes, I need a drink," he replied.

Two men came in and sat at the bar. "She was beautiful, never seen anything like it in my life. I'm going to try to get on her next time she's in port. A wonderful ship that Titanic, saw her leave this morning, saw her sail," the man said to Fanny. She glanced over at Nigel, as if she knew he would get into the conversation, and he did. "That's the last time you'll see her my friend, she won't be coming back to this port, that's a certainty, she's a doomed ship." The two men looked at Nigel in amazement, as he continued, "The truth is she hasn't left yet, she's still held up in the River Test, after nearly colliding with another ship. And the name of that ship is the New York, tied up at berth 38 next to the Oceanic. It's a pity really that they didn't collide, because then the Titanic may have been delayed and things would have been different. To think, just four feet, they missed one another by just four feet!" Nigel took a sip of his beer, and shook his head, a sad expression on his face.

"You're very knowledgeable, sir, how do you know all this? Are you making it up for a joke? Because I don't like your sense of humour," the man blurted out.

"This is not a joke, far from it. I have been saying it for days now, that the Titanic is on its last voyage. It will sink next Monday morning, 15th April, after hitting an iceberg, it's a fact," Nigel said in a definite way. "I bet my life on it."

"Right then, so you want to bet," said the second man, "what odds are you giving?"

"A hundred million to one," Nigel retorted.

"Now don't be bloody stupid, give me real odds, and I will have a bet with you that you are wrong, and the unsinkable Titanic ship will return to Southampton," the man said, looking at his friend, and smirking. "Got a nut-case here Bert," he whispered.

By this time three other men had come to the bar, and had overheard the conversation.

"I'll have a flutter on that one," said a short stocky man.

"Me too," said another.

"Right, if that's the way you want to lose your money, I'll give you one hundred to one. Who wants to bet?" Nigel said, getting up from his stool and facing the men. The five men were in.

"Fanny, will you get me some paper and a biro, and I'll make out the betting slips?" Nigel asked.

"I'll get you some paper and a pencil, but I don't have one of those things you mentioned, biro, never heard of it."

"No, sorry, a pencil will do," he said. The five men had walked away from the bar, and were huddled in the far corner of the pub, talking in an exciting manner.

"Nigel, are you sure you know what you're doing? A hundred to one, you haven't got that kind of money to pay out. I know these five men, they are real gamblers, they'11 take you for a ride." She looked concerned. Fanny had taken a real liking to this fascinating man who made her laugh from the first moment she set her eyes on him, something had stirred in her.

"Don't worry, I'm certain. I would bet a million to one. Anyhow, I can pay you back the pound I owe you, and I can now get the brakes fixed on your bike, pay my lodgings, and for your kindness to me." He smiled at her, and indicated one more drink, before a little afternoon sleep; he was on duty later on.

The men returned to where Nigel was sitting. The short stocky man had taken on the role of spokesman. "Now, me and my friends here," he indicated, "want you to say it one more time, to get it right, and make sure there is no misunderstanding on both our parts. That you are willing to take a bet that the ship, the unsinkable Titanic, that left here today, will sink in a few days' time, and you are offering one hundred to one, is that correct?" The men all fixed their eyes on Nigel.

"I'm saying for the very last time that the Titanic will go to the bottom of the ocean on Monday morning at two twenty, after hitting an iceberg. Seven hundred and five will survive and one thousand, five hundred and twenty nine, or there about, will die. So the bets are on."

"Bloody amazing," said one man.

"Brilliantly stupid," said another.

Nigel took ten pounds in minutes, and made the slips out to the men. "Don't let us down," one man said in a menacing way.

"Don't worry I won't, and spread the word around to your friends, that I will be taking more bets tonight. We're having a sing-song, and Peter the piano player will be here. I may even sing a few songs I know. Yes, another thing you didn't know, I'm a Karaoke singer."

The men laughed, as Nigel drank the remainder of his beer, and went behind the bar to go to his room at the back of the pub, and up the stairs.

Fanny joined him in the kitchen. "Here," he said, handing her the pound she had lent him, "and thanks for lending it to me in the first place. You have been so kind to me, giving me a job and a room; you are truly a wonderful person." He leaned forward and gave her a light kiss on her cheek; her face looked reddish at his praise for her. No man had ever spoken like that to her in her life, not even her husband.

She grabbed his arm. "I'm worried Nigel, those men are not the best. When you can't pay your debts to them, they will get really nasty. I'm worried what will become of you."

"Look, I've already told you, don't worry, I'm in the money now, by the end of this day I will be a rich man, and I'm here to help you out like you helped me." He smiled. "I'm going to have a little sleep for an hour or so, got to get ready for a good night, I have to work you know. But tonight I am going to entertain as well. You haven't heard me sing yet, have you?" "No," she said laughing.

"Best in the world," he laughed, as he went up the stairs to his bed.

"Fanny," shouted one of her customers, "are you working, or do we have to go down to the Bull's Arms?"

"Coming," she shouted back as she watched Nigel disappear up the stairs.

"Strange barman you got there," said one of the men. "I've heard of 'crooners' and 'altos', but never 'karaoke'."

The group of men laughed again. "By this time next week we will be very rich, yes my good friends, very very rich." Once again all the men laughed loudly. Fanny smiled, but said nothing. She was inwardly very concerned for this strange, but delightful man who had suddenly appeared from nowhere, and made her last few days seem somehow different. A mellow feeling filled her being whenever he was near her. She loved his whole demeanour, his smile, he made her happy. She hadn't heard from her husband for a while, yet she didn't miss him as much as she once did. And since Nigel had come along, she hardly thought of her husband. Just thinking of Nigel made her happy, but she was still worried.

The pub closed at two in the afternoon, and re-opened at five o'clock. Fanny tidied up, and went for a little walk, thinking about her life. She was pleased that her mother-in-law had taken Brian for the day, it gave her a little break from looking after the baby. She did wonder why she hadn't heard from her husband for a while, but her thoughts were mostly about Nigel. An hour later she got back to the pub, and went to lay down for her afternoon rest. When she came down she saw Nigel sitting outside at the back of the pub, on a chair he had taken from the kitchen. She picked up a chair and joined him outside in the afternoon sun.

"You know Fanny, have you ever thought of placing some benches and chairs out here for your customers? They could drink their beer in the sunshine instead of in the smoky bar, a lot healthier, then the customers who don't smoke could drink without getting smoke in their lungs. Smoking is bad for you, it can cause cancer and all sorts of ailments. Anyhow, just a thought." He took a slurp of his tea.

"A lovely idea, but I couldn't afford to pay for tables and chairs out here. It's hard enough to do repairs on the inside of the pub. It's been a struggle, these are hard times," she replied.

"Maybe I could help, maybe we could do a few things, entertainment for our new customers; like light lunches in the summer, in the garden, more entertainment in the evenings; singing contests, we could buy meat from the butchers and run meat raffles on the weekends, have card games, with other pubs, we would go to their pubs, then they would come to ours for a night of cards. I've seen pubs packed out on meat draws and raffles nights, I have lots of ideas for this pub."

"You certainly have," Fanny said with a broad smile, "but it all takes money, it takes money to get new things going. Money that I haven't got, and never will have."

"I have, or will have by tonight. I would help you get fixed up." "No," she interrupted, "I wouldn't take your money. Anyhow my husband might not want to do it. The last time he wrote to me he said that he may sell the pub. I'm sure he wouldn't want it expanded, he lost interest in it a long time ago."

"I'm sorry, for a moment I forgot you were married. Don't think that my motives are anything more than helping you out like you helped me. Maybe I just got carried away, I have always had ideas for this and that, sometimes they come true and others just fade into nothing. Like I had a good idea once, of living in a grand house on a hill with the girl of my dreams, for ever and ever, and have children." Nigel's eyes glazed over, and became moist so he stopped talking. "And did that one come true?" she enquired. "No, that one got away," Nigel sighed.

"I will have to get ready for opening time." She got up and went into the kitchen. A tear ran down Nigel's face. With both of them behind the bar, the first customers entered for an evening's sing-song. Peter the piano player was a very talented musician, and could play by ear as well as read music. All anyone had to do was hum a tune and Peter would soon be playing it. Everyone seemed happy enough singing the songs of the day, and the drinking never waned. Some of the Bull's Arms customers had come because of Peter, but a lot came because of the news that the barman was giving odds of a hundred to one, on the Titanic sinking. So in-between serving drinks, Nigel was writing out betting slips. One poor customer put six pennies on, knowing that he would be pocketing six pounds in less than a week, a fortune to him.

Nigel refused one man, who wanted to bet his life's savings, thirty pounds. The man wasn't happy, so he asked others to do it for him in smaller amounts. Nigel couldn't stop it, and by closing time he had one hundred pounds, a grand fortune in nineteen hundred and twelve. A rich man Nigel was now, two years' wages for an ordinary man. And with what he knew, he could make more money as time went along. If he had to suffer, he might as well do it in luxury, he thought. Nothing could compensate for the loss of his life with Jane and his mum and dad, but a bit of wealth might help him in this strange new life. At least he was having fun working alongside the landlady. They seemed to gel together, and although they were busy, kept the customers served quickly, and at the same time had time for a few laughs. Nigel took time out to have a word with Peter when the singing was over, to hum a few tunes to him, and see if he could accompany him with some new songs. It didn't take Peter long to pick up a tune.

"Ladies and gentlemen, Nigel our barman, has a new song he would like to sing to you, so put your hands together for him."

Nigel smiled broadly. "Thank you Peter, now a lot of you have asked me where I came from and where I was born, so I will tell you now." He then went into the Lee Marvin song from the film 'Paint your Wagon' I was born under a wandering star. He had a low voice, and although the customers had never heard the song before, gave him a good round of applause. Then Nigel sang an Elvis number, 'Can't help falling in love with you!' He looked over to Fanny behind the bar, and she smiled and blushed. Another round of applause ended his singing debut, and he returned behind the bar. A good night was had by all.

"You have a nice voice," she told him as she gave him his supper after the pub had closed.

"Thank you very much," he said in his 'Elvis' voice. She had offered to get a tankard for him, but he had declined. He had been drinking too much just lately, and had decided to ease down, so it was tea, bread and cheese and pickles.

"I did well tonight with my bets, I took a hundred pounds," he said.

"One hundred pounds," she repeated, truly amazed. "That's a fortune; I don't take that in a month, in the bar!"

"I could have had more, but I didn't want to take their hard-earned money from them, I'm not that callous. One man tried to bet his life's savings, I refused; it would be like taking money from a beggar. I tried to dissuade them, but they insisted, so what could I do?"

"You were forced into it Nigel, I was there as a witness. You seem so sure you'll win."

"I'm one hundred percent sure," Nigel said, as he got up to go to bed. "If you feel like a cuddle, you know where I am?" he said, laughing out loud.

She looked surprised. "You naughty boy," she said smiling, as she washed the dishes. He went up to his little room, and fifteen minutes later, she slid in beside him, and lost in one another's arms they went off together in sleep.

Nigel woke up abruptly as Jane's engagement ring hit him on his face. She was shouting at him, the dream was very vivid. He was alone, the rays of the sun crossing the room through the holes in the curtains. He suddenly felt guilty, what had he done? In normal circumstances, he would never have contemplated being unfaithful to his fiancée, and now he had. He slowly got out of bed, and dressed in the clothes that Fanny had given him. His jeans, tee-shirt, trainers and other things were in a drawer in an old dresser that stood just behind the door.

'Have to buy something new soon,' he thought, as he dressed in the old clothes, he tucked the betting money in the drawer. He gingerly made his way down to the kitchen, she was making his breakfast.

"Nice day," Nigel said, not knowing what to say. "Yes," she said, not turning around from her cooking. He sat at the table, and watched her, she had a petite figure. He turned around in his chair, and looked at the day.

"Eat your breakfast," she said, putting the plate in front of him. She sat opposite.

"Sorry," he said.

"Sorry for what?" she replied.

"I'm sorry for last night."

"Last night," she retorted, "it was a good night. The customers had a good time, you entertained everyone, you did no wrong."

"No, I mean what happened in bed," he looked at her intently.

"Oh, so you're sorry for loving me, are you? Was I that bad?"

"No, no, you were wonderful, but I feel like I took advantage of you, and I would never do that."

"Look, eat your breakfast before it gets cold, then we will talk." She gave him a smile. "Tea?" she said as she got up from the table.

"Please," he replied. Breakfast was eaten in silence, he avoided her eyes. He felt he had betrayed Jane, he had been unfaithful for the first time.

She cleared the table, putting the plates in the sink, and sat down.

"I'm not sorry for what happened last night, if it was anyone's fault it was mine. After all it was me who got into your bed, I'm really to blame for what happened. I hope you don't think I have done this kind of thing before, because I haven't, I was always true to my husband. I have wondered many times if he was as true to me, with his travelling all over the world. I bet he's got a woman in every port. I haven't heard from him for ages, maybe he'll never come back to me. How long does he expect me to wait? Anyhow, once again Nigel, I'm not sorry at all, it's a pity you regret it."

"I don't regret it, as I have said, it was wonderful. Sometimes people do things then regret it later on."

"Nigel, I don't expect you to love me. Let's just say it was something that happened, something we both enjoyed, we have shared a moment in time."

"That's true," Nigel interjected.

"I hope you are not going to leave?" She looked at him with enquiring eyes.

"No, I'm not going anywhere, I'm stuck here for the duration, I have nowhere to go."

"Where are you from Nigel? How come you turned up at the pub out of the blue, so to speak? No money, if I remember rightly?"

"I will let you into my secret, only if you promise to keep it a secret?"

"I will, I promise you."

"Well, I'll tell you the full story next Tuesday the sixteenth of April, after we find out that I was right about the Titanic."

"Oh, that again," she retorted.

"Yes, that again." He got up from the table, took her in his arms and kissed her full on the lips. "Thanks for your faith in me, and I'm not sorry for last night." She hugged him tight.

"I'd better start on my chores, otherwise you may sack me," he joked.

"Yes, get to work," she laughed. "Break at eleven o'clock."

Nigel went to do some painting he had intended to do, the place needed brightening up. She busied herself in the bar, stocking up. Brian her baby would be back today, and then her hands would be full with him.

At eleven o'clock she had made the tea, and because it was a nice day, she set a little table in the garden at the back of the pub. She knew she had the same feeling in her that she had had when she had met her husband. She was falling in love again, but this time with a man she hardly knew, a complete stranger who had come into her life just a few days before, and would he stay? she wondered. He could go at any time. She could visualise him staying with her for ever. She would tell her husband that she had met someone else, he wouldn't care, he had been gone a while now with no contact. Her mind was full of these thoughts, confusion reigned, she hoped he would stay for ever. She called him, and he appeared with paint on his face and hands.

"Look at you, looks like you're painting yourself!" she laughed, as she wiped his face with a wet cloth.

"Like my singing, I'm the best painter in the world!" They both laughed as they made their way out to the garden. "By the way, have you seen Bill my friend? He wasn't here last night. In fact, I haven't seen him for a couple of days."

"Bill who?" she asked.

"You know that policeman bloke who you talked to on the day I first came here?"

"Oh him, I don't really know him that well. In fact, the day you came in, he had come in just before you."

81

"Oh, I thought he was a regular customer!"

"No, never seen him before, as I've said."

"Oh well, I guess he will turn up sometime. Funny, he always seems to be around when I'm in trouble, like in the pub in Southampton, when I got into trouble with some sea-men. And the café, once again when I was in trouble. Then the time I was in trouble in this pub with that Irish sea-man, and I remember he said that he was looking out for me. Good friend, I hope I see him again, nice fellow." They enjoyed the break for tea, and did a bit more talking on different subjects, when they heard loud knocking on the front door of the pub.

"There's another three quarters of an hour before opening time," she said, as she went to see who it was. Nigel finished his drink and was looking over the garden at things he might do to attract more customers to the pub, when she came out of the back door.

Her face was full of anguish. "Nigel, there's someone in the bar to see you, policemen."

"Oh, Bill's here," he said standing up.

"No Nigel, not Bill, the police."

They walked through the kitchen and into the bar, two policemen were with a man Nigel recognised.

"That's him," said the man excitedly, "that's him, he was at the house yesterday morning."

Nigel stood and said nothing, Fanny looked at him.

"I went to pick up my friends for the ship, and he answered the door, telling me that they had left for the docks. Don't deny it you bounder," Bertie said with anger.

"Are you Nigel Maythorn?" the policeman asked.

"Yes, that's my name."

"Well, you are under arrest, you are charged with kidnapping, theft and obstructing people, named the Anderson family, from going about their lawful business. You will now come with us to the police station, where is your coat?"

"It can't be true," Fanny said, almost in tears. "Nigel, tell them it's not true."

"It's not true; just have faith in me. All will be well, just wait and see."

"Where is your coat, sir?"

"It's in my room." "Then go and get it, we will wait here. And don't try to escape, because that will only add to your troubles."

"Can I have a word with Fanny, just a few minutes please?"

"Alright, just a minute, then you will come with us."

"I can explain everything, officer," Nigel said as he made his way through the bar and kitchen, and up to his room. A constable went with him, and waited at the bottom of the stairs.

Fanny went upstairs with him. In his room, Nigel turned around and took her in his arms. "Don't worry, everything will turn out alright, believe me."

"But Nigel," she blurted.

"No, listen to me, we only have a minute. While I'm away, take as many bets as you can, in my name, as much as you can, 100-1. Remember, do it. The one hundred is in that drawer."

He picked up his coat and slipped it on. "Sorry, you will have to get someone to help behind the bar while I'm away. And give little Brian a kiss for me when he comes back. Look after yourself, I'11 be back," he said, remembering that saying from a film he had seen. He kissed her, and walked down the stairs, with her trailing behind. In the bar the police now took hold of him, one on either side, and he was led to the door.

"Search him," shouted Bertie, "search the blaggard." The policemen went through his pockets, and found a knife and a pocket watch.

"That watch belongs to Gerald," Bertie pointed. "I know, I gave it to him as a gift. And that's the knife that he threatened the little girl with, the bounder."

"Are they yours sir?" a policeman asked.

"No, they're not," Nigel said, as he was led out of the door. By this time Fanny was crying.

"Trust me Fanny, please trust me," he shouted as he was placed in the car, and led away to the police station.

It seemed strange to be driving up to the house and through

the gates, the same thing he had done just five days before with his beloved Jane. The police car stopped outside the house, they thanked Bertie for his help. At that moment the Andersons came out of the house, and came to the car.

"We've got him, sir. Is this the man who stopped you going about your lawful business?" said the driver of the police car.

"Yes, that's him," said Mrs. Anderson, glaring at Nigel.

"Are these your property, sir?" said the policeman, producing the pocket watch and the knife. Gerald took them, and declared that indeed they were his.

"We would like to keep them for evidence at the trial, if that's alright with you, sir?"

"Yes, take them."

Gerald handed them back to the policeman. He then directed his attention to Nigel who was in the back of the car.

"I mis-judged you. I thought of you as a gentleman my friend, and you did this to us. You upset my wife so much that she has trouble sleeping now. We were worried about our little girl. You are a cad and a bounder, and I hope you will be punished severely for it. Goodbye to you sir." With that, Gerald turned his back and walked back into the house, taking his wife by the arm, and Bertie trailing behind. As they reached the door, Bertha came bounding out and, seeing Nigel in the police car, came running towards him.

"Nigel, you've come back. Are we going to play another…"

Gerald stopped her, and held her back. "Inside Bertha," he demanded.

"But Papa," she protested.

"Inside now," he said in a stronger tone.

"Yes Papa," Bertha said, waving to Nigel as she disappeared in the front door.

"They don't care for you laddie," the policeman said sarcastically.

"They will, just wait a few days and I'll be their hero, I saved them."

"We will take your statement when we get to the station.

For now, keep your comments to yourself," the policeman said. "You're in a lot of trouble, I would think twenty years in prison, kidnapping is a serious offence."

Nigel said nothing for the rest of the journey to the Central Police Station in Southampton. It was the first time in his life that Nigel had seen the inside of a police station, or indeed had any dealings with the police, so this new experience didn't bother him too much. In a strange way he was enjoying it, he was sure that he would be freed when his predictions were found to be true. There was only four days to go before the historical event took place. He couldn't visualise going to prison, he was more concerned with how Fanny would manage without him.

The police put Nigel in a 'holding' room, just a room with a small desk and two chairs opposite one another. He was left there for half an hour, which gave Nigel time to think of how he would go about explaining it all! He realised it was pointless trying to explain where he had come from, he would have to devise a brand new identity. He looked down at his shoes and old clothes, and decided he would have to buy new ones soon.

The door opened and into the room came a big police sergeant who sat down opposite Nigel and fumbled with some papers.

At last he spoke. "Now then, what's all this about? The constable who arrested you has told me that you kidnapped a Mr. and Mrs. Anderson and their daughter. You have also been charged with robbery and threatening behaviour. What have you got to say for yourself?"

"Don't you have to read me my rights?" Nigel asked.

"What?" the sergeant said in surprise. "Rights? You have no rights, you have been identified as the man who put these good people to a lot of trouble. They feared for their lives, and you talk about 'rights!' Let me tell you this, these are serious charges, so I would advise you to tell the truth." He looked at the paper work and continued. "Why did you steal a pocket watch and a butter knife and nothing more? But first of all, before you answer these questions, I want a few details from you: name, address and so on. Name?" the policeman asked, pen posed.

"Nigel Maythorn, I'm twenty three years old and I live at the Fox and Hounds pub."

"How long have you lived at the pub?" asked the policeman. "Just a few days."

"A few days," the policeman muttered, writing the information into a note book. "Now tell me, what's all this about? You seem to me to be a decent sort of character. Unfortunately you have been arrested for kidnapping, theft and endangering a little girl's life. Let me warn you that the magistrate won't take these charges lightly. I can foresee twenty years in prison, at least. So tell me the truth and I'll do my best for you."

At that moment another higher ranking policeman came into the room and pulled up a chair and sat next to his colleague. This burly man with a squint in one eye that made him look menacing to Nigel said, "What's this all about? I've been hearing some bizarre things about you laddie." He looked at a page of a portfolio, and picked one out. "You have said that you come from the future, and you did this to look for a house you thought was for sale. You stopped people from going on a ship, and worst of all, you think that the Titanic will sink!"

Both policemen looked at one another and burst out laughing.

"It's not funny," Nigel blurted out, "just wait and see!"

"Oh, so you still believe that the Titanic ship will sink?" said the smaller policeman.

"Yes," Nigel replied, sighing and looking down at the table.

"Is there something wrong with your mind? Are you going to plead insanity? Because let me inform you, it won't work. I can see a long prison sentence coming your way laddie. So tell us the truth, as to why you imprisoned the Anderson family for three hours or more, and stopped them going about their lawful business."

Nigel was beginning to sweat, little beads started to form on his forehead! He knew he had to concoct a new story, and fast! He said, "I had a dream the other night that the Titanic was going to sink on her maiden voyage. It was very real, very weird, I could see people drowning and screaming in the cold water of the North

86

Atlantic. I found out that the Andersons were going on the ship, and I felt a duty to warn them, but when they took no notice of me, I had no option to help them, but to stop them going. I had no intention of hurting any of them, and I needed to know the time, so I just borrowed the watch. I don't remember how the butter knife ended up in my pocket though! I've saved them, and they will be grateful to me by next week!"

"Rubbish, utter rubbish," said the higher ranking officer, getting up from his chair. "I've never heard anything so stupid in my life. You're for it laddie, that's a certainty. Put him back in the cell sergeant. Court for you tomorrow, we'll see what the magistrate has to say about this. I'm off home." With that he walked out of the room, and slammed the door.

"You've made another enemy; we are not getting very far are we? Better think of a better excuse than a dream. Twenty years I reckon." The sergeant put his notebook back in his pocket and took Nigel to a cell. "You'll be getting some tea soon, then I suggest you get a good night's sleep, you've got a busy day tomorrow, court is at ten a.m."

"What about a lawyer?" enquired Nigel. "Don't I get a lawyer? Haven't I got a right to see one?"

"As I have said before, you have no rights, understand? No rights! Your tea will be here soon." With that he locked Nigel up. The cell was small, a bed, one blanket, a bucket and a chair, that's all. A small barred window full of dust and cobwebs showed that the day was ebbing away. He sat on the bed that was hard, and his head in his hands, he cried like a baby.

Bread, cheese and lukewarm weak tea. He wasn't very hungry, the policeman who brought him his meal didn't utter a word. At eight o'clock the light suddenly went out, the utter darkness overwhelmed the cell.

Nigel slept fitfully, and at six o'clock the light came on again. A sparse breakfast was served, and at nine a.m. he was taken from the cell and to the Magistrate's Court. Nigel was remanded in custody until a 'mental' report was made; it was all over in a few minutes. The charges were read out, after his name and address were verified. The charges: false imprisonment, robbery, and endangering life.

"Not guilty," replied Nigel to the question. The inspector asked for remand to ascertain the defendant's mental health. Nigel was taken to Winchester prison and put in a cell with another inmate also on remand.

"Dick Flint's me name, I'm thirty one, from Portsmouth. In for grievous bodily harm, if they can fookin prove it. And that's all you need to know. You, top bunk," the burly unshaven man said with menace in his voice. "Don't ask me any fink more, understand?" "Yes," said Nigel, climbing up to the top bunk. Half an hour of silence between the two men ensued, then Nigel said, "I'm not your enemy you know, so why can't we be friends? It seems we are in the same boat so to speak."

"Why the fook would I want to be friends with you? You don't know fook all about me, and I don't want to know fook all about you, so shut your fooken mouth, or I'll shut it for you, understand?"

"Yes," said Nigel, turning over and pulling a blanket over his head. The man swore under his breath as he got his clothes and things together. Within the hour he was taken away, and Nigel was left alone for a short time.

Tea was taken in a big hall at long tables. Nigel collected his meal and quietly ate, not talking to anyone, before he was taken back to his cell.

"You will be getting a new cell-mate. Bruser Flint has gone down for twenty five years," the warden informed Nigel.

"That's good to know, he wasn't the friendliest of people," Nigel said as he got up into his bunk.

"No, there's no friendliness with him. He just killed his wife and her boyfriend, bad one that one. You may get to meet him again when you go down," he said sarcastically as he locked Nigel in for the night.

He paced his cell for an hour or more, nothing to read, no TV like modern prisons. This place, this time, was no place to be. He had been in more trouble in five days than he had been in all his past life, and there was nothing he could do about it. He thought of Jane and his family, and had one more cry before he drifted off to sleep, and another dreadful day had gone by.

Word had got around to the Bull's Arms betters, and they descended on the Fox and Hounds like a swarm of locusts, not wanting to take bets, but demanding their money back, when they heard of the barman's arrest. Fanny, on hearing that Nigel was likely to go to prison for a long time, got the betting slips together and paid them all off.

"If we ever get our hands on him, he's in for a hiding, and when he goes in, we have friends inside who owe us a favour, so he's in for a beating no matter what," said one of the men, all the others agreed.

Fanny was relieved that Nigel had told her where the hundred pounds were kept, so at least the gamblers had got their money back. She felt relieved also, that she had found his wallet and looked at the contents. There was a picture of a pretty girl, 'with love to Nigel 2006'!; paper money with a Queen she had never heard of, Elizabeth. Driving licence, once again with the date 2005. A cutting of a school history, dated 2006, cut out of a newspaper! She could not make head or tail of it. She was pleased when she shut the doors, hoping that the customers from the Bull's Arms would now return there to drink. She checked on Brian who was sleeping soundly, and went to bed. Little did she know that the next day her husband would return, and this time to stay, his life at sea over, for a while.

Nigel's door was opened again, after he had returned to his cell half an hour after breakfast, and he was told that he was to be interviewed by a doctor. He was led to a little room that looked like a consulting room and told to sit down.

A thin man with a white coat sat opposite him. "Nigel," he started, as though an enquiry.

"Yes sir," Nigel replied.

"I want to ask you a few questions, so listen carefully. Do you like children?"

"Of course," he replied in surprise.

"Then why would you threaten a young child's life with a knife?"

"Oh that. I know what you're referring to, the little girl Bertha, a lovely child. I had no intention of hurting her or anyone else. I had the knife to cut some cord to restrain Mr. and Mrs. Anderson and stop them from leaving the house. I had to delay them to miss the ship they were going on to America."

"So you admit you did this," said the doctor, writing something down on a sheet of paper.

"Yes, I did it deliberately," said Nigel with a broad smile.

"Why?"

"Because, as I have said a hundred times, the ship the Titanic is going to sink. I'm fed up with saying it, nobody believes me."

"You stole a time-piece, I have written down here. He pointed to the paper.

"No sir, I slipped Gerald's pocket watch into my pocket, and just forgot to return it."

"You call Mr. Anderson by his first name, don't you think that's presumptuous of you?"

"Why should I? We're friends, he's my drinking partner."

"Your friend?" the doctor interjected. "You treat friends in this way, tie them up and stop them doing things that normal people do? Hardly the way to treat a friend."

"Well, he is my friend, and so is his wife. They have been good to me, I've drank, eaten and been shown friendship. We have talked and laughed together, and I call him my friend, and in a few days' time they will love me, when the news comes through on Tuesday 16th April."

The doctor looked at Nigel intently. "If you were cast on a desert island on your own or with anyone else, what do you think you would miss the most?" the doctor enquired.

"Music, my music."

"And what do you listen to?"

"Beatles, flock of seagulls, animals."

"Who?" said the doctor.

"Yes, sometimes."

"Who?" repeated the doctor again.

"I've just told you, yes. But the best of all would be the American group The Byrds, and of course Grateful Dead."

"The Birds," the doctor muttered writing it down. "Do you enjoy telling stories?"

"Yes," said Nigel, "I was once a school teacher, and I taught history, so I like telling stories on history."

"If you could have been born in the past, what era would you have liked to live in?"

Nigel replied, "I wouldn't want to be born in the past, but in the future, 2007 would be a nice place to be right now."

"Why is that?" enquired the doctor.

"Because that's where I come from, and that's where I belong, where my life is, my loved ones, my work, not here in this prison. I don't belong here, I want to go home. Help me, for Christ's sake, help me please doctor? I can't stand this for much longer, I'm going out of my mind. Doc please, I'm cracking up. You have to believe me, I don't come from here, I'm an alien, a bloody alien!" "Calm down Nigel, calm down," he could hear the doctor say, as he ranted on and on.

"I want to go home, to watch my television, fly to America, live in my own world, not this one." Tears flowed down his cheeks. Two wardens were standing him onto his feet, and he was led away from the consulting room and back to his cell. The doctor made his report, that he would present to the inspector, recommending that Nigel Maythorn was to be put into a psychiatric hospital, and that he was mentally insane. 'He says he listens to the animals and beetles, and thinks he can fly! I have never come across such an acute case,' he wrote in his report, 'he needs long term care.' He signed it and closed the folder, and it sealed Nigel's future. In the meantime, Nigel was having to deal with another, new cell-mate, who happened to have taken a fancy to him!

Monday morning didn't come too soon, and Nigel was pleased to be in front of the magistrate. He was going to ask if it was possible to wait for one more day before his case was heard. Because then the news would hit the streets on Tuesday. He could see the headlines: 'TITANIC disaster, great loss of life' in the evening news. He even remembered a picture of the news-boy, with a bundle under his arm, and people standing around reading the dreadful news. He had seen that picture many times in the books he had read. He came up from the cells; the old wooden stairs creaked under the weight of the two burly wardens who accompanied him to a box in front of a stern looking magistrate.

"Is your name Nigel Maythorn, of the Fox and Hounds public house, on Maypole road?" the magistrate said, looking over his black spectacles, which made him look more severe than may have been the case.

"Yes sir," Nigel spluttered.

"How do you plead to the charges brought against you?"

"Not guilty," Nigel replied, looking around the court, which seemed old and had an air of neglect with plaster missing in parts, and the window showed little light. There weren't many people in the court, but he could feel their eyes fixed on him.

"Are you paying attention Maythorn?" the magistrate said in a rebuking way.

"Yes, sir."

"Look at me then. First witness," he demanded. The arresting policeman was the first to give evidence, and he told the court about being called by a Mr. Albert St. Clair, who was concerned about the whereabouts of his friends Mr. and Mrs. Anderson, who he was going to take to the docks to sail on the Titanic who were not at home, or down at the docks. Mr. St. Clair later identified the defendant as the man he saw at the house of Mr. Anderson.

"Is Mr. St. Clair in court?"

"No sir, he was taken ill, but Mr. Anderson is here to give evidence."

Mr. Anderson gave his story, and pointed out Nigel as the man who stopped them sailing. After he left the stand the magistrate asked Nigel to explain himself.

"Did you do these things that Mr. Anderson has said that you did?"

"Yes sir, I did, but time will show that I was trying to help the family. I didn't hurt anyone, nor did I steal anything, I've never stolen anything in my life!"

"And do you still insist that you are from another time?" He looked down at some papers. "Two thousand and seven in the future."

Nigel hesitated at that question for a moment, his mind working overtime. "No sir, that was a story I made up."

"You like telling stories do you?"

"No sir."

"I have a report here from a psychiatrist, and in it it says that you like to listen to the animals, birds, insects, like beetles, you want to fly like a bird! Is this the way a normal man would talk? I think not. I was going to send you to prison, but with hearing the evidence and the report, I can only for your own good, put you in a proper place for a man of your disposition, and that is a mental institution, for as long as you continue to act like you have been doing."

"But sir, just wait until Wednesday, just two days' time, and it will be on the television news; The Titanic, then you will know that I was telling the truth. But I realize you don't understand me do you? You've never heard of television have you? Because it's not been invented yet, nor has radio, all that's to come in the future. But one day it will, then you'll believe me! I don't belong here, you don't understand, I want to go home."

Nigel was very distressed by now.

"Take him away," ordered the magistrate.

"You'll see I'm telling the truth! Wait until Wednesday the seventeenth April!" Nigel shouted as he disappeared down to the holding cells.

The hospital wasn't too far from the prison, and in no time at all Nigel was in his new home. The hospital looked as grim as the prison, there was no doubt that it had a need of a face lift. It was the kind of place that Nigel had read about in Dickens' books.

He was placed in a single room, and told to go to bed after being given a tasteless meal of boiled potatoes and cabbage, bread and a cup of weak coffee.

"How long will I be here?" he had asked an attendant in a white coat.

A one word answer came as the attendant went out of the door: "Indefinitely."

The door was locked, and he was left alone to wonder how he had got into this mess. Eight days of trouble, nothing but trouble. He now knew it was useless telling the truth about himself, nobody had believed him, and nobody would. He would have to devise a plan to escape from this place. And then he thought, there would be no reason to escape, because when the news hit the streets on Tuesday evening, they would believe him, and he would be released. Nigel felt a little better as he got into the little bed and went to sleep.

The next morning he woke up refreshed and optimistic, the news of the sinking would hit the streets that day, and the authorities would at last believe him. He saw another man and was asked a few questions, but it was a short interview. He went out of his room, and was shown the dining hall. He was introduced to a few patients, and the staff, but after he had been told to take some pills, he had felt tired so he went and lay on his bed. He had his meals in his room, and the first day passed away.

The next day was much the same, apart from a job of helping to lay the tables in the dining hall, and to help in the kitchen. He asked if the newspapers were out yet, and was told that there were no papers in the hospital.

The rest of the week slipped by, and still no news at all. It was not until Tuesday of the following week that something happened to Nigel, something very surprising. He was sitting on his bed, despondent, when the man in the white coat came into his room. "Get dressed, you have to go to the police station for another court case. This time it may be prison for you. Two policemen are waiting for you in the office."

Nigel got dressed and followed the attendant down the

corridor to a room near the entrance at the hospital, and went in. A policeman with pips on his lapel was bent over, signing a piece of paper on the desk, with his back to Nigel. The other policeman approached and put handcuffs on him. Without saying a word, he was led out of the hospital door, into the sunlight of a lovely day. A car was just outside the grounds on the main road.

"Why do I have to go to court again? Has the magistrate heard the news? I'm being released, aren't I?"

"The inspector will explain everything, get in," he ordered.

He opened the car door and got into the back seat, the inspector got into the driving seat, and drove off to a public toilet, and stopped the car.

"Stay where you are," the policeman said, as both men got out of the car. Picking up a suitcase he disappeared into the toilet.

They had only been gone for five minutes, when both men came towards the car, now dressed in ordinary civilian clothes, and got back in the car. Without talking, the driver started the car up again, and drove for half an hour when they stopped again and the men got out and took the handcuffs off Nigel.

"Thanks Steve, you did a good job," the driver said and handed some money over. The man walked away and disappeared around a corner.

"Get into the front seat," the driver ordered.

"What's going on?" said Nigel, feeling a little concerned. No-one had spoken throughout the journey.

"Get in the front seat," he was ordered again. Nigel got out and slipped into the front seat.

"What are we doing?"

"I'm looking after you, just keeping an eye out for you." He turned to face Nigel, a broad smile ensued.

"Bill," Nigel said with delight, "where the hell have you been? I haven't seen you since that day in the café, the day I went on the Titanic, remember?"

"Yes, I remember it well," said Bill.

"So now you know I was right all along, you must have heard

the news by now. I've been trying to get a newspaper all week, but to no avail. I'm not going back to that hospital or prison, am I Bill?"

"No, I've told you before, I'm looking after you, and I'm going to answer all your questions. But first, I want you to see something, and this will really surprise you. We must drive there, then we will go on a fantastic journey, but this time I'm going with you my friend," said Bill reassuringly. He started the car, and headed towards Southampton docks, where he parked.

"Come with me," Bill said. Both men walked towards where the liners came in, and as they turned into the docks gates, there she was in all her splendour, the beautiful liner, called the Titanic.

Chapter 7

ANOTHER WORLD

Shock was the only way to describe how Nigel felt as he looked at the ship.

"How did this happen? It's unbelievable Bill!"

"I know it's not what you expected, but there it is, the Titanic back from its maiden voyage. And it's sailing again in a couple of days' time," Bill said with a slight smile. "Best liner ever built, and like it's been said, unsinkable."

"But what about the iceberg?"

"No icebergs at this time of year, the ship sails too far south for any danger."

"But history dictates it," Nigel blurted out.

"Not this history, all will be revealed. But first I have to go back to the car, I have to pick up something I've forgotten. I just had to see your face first, and it did go white, I can tell you. Wait here, I won't be long."

Bill went towards where he had parked the car just up the road. Nigel stood looking in amazement at the ship, and didn't notice a group of seamen walking from the ship towards the gates, before they were alongside him.

"That's the bloke who said our ship was going to sink," said a burly man, with a seaman's bag on his shoulder.

"Yes, I recognise him as well," said another. Nigel recognised the big man as the café owner, and the other one as the man he had met in the pub.

"Fucking idiot," said the Irish man. "You ever upset my wife again, or go near my café, and you're a dead man, understand?" hissed the burly man, pointing his finger at Nigel's face.

Nigel said, "I had a dream."

"None of your bloody excuses. Be warned, fucking idiot," said the Irish man again, and the men walked away.

"To the pub Mr. Frederick Fleet, to the pub," he heard the big man say to another of his mates.

So that was Fred Fleet, the man who had seen the iceberg from the crow's nest. What had happened? How could this be? Was this part of history made up, was it just a myth? Nigel thought there had to be an explanation. Bill would tell him, he was sure.

He looked up the road to see Bill coming towards him with a small bag in his hand.

"We have to leave here Nigel, remember you are a wanted man, and the police will be out looking for you very soon. You are in a very dangerous position, you are an escaped mental patient, remember?"

"But you're a policeman Bill, I thought."

"Well, whatever you thought was wrong," he interrupted. "Yes, I'm a policeman, but not of this force. But we have no time for explanations now, we must leave this area."

"Where will we go?" Nigel asked.

"Where would you want to go right now, if it was possible to go anywhere?"

"Home, back to Jane and my parents, my job, my own time, two thousand and seven. But I guess that's not on the agenda right now?"

Bill just smiled, and Nigel didn't know why, but he was soon to find out.

"Come with me," Bill said, and both men walked back up the street, past the car, to a park area with trees, a pond, and plenty of shrubbery. Bill stopped, opened the bag and got a belt out, which he gave to Nigel, telling him to put it on. It was in fact two belts attached with clips to one another. There was an instrument panel on the front, with a lead to a sort of control, like a TV Console.

"As you can see, I have a belt identical to yours, two belt sets. The reason for that is, if I lose my belt, and I won't, but if I did then you could give me one of yours, and vice versa. But guard that belt with your life; your future depends on it. Always wear it, ALWAYS!" Bill emphasized the word always.

Nigel was at a loss as to what was going on, but somehow he trusted his friend. He had always helped him out when trouble came his way, and he had got him out of the horrible mental hospital. His life was surely in this man's hands.

The place in the park was quiet, there was nobody around.

"Take the console Nigel, and punch in the time it is now. Do not touch the red button until I give you the word."

"I haven't got a watch, mine stopped and I gave it to Fanny as a guarantee for a loan." He remembered the one pound she had lent him.

"There's a church clock behind you, it's twelve thirty, so punch in the time and today's date, twenty third of April nineteen hundred and twelve." Nigel did as he was told, he watched Bill do the same. "Now punch in twelve thirty on the right hand side and the date twenty third of April two thousand and seven."

"Two thousand and seven," Nigel said, looking at Bill surprised.

"Yes, two thousand and seven," Bill said again, "that's where you said you wanted to be."

"What good will that do? Is this a game? Is this a joke? Please Bill, tell me what's going on, don't play with me, you are my friend, so please don't mess with my mind. I've been through a lot in this last week, I think I may be going mad! My mind can't take any more of this, please Bill?"

"Trust me, just trust me, two thousand and seven, punch it in."

Nigel punched it in the console.

"Right. When I tell you, I will count down to three, and we will both press the red button on the console. Close your eyes as you press it. Ready, three, two, one, press!"

Both men pressed their red buttons. Nigel felt nothing at all.

"Open your eyes," Bill said, "you have your wish and you are now in the year two thousand and seven, just where you said you wanted to be."

Nigel burst out laughing. "Very funny," he said, "what was the use of all that nonsense? Are you really a policeman or just a con-man? I don't know what your motives are, but you can't pull the wool over my eyes, I'm not that stupid. Bill, come clean, what's your game?"

"Look around Nigel my friend, look around," Bill said, pointing towards the park area. Nigel looked towards the pond but it was gone, and a building that hadn't been there before was there now! There were more trees, and a roadway that he hadn't noticed went directly across the park where grass had been. He was dumbfounded for the third time that day; leaving the hospital, seeing the Titanic, and now this! He was at a loss for words.

"Let's go and get something to eat, I've had nothing all day, and we have travelled a long way. Don't lose your belt or console. Let's go," Bill said, "we'll buy a newspaper before we eat. Maybe that might prove something to you."

They walked towards the road they had taken when they had entered the park. All the old cars and the trolley buses had gone. Modern buildings reached for the sky. The news-stand had modern books, pictorials, magazines and newspapers that said Monday 23rd April 2007. Nigel looked at Bill and just shook his head from side to side in disbelief! He felt like hugging him, but resisted, people were staring as they passed by, but Nigel didn't understand why.

Bill came to his rescue once again. "Got to get some new clothes my friend, we both look like we come from the year nineteen twelve, or that era." Both men laughed.

"But I've got no money Bill, not one penny."

"I have," Bill smiled, "let's go eat."

They entered a modern store called BANES, and got a table overlooking the street. Nigel ordered steak, chips and peas, and a cake that was called PANAL. He had never heard of it, but it was wonderful. He asked the waitress for Tetley tea, but she said she had never heard of that make, so gave him DIPSON instead. It was good, but Nigel had never heard of it either. Both men ate their fill.

"Nobody's after you now Nigel, so you have no worries there. But I must give you a warning, watch what you say. You seem to have got yourself into a lot of trouble. Try to listen, and soon you will understand. I can't be with you all the time, but I will meet up with you at this caféteria in a week's time at mid-day. We have to make another journey. I've been instructed to give you assistance in any way I can. So, here's some money." He gave Nigel five thousand pounds in notes.

Once again he was shocked. "Why so much money Bill? I won't need that much. I'll be at work soon, teaching again, and I'll have money as soon as I get home."

"Believe me, you'll need it, and if in a week's time you have any left, then you can give it back to me, agreed?"

"OK, agreed."

"You will need to buy a watch and new clothes, and you never know what life brings," Bill said, as he called the waitress over to pay the bill.

"You can say that again," Nigel said, putting the money in his pocket. "Do you want the belt back now?"

"No, as I've told you, guard it with your life. I can't emphasize that enough. WITH YOUR LIFE!"

"If you say so, Bill. I'll look after it; I'll put it in my bedroom when I get home. It will be safe there, and when I see you next week you can have it back then." Bill nodded.

"Sixty three pounds," said the waitress.

"Thanks," said Bill, not blinking an eyelid.

"Hell, that was expensive," Nigel spluttered, "sixty three pounds for two snacks!"

"I told you you would need the money I gave you," Bill said, getting up from the table.

"Let's stay here a while longer, I want to know a few things before I go home. And I wouldn't mind another cup of that tea, what's it called?" Nigel asked.

"Dipson," said Bill, taking his seat again. He ordered two more cups of tea, and looked at Nigel. "Tell me what you want to know."

"How did you do this, get me back home? You certainly have powers that ordinary men haven't got."

Just then the tea arrived and the bill was paid, it cost fourteen pounds. "That's heavy for two cups of tea," Nigel remarked.

"It's cheap in this day and age, considering the wages people get. She," he pointed to the waitress, "must be on a thousand pounds a week, maybe more."

"The wages must have gone up in the short time I've been away, because I wasn't getting that amount as a school teacher, I can tell you that."

Bill ignored the comment then said, "Now to answer your question of how you got here. It was the time belt you've got on, now don't ask me how it works, it's beyond me, that's in the science world, the work of scientists, not me, I' m just a policeman. Now, I will tell you the truth about myself. I'm in the Time-Patrol section of my unit, and I come from the year two thousand and sixty four, fifty seven years from now. But I never tell this to anyone, because nobody would believe me. The only reason I'm telling you Nigel, is because you are a time-traveller yourself. So, you will understand that time-travel is possible, because you have done it, and are still doing it."

"Oh no I'm not; I'm not going anywhere again. I'm here to stay, you can bet your life on it."

"I wouldn't do that," said Bill with a smile. "My job is to go back in time whenever someone like yourself comes into it, and can't get back. My job is to get you back where you belong, before you try to alter history, which may I say is impossible, and get yourself into trouble that you can't really understand. I don't mean going to prison or a mental institution, I mean losing your minds. I have saved quite a few minds in the past, that's my job. And may I say, I love it."

"But why did you not let on the day you met me in the bar, the 'Fox and Hounds'? I thought you were one of the locals at first; you put on a good act. I remember you didn't know what a biro pen was, or a pound coin."

"I had to put on an act, I couldn't say, 'Oh I know what that is!' now could I? But the fact is I was telling the truth, because I have never seen a biro, as you call it, or a one pound coin."

"That's odd," said Nigel, "why didn't you rescue me there and then? Why let me go through all that turmoil and strife?"

"Orders," said Bill, "and for the moment, that's all I can say, Nigel my friend."

"Orders? Orders from whom?"

"From the top, from the Big Boss. That's all for now, I may tell you more in a week's time."

"Why a week? Why can't I meet you tomorrow or the next day?"

"Because that's my orders, but if you get into any more trouble, just push the blue button on your time belt, and I will come to you."

"How will you know where I will be?"

"Don't worry about that, I'll know, believe me."

"One last thing before we part, this time-travel business, I've seen in films, and in the films to go back in time you had to get into a time-machine, and after a lot of flashes and whirling around, sometimes in puffs of smoke, you would find yourself in the past! Yet we travelled through time in a split second, without that palaver, it was incredible, miraculous!"

"I know what you mean, I've seen similar films, all made up by people who have never travelled, quite obviously."

"Like Dr. Who in his silly Tardis or Well's Time-Machine film," said Nigel.

"Never heard of those," Bill said.

"Never heard of Dr. Who? Now that's strange. I thought everyone knew Tom Baker or Bill Pertwee."

"Not me," said Bill. "Anyhow, you have to go now, and so have I. I have more travelling and work to do." He started to get up from the table but Nigel seemed reluctant to leave this cosy spot, overlooking the street and the hustle bustle of the people going about their lives.

"Bill, there's a lot more I want to know. This has been a strange experience for me, and at times I must admit, it was enjoyable."

The night with Fanny came to mind, and his singing, and working behind the bar. Meeting different ordinary folk.

Bill sat down again. "Just five more minutes, then I'll have to go."

Nigel continued, "You have said that history can't be changed, but I'm sorry to tell you my friend, I did change history by stopping the Andersons from going on the Titanic!"

"No Nigel, you didn't, because the Andersons were never going to go on that ship. They were destined to miss it, and I'll tell you why. Because Mr. Bertie St. Clair, after leaving you at the door that day, left to go down to the docks to look for his friends, but never got there, because just a few minutes after he left the mansion he crashed his car and careered through a field where he got stuck in a small pond! It took him more than an hour to get help, then as he set off again, he ran out of petrol. And by the time he had sorted that out, the ship had sailed. He lied to the police because he couldn't admit to his friend that because of his fault, they would have missed the ship anyhow! So you see, all your efforts were in vain. He pretended to be ill, not to go to court. Once again Nigel was shocked, and was lost for words for a moment.

"I have to go my friend, remember the blue button. You know your way now don't you?"

"Like the back of my hand," Nigel said, as he shook Bill's hand firmly. "See you soon," he said, and Bill left. But before he got ten feet away Nigel said, "Where are you going Bill?"

"Home," said Bill smiling, "home."

Nigel left the caféteria a few minutes later, and found himself on a street he knew well. The street took him to the Bargate, a mediaeval gate with remains of walls that the authorities had retained, to remind people of the city's history. The city, like many others in England, had had in olden times high thick walls to keep out armies from other countries.

As he walked up the street, before the High Street, he saw shops with names on he didn't recognise. As he passed his bank, Lloyds TSB, he noticed that the name had changed. HICKS BANK it said in big golden letters. He noticed that the McDonald's hamburger joint had also gone and was a greengrocer's shop. Even the shop where he had ordered a new suit for his forthcoming wedding to Jane had gone, so no more Burtons. Nigel put it down to not going into town very often, and continued on his way. People were still looking at him when he came across an old shop that sold second hand clothes. He went in and a young girl came to his aid.

"Can I help you, sir?"

"Yes, I would like some clothes please," he stammered, feeling a little foolish as she looked him up and down.

"Been to a fancy dress party have you, sir?" she said, almost laughing.

"Yes," Nigel said. "I want the whole outfit: trousers, shirt, socks and shoes. Are your clothes cheap?"

"Cheapest in town," she replied.

He picked out the things he needed, and went into a closet to change into them. She then put his old clothes in a paper bag, and told him he looked very smart.

"Thanks," he said, looking in a mirror, "do I look like a pop star?" he joked.

"A who?"

"You know, like Elvis or Tom Jones or Elton John!"

"Don't know them, are they models?" she enquired.

"In a way they were," he said. "How much is that?"

"Two hundred and fifty pounds," she said, opening the till.

"Two hundred and fifty pounds for second hand clothes. That's expensive."

"No sir, the cheapest in town, as I've told you."

Nigel took the money out of his old trousers that were now in the bag, and gave her a thousand pound note. He hadn't looked at the money, and hadn't realised that you could get a thousand pound note, a fifty was the biggest amount on a note that he remembered.

"How long have these big notes been out?" and he held out the note.

"Years, but don't you know that? Where have you been?"

"Away," Nigel said, he could see that she was looking at him as though he was not a normal person, that's what he imagined, so he thanked her, took his change and picked up his bag and left the shop. As he was putting the change into his pocket, he noticed that the notes were different, there was no Queen Elizabeth portrait on them! Now he knew that something was wrong, how could the price of things go sky-high in just over a week? Shops he remembered all his life had gone! Surely he would have heard about them, or read it in the papers, or seen it on the news. He decided to check his bank balance, so went to his bank. They knew him there, so they would explain why the Queen's portrait was missing on the notes. 'They may be forgeries,' he thought. But then the girl in the shop had taken the money without blinking an eyelid!

The bank looked the same as normal as he entered: the big staircase at one end, the same familiar counter, and a woman behind who he knew, who had dealt with him on many occasions. "Good afternoon sir," she said with a smile.

"How long has the name change been in operation?" "What name change, sir?" "The bank's name change," Nigel said.

"This bank has always had this name, sir; it's always been HICKS BANK."

"Don't give me that rubbish, are you kidding me? This is the TSB Bank, and always has been. You served me a few weeks ago!" He was sounding stern.

"I'm not kidding you, sir, it's always been HICKS. I've been here ten years, now can I help you?"

"Yes, I want to check my bank account."

"Name?" the lady asked.

"Now you're kidding me again, you know my name, I've been a customer for years."

"Sorry, sir, but I don't know you; I've never seen you in my life!

"Oh, you are funny; you're having a joke aren't you?" "No sir, as I have said, I don't know you."

"I'm Nigel Maythorn, could you check my account?"

She looked on a star-shaped TV monitor, with no sign of a keyboard, pressed one button and said, "You have no account with us sir." "That's preposterous," Nigel blurted out, he remembered for a split second Gerald Anderson saying the same thing to him back then in another time. "Get the manager now," he spluttered.

"You're being very forceful sir, if you don't mind me saying."

She pressed another button, but the manager was already on his Way, descending the stairs.

"I'm the manager of this bank, can I help you sir?"

"Yes," said Nigel, anger now rising. "This lady said I haven't got a bank account here, when she only served me a few weeks ago, maybe two weeks, I've lost track."

"You have no account with us, sir. May I ask you a question? Have you got more than a million pounds in this so-called account?"

"Of course not, but I've got five' thousand in here."

"I'm afraid you haven't, sir, because we only take deposits of a million each transaction."

Nigel was shocked once again. He looked around for help, but there was no help forthcoming. He felt like pressing his blue button for Bill's help, but had second thoughts. After all, he would be on his way home by now, and anyhow he had only left him half an hour before.

"Why is there no Queen's portrait on these notes?" he enquired, showing him the money.

"Now that's a silly question sir, if you don't mind me saying." "Why?" Nigel said again.

"Because she isn't our Queen, and never has been, that's why. But surely sir, you should know that, where have you been?"

At that moment the manager was called away. "Sorry sir," he said as he walked away.

Nigel returned to the counter, but another woman had taken the place of the one he had been speaking to. He walked out into the street, bewildered. Jane would have the answers, he would go and see her, but first he had to see his parents. His first thoughts were to take the bus, but decided on a taxi.

"Do you know the mansion on Eastern Hill, called THE BRIARS?" he asked the driver.

"Yes sir," he replied. Nigel gave a sigh of relief; at least the mansion was still there. But what had happened? Things didn't seem right! He would sort out his account at a later date, it was a mistake.

The driver slipped a small chip into a slot in the car, and set off.

"What did you put into that slot?" Nigel enquired. "Here?" said the driver, indicating the slot.

"Yes, that thing you put in there?"

The driver looked at Nigel in a strange way. "Oh, the power chip you mean?"

"The power chip, what's that?"

"Makes the car go, sir," said the driver laughing.

"Don't you fill up with petrol?"

The driver laughed louder. "No sir, we don't use that old-fashioned stuff any more, been twenty years or more. No sir, this atom power is so much better and cheaper than it was."

"Atom power! How does it work?"

"Just two atoms that bounce against one another and gives off the power to drive the car for years. No more waiting to fill up like the olden days. Much better for us all, don't have to rely on the Arabs to supply anymore. Anyhow, where have you been?"

Nigel was beginning to get fed up with that saying. This was not the world he knew, something had gone wrong. Bill would know what the hell was going on. He had another shock, because as they drove up the High Street in Southampton, the Army Recruiting Office had gone! "No more Army Recruiting Office I see," Nigel said, pointing at the place he remembered it being.

"Army, what army? We haven't had an army since the war, if

you'd read your history books you would have known that! No need for an army in this peaceful world that we live in. We've had no wars since the war to end all wars."

"What, the 1914-18 war you mean?"

"Don't know that one," said the driver, "the Boer War I'm talking about, and that one ended in nineteen hundred and two. After that one I reckon the 'bosses' decided that it was pointless, so the world countries banned all wars. And we've had peace ever since. Anyhow why am I giving you this lesson? I'm only talking to pass away the time. I talk to all my customers as I'm driving. This is the best job I've ever had, my brother is going to be a driver like me when he gets older."

Nigel was not listening, his mind was trying to decipher the information he had just received. 'No wars,' his mind shouted out, 'No wars!'

"What about the war in the Middle East, in Palestine, the war there with the Jews?" Nigel said. Where the hell is the Bargate, the old gateway? It wasn't there, no sign of any old walls at all!

"Where's the Bargate?" he shouted.

The driver became startled and stopped the car. "Get out," he ordered. "I've had nutcases in here before, and I'm sorry, I can't deal with them, no charge. Get Out," he demanded.

"Sorry I shouted, but I was so surprised at something I saw, or not saw as the case is. I thought there was an old gate there," he pointed, "but I must have been mistaken," Nigel lied. "I'm sorry, I won't shout again."

"OK, but this is your last chance, I can't deal with people who shout."

"Sorry," Nigel said for the third time. He wasn't surprised when they passed the Titanic monument at the top of the High Street, it had been there as long as he could remember. As a boy at school he remembered the class was taken there to view it, as a history lesson. It was dedicated to the engineers who had lost their lives, because they had stayed at their stations, those brave men who went down with the ship, the plaque said. It was no surprise at it not being there, in its place was a derelict bit of land. He now knew he wasn't in the right time-zone, something had gone tragically wrong. He knew it wouldn't be a week before he pressed his blue button on his time-belt. Silence descended in the car as it made its way to the mansion. He had to see it before going to see if his family was in this world, but somehow he was doubtful he would find them.

At last Nigel broke the silence. "The war in the Middle East between the Palestinians and the Jews, that's an ongoing war isn't it? And what about the Vietnam, and 1939-45 and 1914-18 wars? Not counting the Korean war?"

"Sorry my friend, as I have told you, I have never heard of those wars. And the Jews are not at war with anyone, never have been, they have always lived in peace, and the Palestinians are the same, they are peaceful people, nice people."

"But Israel has been fighting for years," Nigel stressed.

"Never heard of Israel," said the driver, not understanding his 'nutcase' passenger. Because that's what he now thought of Nigel. "As far as I understand, the Palestinians live in Palestine, and the Jews live on an island. Madagascar off the coast of East Africa."

Nigel just shook his head in disbelief. He had read somewhere that the Jews had been offered the island of Madagascar for their homeland, and it had been rejected, but not in this world it seemed.

He saw the house in the distance, not so many trees obscuring the view. The car stopped at the gates.

"Can I ask you just two more questions please?" he asked the driver, "But first I will explain my shouting. I have been under a lot of stress lately. I've lost my loved ones, my family, my wife-to-be, I have lost everything that I hold dear to my heart. I have suffered more than most men could ever think about, so please forgive me?" He looked at the driver with sadness in his eyes and the driver felt sorry for him.

"Yes, you're forgiven, what are your questions?"

"You do remember the Titanic liner, do you?" he asked.

"Well, I don't really know much about ships, but I believe there is a ship in a museum that's in Ireland, yes in Belfast. Why it's there I don't know, I don't have any interest in liners. Why, are you looking for a cruise?" he asked.

"No, I was just wondering. Anyhow, how much do I owe you?"

"That will be two hundred pounds."

"I'll give you two hundred and fifty pounds, if you wait for me. I'm going up to the mansion, won't be too long, maybe half an hour."

"Four hundred pounds," the driver said.

"Alright, four hundred pounds, when I get back."

"No, pay me two hundred pounds now, and I'll wait for you."

Nigel paid, and promised that he wouldn't be long. He shook hands with the driver, then with a wave, he went through the gates and up to the mansion. The trees on either side of the drive seemed thicker and they arched towards one another like an embrace. Everything looked different to when he had walked up this avenue with Jane. The fountain was in full flow, and the gardens well kept. No broken branches littered the avenue, the gates hadn't creaked. 'It is the same place but a different time,' Nigel thought. One thing that he was certain of was that he didn't expect to see Jane at the house. He remembered the date, April the twenty third, in his own world. He hadn't even got that far in his life! He had had enough shocks today to last him a lifetime, and didn't want any more. He thought of saying that he remembered his father telling him as a boy, 'He who expects nothing shall not be disappointed!' He even had doubts that he would get to see his parents or Jane, but he would try.

The big oak door looked the same as he remembered it, he rang the bell. He had thought of a story to tell the occupier of the house, he just wanted to get in to see the big fireplace, one last try. He thought that with his belt, his time-belt, he might make it this time. The door opened and a middle-aged lady smiled as she said, "Hello, and what can I do for you young man?"

"Don't worry, I'm not selling anything," Nigel said, smiling back. "I've come a long way for this moment," he continued, "you see, I used to live here many years ago, as a boy, and I was hoping you would let me have a look inside the house again, for nostalgic reasons. I promise you I wouldn't be long."

"Oh," said the lady, with a surprised tone in her voice, "what's your name?"

"Nigel Maythorn," he replied.

"Nigel Maythorn," she repeated.

"Yes, Nigel May   "

"Do you come from Stockton?"

"Yes, I lived there."

"But I thought you were in hospital in Winchester! And don't lie, that's not your real name. Have you escaped?" She seemed alarmed. "Sorry," she said, "you can't come in here, leave this property now." And before Nigel could say anymore, the door was shut in his face! He stood there for a moment, then made a hasty retreat down the avenue.

The taxi was waiting. "Thanks for waiting," he spluttered.

"You weren't very long," said the driver, starting his car.

"No, I didn't get to do what I wanted, just to look at the house. You see, I've been here before, but that's another story. Can you take me to Claymore Street, in Stockton?"

"Don't know where that is, you will have to show me the way," the driver said driving off.

"Past the Fox and Hounds public house, if it's still there, then first on the left down the lane, towards the valley."

"The Fox and Hounds pub has always been there," said the driver, "I drink in there at times."

"How much is a pint of beer now?" he enquired, thinking how expensive he had found things.

"Only thirty pounds a pint."

"Only," said Nigel with a laugh. They passed the pub, and Nigel's thoughts went back to the few days he had worked there, and how he had met Fanny. He wondered how she was faring without him, but then he thought that that was back in nineteen hundred and twelve, she must be dead by now. His mind was full of things; the woman's attitude at the house. How did she know he had escaped from prison, well not prison really, but the mental hospital was a sort of prison to him. There were a lot of things he had to find the answers to before he would be happy again.

Bill had said he was going on orders, whose orders? And for what? Why had he transported him here when it was blatantly obvious that this was not the world he knew or came from.

"Right, here you said?" The driver slowed to a snail's pace.

"Yes, just up this street."

In half a minute the car pulled up outside Nigel's house. "Thank you," he said to the driver, as he handed him four hundred pounds. The driver handed him back one hundred pounds. "You weren't as long as you said you would be, so three hundred pounds is fine."

"Thanks," said Nigel, extending his hand. The men shook hands, then he watched the car disappear up the road and around the corner. He walked up to the front door of the house and tried the door, it was unlocked so he went in. Everything seemed in place, and he walked towards the kitchen at the back of the house. He saw his mother and father sitting at the table having a talk. The room was the same as he remembered it.

"I'm back," he declared. They looked around with shock written on their faces, the old man nearly choking on his drink!

"What are you doing here?" the woman asked, as she stood up and embraced him.

"Mother, you wouldn't believe me if I told you, it's such a relief that I found you again. I've been on a fantastic journey beyond anyone's imagination. I've got myself into all sorts of trouble, now I'm just glad to be home. I need to rest, it's been a hectic day, a hectic time. I'll see Jane tomorrow; I just hope she will understand."

"Sit down," his father said. "Now tell us why and how you escaped."

"How do you know that father?"

"Well, you wouldn't be here otherwise, would you?" he said. "No, I suppose you're right." "Who's Jane?" his mother asked as she cut a slice of cake.

She was just about to put the sugar in his tea when Nigel said, "Mother, you know I don't take sugar, I've never taken sugar."

Her face showed her surprise. "Since when?" she said, putting the sugar back into the bowl. "You always take sugar, anyhow who's Jane?"

"Mother, are you getting forgetful? Jane's my fiancée, she works with me at the school, she's the English teacher."

"What are you talking about? Have you completely lost your mind? What have those people done to you, my poor boy?" the old man said.

He knew what his father meant. Bill has a lot to answer for, he couldn't understand what was going on. Orders, he had said, Bill had orders. 'What orders? And from whom?' he asked himself.

"Look, tell us what happened, how did all this come about?" his mother said. "You were meant to leave hospital today, but the doctor advised that you stay longer, for another week."

"Mother, I think we're at cross-purposes here." He sipped his Drink. "Have I been ill?" he asked.

"Yes my love, you have had a sort of mental breakdown, you won't get better if you don't get your full treatment."

It was at this point that Nigel knew something was really wrong. He looked at his mother and father, who were now sitting opposite him.

"Who am I to you?" he asked.

The old man looked at him in Disbelief. "You're our son Simon, why are you asking these silly questions?"

"Simon, Simon?" Nigel repeated. "Nigel you mean."

"Simon, stop this nonsense," his mother demanded, "at once. Now, tell us, why did you leave the hospital? You'll have to go back. To think you had a nice job working as a gardener, and then you had a breakdown. The hospital said that you are doing well, and can come home soon. Simon, what will become of you? You know you are loved, and you promised us that when you get better you will get a job again and settle down. That's all me and your dad want, to see you happy, son." She had a sad look as she put her hand on his shoulder.

114

"How old am I mother?" he asked.

"You're twenty three, son."

'That's right,' thought Nigel. "And are you telling me that you have never heard of my wife-to-be, Jane?"

"No son, we both have never heard of her. Why are you making up these stories? What have they done to you in hospital?" The old man sighed.

"Have you a picture, a photograph of me?" Nigel asked.

"There's one on the sideboard, I'll get it." She got up and went into the front room.

"What's your name?" Nigel asked his father.

"Son," his father said, "please son, what's up with you?"

"Please answer me?"

"Clarence Maythorn."

"And Mum's name?" Nigel asked.

"Clare," came the reply, as the old man shook his head from side to side in disbelief.

'Well, that was right,' Nigel thought.

She came back and showed him a photo, and the picture was of a man that certainly looked like himself, split image, but he knew it wasn't him. And the other people in the photo were strangers to him. He knew that these two lovely people were not his true parents and he wasn't their true son. At that point Nigel had to alleviate the worry that was etched on their faces.

"Don't worry about me, I'm going back, you will get your son back, and everything will turn out alright in the end. I will go now, I have things to do." He stood up and went to the door.

"Look after yourself son. We both love you and miss you."

"I will." He kissed her lightly on the cheek, shook hands with the old man and left, as the daylight was leaving the day.

"See you in a week's time," his mother said.

He looked back at the house, the house that at one time had been his home, and walked towards the Fox and Hounds Public House.

It was dark when he reached the pub. The light lit up the car park, and the interior of the bar was the same as it had been the last time he had been there with Jane, just two weeks before. There was no-one behind the bar as he pulled up a stool and felt for his money in his pocket. The barman appeared from behind a curtain at the far end.

"Hello Simon, they let you out early did they?" he said with a laugh.

"I was found to be sane," Nigel said, laughing as well. Maybe it was better this way, to go with the flow, so to speak. "A pint of bitter please," Nigel said.

"Oh, you've changed your drink have you?" the barman exclaimed.

"Yes, a change is as good as a rest, don't you think?"

"Nice saying, can't say I've heard it before, but it's a good one." He poured the pint. "Thirty pounds please."

Nigel paid without comment, his money was going down fast, he thought.

"I just got here today," Nigel said, "and I don't want to go home just yet. I want a few drinks to celebrate getting well again. I've had a breakdown you know."

"I know," Brian replied.

"I'll see my family tomorrow, so I was wondering if you still have a room for the night?"

"As it so happens there is a vacant room, it's yours Simon, if you want it. I'll let you have it at the cheaper rate because I've known you all your life, since you were a little boy. So that's two hundred and twenty five pounds for the night, and I'll chuck in a breakfast, how's that?"

Nigel swallowed; did he say a cheaper rate? he thought, but said, "Thanks Brian, that will do fine." He was happy that he got his name right, because this was the same landlord that he knew in his world. Nigel knew for sure that he was in another world, a parallel world. He had read books and seen films on the theme many times. But how he had got here was a question he didn't know the answer to. He was sure Bill would explain, but right now he would relax, after all no police were after him! His 'twin', so to speak, Simon, was in hospital, so he would go on for the time being, answering to his new name of Simon.

He checked how much money he had left, the way it was going, he wondered if it would last a few days, let alone a week! He calculated that he had spent two hundred and fifty pounds on clothes, taxi three hundred pounds, his room for the night, two hundred and twenty five pounds, and his first pint! He quickly calculated that at eight hundred and five pounds so far on his first afternoon, without his evening meal, plus a few pints, the money Bill had given him wouldn't last long at this rate!

He accepted the key to his room, and ordered a meal and another pint. At that moment the door of the pub opened, and she walked in, it was Jane.

Chapter 8

NEW ROMANCE

Nigel nearly fell off his stool. He knew she wasn't his Jane, but she looked exactly like her, split image: same height, same figure, even the same smile! She came over to the bar, just three feet away from him, and ordered a small drink that had a strange sounding name.

"Hello Janice, how are you today? You haven't been in for a while," said Brian the landlord.

"No," she said with that certain smile that Nigel knew so well. "I've been busy at the hospital, being a nurse is a very hard job you know."

"I know it," he replied, as he placed her drink in front of her on the counter top.

"Are you still serving food?" she asked.

"Of course," he said. So she ordered a meal, and sipped her drink. She looked Nigel's way, and gave him a smile.

"Hello, I'm sorry but I overheard you; you're a nurse, are you?"

"Yes," she replied demurely.

"I've always admired nurses, they do such a wonderful job, and normally for so little money!"

"Oh, the money's very good, but it is a very demanding profession. At one time I was going to be a teacher, but didn't have the brains for that, so I became a nurse." She laughed out loud, so did Nigel.

They talked about various things for the next twenty five minutes, and seemed to be getting on quite well, when the meals arrived together.

"Will you join me at my table?" Nigel asked, picking up his meal.

"Sure, why not," she replied. He smiled and went towards the same table where he had had a meal with Jane the night of the storm.

They both enjoyed their meals, when Nigel asked her if she wanted a glass of wine, she replied in the affirmative. He went to the bar and asked Brian for a bottle of nice, but his Cheapest, wine. Brian came back within a minute with a bottle and two glasses.

"You seem to be getting on well with her!" He winked.

"Yes, sometimes it seems I've known her for years," he winked back.

"Seventy five pounds," Brian said.

"Fine," Nigel replied, trying not to faint! He paid and returned to the table. "Hope you like this one," he said, looking at the label, BLUE ZEST it read. "Never had it before."

He unscrewed the top and poured the wine, lifted his glass and said "cheers."

"Chairs," she said.

"No, cheers," he repeated, laughing.

"Oh, I thought you said 'chairs', never heard that expression before."

"What do you say then?"

"When? What do you mean?"

"When you drink wine and clink glasses," he said.

"Clink glasses, what's that for?" she enquired.

"It denotes friendship and togetherness, love sometimes," Nigel explained.

"I've never heard of that before, but I'll give it a go, for friendship."

They both laughed aloud every time the glasses were clinked. He felt a glow come over him; the wine was strong and rich. But he was sure the glow came from being with her, it was just like old times. They talked on as the evening passed by. Nigel didn't know the time, as he had forgotten to buy a new watch. But time passes quickly when one is enjoying oneself, and he was certainly doing that.

He ordered another pint after the bottle was emptied, and bought her a drink as well. She told him that she had only moved to this area in the last year, and lived with her mother and father in Heather Street off Moreland Road. He had enquired if she had a boyfriend or was married, she had said 'no' to both questions. She felt a warmth towards her new-found friend; they were getting on so well. So when Nigel asked her if it was at all possible that they would meet again, she agreed to meet him the next day, her day off work. Nigel was over the moon, he had called her Jane a few times during the evening, but Janice had let it go, because sometimes at home her mother called her Janey.

When she asked Nigel his name, he said, "Around here people call me Simon, I'm known as Simon." She just smiled. The time came when she said that she had to go home, Nigel offered to take her, but she told him she had a power bike, and would be home within five minutes. They planned to meet at the pub the next day at ten o'clock in the morning, for a day out in Southampton. Nigel took her hand, and she bent forward and gave him a light kiss on the cheek. He saw her to the door and waved as she took off on her power bike, which was worked by a small atom box. Nigel went back into the pub and had one more pint before going up to his room.

"That will be eighty six pounds please," said Brian.

"What for?"

"For two meals," Brian said.

"Oh, sorry," said Nigel, as he paid the money over. Bill was right when he had said the words, Believe me you will need the money! His wad of notes was going down as though there was no tomorrow, but he knew there would be, and he was certainly looking forward to seeing her again. It had been a lovely evening, and he hadn't got himself in any sort of trouble, as he had done in his explanations of his time-travelling. No one had believed him, so he decided not to talk about anything again, but to listen and learn about this new world he had discovered. For a time he had forgotten his woes, and was beginning to enjoy himself again.

"Goodnight Brian, I don't owe you anything do I?" he said, as he finished his last pint of the day, and got up from his stool.

"No, you've paid for everything. You have your key, so I'll show you your room."

"That's alright; I know where it is, through the kitchen and up the back stairs, first room at the top, I've stayed here before," Nigel said in a slightly inebriated way.

"I don't remember that," Brian said.

"You weren't here then."

"I've always been here."

"Well, you must have been on holiday then," Nigel laughed.

"Goodnight," said Brian with a shrug.

Nigel went through the kitchen, and he could see where Fanny had stood at the sink, the table where he had eaten with her changed now, but he could picture it in his mind's eye. He climbed the stairs, each step getting harder it seemed, and opened the door to the small room, now with mod-cons, and an en-suite bathroom. He undressed and thought about this unbelievable day that he had just lived through. Sleep came to him within a few minutes.

The next morning he woke with no hangover at all. After a shower, a wonderful power-shower, with shower gel that made his body come alive, he felt like a new man, he felt good. 'Life' was the name on the gel, it was a better brand than he had ever used.

'I will look out for that make,' he thought. Then thought otherwise, when he remembered where he was. Breakfast was a hearty one, and he ate the lot. Coffee was strong and sweet, although he never had sugar in his tea, he always liked sweet coffee. Brian wasn't around; a young man served him his breakfast.

He sat alone in the kitchen, then he went back up to his room. He made sure he put his time-belt on under his shirt, and at ten o'clock on the dot, went downstairs to the bar.

"Can I stay here tonight?" he asked the young man who was stocking the bar.

"I can't see why not, I'll ask my grandfather when he comes in at noon."

"By the way, what's Brian's surname?" Nigel enquired.

"Small, my grandfather's name is Brian Small."

"Thanks." 'Well, not everything is different in this time, some things seem to be the same as in my time,' he thought, as he walked out to meet a new day with Jane, or Janice.

She was waiting, sitting astride her machine, and smiling like the sun.

"Morning Simon, good sleep?" she asked.

"Wonderful."

"Get on then," she indicated.

"Don't we need crash helmets?" he asked.

"No, they were banned a few years ago. It was said, rightly or wrongly, that they caused more head injuries than people who didn't wear them, you know what politicians are like?"

Nigel nodded. 'There is no change there then,' he thought, as he got on behind her.

"Hold tight," she shouted above the roar of the machine, and they pulled off at a fast speed down the lane towards the city.

Half an hour later they arrived, and after parking the bike, they walked along the river for a while. The birds were singing, the sun was shining, and people were very friendly as they passed by with greetings and smiles. Nigel felt good, and even better when she slipped her hand in his as they walked and talked.

At lunch time they found a little café and both indulged in a light snack. She fed the hungry ducks and laughed at their antics, they were both enjoying the day. As they were leaving, Nigel remembered that he hadn't paid for the food.

"I've paid for it," she said, "after all, you paid for mine last night, or did you?" she asked with a laugh.

"Thank you, and of course I did. But you didn't have to you know." She put a finger on his lips and smiled, he got the message, they walked back to her bike. That afternoon they visited the cinema and saw a wonderful film in multi colour, smellorama and Four D, that Nigel had never heard of, and it was a great experience, so advanced from his time, he pondered. This was surely a different world. At six o'clock she took him back to the pub, with a promise to meet him the next day after her shift at the hospital.

"Thanks Simon, for a lovely day, I really enjoyed it, we'll do it again soon if you want to."

"It's a date," Nigel said quickly, making her laugh out loud. They kissed on the lips lightly, for the first time. She tingled and so did he. Love, it seems, was waiting in the wings. He went to his room and had a lay down for an hour, before going down to the bar.

There weren't many people in the bar, as he pulled up a stool and sat in his normal place. He ordered a pint from a barman he had never seen before.

"Brian not here tonight?" he enquired.

"He starts at eight," came the reply. Then the man disappeared into the back room. Two people in the far corner of the bar left leaving Nigel alone with his thoughts. What a world this was, a place with no wars, hardly any crime, friendly people, wonderful things like atom-powered cars and bikes, cinemas where you experience being in the actual film, Four D put you inside the movie, wonderful. The only thing that continued to shock him was the cost of things, but then he hadn't yet found out what the wages were. Bill had said that the wages were high; one thousand pounds a week for a waitress, even Janice had said that her nurse's pay was good.

At times he thought that he could get accustomed to living here, it was certainly better than nineteen hundred and twelve. At least here he had been in no trouble at all, apart from the incident in the taxi, he remembered the shock at seeing the old gate and walls at the Bargate in Southampton were no longer there! He had also been very angry at the bank, but that was before he had realised where he was, and after seeing the people he thought were his mother and father it had dawned on him that this wasn't his real home, but the same time, same people, but different time-zone, a world that ran alongside his. These were his thoughts when the barman reappeared, and he ordered another pint, and asked him if there was any music available. "What do you want to hear?" the barman asked.

"Elvis, Sinatra, Elton John, anything really. It's pretty quiet tonight, is it always like this?"

"Yes, it's always the same; pubs are going out of fashion. In a few years time they will be history. People meet in their homes, they can get cheaper beer, at ten pounds a can, and with all the entertainment at home these days. With the new transporter you can, in an instant, be in someone else's home! Anyhow, why am I telling you this, you already know that. Excuse me, I do talk a lot, a fault of mine. I'm getting treatment for it at the moment. I may have to have an operation on my brain, to kerb my talking! They say it's very successful, and quick. Many people have had it done, mostly women. Some men think it's the best invention that man has devised, apart from the cure for cancer. Mind you, the pills that are available now, that give you extra life, are the best, people live to be one hundred and thirty years old, some slightly longer. Never heard of those singers you mentioned, how about my favourite, Lance Summers?"

"That will be fine," Nigel said. The barman smiled, and disappeared once again into a back room. Almost immediately this beautiful sound and voice came through to the bar through speakers that were invisible. Nigel sipped his beer and relaxed, tapping his fingers on the counter. Another day was coming to an end, it had been a good one. Jane, or Janice, but he always thought of her as Jane, had been wonderful company. He was missing her, and he had only seen her a few hours before, but it seemed like a lot longer.

He hadn't spent so much money today, but he had had a good time. He was, in a strange way, enjoying this life. He looked around the empty bar, glancing over at a window, and could see that darkness was coming to stay awhile. A tap on his shoulder surprised him, he turned around and Bill was sitting on the stool next to his.

"Bill, don't do that, you'll give me a heart-attack! I didn't see you come in."

"I'm looking after you, I've told you that before," he said, with a broad smile across his face.

"But I'm not in any trouble; in fact I like it here, where ever we are. It's certainly not where I come from, but you know that already, don't you?"

"Of course I do, and you will be told everything, but you must realise that all the information I give you must be imparted slowly. Your mind couldn't take it in all at once, so Nigel, be patient."

"I'm glad you know who I am, the people around here think I'm a man called Simon who's in hospital at the moment. Even his parents thought that I was him, we are the spitting image of one another! Brian looks the same as in my time, and Janice, a girl I met in here last night, is the spitting image of my wife-to-be Jane. So please tell me something, please Bill, something?" Nigel said in a pleading way.

"I will tell you just this, I know everything you do. And I know you must have guessed by now, you are an intelligent man, you are in a parallel world, you are in Zone Two. The reason for that is when you time-travelled back from your time in Zone One, you came out of the big fireplace just that split second too early. You see, there are twenty five zones, and the time zone clock, to put it as easily as I can, because believe me it is complicated, the clock was in Zone Twenty Five, and when you felt the 'force' pulling you, you resisted at first, am I not right?"

Nigel nodded. "And then you let yourself be pulled out into this zone! The clock was counting down, and got to Zone Two when you came out of the fireplace. One split second more and you would have come out into your own Zone One, your own world. Just back through the gateway that was created because of a lightning strike, and the entrance, that for years had been sealed up, a breach was made, and you were there at the time. Do you understand what I'm saying?"

"You say that there are twenty five parallel worlds or zones, so there's twenty five of me about, that's unbelievable! I thought one of me was enough," Nigel laughed.

"Yes," said Bill, "there are twenty five of all of us. Some, I have met myself, being in the Time-Control police, I've had lots of encounters with people who look exactly like me! But that's another story. All zones are different in some ways, in this zone, as you already know, there have been no wars since the Boer War ended, in nineteen hundred and two, a hundred and five years ago. But other zones have always been at war. In Zone Three for example, the great liner The Titanic, was never built. In this zone it sailed for thirty five years and ended up in a museum in Belfast in Ireland. And in your own world Zone One, it sank on its maiden voyage. In Zone Twenty three the dinosaurs still roam about! In some zones you are a caveman even in this day and age, progress is slower. In other zones you are richer than in your wildest dreams!"

"Have you been to every zone?" Nigel interrupted.

"Most only once, because they are too dangerous, but we, that's the Government, have sealed off the gateways to these other zones. Work goes on all the time. We don't want diseases and dinosaurs in this world, now do we? We live a good life here, and where I come from, two thousand and sixty four, life is fantastic, and the Time Police and the Government want to keep it that way. "

"How far can you go back in this zone?"

"We can only go back to nineteen hundred and twelve, because as we go along we seal up the gateways, which are really defects in time. It's the same in your zone; you can only go back to nineteen hundred and twelve. In some worlds you can go back to the beginning of time, but it's too dangerous. We are forbidden to go there, so we block off the entrances as we discover them."

"Absolutely incredible," said Nigel shaking his head from side to side.

"Now, you can understand why this information must be kept secret! The majority of people don't know anything about time-travel, ask anyone, nearly everyone will say it's impossible, and we, in the Time-Police, want to keep it that way, so does the Government. Just imagine if people knew they could go back in time, they would flock to get souvenirs to bring back and sell! Imagine people having access to things on the Titanic in your zone? They would steal anything they could get their hands on before she sank, and sell their spoils. Some would get lost, and most would get themselves in trouble, as you did."

"Don't rub it in, Bill," Nigel remarked smiling, "I realise I was an idiot, but I didn't know what I know now. I've certainly learnt my lesson, and I will never tell anyone of these experiences I've had, ever again. I've told nobody here, and I'm enjoying it. I can imagine telling people here that I have just come from nineteen hundred and twelve in time-travel, and I would end up in the nearest mental hospital again!"

"You would Nigel, you would," Bill said in a definite way. He handed him an envelope and said, "Blue button if you need me. If not, caféteria in six days' time. Nice to see you and the lady are getting on well. I have to go, take care." He got up, went to the door and walked out, the door shut.

"Bill, one more question," he shouted as he ran to the door. He opened it, but Bill had gone. In a split second, he had gone! The question he had wanted to ask was Could Bill get him back to his zone, his world? For the moment the question remained unanswered. Also, he wanted to find out why he was here in the first place. Bill knew that this wasn't his world. What was the motive for bringing him to this world? There were a lot more things that baffled him, as he returned to the bar.

Brian appeared from the back room. "Hello Simon, you're staying with us another night I believe, you must like it here?"

"Yes Brian, and you never know, I may take up permanent residence."

You're welcome to stay as long as you like. You're a good lad; I've always believed that you couldn't help your breakdown. What was it like in there? Pretty grim I would imagine?"

"It was grim," Nigel replied, "but I would rather not talk about it, I'd rather think of my future."

"I saw Jimmy Smith today; he was surprised when I told him that you were out. He reckoned the only reason you're out is because you escaped! I said that he must be joking, and he said that he wasn't. When he saw you last week on a hospital visit, you never said a word to him that you were going to be released. Anyhow, he's gone away for a few days to do a job in London, but said he would come and see you when he gets back. He said that you have some explaining to do, real villain he is, Simon, why did you ever mix with the likes of him?"

"Oh, Jimmy's alright, he's just misunderstood that's all. He's always joking with people, and with his dead-pan expression, you never know when he's joking or not!"

Brian just nodded, and poured Nigel another pint into his empty glass.

"I don't want any trouble in here," Brian said as he took the money and put it in the till.

"Don't worry Brian, they'11 be no trouble." But Nigel was worried, he had never heard of this Jimmy Smith, not even in his own world. He would need Bill's advice on this one. In the meantime he would stop worrying and continue to enjoy his new world.

One thing he wanted to do was to go and see his work place, the school, see if his colleagues were the same. Although he realised that here he certainly wasn't a school teacher, he was a gardener who was in hospital with a mental breakdown!

"Brian, how long have you been running this bar?" Nigel needed to talk to someone, the bar was dead, the music had stopped long ago, and at one time the thought had crossed his mind to have a very early night! Brian pulled up a stool after pouring himself a drink, and sat opposite him, behind the bar.

"This pub has been in the Small family for one hundred and twenty years. My great grandfather Brian Small, owned it, then my grandfather Brian Small, then my father Brian Small, and now me, Brian Small, all Brians, it runs in the family!" He burst out laughing. "What imagination my family had, it's all we've ever done,'publicans'. But I don't think my son will carry on when I'm finished, and that won't be long the way things are these days. Look around…" He pointed around the bar. "The customers are few and far between, since the Government said that alcohol might soon be banned, apart from in private houses. Public houses are on the way out! I'm getting ready for my retirement anyhow." He sighed, and filled his glass again.

"All Brians, and what was your great grandmother called, do you know?" Nigel asked.

"Yes, I remember her as well, she lived to a ripe old age, her name was Fanny. She was a wonderful woman, full of fun, she died in nineteen hundred and eighty, at ninety years old.

"And her son Brian was your grandfather?"

"Yes, but he died before his mother and sister."

"Oh, Fanny had a daughter then, when was she born?" Nigel asked.

"April was born in January nineteen thirteen, she also died before her mother. I have done a family tree, that's why I know all this," the landlord explained.

"That's very interesting," Nigel said.

"Why is my family history interesting to you, Simon?"

"It's just the way you tell their story; it seems that I know them. You tell a good story Brian," he laughed.

"I expect I do, a story worth telling, is worth telling well," he said with satisfaction.

"That's true," Nigel said as he stood up from his stool and finished his drink. "Early night for me Brian, thanks for the chat, I enjoyed it."

"What chat? I haven't given you a chat, whatever that is?"

"I mean talking, the information you gave me about your family, that's what I meant."

"Alright, goodnight then. Will you be staying here tomorrow night?

Or are you going home, won't your mother and father wonder where you are?"

"Oh, they know where I am alright; I'm having a break from home. I will be here tomorrow and most probably for the next few days, then I'll be gone, goodnight." He made his way through the door that led to the kitchen and up the stairs to his room.

For the next hour he had a bath and then got into his bed. Chatting was coined during the nineteen fourteen-eighteen war when soldiers would sit in circles and talk as they searched for lice in their clothes. So, it was no wonder that Brian had never heard of the saying, in this world with no wars!

Nigel slept well, and was up early. Today he was going to see Janice after she finished her day shift. He had all day to fill before meeting her, and he knew what he wanted to do, he would go to his school to see what differences were there.

After breakfast he left the pub and walked towards the school. He had plenty of time to explore, and the walk along the country lanes past the house on the hill would do him good. It was a lovely day and a blue sky seemed to welcome him as he set off, passing The Briars. He stopped briefly at the gates of the mansion, where all this started. It was very much the same as he remembered it. He thought of his Jane, and of the last time he had seen her, in the big room with the fireplace. The fireplace that had started this adventure. If only he hadn't ventured inside, he wouldn't be in this place now! But on the other hand, he wouldn't have had this experience he was having, and at times, enjoying it.

As he walked on he passed places he knew. After two hours he stopped at a café and had a meal, the tea he enjoyed, and watched the world go by. His mind was full of thoughts. Fancy Fanny having a baby nine months after he had known her, that night all those years ago. Yet, for only eight or nine days, or whatever it was, it was hard to really understand. But Nigel could understand better than most people, being a time-traveller'.

He saw the school from afar; it looked pretty much the same as he remembered. Entering the main door, the something different was a small reception desk, with a woman he knew sitting behind it, Mrs. White the cleaning lady of his school.

He approached the desk. "Mrs. White, how are you?" Nigel said smiling.

"Good morning sir," she replied. "Can I help you?" It was obvious she didn't know him.

"Is the Headmaster and History teacher Mr. Smigging here today?" he enquired.

"Have you got an appointment?" she replied.

"Oh, he's a good friend of mine. I'm a History teacher myself, and we once worked together. I'm in town so I thought I would look up my old friend."

She was convinced at this young man's sincerity, and said that the professor was in his office just down the corridor, and directed Nigel. He thanked her, and went down the corridor to the office, and knocked on the door.

"Come in." He opened the door and entered the neat little office, the professor was sitting at his desk.

"Good morning Tom, how are you?" Nigel said. There was no recognition, once again it was obvious.

"How do you know me sir?" he asked.

"Oh, I worked with you once, not too long ago."

"I don't recollect you at all," the professor said.

Nigel knew that trying to explain himself would be in vain, so decided on another ploy. "Well sir, I was hoping that you could spare a little of your time, just to explain a few questions I would like to put to you concerning the history of this century. I want to become a History teacher like you, I am on holiday from college, and I was told that you were one of the best teachers on the subject. So please sir, if you have the time?"

"Take a seat young man; I have a little time to spare before lunch," he said, indicating a chair.

"Thank you, sir, that's good of you. My first question sir, is this; have you heard of Archduke Franz Ferdinand of Austria? Or Adolf Hitler, or the Kaiser?"

"Hold on, one at a time," the professor said smiling, "you're a very keen young man. To answer your questions, yes, but what do you want to know about them?"

"Somebody once told me that Adolf Hitler the Chancellor of Germany, invaded Poland in September nineteen hundred and thirty nine and started a war!"

"Yes that's true he did, and the British Government issued an ultimatum, that if he didn't withdraw his troops from Poland before the third of September nineteen thirty nine, a state of war would exist between us. So Chancellor Hitler withdrew, and so avoided any war. His role as Chancellor lasted only four years, and it was taken over by a more moderate regime. But he did do a lot of good for Germany, with new building projects and motorways."

Nigel listened in amazement at this new history unfolding.

"And what happened to Poland?"

"The Russians, who had taken half of the country, also went back to their homeland, so that was that, Poland was once again intact. Everyone, including politicians, saw sense after the war in South Africa, and there's been no wars since. We live in a peaceful world, and I hope that's the way it will always be."

He looked at his watch, which reminded Nigel that he still had to buy one. The professor continued, "Now, you wanted to know of the Archduke Franz Ferdinand of Austria. Well, he was killed in nineteen twenty seven in a car crash, not fulfilling his dearest wish. It was stated that he had always wanted to go and visit Sarajevo in Yugoslavia, but never got to do it. Although he was going to go there in nineteen hundred and fourteen on June twenty eighth, but at the last minute his schedule was changed so he never got there."

"I heard that he was assassinated there on that date," Nigel ventured.

The professor laughed out loud. "My dear boy, who has been putting this rubbish into your mind? Next you will be saying that the Kaiser started a war with everyone! That dear man also did a lot for Germany. They are a great people, very peaceful, as we all are, all over this lovely planet." The professor looked at his watch again, making Nigel feel uncomfortable for a moment.

"Can you tell me this, sir, have you ever heard of Al Qaeda? The terrorist organization? Who were responsible for the destruction of the Twin Towers sky-scrapers in New York, America?" Nigel stopped abruptly, knowing he had said too much.

The professor looked at Nigel with a certain sadness in his eyes.

"I don't know what college you are attending my boy, but whoever is teaching you this rubbish is doing you no good at all. I suggest you look for another learning facility, or you will never make a good teacher. Take my advice, look for another school!"

"I will sir," Nigel said sheepishly.

"To answer your question: no, I've never heard of the terrorist organization, there's no such thing in our society. And the Twin Towers were there in New York last month, because I had lunch in the restaurant on the very top." The professor looked at his watch again, and declared it was time for his lunch.

"Thanks for your time, sir. I will take your advice. But one last Question, sir, if I may, in a little form of a quiz. Who was born in Tupelo, started a musical trend that took over the world, made millions of records, films, and is the idol of millions? Here are three names: Elvis Presley, Tom Jones and Frank Sinatra?"

"Ha," said the professor smiling, "a trick question, because those three names I have never heard of. But the answer is Lance Summers, isn't it?"

"You're right, sir," Nigel said with a laugh, "it's Lance Summers."

Both men shook hands, and Nigel left the professor laughing at his desk. Nigel said 'goodbye' to the receptionist.

"Lance Summers is better than Elvis Presley," he told her as a parting shot.

"I don't know who Elvis is, but Lance Summers is better than anyone," she said knowingly. He smiled and walked out into the sunshine. He felt satisfied with his encounter with the professor. He had learned a great deal of this world, this 'time' he found himself in. He heard the school bell ring out, and within a minute the children poured out into the playground, all going their various ways to have lunch. It was at that moment that Nigel saw two boys he knew.

"Jarvis, James," he said aloud, above the chatter of the children. The boys stopped in their tracks.

"Your names are Jarvis and James, aren't they?" he said smiling.

"Yes, sir," said Jarvis, "are you a new master?"

"Oh no, I'm a friend of the professor, just paying him a visit."

"How do you know our names?" said James. For a moment that question took Nigel by surprise. How could he answer it? He had to think fast. "Oh, my friend the professor told me that you are both good pupils, and he actually pointed you out. But being an ex-teacher myself, I thought you were two boys I used to teach at one time, but I was mistaken. I'm sorry I'm keeping you from your lunch, anyhow boys, I won't keep you, thanks for your time."

"Oh, that's alright, sir, we're only going to the café down there." He pointed.

"Café! I could do with a bit of lunch myself. Maybe you young gentlemen will allow me to accompany you?"

"Yes, that will be fine, I'll show you where the café is," said Jarvis. The café was only a short walk from the school. Nigel ordered a sandwich, and the boys ordered chips and eggs, and they sat down at the table.

"This is nice," Nigel said. "Tell me Mr. Jarvis, what will you do when you leave school?"

Jarvis looked at his friend and smiled. He had never been called 'Mr' before. It sounded funny, yet important to him.

"Me, sir, I'm going to be a fireman."

"And I'm going to be an accountant," said James.

"Good professions, both jobs," Nigel volunteered.

They talked about school and their dreams, ate their food, and said goodbye to their new friend, after he paid for their lunch.

Nigel wished them the best in life, left the café, and walked towards the hospital to meet Janice. She flew out of the hospital and flung her arms around his neck.

"I've missed you, where have you been all my life?" She laughed. Her eyes sparkled, she knew she had found her soul mate, it was the feeling she had in her stomach.

"I've got butterflies here," she said, pointing.

"Really!" said Nigel.

"Really," she replied, "I know we have only known one another for a short while, but you're the one for me."

"Really?" he said again.

"Really," she laughed again, "jump on."

"Where are we going?" he enquired.

"I've got to go home to wash and change, before we go out tonight. It's alright with you, is it Simon?"

"Yes, it's perfectly alright," he said as he got on the back of her fast machine. Within ten minutes he was at her house, and sitting in her living room, while she got ready. The room was as any normal sitting room in his 'time' might look: TV, hi-fi, but a strange looking contraption caught his eye.

"What's that thing there?" he asked, pointing, as she entered the room.

"What?" she enquired.

"That thing there."

"Oh, the Transporter, have you never seen one? Have you never tried one out? Where have you been Simon?"

'That saying again,' he thought. "No, I've never seen one, explain?"

"Well, I know they are comparatively new, and not everyone has one. It's a Transporter; it takes you wherever you want to go. As long as there's a Transporter at the other end. Do you want to try it? It's fun really." "I'll try anything once," he said eagerly.

"Right, well I have friends who are selling their house, and I'm going to buy it in three months' time. It's just near the hospital where I work, we could visit there before we go out."

"Where is this place?" he enquired.

"It's in Moreland Road," she said with a smile. "Just sit there, and I sit opposite, pull the curtain." She demonstrated.

He did what she said; she smiled and pressed a button. Nothing happened, no movement, no sounds, no whirling, nothing!

"One second," she said, "here we are." She slid open a curtain, they stepped out into another living room. He looked around, it was different, no TV, no hi-fi.

"Jean," she called out, and a voice came back from the kitchen.

"Hi Jan, I was wondering when you where coming round."

"That's Transportation," she smiled, "one place to another in a flash."

"Bloody marvellous."

"Simon, please don't use that bad language, you know it's not allowed. It's against the law, five years in prison, but why am I telling you this, you already know?"

"Yes sorry, I just forgot for a moment, I was so surprised. First time I've been in a Transporter."

"These are just 'home' models, they are trying to get bigger ones where anyone can go from country to country. But I believe some people in government and the police are against them. Also there are rumours that they may be withdrawn very soon, I can't understand why, I reckon they are a good invention. One day we may be able to travel back in time! Now that would be something else, what do you think?"

"Yes, sounds good to me, but I can't see that happening," he said. Jean appeared in the doorway. "Janice, I thought you were talking to yourself, who is this good looking man?"

"This is Simon, my husband-to-be, if he wants to be?" she looked towards him, and her smile lit up the room. Nigel just smiled back, but said nothing.

"And where did you come from?" Jean enquired.

'Next question,' he thought, but said, "Not far from here, Eastern Hill."

"Oh, local then?"

"Yes, local."

"And where do you work?"

Janice could see that he was looking uncomfortable, so stepped in. "Jean, enough of the interrogation, leave the poor man alone! We have just popped in to say hello, and to show Simon how the Transporter works, he has never seen one."

"Where have you been?" Jean enquired. Nigel just shrugged.

"We won't be here long, Jean, so how about that drink, we're going out on the town tonight."

Jean went into the kitchen, and came back with some biscuits and tea. They sat down, and the two women talked about the sale of the house, and other things that had no interest to Nigel.

His mind was on other things, how would he say goodbye to this woman who he knew he was in love with? Maybe he could live in this 'world'? After all, he thought, it was a better world than the one he lived in; no wars, hardly any crime, good living, very good wages, the almost perfect world! He would certainly get a job, not as a History teacher, but maybe a publican! He remembered he had loved working as a barman with Fanny! Maybe this was his future? He would marry Janice, and live happily ever after! He was sure he could do well, with his knowledge, his experiences! But something was worrying him, this villain Jimmy Smith, he might make a lot of trouble for him? He had to find out why the real Simon was in hospital. There were lots of things he had to get answers to! Why did Bill bring him here? Surely he knew beforehand that this wasn't his world! Orders, why? What orders? And from whom? He sipped his tea, and looked up and smiled from time to time at the two women who were in deep conversation. He came to his senses when he heard the name he had been thinking of just a moment before.

"What will happen when Jim comes back from London?" he heard Jean say to Janice. "He won't like it, and you know how the Smiths are."

"I only went out with him the one night, and it didn't work out, we had nothing in common, and that was with other people! He thinks he's got a chance with me, but he's very much mistaken. No, this is my man." She put her arm around her Simon.

"You didn't say that you knew Jim Smith," Nigel said.

"Well, you haven't told me if you have another woman, have you? Anyhow, he means nothing to me, nothing at all."

Nigel looked at her and said, "The only woman in my life at this time is you." He leant forward and gave her a little kiss.

"Then that's it then, we both have nothing to worry about. Have we?"

"No, nothing." But he didn't mean it really, he had his doubts.

"Do you want to look at this house? I'm going to buy it in the next few months. " She got up, took him by the arm, and showed him the rooms upstairs and downstairs.

"Nice place," he remarked. The very same house that his Jane had wanted to buy in his world. It seemed that this parallel world was indeed the same as his own, apart from minor things. As far as names were concerned, and jobs, but people looked exactly the same; Brian at the pub, the professor, Janice, Jarvis and James. The only big difference was the history. He would have to find out once and for all what the motive was, why was Bill doing this to him? And could he ever get him back to his own world? He had never said he could! He would summons Bill, he had said just press the blue button, and he intended to do just that later on that day. And if Bill didn't give him any answers, he had decided that he was prepared to stay on in this world, get married to Janice, get a pub, and start a new life.

Back in Janice's house she got ready and they headed out for a meal and drinks at a restaurant overlooking a river.

"Now you have experienced the Transporter, how did you find it?" she enquired.

"A great invention, a great time-saver when you want to visit friends and you can drink as much as you like. Just get into it, and in a split second you're back in your own home. No traffic accidents, no worries about going out in the rain, or bad weather.

"Wonderful. But one thing I've wondered about, what happens if you transport yourself at a time that is inconvenient to your friends? I mean, they may be making love, and all of a sudden you are there with them!" he laughed.

"No, that can't happen, you can only transport with people you know very well. No-one can just appear, it's all computerized. When they are out then they shut the machine down, and when they want company they switch it on, it's so easy. Before we left home didn't you see me press the 'OUT' switch? Now my friends will know I'm not available at the moment. But most times when I visit my family I phone them to let them know I'm Transporting. It's easy when you know how."

"They should have one in every pub in the land," he said, and he ordered their meals.

The evening passed by, as all evenings do, fast when there's love in the air. They laughed, she told him about her life. He tried his best to tell some of his beliefs, but very little of his past life. He learnt that she was twenty five years old, the same age as his Jane. Her mother and father had names he remembered, every thing about her was the same, apart from her job. As he kissed her goodnight outside the pub, he knew for sure that he was madly in love with her, as she was with him. How could he leave her? He made his decision as she waved goodnight, and drove away on her fast motorbike. He would get in touch with Bill and cancel the meeting, he was going to stay. The bar was empty, and Brian was just about to lock the door.

"Simon, there's been someone looking for you tonight."

"Oh, that must have been my friend Bill."

"No, it was Jimmy Smith, and he's not very happy with you, so he said. He came back from London earlier than he thought he would. He said he'll be here tomorrow night, and a warning, you had better be here."

"That's no problem," Nigel said, not meaning it.

"And another thing I would like to know is, how long do you intend to stay? Because I have a friend who wants to visit me, and you have the only room."

"Oh, a few days, but I may move out sooner. I'll let you know for sure tomorrow. Are you locking up now? I was going to ask you for a pint before I go to bed," he asked.

"I was going to shut up, but seeing that you are a resident, a paying guest, you can have a pint." He then went behind the counter.

In his room, Nigel pressed the blue button on his belt. He remembered that Janice had told him of her intentions to leave her job, and go to live elsewhere, the only reason she had decided to stay was the night she had met him in the bar. He was the only reason for her to think of her life and her future. They had talked, and he had told her that he was a gardener, and had had a breakdown and had been in hospital. He could hardly tell her the truth. He assured her that he was on the mend, and all would be well in the end. They had laughed a lot, and kissed and held hands, it had been another magical evening. He pressed the blue button again, just before he got into bed.

Chapter 9

TRUTH EXPOSED

The morning came, and Nigel knew that this day was going to be the beginning of a new life. He had to sort things out, get some work, a place to live. He would see Bill and tell him his intentions to stay in his new world. He would marry Janice, and live happily ever after. But what goes on in the mind, doesn't always work out, what he didn't know, he would soon find out.

After breakfast he left the pub and caught a bus to go into Southampton city centre. He had all day to fill before he would meet Janice again. The countryside passed by as he sat on the bus, and his mind wandered; his Jane would be getting on with her life now, he supposed, and he would never see her again. But he had Janice, and they were one of the same. The pub idea had been a good one, he had enjoyed that work. It would be no good him trying to go back to being a History teacher, in this world there was no history, well, at least no military history. In most ways the world he found himself in was a better world than his. It seemed that a world at peace was surely a better way to live one's life. There were certain differences with people; names and their professions; a few inventions, like the 4D cinema, and the Transporter! There was certainly less crime, and people were very friendly and courteous, yes, a nice world to live in. He noticed also, that there wasn't so much traffic congestion, and no-one seemed to smoke!

He arrived in the city centre, and alighted the bus.

"Thank you sir," the driver said.

Nigel walked the streets he had known all his life, saw people in shops that he knew, Mr. Wilcome in the butcher's, and Tommy the young man who helped him. But there was no recognition. He went to the shop where he had been for a suit for his forthcoming wedding. The people who ran the shop were the same people he knew, but he wasn't surprised when enquiring about his order, that there was no such order in place.

He went to a coffee bar near where the Old Gate had been, and went in. The waitress that he knew well was there, but she didn't recognise him at all. Nigel surmised that his 'twin' didn't frequent coffee bars. He realised that he would have to make friends all over again, but that was OK, he would do that. Although this was a different world to his own, he didn't feel ill at ease, in fact there were so many new things to learn, see, and discover. People smiled and some talked to him, to wish him a nice day. The sun was shining, and he felt on top of the world, and he was in love!

He had to see Bill, and he pressed the blue button, after a nice lunch that cost ninety two pounds! He spent the afternoon watching the boats and ferries going to and fro. He enjoyed the sun and had a little sleep on the banks of the river. His time-travelling days were over, whatever Bill had to say. Where was he anyhow? he thought. 'Press the blue button if you want me,' he had said. So he pressed it again, and again, and again!

His money was going, things were so expensive. He got up from the grass, brushed himself down, and made his way back to the city centre. Then he caught a bus to Janice's hospital, where once again she was waiting for him. Her smile lit up his heart, he kissed her passionately and they were soon speeding towards her house. Her parents greeted him in a friendly manner, she had told them about the man she had met, and who she now loved, and they were happy for her. They had a meal then Janice got ready to go out.

"Thank you for coming along at the right time," her father said. "We were about to lose her, she was going away for good, and we didn't want that to happen. She's a wonderful daughter, and because of you she is staying here. She loves you, Simon, and hopes you will marry her some day."

"I hope that will happen as well, sir."

Her mother looked at him and smiled. "More cake Simon?" she asked.

Janice came bouncing into the room. "I hope you're not talking about me, Father? I know you want to get rid of me, you want me to marry and leave, don't you?" she laughed.

"Of course we want you to leave," her father laughed, "don't we dear?"

"Only if it's as far as Moreland Road," she replied. "To think that just a few days ago you were going to leave here, and the next day after you met Simon here, you went to look at that house and decided you wanted it, that was a quick decision wasn't it, dear?"

"Mother, I had this feeling that I can't even begin to describe to you, but I knew that's where I would end up, but only with my Simon." She took his hand and squeezed it, they looked into each other's eyes, and they both knew.

"Enough of this lovey-dovey, it reminds me of when me and your mother met! And I don't want to be reminded of it; it was a long time ago anyhow." They all laughed, and Nigel and Janice left for their evening out. Tonight he would tell her of his intentions.

He wondered why Bill hadn't answered his call, he had pushed the blue button a few times, but there was no sign of him. The evening was the same as always for the lovers, they danced, laughed a lot, love has a way of making people happy, and Nigel forgot everything as he danced in her sweet embrace. She told him that she had the next week off, and looked forward to them spending more time together, and he agreed eagerly.

The evening passed as all good times tend to do, and soon they were kissing goodnight once again outside the Fox and Hounds public house. They made plans to meet at ten o'clock the next morning. He waved and blew her a goodnight kiss, as she rode away on her bike. He was smiling as he entered the bar, there were a few customers sitting around as he went to the counter to have his normal night-cap.

"Simon, there's someone here to see you," Brian said, as he poured his pint of beer. "Over there in the corner," he pointed.

Nigel looked around and saw a stocky man he had never seen before, even in his own time.

"Jimmy Smith," Brian said. "Any fighting then take it outside," he warned. Nigel paid, picked up his beer, and went over to the corner table.

"Simon, nice to see you," Jim said. "Sit down. How are you feeling?"

"Fine," said Nigel, sitting down opposite the man.

"So they let you out early, I was surprised when I heard. You were very depressed last time I saw you. So, you are better then?"

"I'm fine now," Nigel said, not really knowing what to say. This man seemed friendly enough, not like Brian had portrayed him to be. Nigel decided just to listen, and try to bluff his way along. "They let me come out earlier than I expected," he volunteered.

"That's good, I bet your mother and father are pleased?"

"They are," he lied. "Look Jim, I'm sorry to say this, and although it's nice to see you again, I'm very tired so I must go to bed soon. I've had a traumatic time just lately."

"So I understand, but there's another thing I want to have a word with you about," Jim said, but with a smile.

"And what was that, Jim?"

"Janice."

"Janice?" Nigel repeated.

"Yes, Janice. I hope you are getting on alright with her, she's a wonderful girl. And I believe she had designs on me, but I've got myself a woman in London who, may I say, I love. I would have had to tell Janice and let her down, and I didn't look forward to doing that. Now, I've heard that you have been going out with her, so you have done me a favour, and now I won't have to tell her anything, see?"

144

"Yes, I see. How long did you go out with her for?" Nigel enquired.

"Oh, only once, but I think she liked me. Anyhow, you've let me off the hook. I'm away back to London tomorrow, and I'm not coming back."

Nigel sipped his beer, just listening to Jim talk about how he had met his woman in London. He told Nigel that he was welcome to visit him at any time. Ten minutes later he was saying his goodbyes. Nigel was relieved that there was no trouble, and took a liking to the man he had never met before. One thing he knew was that the real Simon must be identical in every way to himself, because according to Jim, they had known one another at school, and had been friends for years! "Give my love to your mum and dad will you, Simon? And I'm glad you have recovered from your breakdown. You'11 be OK now and don't let things get you down." was Jim's parting advice. With that they shook hands, and he disappeared through the door.

Nigel went to the bar for a re-fill before he went to bed.

"Have you sorted out your differences?" Brian asked.

"There was no problem; he's going off to London for good, he's a nice sort." Brian didn't say anymore, apart from asking how long he intended to stay. Nigel said he would let him know the next day.

As normal she was on time, and somehow she always had a surprise for him. This time it was a picnic hamper, she had planned a picnic on the downs, the view towards the sea was magnificent. The morning air and the sunshine were like a tonic to him as they whizzed through the lanes, with fields so green, lambs at play, and love all around. He clung to her as though he would never let her go. Her lovely face competed with the sun when she smiled. Her laughter was infectious, Nigel was a very happy man. He had lost everything, but now at least she made up for most of it.

When they were having their picnic, he told her that he would be leaving the room he had at the pub and then he would have to find a place to live, he would also get a different job. There was no mention of marriage, she told him that she enjoyed her work, and that she wanted to buy the house in Moreland Road. They held hands and kissed lightly from time to time. In the afternoon they both had a sleep on the rug under the tree that sheltered them from passing planes. The sun seemed to linger that much longer, and the sea in the distance was like a big sparkling jewel. He woke before her, and looked at her sleeping. What world was she in now? She looked so content, and so was he. He sat up, and on hearing a noise behind him, turned around. And there he was sitting on the rock just a few metres away. He gave Nigel a broad smile, and beckoned him to go over. He glanced down at his princess, she was still sleeping. So he got up and went towards where Bill sat.

"Where have you been? I've been calling you, I've pressed the button, the blue button many times, but you didn't respond."

"I've had no calls, let's see your belt." Nigel took his belt off and handed it to Bill. He examined it.

"A crystal has blown, and now the belt is useless. It's been in a strong force, not what it was designed for. Have you worn it every day as I told you to do?"

"Yes, I have, all the time, apart from when I'm in bed."

"Have you been near any magnetic electric forces?"

Nigel thought for a few seconds, then said, "There was the Transporter, that's all I can think of."

"That's the reason, the Transporter. They haven't been fully developed yet, in my time they are far more advanced than now. Anyhow, it's not your fault, but I have to go back to my time to get it repaired. Stay here," he commanded, "won't be long."

He walked behind the rock out of Nigel's sight, and walked back again within a second. "It's working now, don't go into any more Transporters with it on."

"That was fast, you were gone just a second and you say you have been back to your time and got it repaired, that's unbelievable!"

"It wasn't easy to repair Nigel, it took a week, I've been gone a week. Time-travel is something else, and I'm going to let you into a few more secrets, so listen carefully." The two men sat down on the edge of the rock, and Bill began.

"First you must realise a few facts, at this moment in time I haven't been born yet. I was born in two thousand and ten, this is two thousand and seven. You must also realise that you haven't been born either, not in this zone. So therefore if you have never been born then it's just logic that you can never die! In this zone you, my friend, have eternal life, you will never die!"

"What?" Nigel spluttered. "Eternal life, I'll live forever, that's wonderful!"

"Is it Nigel? Think about it, you will never age, you will remain as you are now, forever! You'll never get ill, and your life will be a misery. As your loved ones grow old and die, and you start again with new friends, again and again for eternity. Do you really want that?"

"Give me time to think about it," Nigel joked.

"It's no laughing matter; people may be envious of you, jealous. You will be scorned as time goes by. No Nigel, it can't be allowed, the 'forces' wouldn't allow it. So if you think that you are going to stay here, you have been under a misapprehension! You have to go back."

"I'm not going back anywhere. Why would I go back when I have found love here? This is a nice place to live, I lost everything I'd held dear to me, and I don't intend to lose it all again, I'm not stupid. Anyhow, back to where do you mean?"

"Back to nineteen hundred and twelve."

"No way," Nigel blurted. "All I did was get myself locked up there, and the police are still after me! No Bill, I'm not going back there. Why can't I go back to my world in Zone One, as you called it? Why can't I just flip a zone now, we are in two thousand and seven?"

"Because that is not possible, the only way you can get back, is to go back to nineteen hundred and twelve, and go back through the same gateway that you came through."

"But I tried that and it didn't work!" Nigel protested.

"I'll explain that," Bill replied. "I realise all this information at one time can baffle the brain, that's the reason I've imparted it slowly in dribs and drabs, so you can absorb it better. Time is a strange phenomenon, even the top brains in the world can't get to grips with all of the quirks. Time has its flaws, it's not a pure thing, like everything, it has flaws. The reason you couldn't time-travel when you tried was because the gateway has been sealed, so there is no longer a way to get through there. The only way to go back to your time is not to come here to two thousand and seven, but to get to Zone One in nineteen hundred and twelve, it's a sideway thing, then you can go back to your time. So that's why I have said we go back to nineteen hundred and twelve. Go to the mansion, and the fireplace, transfer sideways from Zone Two to Zone One, then you will time-travel to your own time. It's easy, the hardest thing will be getting you back to the mansion without being caught by the police, remember you're a wanted man there?"

"You don't have to remind me of that. But if I have to leave here, you can get me back home can you?"

"I can, and I will," said Bill smiling. Nigel couldn't contain himself; he hugged Bill.

"Thanks, Bill," he said, his eyes starting to get moist. "I'm going home!" Excitement started to overwhelm him.

"Hold on," said Bill, "don't get too excited, we have to get to the mansion yet."

"What will happen to Janice over there?" he pointed to her, still asleep.

"Don't worry about her, it's been taken care of, she'll be fine."

"How do you know that? Or maybe that's a silly question? I suppose you have taken care of that as well?"

"No Nigel, you have," Bill said with a smile.

"I have?"

"Yes Nigel, you have," Bill repeated.

"And just how have I done that?"

"Because she has fallen in love with you, well not you exactly Nigel, but she has well and truly fallen for a man named Simon. And where is Simon? He's in hospital at the moment, but he will be out on Monday, that's the day we go back. And Simon will go to the pub to celebrate the fact that he's now well again after his breakdown. He will meet Janice who will be in the bar, and he will carry on where you left off. And because you are identical in every way; physique, looks, personality, she will never know. She will still love him, as she loves you."

"Isn't that deceitful?" asked Nigel.

"No, it has to be that way. It's been set up this way, everything has been set in motion. It will happen; it has to for my sake."

"For your sake?"

"Yes, for my sake." At that moment Janice moved, she was waking up.

"I'll tell you more tonight, Nigel. Here, put your belt back on, and no more Transporters! See you at the pub later tonight, we have something to do tomorrow morning, so arrange to see Janice in the afternoon, I'm going now." He went behind the rock.

"Bill, why did you bring me here in the first place?" he asked as he followed Bill. But once again Bill had gone. Nigel shook his head in disbelief! He had learned a lot in this short time. He understood more now, inwardly he was elated to think that on Monday he would be going home, just two more days! But what did Bill mean when he had said that he had taken care of things? There were still more questions he needed to ask. He walked over to her, lay down alongside and leant over and kissed her on her lips.

She opened her eyes. "Simon, I had a dream that you left me, it was more of a nightmare really."

"Don't worry, Simon will never leave you," he said. She smiled a contented smile and they kissed again. The sun was telling the world that the moon wanted to have its turn to light up the sky, so the lovers packed up the picnic things, and returned to the pub. She wasn't able to see him that evening, so instead of leaving him right away, she went into the bar with him to have a drink and a bite to eat. They had a nice meal and she left at eight o'clock, she was going to Moreland Road to help her friend with some packing. As she had to work all day Sunday, they made a date to meet at seven o'clock the next night, Saturday. He watched her leave from the doorway then went to the bar. He sat at his normal place, wondering what the evening would bring. Then he noticed people coming in, more than normal, and a couple of men were setting up some equipment.

"What's happening tonight?" he enquired.

"Singing contest," said Brian the landlord, "you singing?"

"Why not," Nigel replied. "Oh, by the way Brian, I will be staying just two more nights, I'm going home on Monday."

"That's nice, I bet your mother and father will be pleased to see you back again."

"That's a certainty," said Nigel smiling broadly. "And to be honest with you, although I've loved it here, it will be good to go back," and Nigel meant it.

Bill appeared before the singing started. "Hello again Bill, please don't tell me you have been gone a week this time?" Nigel laughed.

"No," said Bill, "that would be a lie; the fact is I've been gone a month. I've been to New York on holiday with my family. I have a wife and two kids don't you know?"

Nigel spluttered on his drink. "What would have happened if I had pressed the blue button on the belt, with you on holiday?"

"All was taken care of, believe me," Bill said.

"I believe you Bill, believe me, I believe you," he repeated.

Nigel tried to buy Bill a drink, but he refused."I never drink on duty," he said. "Now is the time to let you in on the main reason why I brought you here, I'm sure you have been wanting to know?" Nigel just nodded.

"In parallel worlds," Bill started, "everyone is duplicated. Some people die at the same time, but not all necessarily of the same cause. They get married on the same date, their children are born on the same day; for example, Simon and yourself will get married on the same day, and die on the same day as one another. And your children will be born on the same day. The only difference is that names can vary, and professions. Although the zones go along hand in hand, there are sometimes when events are not the same; war in Zone One, no war in Zone Two, for example. But when people were being killed in the trenches of the World

Wars, their duplicates were dying here, but of other things like the plague or diseases. There's no perfect world you know. In a zone I know there were no wars, no diseases, and people just died of boredom! Anyhow, I don't want to complicate it too much, so I'll just concentrate on our zones for the time being."

Once again Nigel nodded in agreement, and sipped his drink. It was complicated, he was getting the drift of it all, but he still wondered what he had to do with it all.

Bill continued. "Sometimes we get a blip, and when that happens certain action must take place. A blip occurred a few weeks ago in this zone, this world. Simon was taken ill with mental problems, and was put into hospital. He was supposed to recover but didn't, and it was obvious he would be staying in hospital longer than he was supposed to. When things happen like that incident, which may I say, are rare, but I've known cases of a similar nature in the past, and our warning systems go into action, our atomic computers take over and give the warning, and the blip I'm talking about was picked up, and has now been dealt with. And that's thanks to you Nigel, and this will surprise you even more," Bill hesitated at that moment because he saw Nigel's surprise, "And your son." Bill expected this reaction from Nigel, who was now choking on his beer.

"Son, my son! Now that is preposterous, I'm not even married, let alone have a son!"

Bill interjected, "You haven't got a son at this moment, but you will have, and he will be born to you and your wife-to-be in two thousand and ten, the same date I will be born."

"Is he your duplicate, Bill?"

"Yes Nigel, he is, he's in the police force right now, and is the same age, living in the year two thousand and sixty four.

"My son, alive now! Although he hasn't been born yet! Now that's a hard one to believe!"

"Why Nigel? How can you say that, when you have lived in nineteen hundred and twelve? That was before you were born. This time thing is a complex phenomenon. As I have said before, the best minds in the world can't understand it fully. It's like the end of the universe, where does that end? No-one knows. Some things are impossible for us humans to understand. Aliens, do they exist in far off worlds? No-one knows, and it's the same about 'time! We stop time every time we take a photograph, but maybe people shouldn't delve into it. The governments and wisest men in the world don't want the public to know that it even exists. It would be chaotic if people travelled back and forth in time."

"So where did I help in all this?" enquired Nigel.

"We all have a destiny, it's pre-arranged by another greater being, some people call it God, but at times these events don't happen because of human influences, and in this case, this is what happened: Simon was destined to meet my mother at a certain time, some people call it fate, but because he unexpectedly had a mental breakdown, he would have never met my mother who was going to leave the district, they would never have met, and yours truly would never have been born. And this is where you came in, you filled in the time that Simon wasn't available, and now my mother is truly in love with Simon my father."

"So Janice is your mother, you say?" Nigel enquired.

"She is my mother, just not at this minute; I'm not destined to be born for another three years! But as you can see I was born, so she is my mother now. In my time she is still alive and she's eighty two years old, my father is still active as well. Hard to believe, eh Nigel?" Bill laughed, but mostly at Nigel's expression on his face.

"So you brought me here to fill in the week that Simon would have if he has left hospital that fate predicted?"

"Yes, without you I would be nothing, you are my duplicate father." Nigel shook his head from side to side in disbelief. He remembered he had always had a good feeling about Bill, a sort of kinship.

"Will my son look like you, Bill?" Nigel enquired.

"He does, he's the spitting image of me, you will see when you get to be eighty years old, and he is in the police force, just like me."

"Incredible," Nigel said. He ordered another pint of beer, and bought his duplicate son a soft drink.

"When the computers saw the discrepancy, it suggested that we get help from the Time-Police in Zone One. So I contacted my duplicate brother Zane, and he set up this plan to help me get born. Do you remember going to the doctor for a check up three weeks ago?" asked Bill.

"Yes, I do, I was passed A.1."

"Yes, but what you didn't know is that you were implanted with a very small device called a 'suggesting chip'. It was implanted in the back of your head, and the information on it has made you do what you did. First, it put into your mind that you wanted to leave home and buy a new home and you were guided to the mansion, where a gateway had been made for you to come here. The lightning that struck the chimney was arranged by the scientific department of the police. As you drove home from school that day, you were aided on your way. Do you remember the tractor that slowed you down as you drove through the lane? If he hadn't slowed you down you would never have seen the sign that had been hidden by tree leaves and foliage. Once again the scientific department made the sudden gust of wind to expose the sign as you passed. Remember the day was fine, there was no wind? The storm would come the next day."

Nigel nodded in remembering.   "The driver of the tractor was a Time-Police-Operative, your son. Then do you remember the force in the fireplace, as you got to nineteen hundred and twelve? That was with his help. He pushed you into this zone, Zone Two. You didn't see him because he had an invisible suit on."

"Invisible suit?" Nigel blurted.

"Please Nigel, let's not go there at this minute, it's complex enough, don't you think?"

"This chip I have in my brain," he touched his head.

"Don't worry, it's harmless, it will be removed as easily as it was put in, when you go home. Now, your job here is almost done, and on Monday we will go back. But first we have to do something else, you have to meet your duplicate brother Simon, and I have arranged that for tomorrow morning."

"I'm to see Simon," Nigel said excitedly, "that will be something else, that's great. I'll tell him about Janice, and how wonderful she is, and tell him to meet her in here at seven o'clock on Monday evening, the day I go home. I'm looking forward to doing all this!"

"I see the 'suggesting' chip is working well," Bill said, laughing out loud. "The other thing is that since your work in helping me has almost come to an end, a little holiday is in the pipe-line for you, and I'm going to take you to my time, two thousand and sixty four for a month of the most fantastic holiday of your life. You'll be amazed what two thousand and sixty four is like, and what a wonderful world I live in. That's my gift to you. After all, Nigel, you have helped get me life, without you I would never have been born, thank you, Father!" Both men laughed at his joke. The bar was now getting very crowded and the first singers were being announced.

"We will continue with the explanations when we meet tomorrow. In the meantime have a nice evening; I have a wife to go home to, after all!"

"Before you go Bill, will I need to pack a bag for my holiday?"

"You won't need a thing; it's all been taken care of." He finished his drink and they shook hands. Nigel stood up from his stool and hugged his duplicate son, the bond felt strong. He left the pub.

"Eleven tomorrow morning, don't be late, outside in the car-park," his parting words were. Nigel sat there and smiled to himself, as he ordered another pint, and put his name down for the singing contest.

"Hello Simon, you're better now, I see," said people he didn't know. But they were very friendly, and everyone had a good time as the evening progressed. He sang 'ARE YOU LONESOME TONIGHT', an Elvis Presley song and the applause was overwhelming.

"You sound just like the main man, Lance Summer," they said.

Nigel was in his room, before the music had died down, trying to digest all he had been told by Bill. He felt happy that he had helped in making someone's life happy. He wondered about

Janice, in a way it was a deceitful thing he had done. He had made her fall in love with him and now he had to leave her! But on the other hand, without him, what would have happened to both of them? He went to sleep, but now his mind was on his very own true love, and that was Jane, in Zone One, his world.

Nigel was up at the first sign of light, he felt excited about a day full of promise. He looked at himself in the mirror and realised that he didn't need to shave. He hadn't shaved at all since he had come to this world! No change, everlasting life! How many people had this chance? How many people would jump at the chance?

He showered, and went down to breakfast. The same waiter gave him his breakfast without talking. Nigel was outside when Bill came, the funny thing was that he always appeared from out of Nigel's sight: from behind a rock or a building, he didn't materialize, as in the films he had seen, like Star Trek.

"Morning, ready for your adventures?" Bill asked.

"I'm as ready as I will ever be, and looking forward to going to the future, just inquisitive, you understand!"

"I understand," Bill said with a smile. They walked to the bus Stop and while waiting for the bus, Nigel said, "Why the bus, Bill? I would have thought that you could get us to our destination a lot easier?"

"We don't abuse the powers we have. Anyhow, the hospital is not too far away, and it's a nice day for an old fashioned ride."
"Old fashioned, this is old fashioned?"

"We don't have buses any more in my era. The people have different ways of getting about, you'll see. Just for now, relax and enjoy, here's the bus now."

In the back of the bus, Bill told Nigel what he would have to say to Simon when he met him, to tell him to meet Janice in the pub at seven, she would be expecting him.

"Don't say anything about where you really come from. Make up any story you like for the reason you are visiting him. And just half an hour, not longer." He told Nigel he would wait in the grounds; he didn't want to meet with his father-to-be! Anyhow, he had been advised not to, for emotional reasons. The hospital was just an hour's bus ride, and soon the two men were in the grounds of the hospital.

"I'll wait here under this tree, nice sunny day, I might just have a lie down for half an hour."

Nigel left Bill, and made his way to the main entrance, it was the same hospital he had been in in nineteen hundred and twelve, but modernised. As he approached the reception, he felt as though someone at any time would stop him, and re-arrest him! But it was only a fleeting thought. From nowhere it seemed, the man was standing in front of him. Nigel had been looking around and remembering how he had lived here all those many years before.

"You're going back on Monday, to your past life I believe," Nigel heard him say, "it must have been a traumatic time for you, but we're here to look out for you, you know. Have you seen your friend Bill this morning?"

"Bill is outside, under the tree over there." He pointed to the tree that could be seen through the open door.

"Thanks, he's a nice man that Bill, he has helped so many people over time, as he's helped you."

"Is he your colleague? Are you also helping 'lost' souls?"

"Very much so, as you know, we've done alright in getting you back on the right path."

"You've certainly done that. It's strange how certain people take up, and love to work on projects that deal with people who are lost in this world," Nigel said.

"I've always been in this business, it's my vocation."

"Yes, the rewards are good in the police force," Nigel volunteered. "That may be so, but I wouldn't want to change my job."

"In the Time Police, you mean?"

"The what?" said the man. "I don't know what that is, I'm happy being a nurse." At that moment another man in a white coat came around the corner, and came towards the pair.

"Oh Bill, I've been looking for you. Don't forget the meeting, what have you been up to, sitting in the grounds? I saw you lying under the tree. I was just about to come and get you." Nigel looked towards the door, and he could see the figure of a man still lying under the tree!

"I was just saying that you have done a good job getting Simon here on the road again." Bill the nurse nodded, just nodded. Nigel now realised once again, that he had misunderstood the situation, and this nurse had mistaken him for Simon.

"Oh I'm sorry," Nigel said, "I'm not Simon, I'm his twin brother, and I've just come to visit him."

"Twin brother, you're having us on?"

"No I'm not; I have just arrived here to see him."

"But we were talking about your friend here Bill, who has been looking after you.'"

"No," Nigel responded, "I was talking about my friend Bill, who's waiting for me in the grounds under the tree. We were talking at cross-purposes!

Bill the nurse looked at Nigel intently. "It's incredible, and you're identical!"

"Yes, we're twins. Can you tell me what ward or room my brother is in?"

"I'11 take you to him," said Bill the nurse. They walked down the corridor and came to a room. Simon was sitting on his bed.

"You've got a visitor Simon." And the two nurses walked away, saying how the two men looked the same and it was amazing.

Nigel shook hands with his image. "I'm your twin," Nigel said with a broad smile, Simon smiled back.

"You know they say that everyone in the world has a double, and you are mine," Nigel said as he sat on the chair opposite Simon. He told him that he wanted his help. He had come to this part of the world on holiday and everyone he met had mistaken him for someone else.

"They all thought that I was you, and called me Simon, it's been very confusing. I've even met your friend Jimmy Smith in the Fox and Hounds, and he thought I was you, so did Brian the landlord. Everyone has mistaken me for you!"

Simon sat and listened intently. "Well Nigel, you did say Nigel didn't you?"

"Yes," Nigel said.

"How can I help you then?"

Nigel handed over an envelope containing money that he owed Brian for his room. "When you leave here on Monday, can you give this money to Brian in the Fox and Hounds pub? It's money I owe him; just tell him that it's money for the room, that's all, he will understand. And a beautiful woman will be there in the bar, she will speak to you, and you will like her very much. Have a meal with her, you will get on well. Don't say anything about meeting me because nobody will understand you."

"I understand this, but why would you trust me?" Simon said.

"I trust you like a brother, we are one of the same. Can you do this for me? I have to leave; my holiday here has come to an end. I'm sorry, but there will be a bit of confusion, because I have been here for nearly a week now. I even met your mother and father, and they thought I had escaped, that's how I found out you were in here, even they mistook me for you! Janice is the woman I've mentioned, and she is the woman for you, believe me. She will be waiting for you at seven o'clock in the bar on Monday night. I realise you have had some problems in the past, but Simon, you're better now. I'm sorry that I have confused things, but I answer to your name, because everyone believed I was you. And you can't blame them can you, look?" He took Simon's hand, and put him in front of a mirror, standing alongside him.

"See, we are one of the same. I have to go now; it was good to meet you. You won't see me again, but I hope you have a good life. If Janice asks you anything you don't understand, just tell her your memory's been bad, but it's improving."

Simon, who had been listening, talked at last. "You know Nigel, somehow it seems that I have known you forever, and I will do as you ask, I'll pay Brian your money. I intended to go to the pub anyway, to ask him if he had a job for me. I've had enough of gardening to last me a lifetime. It was because of it that I was so depressed, I hated my job. And I must tell you this; I have never had a girlfriend, that's another thing that led me to despair. I've had a breakdown, and my doctor said I should have a short time in this hospital to get better. I'm fine now, and I'm going to change my entire life, maybe this woman you've mentioned, who knows what will happen. But how will I know her?"

"Don't worry about that Simon, she will know you. I've been seeing her for the last six days, and she'll think I'm you. But I have to go back home, I have my own woman. I know I should have told her that I was Nigel not Simon, but I didn't. Maybe I was wrong, but it's too late now. Her fate is in your hands, my friend, I know you'll love her. By the way, just to set your mind at ease, we were just friends; there was no sex at all, please believe me." Simon saw in Nigel's eyes the truth, and recognised it.

"Tell your parents that it was you that visited them on Monday last, but that you had to come back to the hospital, because that's what I told them I was going to do. Jimmy Smith has gone to live in London, so you won't see him again. He's fallen in love with a woman up there. That's about it Simon, it's been nice meeting you, I must go now, I have a good friend waiting for me in the grounds."

"Anyone I know?" asked Simon.

"Not at the moment, but you will meet one day, and you'll get to know him well."

"How do you know that?"

"Put it this way; let's just say that I do!"

Nigel shook hands with his 'other' self, hugged him, and left the room. He looked back to see Simon smiling broadly and waving.

'What a strange experience that was,' Nigel thought as he made his way out of the hospital, and went across the grounds to where Bill was sleeping under the tree.

"Wake up Bill, mission completed." He went on to tell his friend how he had developed his story, and that Simon would be in the pub at seven o'clock on Monday night.

"Well done Nigel, you did a great job, you deserve your holiday.

Chapter 10

THE HOLIDAY

"All systems go," Nigel exclaimed with enthusiasm.

Bill instructed him to punch the year two thousand and sixty four into his belt, to shut his eyes, and as before, check the time, it was one o'clock.

They pressed their buttons, closed their eyes, and a split second later, Bill said, "Home sweet home, we're here."

Nigel opened his eyes, the hospital had gone, in its place was a much bigger building and the whole district was different. They walked towards the main road, and the first surprise for Nigel came along. There were no cars about, but a rail system, with capsules lined up like a sky lift. As one left the station, another one took its place. No queues, people arrived, got into a capsule and it moved off, slowly at first, then with a joy stick the operator, that was Bill, would go left or right, to follow the destination plan. Eight lanes, the eighth lane was like car lanes, very fast, with exits all along the way. Bill explained how it functioned, and in no time they were whizzing across the countryside towards the city.

Just fifteen minutes and they alighted and were standing outside Bill's house. It was a magnificent place, and beautifully decorated. Bill's wife Grace was a delightful woman, and welcome was written in her smile. Bill introduced Nigel as a friend, and had warned him not to mention anything of his time-travelling. His job in the Time-Police was top secret, and Bill never discussed his work with his wife, Nigel understood. Bill told his wife that Nigel would be with them for a month's holiday, and she accepted it without blinking an eyelid. His room was luxurious, thick carpet wall to wall, velvet bucket chairs, a TV screen covered one wall! Power shower with four shower heads, jacuzzi, everything a person would want to live in a 'perfect' life.

After Nigel had eaten, Bill took him on his first tour of the city. To his surprise, the first stop was to visit Bill's mother and father.

"What, Simon and Janice?" Nigel spluttered.

"Of course, mind you they have aged, mother is eighty two years old now, and father is eighty, but healthy enough. Have a guess where they live?"

"Moreland Road," Nigel replied.

"You're right," Bill smiled. They walked the quiet streets, no car congestion here. People were friendly, and Bill explained how in his world there was harmony, no gangs were allowed, the police had banned that culture years ago. There was no country that was at war, no conflicts at all. Everything was peaceful in this Zone Two world. Nigel just marvelled at all the information coming his way. He compared his world to this one, and wished he could live in the very place he found himself. But everlasting life? It sounded great, never having to die! But Bill had explained the hazards of that.

The men got into the individual transport system again, and this time Bill let him take the controls with instructions. Nigel found it easy and twelve minutes later they got off. He saw the sign Moreland Road, number thirteen. The house looked much the same as they went through the gate, and up towards the front door.

"Won't he recognise me?" Nigel said."After all, I only saw him a couple of hours ago."

"No," Bill said, "remember, it was fifty seven years ago?"

"Oh yes, fifty seven   years," Nigel replied. He shook his head; he still had a job to come to terms with this time-travel business! Bill went in the front door, and Nigel followed, a little apprehensive.

They were in the back garden sitting at a table having a glass of wine. She got up as Bill shouted out, and there she was. Nigel could see her beauty had remained, all these years, and her smile was still as radiant as he remembered. She kissed her son affectionately.

"This is my friend Nigel," Bill said to his mother, "he's here for a short holiday and staying with me and Grace."

"Hello Nigel," she said, extending her hand. Nigel took it, and remembered.

"Come and have a glass of wine with us, Simon, Bill is here with his friend."

Simon looked around, and his smile said it all, 'welcome' was the word. They all sat in the afternoon sun sipping wine, talking and laughing. Nigel felt at ease as he watched her intently, knowing that this was his Jane at this age, and Simon was 'him' at the same age!

Nigel felt happy. Bill told his mother about new plans for his house and how her great grandchildren were getting on at school. She reminded him of their get-together for a party for a forthcoming anniversary. She asked Nigel where he lived, and Bill helped out when he saw the look in his eyes.

"My friend comes from a different land far away."

"What, like Australia?" she asked.

"Further than that," Bill laughed. "No mother, only joking, he's local, he lives in Stockton."

"Near the pub the Fox and Hounds," Nigel volunteered.

"That was a lovely place; I met Simon there all those years ago, didn't I dear?" she said, talking to her husband.

"Yes, oh memories," Simon replied. "I worked there for many years, behind the bar. It's a pity it's no longer there, they pulled it down a few years ago, if my memory serves me well. So you are talking about the site of the old pub?"

"Yes," said Nigel, "the old site." But inwardly he was surprised to hear that the place that had been so important in his life had gone!

"I met him in that pub, and we have been together ever since.

Simon had been in hospital, and his memory was very poor. He had even forgotten what had happened in our first week together, we walked the river, went on picnics, and Simon didn't remember any of it! He didn't even remember the watch I gave him on the Saturday night, and by Monday he was sure that the barman had given it to him, even though it had my name on it! Look at this photo, it was taken the night I gave it to him, yet he still didn't remember! But his memory now, is better than mine," she laughed.

Then she went into the house and made some sandwiches and a very pleasant two hours ensued. She talked about her life and about Bill when he was a little boy. She did at one point, say that Nigel reminded her of someone she once knew a long time ago.

"That must have been dad when he was young," Bill volunteered. "Maybe," said his mother. Nigel discovered that she had had, and still had a happy life. He could see that his life with Jane would take the same course; at least he hoped so, if and when he could get back again. It had been a very enjoyable afternoon, when Bill said that it was time to go. They said their 'goodbyes', Nigel hugged the old woman. And a certain love lingered in his heart as he left with Bill. He looked back at the house, and knew he would see this place again one day. Same trip across the town, and soon they were home again. After a wonderful meal, Bill joined him in his room, with more information on the holiday of a lifetime. In the pipeline was a trip to New York, a meal at the restaurant at the top of the Twin Towers, a week's beach holiday in Florida, and to take in the rides of Bart Disney. To go and see the blast-off of the latest rocket, with astronauts heading for the base on Mars. Nigel was informed that people had been living on the planet for ten years, the amount of personnel there now were in their hundreds! Once again Atomic Power had been the answer to the propulsion question.

Two shorter holidays of four days were planned for a break in the most peaceful cities in the world, Johannesburg and Mexico City, with no crime whatsoever in these places. "They are paradise on earth," said Bill.

Nigel sat in his bucket seat, drinking his wine that Bill had said cost three hundred pounds a bottle, amazed, excited, gob-smacked, and he smiled a lot. The holiday would start the next day and so Bill said goodnight. He left Nigel with his 'wall-to-wall' TV on. He was in Utopia for the rest of the evening.

The plane to New York took just one hour. The airport was a 'piece of cake': no queuing, no security, they just got straight on to the plane. Good food served ten minutes into the flight, capsule to the hotel room in no time at all. People all friendly, greeting each other at every turn. 'What a wonderful world,' Nigel thought.

As Bill had promised a great time was had, the Twin Towers stood tall, and the restaurant was wonderful. The sights were much the same as in his own world, but most were better by far! At times Nigel thought that the year was two thousand and seven, forgetting that this was two thousand and sixty four in a different zone to his! The shows were out of this world, spectacular was hardly the word! Nigel was fed, had everything he wanted, with all expenses paid!

"I could live like this for ever," Nigel said.

"Do you think so?" Bill replied in a quizzical way. "I doubt it, not the human way, everyone gets fed up after a while, even of this kind of luxury. Human life needs to be continually challenged, that's why we have gone to the stars. People in their thousands have applied to go to Mars and other planets, and yet they live in this near perfect world, it baffles me."

Nigel made mental notes; he hardly saw any police about, no people begging, no police car sirens, everyone seemed happy. He asked Bill about the global warming and was told that because of the atomic cars, and the gradual reduction in the use of gas and oil, carbon monoxide in the atmosphere had reduced by seventy percent over the years, and the earth's weather had stabilized. There was crime, but mostly by people of low mentality, and most perpetrators were helped when caught, instead of being sent to prison.

The hotel the men stayed in was fabulous, and the rooms were the best that Nigel had ever been in. The days were spent sight-seeing, having fun, and relaxing with a few bottles of expensive wine in the evenings. The days in New York were magical, but came to an end too fast as far as Nigel was concerned. Florida was much the same; Bart Disney Pleasure Parks were great. The days on the beach in Miami were filled with lazing around, swimming and drinking. He saw the launch of a rocket to Mars, and marvelled at the sight. Mexico City and Johannesburg in Africa were as Bill had said, places of peace. The shanty towns that Nigel remembered reading about in his world were non-existent, so was crime. Wonderful holiday destinations. 'Time waits for no man', so the saying goes, he was aware of it, and enjoyed every minute! The only thing lacking was the company of the female sex, but funnily enough it didn't enter Nigel's mind.

The holiday was coming to an end; he found out that Bill had understated his position in the police force. Nigel had thought that he was just a policeman, but he was to find out that Bill was the Superintendent of the Time-Police, the Top Man. He was shown the headquarters, and the control room that looked like a space centre, the kind you might see in Houston, for space flights. Computer screens filled the walls, with personnel sat looking into monitors. The tour of the complex lasted an hour, Bill had tried to explain the idiosyncrasies of time and space, most of this information went over Nigel's head, but he had enjoyed the tour.

On the last night of the month's holiday, they all had a farewell meal at Bill's home; his wife was a perfect host. He thanked her profusely for the hospitality he had received. Then Bill shocked him with a question. "How much do you think your holiday has cost, Nigel?"

"I wouldn't hazard a guess. Go on, surprise me."

Bill did. "One hundred thousand pounds," he said. Nigel nearly choked on his wine. Bill just laughed at him.

"And where did this money come from?"

"Expenses," said Bill.

It had been the most wonderful holiday Nigel had ever had in his life, or would ever have. He had been truly paid for his help in getting the blip in time back on track. He had always got on famously with Bill, who had been first class in looking after his duplicate father from Zone One.

The two men laughed and talked about their holiday experiences, as they made their way across town to the hospital site, where they entered the Time Zone. As they walked into the grounds of the 'used to be' hospital, and positioned themselves under the old tree, Nigel looked at Bill for the next instructions. At one on the dot, they both pressed the buttons on their time-belts, and with eyes closed were back in 2007. On the clock the time said one o'clock, the same time they had left. Nigel noticed that people he had seen just before he had gone on their adventure, walking in the grounds, were there, continuing their walks. The hospital was standing just where it had been.

"How was that?" Bill asked, with a broad smile. For a moment Nigel didn't say a word, his smile, his look, said a thousand words.

"One thing I missed, I completely forgot to ask you when we were in your time Bill, I wanted to visit the mansion on Eastern Hill? I never got around to mentioning it."

"It would have been pointless, because the mansion is no longer there. It was demolished in 2008, and it's got a three metre concrete topping on the site because of the 'time-fault', a gateway, so the Government sealed it over, the site is out of bounds to the public. Every time we find a gateway we seal it in. But there are hundreds all over the place, so we keep plugging."

Nigel listened to the explanation. "Hope the Government hasn't plugged the gateway to my zone?"

"So far they haven't, so far." He didn't seem to be convinced, but Nigel let it go. There was something else on his mind; he told Bill that he just wanted to go over to the hospital reception to ask a question.

Bill just nodded, "I'll wait here for you," he said.

Nigel made his way across the grass to the hospital entrance, entered the big door, and walked to the reception.

The lady behind the desk was friendly, and went through the ledgers to answer Nigel's questions

"Yes," she said, "here it is, a Nigel Maythorn was admitted here in April nineteen hundred and twelve, but absconded with the help of two bogus policemen, and nothing was ever heard of him again. Was he an old relative of yours?" she asked, looking up from the paper work.

"Yes, I believe he was," Nigel smiled.

"And what became of him? Just for interest sake, you understand?"

"He went on to have wonderful adventures, so I'm led to believe. He lived a long life, and he wasn't guilty of the offences that the police said he had done. And he certainly wasn't insane!"

"Well, I'm pleased to hear that," she said with a smile. "And may I have your name?"

"Nigel Maythorn," he said, smiling as he walked away.

She closed the ledgers and replaced them on the shelf. She was used to dealing with all sorts of people, 'but he was nice', she thought, 'a little strange in a nice sort of way.'

Nigel told Bill of his enquiries, but Bill had other things on his mind. "Got to get back to work, remember I've been away on holiday in my time for a month. You can find your way home from here, so I'll say have a nice time tonight with my mother, and treat her good," he laughed. "Oh by the way, you have to continue your good work. Tonight you will have to tell her that you have memory lapses, a little white lie. But you have to understand that when she meets Simon, my father-to-be, on Monday night, he won't remember the picnics, or walks, or meals that you have been having with her this last week. So if you haven't told her yet, tell her of your mental breakdown."

"I've mentioned it before."

"Well, tell her again gently, she has to be primed for Monday night."

"I'll do my best."

"See you Monday morning, have a good last two days, then I'm going to try to get you home."

"Thanks Bill."

"Look at that magnificent building over there Nigel."

167

He turned to look where Bill had pointed. "Yes, it is a beautiful building," but he was talking to himself, Bill had gone!

With mixed feelings, Nigel made his way to the bus stop. The plan that Bill had devised was going to plan. But he still had this thought in his mind that it was deceitful. He was in love with her, but he still loved his Jane as well! It had been a strange experience meeting his duplicate self in this world. It had been like talking to himself in a mirror when he had met Simon. He was happy to be going home, yet sorry to be leaving this 'perfect' world.

The bus came, and the journey back was a blur, as the countryside slipped by. His head was full of thoughts, it had been an amazing adventure and it was coming to an end. He decided to go back to the pub and sit in the garden with a cold beer on this nice sunny day, then get ready for his meeting with Janice at seven o'clock.

He walked into the bar and ordered a pint of beer from the landlord's grandson, who had a big smile on his face. "Why so happy?" Nigel asked.

"Got another job, this is my last weekend. Wanted to leave this job for a while now," he said, as he wiped a glass and put it under the counter.

"So if I wanted a job here, there is a vacancy?"

"Sure is, do you want to take over from me now?" he laughed. "I'll apply on Monday night thank you. I've a busy weekend myself coming up," Nigel said, as he took his pint out into the garden.

He spent the next hour in the sunshine, feeling the warmth of the sun, contemplating his trip home. Later in the afternoon he had a sleep, and then got ready to meet Janice.

She was on time as normal, and looked radiantly beautiful. She placed the package on the counter as she sat opposite.

"What's this?" he asked with a smile.

"Open it; it's a gift for you."

"A watch," he said, "how did you know I wanted a watch?"

"Because you have told me often that you were going to get one, so I bought this one for you. Read the back of it." Nigel turned the watch around, and read: 'With love, Janice. To Simon' engraved on the back.

"Beautiful, but I don't remember telling you that I wanted a watch," he said.

"On the picnic the other day, for a start."

"Picnic, what picnic? I don't remember a picnic; my memory's not that good."

"Don't tell me you've forgotten that wonderful day we spent on the downs?" "Yes darling, at the moment I have I'm afraid. I've told you I've been in hospital, my memory is real bad at the moment, but it will improve, so the doctors have said."

"I hope so," she laughed. "I hope you don't forget me."

"That's one thing I'll never do," he replied, as he turned and ordered another drink for both of them. As the evening wore on she told him that she would be moving into her new home in Moreland Road on June 1st, and was looking forward to it.

He watched her intently as she spoke with enthusiasm about her life, and her hopes for the future. He felt he didn't want to let her go, but it was out of his hands. He imagined her getting older, and himself staying as he was now, eternally young. He felt his chin, and realized that he hadn't needed to shave the whole time he had been in this zone! It would always be this way, never getting a day older than he was at that moment. Seeing her die, and everyone about him, it was unbelievable!

She put his watch on his wrist, and admired it. "It will hide the freckles on your wrist." He smiled and looked at the watch.

"You like it then?" she asked.

"Beautiful," he replied, "I'll have it for ever more."

She smiled, and sipped her drink. Then she took a photograph of him showing off his watch. He sang a song and dedicated it to her. She told him that he had a good voice, and sounded a bit like Lance Summers.

"That's nice to know, everyone likes that singer it seems."

"Don't tell me that you have never heard of him?" she said.

"Of course I have," Nigel lied. Although the barman had played some of his songs over the pub's system a few

169

nights before, and the professor had also mentioned him.

"That's not his real name; he changed it from Elvis Presley. He would have got nowhere with a silly name like that," she laughed.

"Oh, I don't know," Nigel said, "stranger things have happened."

"You are a bit quieter tonight Simon, have you got something on your mind?" she enquired.

"Sorry, I've been thinking, as I have told you my gardening work is coming to a close and I'm fed up with it, so I'm going to apply for the vacancy here, working as a barman. I once worked in a pub just like this one, and I enjoyed it."

"That would be good, I could get free drinks," she laughed.

"And me," he responded.

After their meal, other people joined them, and after more singing, a very nice evening was had by all. Time is a funny thing; it has a habit of flying by when one is having fun. The evening had come to a close. He saw her ride away on her bike as he stood in front of the pub. She had a full working day at the hospital the next day, and so they had made a date for Monday at seven p.m. at the bar. He stood there remembering the passionate kisses and waved, knowing he would never see her again. His duty was done, and he cried like he had never done before. He went straight up to his room, and lay on his bed. He felt some regret for the deception he had put her through. But then again, it was Bill's idea and it had worked, so that was that. Now he was ready to go home.

Sunday passed by in a flash, Nigel walked the countryside and after a few drinks had an early night.

After breakfast on Monday morning, Nigel got his things together. He still had his old clothes in the bag the girl in the clothes shop had given him. He counted his money and took one last look at his little room that had been his home for a week, and went to the bar.

"I'll be going home this morning, but I'll come in tonight to pay for the room," he said to Brian.

"I won't be here tonight, going on a little holiday, so leave the money behind the bar, and give my best to your mum and dad, hope you enjoyed your stay here?"

The two men shook hands, and Nigel left. But as soon as Brian disappeared behind the counter and into the kitchen, Nigel took off his watch, kissed it and left it on the side of the counter.

Bill was waiting outside the pub; they walked to the bus stop, and made their way into the city of Southampton.

"You did a great job Nigel, now it's time for you to go home," Bill said.

"I feel sorry for Janice, I have been deceitful, and I should have told her the truth," Nigel said.

"She wouldn't have believed you, you wouldn't have succeeded at all. She won't notice the difference between you and Simon. You are the same person, she fell in love with you, and I know she always loved my father, so forget about the deceit, there was no other way. As I have said, you did a great job. Anyhow, you have your woman, your life, your world."

"I suppose you're right," Nigel said.

"You've had a good time, an amazing adventure, not many men have had that, a time you will never forget."

"That's true, and now the job is over I can have the transmitter that was put in my head removed?" he enquired.

"That's all in hand, so don't worry about that, enjoy the bus ride."

The two men sat in silence as the countryside slipped by, and they arrived in Southampton. The walk through the city, past familiar places, some not so familiar, past the site of the 'non-existent' Bargate, towards the docks, took half an hour. As they got near the park, Nigel recognised it as the place he remembered on the day that he arrived.

"We need to change into our old nineteen twelve clothes. We would stand out like a sore thumb if we got back there dressed like this," Bill said, pointing to himself.

"I'd forgotten about that," Nigel said.

"I forget nothing. I'll have the money back too, it's no use to you where we're going." Nigel handed him the money, and Bill gave him some money dated nineteen hundred and twelve.

As they were getting changed, Simon had left hospital, and was going inside his mother and father's front door. His new life had just begun.

Bill took Nigel to the same spot that they had arrived at. After setting the time-belt to the time and date twenty third of April nineteen hundred and twelve, the men closed their eyes, and pressed the red button. And in a split second they were back in nineteen hundred and twelve. Nigel looked up at the church clock, it said twelve thirty, and just up the street in the dock was the liner the Titanic it was back from its first voyage to America!

There was no-one to see the two men appear from nowhere. The park was empty; Bill sat on the grass and indicated to Nigel to do the same.

"Now, I'll tell you the plan," Bill started, "first, we must make our way back to the pub, where you will pick up your belongings. I mean all that you came with, that's important. Without everything, it's impossible to go back to Zone One."

"Hold on," Nigel broke in, "that might not be that easy. I gave little Brian my phone on the first day I arrived, he may have lost it."

"It must be found," Bill said, "it's imperative."

"But there's the one pound coin I gave Fanny as a memento and the pen I gave you."

"This one?" Bill said, producing it from his pocket, he handed it back.

"Yes that's the one," Nigel said, examining it thoroughly.

"You must get all that you came with, then we have to go back to the day you arrived. Then go back to the house, go to the gateway in the chimney, go to Zone One. And then there will be someone who will meet you there to take you home. So, we'd better get going, we have a lot to do. Remember, the police are still after you, so the quicker we get back to the date you arrived the better."

Bill got up and pulled Nigel to his feet, and they made their way to the roadway. "The car we used in the big escape was on loan, we're getting the bus," he explained.

As the bus they were on passed the dock gates, Nigel noticed people with suitcases, waiting to go aboard for their new lives in America, on the finest liner that was around in nineteen hundred and twelve Zone Two.

It was still hard for him to fully understand what had happened to him. He was surely a very lucky man to experience this phenomenon of time travel. But inwardly he was glad that he was homeward bound, to think that in a short time he would be in Jane's arms once again. Deep in thought, he tried to visualize how Janice and Simon would get together. He had been told by Bill that he had done a good job, and he wondered how it would have turned out without his help, he felt satisfied.

"Bill, can you tell me, are you coming with me to my world? Or will we say our 'goodbyes' at the gateway as you call it, the chimney at the house? Because I would like you to meet my family just like I met yours."

"That won't be possible I'm afraid. I have to go back to work as soon as I see you safe and on your way."

"But I have so many more things I want to ask you, I have a hundred and one questions!"

"We still have some time together, and I'll answer as many questions as I can," Bill said as he stood up to get off the bus, just a little way from the pub.

"We must be careful now; the police may be around, so just go into the place, get all your, stuff, and I'll meet you here in a quarter of an hour, I have to go home, I've just been summonsed." Bill went behind a tree, and in a second, he had gone.

The pub was closed as Nigel casually went to the bar door. He went behind the pub, and in the garden sitting at a table in the sunshine was Fanny. She heard his footsteps on the cinder pathway and looked up. A smile lit up her face and she ran to him and flung her arms around his neck. He felt her bosom against his chest, and hugged her.

"Nigel, they let you go? When? I was told that you were in a hospital for the mentally insane, they must have come to their senses."

"Fanny, listen to me. Have you seen any police around here?"

"No, there's been no police here since you were arrested. Why would there be?"

"Look, can we go inside, and I'll explain everything to you?" A look of apprehension came on her face, as she led the way through the back door of the pub.

"Sit down, I'll make you some food I have a lot to tell you as well. There's a lot of people asking after you."

Nigel explained that he didn't have long, and had to leave very soon. He asked about his things he had left in his room. She informed him that nobody had touched anything. She told him of how she had paid back the bets in full. He thanked her for her trouble. There were so many questions she wanted to ask, but Nigel stopped her, saying that he had very little time. To his question about the whereabouts of the little boy Brian, she told him that he was on holiday with his grandmother, and would be gone for a week. And she informed him that he had taken his toy, the mobile phone, with him. Nigel said that it was important to get it back, plus the coin that he had given her.

"I've got that in my bedside cabinet, I'll be a minute, make the tea." She left, and climbed the stairs to go and get it.

He got up, and noticed the time on the kitchen clock, it was four o'clock. He went out the back door, Bill was waiting.

"Let's go," he said abruptly.

"Can't, I haven't got all my things, the little boy is on holiday, he'll be gone a week, and he has my phone with him." Bill thought for a few seconds, and then said that Nigel should lay low for a week, then he would come back in a week's time.

"Bill, I want to ask you for a favour. Seeing that we can travel through time in a split second, I want to go to nineteen hundred and thirty nine, third of September to be precise, at eleven o'clock in the morning. I would like to hear a radio broadcast. Is that possible? Then I have to see Janice one more time, I feel so guilty in deceiving her. I have to witness how she meets Simon. Please, I need peace of mind before I go home. I promise I won't ask for anything more."

"I've told you, you have nothing to feel guilty about, but alright, let's do it later."

Nigel walked back into the kitchen, and the kettle was boiling. He poured the tea and sat down. He heard her come down the stairs.

"Here it is Nigel; it was in my drawer as I said it was."

She handed him the one pound coin. The clock said four o'clock.

She pulled up a chair and sat opposite him. "Now tell me what happened, I want to hear the full story." She gave him that smile, the smile that he loved. He loved smiling women, and this one was high on his list.

"The story's too long, and I haven't got the time. The police are still after me, and I have to leave here. I don't want you to get into trouble for harbouring a fugitive, because that's what I am at the moment, an escaped criminal, and yet I've done nothing wrong. Please believe me; I've never stolen anything in my life!" He looked at her, looking desperately for understanding.

She placed her hand on his and said, "I do, I do believe you Nigel. I don't believe you stole anything from those people in the big house."

"I didn't, I only wish that I could prove it to you. I have to go, the police could be on their way now." He stood up.

"No, stay, you can hide out here, no one would ever find you."

"Where?" he said frowning.

"Upstairs."

"Upstairs?" he repeated.

"Yes, upstairs in the secret room." "Secret room?" he said again, almost parrot fashion.

"Come, I'll show you." He followed her up the wooden stairs that led to her bedroom.

"See where it is?" she asked.

"No, can't see anything that would be contrived as a secret room."

"That's why it's secret," she laughed, and went to a big wardrobe and opened the double doors. A few dresses hung there, she swept them aside and stood inside, a small clip that held a back panel was slid to one side. She came out, lit a candle, and went back inside the robe.

"Come," she ordered. He followed, the candle flame showed a small room, empty apart from an old sea-chest and a few odds and ends.

"The perfect place to hide out for a while if need be. You'll certainly be safe here until you decide to go, Nigel. So you don't have to worry about the police. Only me and my husband know about this room, and he's not here."

"But he will be, won't he be coming home soon?" he said.

"He's written to say he's coming home, but not for a week or so, you'll be gone before he comes back. And anyhow where would you go tonight, you have nowhere? Please Nigel, stay with me for a while? I want to hear the full story."

He looked at her, the candle light showed her sincerity.

"OK, I'll stay, and thanks again for helping me. I can't understand why you have taken all this trouble for me, you have enough on your plate with the pub and little Brian to bring up, and a husband who is never home, yet you do all this for me?"

"That's easy Nigel, it's because I love you," she said in a matter of fact way. "I realised it the day the police took you away. I missed you so much; I couldn't sleep or eat for days after you left, it was then that I realised. I'm sorry I'm being so forward, but I wanted you to know."

She walked into the main bedroom and he followed. She put the candle down, blew out the flame, and went into the wardrobe to shut it up. Pulling the clothes across the rail, she faced Nigel. He went towards her, took her in his arms and kissed her long and hard. They toppled on to the bed and spent the next hour making mad passionate love.

"I missed you too," Nigel said.

It was early evening when he woke, he glanced over to where she had lay next to him, but he was alone. He got up and dressed and went down to the kitchen. He could hear the customers in the bar laughing, and wished that he could join them. He felt hungry, but put that to one side and went up to his old room to check on his belongings he had left in the drawer. He remembered what Bill had said, that he needed to get all his belongings together. Everything was where he had left it: wallet, clothes, he had his pen and pound coin, all he wanted now was his mobile, then he would be on his way.

He went downstairs again; it was at that moment that he heard a commotion coming from the bar. He heard raised voices, and went to the door that led from the kitchen to the bar and opened it slightly. He saw Fanny remonstrating with three men, she was telling them to leave. The big man was holding her arm and it was obvious he was hurting her.

"The lady has asked you to leave," he said with calmness in his voice, "so be a nice man and let her go."

"It's him," said the oldest of the three. "It's him who took the bets and the police arrested."

"Let her go now," Nigel said with determination now, instead of the calmness.

"Keep out of this you ratbag," the big man said menacingly.

Nigel said, "YOU TALKING TO ME?" Then again, louder, "YOU TALKING TO ME? YOU'RE LOOKING MY WAY; IT'S ONLY ME, YOU TALKING TO ME?"

One of the men made a forward movement, with fists clenched.

"Make my day punk, make my day. Do you like hospital food? Because if you don't back off you'll be eating it, now let her go!"

The man let Fanny's arm go, and swung a blow towards Nigel, who ducked, and with a karate chop to the throat, decked the big man. He swung around and with a kick that landed on the older man's nose, had him sprawling across the room. The third man backed off and ran out of the pub shouting threats that he would be back with the police or re-enforcements.

The two beaten men got to their feet and headed for the door. "You haven't heard the last of this," was the warning as they left, tail between their legs.

"Well done, those bullies deserved what they got, you sure are fast," said one of the customers.

Fanny looked relieved. "Those ruffians should stay in their own pub. I've barred them for good now. They wanted to know what hospital you were in, and I said I didn't know, they didn't believe me. Knowing that lot they will cause more trouble, the police will have to be involved to put an end to it, but I can't call them while you're here. My husband will sort them out when he comes home."

Fanny told her customers that she was going to close early because of what had happened. They all understood and drank up, Nigel went into the kitchen.

As he went through he glanced down at a clutter of toys in a corner, and there it was, his mobile laying in the back of an old farm cart. So Brian hadn't taken it after all! Now he was free to leave.

She came back into the kitchen and he showed her his mobile, he told her he saw it amongst Brian's toys.

"So now I expect you'll be going. I didn't lie to you, I saw Brian with your mobile, as you call it. He always had it with him, he even slept with it. His grandmother must have put it with his toys when she came to collect him. You could still stay in the secret room, where else could you go?"

"I have to go home, back to my world," he said.

"And where is that Nigel? You promised to tell me the full story before the police picked you up on the sixteenth April."

"Fanny, you are not going to believe me, but I will tell you what has happened to me."

For the next half hour he told her that he came from the future, how he was transported, to his utter amazement, through time to this place. That was the reason that he had come with no money, and had been disorientated. He looked at her intently, looking for any signs of her laughing at him, but she kept a straight face.

"I'm a time-traveller, it's as simple as that. But then it's not as simple as that really, because no-one would believe it. That's the reason I've only told one person so far, Gerald Anderson, and he didn't believe me. And I know you are not believing me either. Do you realize that if I wasn't telling the truth I would have to be a nut-case, a candidate for the asylum! This is all a waste of time," he sighed. He felt weak like a child who had just run the hundred yard race.

"No, it's not love," she said with a knowing smile. "I believe you. I have seen the dates on the money and coins you have in your wallet, plus your photographs, all dated. And I've seen her as well, she is very pretty, your Jane. I've seen and read some cuttings from newspapers, dated in years to come. Sorry Nigel, but I read it all when I went to pay the men's bet money that you had left in the drawer with your things. So you see, I do believe you. You are different from other men, the way you speak, the way you act; you're years in advance of anyone around here. It's just my luck that I fall for someone I can never have."

He leaned over the table and took her hands in his. "You are wonderful. I come from another zone, and in my world we run almost parallel with this world. The Titanic sank in nineteen hundred and twelve, on the fifteenth of April, it's in our history books. There's not much more that I can say. Bill is also a time-traveller but he's from this world, and his job has been to look after me, and to try to get me back to where I belong. He's a first class man, and is in the Time Police Force. He's back in his time at this minute, the year two thousand and sixty four. It's unbelievable, even to me, all this time travel business is very hard to understand. That's the reason I haven't told anyone apart from Gerald and you."

"You are my 'time-travel lover', she said laughing.

"Now that's a brilliant password, 'Time Travel Lover', never forget that," he said, squeezing her hands.

"I won't, I'll always remember it. When you go, will I ever see you again?" she enquired.

"Yes, and I'll tell you when." He looked at her intently. "Get me a piece of paper and a pen, no, I've got my own pen, just a bit of paper."

She went to a cupboard and came back with a sheet of paper.

He wrote: 'I WILL COME BACK ON THE THIRD OF SEPTEMBER NINETEEN HUNDRED AND THIRTY NINE, AT ELEVEN A.M. WHEN A BROADCAST IS ON A DEVICE CALLED A WIRELESS.' And he signed it Nigel Maythorn.

"Keep this note in a safe place," he said, handing it to her.

She took it and put it in the drawer of the kitchen cupboards, in a small tin.

"How do you know you'll come on that date?" she asked. "Because it has to happen." He smiled and shook his head. "Please Fanny, don't ask me how, and don't tell anybody about our talk tonight! They wouldn't believe you, they wouldn't understand. Promise?"

"I promise," she said.

He kissed her. "You know, when you see me again, I will be the same as I am now, I will never age. I must go now and get my things together. Those ruffians will have reported the fact that I am here, got to get going."

"I want to thank you for saving me from them. You can sure fight well, where did you learn that from?" she asked.

"It's called Karate, a self-defence, with a bit of kick-boxing. And my verbal warnings were from sayings in films I've seen, from people like Clint Eastwood, Robert De Nero, films like 'Taxi Driver'," but he could see by her quizzical look that she didn't understand him.

"Are these people your friends?" she asked.

"Yes, sort of," he smiled. "I'm going to get changed, I won't be long." He went up the stairs to his room.

"I'll make you something to eat before you go," she shouted up the stairs.

"Thank you," he called down. He entered his little room and lit a candle, then went to his drawer, pulled out his jeans and tee- shirt, checked his wallet, slipped out of his old clothes and got dressed.

He checked his possessions: one pound coin, mobile, pen. It was at that point that he heard some commotion from outside. He looked out of the window, and caught a glimpse of a policeman going to the back door down the side of the house, there were other people with him. He pressed the blue button on his transporter belt to summons Bill. He checked the drawer to make sure that he had everything that he owned, and sat on the little bed to await his fate. He felt nervous; he didn't want to go back to prison or the hospital. He faced the door, and saw the handle lift. The door opened wide then shut again, but to his astonishment there was no-one there, it was as though a ghost had just entered the room.

"Don't worry it's me, Bill," came a voice from nowhere. Then Bill's head appeared, just his head, then his shoulders, then his hands. Nigel couldn't believe what he was seeing: half a man in mid-air, no support. "Give me the button you have in your wallet, I told you once about the 'invisible suit' remember? Now you get to use one. There's no time to lose, the police are about to take you in again. We have to find out where Brian has gone with his grandmother and get your phone back."

"I've found the mobile; he left it here amongst his toys. But you should have known that Bill, you already know how all this business is panned out." He found the button and handed it to Bill.

"Get into this now," Bill commanded, and handed him a little blue button, the size of a finger nail. "This is your invisible suit, you can't see it but the button is your guide to where the opening is. You will feel a force, open it up here," he indicated, "and put your feet in." Nigel obeyed and bent over, lifted his feet and watched them disappear. He pulled the invisible suit up and watched his body disappear.

"Put it over your head and hold the button in your hand, over your head, like this," he demonstrated, and Nigel saw Bill's shoulder and head disappear, the small button floating in the air, hardly noticeable. He did the same, he heard Bill's voice say, "Now we are both invisible move to the corner of the room, and don't say a word." Nigel obeyed, he couldn't see Bill, but he could see everything in the room. At that moment the door opened and there were two policemen standing in the opening.

181

"There's no-one in here," one policeman said.

"Look under the bed, Harry. Do these clothes belong to him?" the policeman asked Fanny, who was standing outside the door.

"No," she said, "they belong to my husband. But I told you, he left a while ago, and didn't say where he was going. I didn't know he would come back, he took me by surprise. After all, he was only my barman, he only worked here for a few days. I can't help you any more than I have. All I can say is he came to my rescue when Fred Bartlett assaulted me in the bar. Now, unless you are going to arrest me for trying to keep an orderly pub, would you please leave?"

"Where is your room? We want to search in there."

"This way," she said. She knew Nigel would be in the secret room by now, so wasn't worried. The bedroom door shut.

"Don't move," said Bill.

"Not moving," Nigel replied.

After the search of Fanny's room, the police went down to the kitchen and took a statement from her. She said that if Fred said sorry to her for the trouble he had caused her in her pub, she wouldn't press charges. Fred apologised, saying that he hadn't meant to hurt her. The police warned him not to come to the pub again for at least a year, there the matter closed. Fanny told the police that if the fugitive called round again, she would let them know. The police bid her goodnight, then they left.

Upstairs Bill said, "Right Nigel, take your suit off, I'll give you an hour to say your goodbyes then I'll meet you outside. We'll then go up to the house, where I'll see you on your way back to your own zone, your job here is over. I'm going to stay in my suit, so when you go downstairs open the back door, pretend to look out then I'll slip out. I'll see you in an hour, keep your suit safe, put it in your wallet. Right, let's go," he commanded.

Nigel got out of the invisible suit, blew out the candles and went down the stairs. Fanny was on her way up as he descended.

"The police knew you had been up there by the lit candle. I told you they wouldn't find you in the secret room," she said.

There was no way that he was going to tell her about the

'invisible suit' so he just said, "I hid behind the door, I was lucky they didn't look there. And now I must leave, you've done enough for me."

"No Nigel, before you go have one last meal with me, you need something to eat," she said pleadingly. "I have some stew ready to serve. The police won't be back, at least not tonight."

Nigel looked at her, and nodded his approval. He opened the back door as instructed, all was quiet, he didn't feel Bill's exit, he then sat at the table and had some food. He had forgotten how hungry he was.

"I have to go very soon," he said, after finishing his food.

"Have you got everything, have you got all your belongings?"

"Yes, as far as I know."

"Not everything," she said, "don't you want this back?" She held out his watch, the watch he had given her in exchange for a loan. Surprise showed on his face, he had completely forgotten. He took it and saw that it was still stopped at four minutes past twelve.

"Thank you Fanny, what would I do without you?" he laughed.

"If you're really going, you had better get used to me not being around. I wish you could stay, but I realise you can't. I know I'm going to miss you so much, I don't know how I will go on without you."

"Oh, you will do fine, your husband will be back soon, and I'll tell you something more that will surprise you, you will have another child by him, a daughter!"

Her face showed her surprise, but it was soon hidden by laughter. "Don't make me laugh Nigel, I'm not having any more children, I can tell you that."

He put his watch on his wrist, and checked his wallet.

"I know you must think me strange, but before I go, I have told you the truth. And you will live a good life, even without your husband, because he'll go back to sea."

"I've always thought he would, he never liked this pub life as I do."

He got up reluctantly, a part of him wanted to go, but another

183

part wanted to stay with Fanny. He realised that this was the second woman who had made a big impression on him, and all in just over a week! Yet he had been away from his world for longer than that, there was that month he had spent on holiday with Bill. He felt mixed up, his emotions were running wild.

"Goodbye Fanny, thanks for everything you have done for me." He kissed her, and saw tears in her eyes as he walked to the door.

"I love you," she mimed, as he walked out into the night. The moon cast its paled light, making shrubs and trees seem like figures waiting to pounce. Bill once again was waiting and was ready to fulfil his promise to Nigel. They set their belts for the third of September nineteen thirty nine, at ten fifty five a.m. Once again, no puffs of smoke, no sensations, just press the red button, eyes closed, and there they were once again, in the future.

They walked around the pub to the front door, and went in. A few people were gathered around a radio. He glanced over at the bar counter, and saw a middle-aged woman serving beer. She was still very beautiful, Nigel thought.

"Quiet," somebody shouted in the bar, as the broadcast started:
"AN ULTIMATUM WAS SENT TO HERR HITLER, THAT UNLESS HE UNDERTOOK TO WITHDRAW HIS TROOPS FROM POLAND, A STATE OF WAR WOULD EXIST BETWEEN OUR TWO COUNTRIES. I HAVE TO TELL YOU NOW THAT HERR HITLER HAS STATED THAT HIS TROOPS ARE TO WITHDRAW AT ONCE. SO WAR HAS BEEN AVOIDED. THAT IS THE END OF THIS BULLETIN."

A roar of cheers broke out. There was some talk about the German leader, and how well he had done for his country. And they couldn't understand why the Poles were being so troublesome!

Nigel went over to the bar. Not much had changed, in the twenty seven years that had passed, a few pictures on the wall, but nothing that was too noticeable. The table and chairs were still there, so was the decor.

She appeared from the outer room that led to the kitchen. The smile on her face radiated sunshine.

"I've waited all these years, I told you that I believed you when you said that you would see me again. I even remember the password: "Time Travel Lover."

She smiled, leaned forward, clasped his hands, and kissed him full on the mouth. "Come out back to the kitchen, it's so good to see you again."

Nigel looked around the bar, indicated to Bill that he wouldn't be long, and made his way through the door that led to the kitchen. She hugged him again, and they both sat at the same old familiar table.

"You haven't changed one bit, as you told me you wouldn't. And as I promised you, I haven't told a soul about you and your 'time travel' because as you also told me, nobody would believe me anyhow. How have you been all these years? Tell me how you got back to your world, tell me everything?"

He looked at her, not knowing what to say. He remembered telling her of his 'time travel', the password, 'Time Travel Lover'! It was all so strange.

"You don't seem surprised to see me again?" he said at last.

"Why should I be? You told me that you would see me again. At the time I didn't understand. But no, I'm not surprised, I still have your note." She stood up and went to a drawer in a kitchen cabinet, and out of a tin produced a note. "look, your note."

He took it and read it out loud, "I will come back on the third of September nineteen hundred and thirty nine at eleven a.m. when a broadcast is on a device called a wireless." And there was his signature, Nigel Maythorn.

"Oh yes, I remember. Tell me Fanny, did you have a daughter after I left?"

"Yes, she's twenty six now."

"She's not my daughter is she?" he enquired.

Fanny looked embarrassed for a moment, but told Nigel that he was not the father. Inwardly he was pleased.

"My husband came home just after you left, but he could

never settle into pub life, and went back to sea. He came home on leave from time to time, but it's years now since he's come home. But I'm happy enough; my son Brian helps me run the bar. Did you see him when you came in, he was serving?"

"Yes," Nigel said, "he looks a fine young man."

"He's nearly thirty years old now," she said.

"He's older than me," Nigel said laughing.

"I'm forty nine," she pointed out. "And you, you're still twenty three? Nobody would ever believe us, would they Nigel?"

"No, they wouldn't," he said as he got up. "Look Fanny, I have to go, it was just a fleeting visit."

"Will you come back again?" she asked.

"No, I'm on my way home. Once again, it's too difficult to explain. Have a good life, and always think well of me? If I could have stayed with you all those years ago, I would have. You know that I loved you, and still do, but I belong elsewhere, in another world," he sighed.

She came to him, and took him into her arms. "I love you as well Nigel, and I always will. But some things in life are never meant to be. You made me understand, but I will never forget the time we had all those years ago. I've treasured that time. Look at me now, I'm old enough to be your mother!"

He stopped her by putting his finger over her mouth. "You are still beautiful, and always will be in my mind and my heart." They kissed, and Nigel made his way to the bar.

There were tears in both of their eyes, as he walked out of the door. He just smiled at Brian; it would have been pointless to talk he thought.

"Someone you know, Mother?" Brian enquired.

"Just a friend," she said, turning away as she wiped away her tear and went to serve another customer.

"That was a strange encounter," Nigel said.

Outside the pub it was a beautiful day. The sound of singing from inside the bar came drifting through the open door. Then laughing people danced the Conga, that trailed out around the car park, then back inside, like a snake sliding down a hole.

Different to his world in nineteen thirty nine, he thought. "No need for Vera Lyn's songs here," he said.

"Vera who?" said Bill.

"Never mind. Can we join the celebrations for a while? I fancy a drink."

Bill's head was swinging from side to side. "Sorry no, it's time Nigel, we have to go. You'll learn as you go along, it's too complicated." Bill produced a beard from a bag that Nigel hadn't seen before.

"Put this on, and we'll go to see Janice and Simon next. But you must not be recognised, and no talking to her or him, understand? It's not in the script so to speak. You have done a good job so far and I don't want you to mess it up. Now, set your belt for seven p.m. on Monday the thirtieth April two thousand and seven."

Nigel did just that, he was expert at it now, 'eyes closed red button, open eyes'. They walked into the pub again.

Nigel sat next to the table where he used to sit with Janice. He looked around the almost empty bar, and saw a solitary man at the bar, that he knew was Simon, his twin.

The barman was handing him a watch, and he was handing over some money, which the barman put behind the bar. Bill came back with one half pint of beer and an orange juice for himself.

On the dot, she came in the door and went up to the man at the bar. Behind his beard, that made him feel slightly silly, Nigel saw her kiss him. He looked slightly embarrassed, but she didn't seem to notice. He heard her order the meals, then she took his arm and they went and sat at the table next to the one where Nigel and Bill were sitting. He heard her say, "Simon, I gave you that watch on Saturday, don't tell me that you have forgotten already?"

Simon remembered what his twin had told him in the hospital, so put the watch on and said, "my mind," and pointed to his temple.

For the next hour Nigel tried to listen to their conversation. He overheard him saying how he intended to work behind the bar, his gardening days over. He realised after a while that they were getting on well. He was laughing, so was she, he was watching himself, it seemed. She had been completely fooled.

Nigel looked at Bill; there were Bill's mother and father sitting at the next table, before he had been born! This was more than his mind could take, it was so bizarre to say the least! This time travel was getting too much.

At last the two men finished their drinks, they talked in a soft tone. Nigel nodded his intentions to leave.

"I've seen enough, time to go back, for good this time," he said. Both men got up and walked out of the door.

Janice and Simon didn't even notice, they were talking about coming events . Outside, the two men set their belts, and in a second they were back in nineteen hundred and twelve.

He took the beard off, scratched his chin, and handed it back. Bill put it in the bag.

"Satisfied now, are you?" Bill said, looking at Nigel intently.

"Yes Bill, I'm satisfied, thanks. I felt that I deceived her. I'm glad it all went well, I just had to go and see her for one more time, I was very fond of your mother."

"I know," Bill said, "and I'm glad she was fond of you."

Soon the two men were making their way through the country lanes towards the big house on the hill.

"Question time," Nigel said at last. "There's some unanswered questions I need to know. Will I be back home tonight? You have seemed vague when I've asked you before."

"I can't say for sure, to be honest. There will be something in place when you get to your own zone, but you know Nigel, there are loads of questions that will never be answered, because no-one knows what the answers are. Even I don't know everything about this business of time-travel. Suffice to say, you've had the opportunity to experience something that very few people have. Like everything in life, you've had good times, and some scary ones, like the short time in prison, but the good certainly outweighed the bad, you must agree!"

"Yes, but why didn't you warn me before I got into trouble in trying to warn people not to sail on the Titanic for example?

When you already knew that the ship wasn't going to sink. You could have told me the truth before I got into that trouble, couldn't you?" Nigel protested.

"Now you already know that you would never have believed me, so I let you learn the hard way, a learning 'curve', and I broke you in slowly so to speak. Just imagine what you would have said to me if on the first night that we met in the pub, you knew that I was going to take you into the future, to two thousand and seven in a different zone to your own. Then on to two thousand and sixty four to meet my mother and father. Told you that there were no wars in nineteen fourteen or nineteen thirty nine! That the Titanic would sail for years, ending up in a museum in Belfast! And to come with me at that moment to help get my mother and father together, by going out with my mother and pretending to be my father! Can't you see how ludicrous it all sounds? Can you honestly say Nigel, that you would have come with me, and most of all believe one single word of it?" Bill stopped walking and stood opposite, putting his hands on his shoulders. "Would you have believed me?" he repeated.

"No Bill, you're right, I wouldn't have believed you for a moment, I get your point."

"This whole exercise had to be done slowly but surely, it has been a success, and you have had some fun along the way. The most fantastic month that you will ever have on holiday, you have been amazed and gob-smacked at times! And now Nigel, it's time for you to go home."

"Thanks Bill, now I understand a lot better. In a way I'm going to miss your almost perfect world, my world is full of wars, religious problems, economical woes, crime, even climate change! And yet I have to get back home, I've yearned for that, all because of one thing, and that one thing is love. Love of my country, love of parents, brothers, sisters, girlfriends, wives, the continual quest in trying to make the world I live in a better place. I think a lot of people would say the same."

"Yes, I know what you mean," Bill agreed. "Although we live in separate zones, we still continually try to make our lives better."

They could now see the house in the distance, quiet in the countryside, apart from the sounds the men made. "Money," said Nigel, "will I need to give you back the money you gave me? I didn't spend any of it, I gave Fanny twenty pounds, or should I say left it on the kitchen table."

"Give me what you have left," Bill said, "it's a different coinage in Zone One anyhow, but I can't see you needing any." Nigel opened his wallet and handed back the money.

"Oh, what about this invisible suit, Bill, do you want that back?" "Keep the suit, but let me tell you, it can be used only twice more, the power substance it's made of gives it only three uses and you have used it once already. You may have a bit of fun with it. The belt you will need as you depart this zone, it won't work in Zone One anyhow, and after a while it will disintegrate."

They opened the gates that lead to the Avenue and up to the house. "How did you know I have a button in my wallet?"

"Just a guess," Bill said.

The clear night sky and the quietness that prevailed gave out an eerie atmosphere as the men walked up through the trees.

"Will I ever hear from you again?" Nigel enquired.

"I'm afraid not," Bill replied, "our work is done, you will go back to your life and me mine."

"Oh well, it's been nice knowing you, and thanks for all you have shown me of this world," Nigel turned towards Bill, hugged him then shook hands.

The house was in darkness. "There doesn't seem to be anyone at home," Nigel volunteered.

"No, they are on the Titanic now, sailing for America, after missing the first voyage."

"How will we get into the house?"

"We're not going to," Bill said. "This is where we say our goodbyes my friend. You have to go back to the day you arrived here, so set your belt to the seventh of April and the time twelve-o-eight, then you must go to the chimney breast, the belt is programmed to take you to Zone One, as you step inside there will be someone there to meet you, do you understand all that?"

"Yes, but will I see the Andersons?"

"Yes, but remember at that time you hadn't met yet, so they will not know you." Nigel looked baffled.

"I know it's bizarre, but that's time travel," said Bill.

"Do you mean that what's happened will happen again if I stayed?"

"Yes, it would, word for word, deed for deed. So don't hang around, go straight to the chimney and get to your zone." Bill checked Nigel's belt. "All set, goodbye Nigel. Close your eyes, press your red button." Nigel did, and the transport began.

He opened his eyes and Bill had gone. The sun blazed down, he stood outside the mansion's big door, he went towards it. He glanced around to see the lawns as he remembered them just a week or so ago. He opened the door and peered in, the luggage was there in the hallway. He heard voices coming from the room on the right. He quietly closed the door and made his way past the labelled trunks and bags to the main room, and to the fireplace. He looked down at his belt and walked into the breast.

He felt no sensations, no flashes of lights, no puffs of smoke, he felt nothing. He looked around for a minute, then came out again. Then he noticed that the room had changed somewhat, different pictures on the wall, different furniture, was this his world? Was he back in his zone? He was soon to find out.

He looked at his watch; it was still stopped at four minutes past twelve.

Chapter 11

BACK TO THE BEGINNING

He went to the door that led to the passageway, and there was the luggage. He went to the front door and glanced out, it was much the same as he remembered, but then once again he saw a few differences. He stood there expecting to see someone to escort him back to his time, (Bill had said 'someone will meet you') but there was no-one around. He heard voices coming from the room on the left, and at that moment the door opened.

"That's the labels done dear," she shouted out. Nigel had heard that before. She looked towards the open front door and said, "Oh, hello there, have you come to see to the chimney, are you the sweep?"

Nigel glanced down to see soot on his hands. "No ma'am," he heard himself say, then quickly realised he was re-living what had happened to him before. A film he once saw flashed through his mind, 'Groundhog Day', where a man woke up at the same time every day and re-lived what he had done the day before! This could become a nightmare, he thought. So he would alter that. "No ma'am," he repeated, "I'm just travelling the country, and was wondering if you could give me a glass of water?"

"Certainly, come in," she said with the same smile he remembered. At that moment a car pulled up in the drive, a little girl got out and ran to embrace her mother. "Who's the funny man, Ma?" she asked. Nigel remembered what the lady was going to say, and almost mouthed the words.

"Now, don't be rude Bertha, this gentleman has come to see Papa." She turned to Nigel. "Sorry about that, you must know what children are like, they find everything and everyone funny."

"Oh, to be a child again," said Nigel before she could. He wasn't prepared to go through it all again, so said, "Could I have that drink of water now please?"

She led him into the study and introduced him to her husband. "This young man was at the front door dear, he would like a drink of water." He was exactly the same man that Nigel knew, it was Gerald.

"Good afternoon sir, how do you do?"

"Very well," Nigel said as the men shook hands.

"Would you like a cup of tea?" the lady asked. Nigel decided to end it here, he remembered he had asked for decaf coffee in Zone Two! "No, water's fine." She went into the kitchen.

"Take a seat," the man offered.

"I have to be on my way, but thanks all the same."

"Would you like to wash your hands? You have a black smudge on your face."

"Thanks," said Nigel.

"The bathroom is in the hallway on your left."

"Thanks again, you are very kind." Nigel went out of the room, straight out of the front door, ran down the drive and towards the gate to the road. He couldn't bear to face those lovely people who would drown on the Titanic, unlike the Andersons in Zone Two who didn't. For a moment he remembered what the landlord in his time had said about that family who had perished. He felt it was pointless going through it all again. No-one ever listened; it was a complete waste of time.

Where was the person who was to meet him and take him home? He wondered if he was still in Zone Two! He ran at times, towards the pub, maybe the meeting would take place there?

He walked into the bar, and it was more or less the same,

familiar faces sitting at the tables, smoking, drinking, and laughing. Only Bill was missing.

There she was behind the bar, with a baby in her arms. "Hello, what can I get you?" she said with a smile.

"It's me Fanny, it's me, I'm back again," Nigel blurted out, forgetting momentarily.

"I'm not called Fanny, my name is Freda. Have we met before?" she asked. He realised that it was pointless to continue, parallel worlds are just that, but with variations, Bill had said so.

"Sorry," Nigel said, "I was mistaken. 'No good asking for a coke,' he thought. "Tankard of beer please." The bar was the same, long tables, men talking, smoke hung in the air in clouds, nobody approached him.

"Three pence please."

"Look, I have to tell you now, I have no money on me, but I will be willing to work for this drink. I'm an experienced barman, I know you do need help with the baby and your husband away at sea at the moment."

She showed her amazement. "How do you know all that?" she said with a slight laugh.

"I'm clairvoyant," Nigel laughed, "what do you say?"

She gave him the once over glance. "Six pennies an hour," she said.

"Done, can I start now?"

"Yes, come around." She lifted the counter top. "Maybe you should wash your face, you have a black mark there," she pointed.

He smiled. "Maybe I should," he said.

"The wash room is in the back room."

"I know," he said as he went into the kitchen. She had a pensive look on her face as she served her customer another tankard of beer.

Nigel washed the smudge off his face, and tidied himself up in the mirror in the kitchen he knew so well. He wandered through to the back door, and went out to see the garden where he had sat with Fanny in Zone Two.

He pressed the blue button on his belt, to summons some

help. 'Someone will meet you,' Bill had said, but there was no-one around. He could see that this must be his own zone, as the garden looked different in a few ways: the table that he and Fanny had talked at was in a different position. So, here he was at the start again, the world he knew, the world of strife, wars, and then it dawned on him, the Titanic would sail and sink, he thought once again of the Andersons, maybe he could help, he had to try. Maybe there was a way without the mistakes he had made before. No more games, no more trying to explain things, he had to get back to the mansion.

He went back into the bar, the baby was crying, as he tried to console him, the baby made a grab for his watch. 'Here we go again,' Nigel thought. He took off the watch and gave it to the boy, who stopped crying immediately.

"You have a way with kids," she said smiling.

"Yes, I used to be one myself once, a long time ago," Nigel responded, they both laughed.

"Look Fanny, Freda, I know this is a strange request, being that I've just been employed on this new job, but I need an hour off. I forgot that I have to see Mr. Anderson from the big house before they leave to go to America."

"Oh, I know the Andersons; they are sailing on the new liner Titanic, in a few days' time. I get seamen in here all the time."

"Yes, and that's the reason I want to warn them of a catastrophe coming their way."

"Really, what catastrophe?"

"I'll explain later, can I borrow your bike?" he blurted out.

"How do you know I've got a bike?"

"I know a lot of things, believe me. Can I have my hour off?"

"Of course you can, see you in an hour."

"Thanks, the baby can play with my watch for now. It's stopped anyhow, it seems to be keeping him happy."

"Good," she said, "Brian's normally a happy baby."

"See you soon," Nigel said as he lifted the counter lid and made his way out of the pub. She saw him riding away, and wondered how he had known where her bicycle was kept.

He arrived at the mansion and went through the front door and into the room.

"Goodness me, you have been gone a long time, we thought you were still in the wash room. Then after a while we realised that you had left without your drink of water. Is everything alright?" the man of the house enquired.

"Yes, sorry about that. I realised that I had to meet someone of importance down at the Fox and Hounds Pub, but they didn't turn up so I came back, not for the drink of water, but for something more important and beneficial to you and your family, sir."

"Are you selling anything? Because we are not in the market for any goods at the moment. We are just about to embark on a trip of a lifetime to America on the Titanic."

"I know all that, could we sit down, I have something to show you and a story to tell. Will you spare me a bit of your time? I'm not a salesman, but what I am about to say to you will affect your life. Can we sit down?" Nigel enquired.

"I like the look of you young sir, so I will listen to what you have to tell me. But before we start, would you like to partake in a little dram or two?" Before Nigel could answer, he directed him to sit down in an armchair in the parlour. He asked his wife to bring the drinks, and also requested that they were not to be disturbed.

Nigel began, "What I am about to tell you will amaze you, and I'm not going to ask you to believe me totally, but I'm going to do my very best to convince you that my intentions are good, and I'm only interested in you and your family's well-being. I say that because I believe you to be a first class gentleman, who has done a lot for other people."

"Well, thank you," the man said.

"I know you well, your name is Gerald Anderson, your wife is Alice, and your daughter is Bertha. My name is Nigel Maythorn, I'm a History teacher, and here is the tricky part, I come from the future, I come from two thousand and seven, the year two thousand and seven." He saw the smile come on the face of Gerald, but ignored it and continued. "I would like you to see this sir," Nigel took out his wallet and showed photographs of himself and Jane, one of them was at a New Year's dance, and the date two thousand and six was in the background on a banner. He showed his identity card, the pound coin, the mobile phone, explaining what it did, although a demonstration wasn't forthcoming as it didn't work at the moment. Gerald examined each item carefully, then looked at Nigel and said, "So if I believed you, and maybe time-travel is a possibility, what's all this got to do with me and my family?"

"Well Gerald, it comes down to this, your life is in danger, and you will die on this voyage on the Titanic, because the ship will sink next week in the North Atlantic, you and your family will die, drown. Now, there's a chance that Alice and your daughter will survive, if you take heed of what I tell you. But you sir, have no chance, and this is where I can help you."

"But that ship is unsinkable, it's been said," Gerald pointed out.

"So they have all said but I have taught the subject in the school curriculum and it will sink. I know I can't dissuade you from going, but you will have a chance if you remember everything I have told you."

Gerald drank his drink and asked his wife to replenish the glasses.

"Are you alright dear?" Alice enquired as she came into the room with the drinks. "It looks like you have seen a ghost."

"I'm fine, I'm fine," he repeated.

"Is there any chance you might cancel? Is Berty picking you up to take you to the ship?"

This really surprised him. "How do you know about Berty? No-one knows about Berty, he's an old army pal; how do you know him?"

"I've told you, Gerald, I am a time-traveller, and I know everything."

"Sir, your story is preposterous, it's impossible to come from the future. I have never heard the likes, and we will not cancel our trip on your say-so. We would be a laughing stock if we cancelled and told our colleagues and family in America that a man from the future told us so! I'm sorry, I've heard enough, I must carry on with our business, and sir, you must carry on with yours."

Nigel realised that this dialogue was the same as he had heard before, and knew the reply. It was there on his mind, on the tip of his tongue; 'look, the ship hasn't got enough lifeboats for everyone on board, and fifteen hundred people will perish', but stopped himself from saying it.

"Don't you believe what I've shown you in my wallet? The photos, phone, coins, dates?" Nigel said.

"I can't explain that, and I'm not sure of your motive."

"Believe me sir, my motives are first class, and if you listen you will find out. You find this story in your words, 'preposterous', so if I can show you something that will save you, will you let me demonstrate? Believe me Gerald, I am like yourself, an intelligent man, I'm a teacher, you Oxford educated." Another surprised look came across Gerald's face. "I have tried, but if you won't listen, then I'll go on my way, I have to find a way back home yet, I'm stuck here at the moment, I'm stuck in time. I have problems, but I feel it my duty to mankind to try to help. Let me tell you the chain of events as I know will happen: you will sail on the tenth of April, on the fourteenth at eleven forty the ship will hit an iceberg, and in two and a half hours the ship will be no more. Women and children first in the life-boats, no place for you. You will, I'm afraid to say, go down with the ship." Gerald was shaking his head in disbelief.

"But there is one chance, and here it is." He showed the little button.

"A button will save my life," Gerald said, bursting out laughing. "I've heard enough."

"No, you haven't, it's not a bloody button, it's an invisible suit." Nigel said, his voice slightly raised.

"Ha ha, an invisible suit!" Gerald laughed louder. Nigel waited until Gerald had stopped his laughing.

"Watch me disappear. This is what you must do, change into it and get into the life-boat. And don't take it off until you get aboard the rescue ship the Carpathia. Then you will be reunited with your loved ones, understand?"

"Yes, I understand," he said sarcastically.

"Don't alarm your wife of what I have told you, because like yourself, she won't believe any of it. Will you ask your wife for another refill? It's a nice whisky," Nigel asked.

"Certainly will. I need a stiff drink after listening to all this. Although I must admit, I find it interesting. Another refill dear, and make it a double," he shouted from the door, and returned to his seat.

"This is how the invisible suit works." Nigel opened the suit from the bottom, and placed his feet inside, stood up, and his torso disappeared over his chest, with just his head hovering in mid-air! He saw the shock on Gerald's face, as his arms went over his head, and he disappeared. The door opened.

"Your drinks dear, don't drink too much. Oh, I didn't know you were on your own, I didn't hear your guest leave. Did you have a nice talk?" She saw his face. "Are you alright dear? You look pale. What's up with you dear? Was it something the man said to you? You look ill."

"Yes dear, I don't feel too good. I shall drink this and may retire early. You know, we'll maybe have to cancel the holiday, and go at a later date, I have this strange feeling that something bad might happen, and I'm not taking any chances."

"It's up to you dear, if you're not up to it then, as you say we'll go at another time. I would, as you know, like to sell up and go to live in America for good, maybe we could do that instead of the holiday?"

"We will discuss it after I've rested darling, will you go and make something to eat, afternoon tea?"

"Are you sure you're alright?"

"Yes I'll be fine; I'll just finish off the drinks." "No more, please darling?"

"No more," he replied, she left the room. "Are you still here?" he said sheepishly.

Nigel's head appeared, then his chest. Gerald's mouth opened as he saw the half body suspended in mid-air. He got out of the suit, and showed the button.

"The invisible suit, that comes from the year two thousand and sixty four. Do you believe me now?"

"I do, I do," he sounded like a man getting married! "It's unbelievable, to think that I would ever meet a time-traveller in my life time. Did you hear what I said to my wife?"

"Yes, every word."

"I'm going to cancel the trip, and if things go to our plans, we are going to sell up and go and live in America."

Nigel went on to tell Gerald how it had all began, with him looking at the house that he had thought was for sale. But he left out the part of going into Zone Two, the story was too much for any normal person, you just had to experience it.

"So you won't need the invisible suit, there's only one use left in it, everything has a lifetime, even an invisible suit!"

"No thank you, I'm not taking the chance. But if you know this disaster is going to happen, have you told the company? Or tried to persuade others to not sail?"

"There's no point, I've tried, no-one believes me. The world is full of non-believers. Anyhow, you can't change history; time-travellers have tried it in the past. No, there's nothing that can be done, but at least I hope to have saved your family. I will come to see you next week when the news comes out, if I'm still here. I expect to meet someone at any moment to lead me back to my world, this world but different dates, to two thousand and seven. I'll be going now, I have to go to the Fox and Hounds, the meeting might take place there."

"I'll walk you to the gate, I need a breath of fresh air to get over the shocks of this afternoon's talking," Gerald said, getting up and slipping on a jacket. He led Nigel to the front door. "I'm just going for a walk to the gates, get a bit of fresh air," Gerald shouted through the door. "I'll be back for tea soon love."

Outside the sun blazed down, and Gerald touched his balding head. "I'll just get my cap, I won't be long." He went back inside, the door shut behind him. Nigel stood there, looked up at the house, adjusted his belt that was starting to sag around his waist and sticking to his skin, and suddenly the rain came down, the sun had disappeared and the night cold bit into his body. He ran inside the broken front door to get out of the down pour. All was dark, he saw a glow at the end of the passage way, he went down shouting out, "Gerald, Gerald."

He opened the door that led to the dining room. The whole room was on fire! He looked down at his belt and it read two thousand and seven, September 13th. He had somehow pressed the buttons as he adjusted himself, or the belt was now playing tricks. He was home in his time. Then he remembered Bill saying that the belt wouldn't work in Zone One. Once again it was baffling. The smoke was now coming down the passageway, so he retreated outside into the rain. He walked across to the water fountain and sheltered under the bowl, although his feet were soaked. He watched as the fire brigade tried in vain to fight the fire. He overheard a fireman say that a bolt of lightning had struck the chimney. He fiddled with his belt, as he saw a man walk towards the fountain, and put the date to the seventh of April two thousand and seven, pressed the button. Maybe this would be it, maybe he would be home?

As he opened his eyes he could hardly make out the house, it was a blur, rain that obscured it, the rain was heavy. He was sitting in chest-deep water in the water fountain. He had to get out, so stuck his head in the downpour. The sun beat down, he scrambled out of the fountain that was in full flow, and went to the front door. Slowly he opened the front door and made his way to the big room down the passageway, he opened the door expecting to see Jane there waiting for him. The room was empty.

"Jane," he shouted, "Jane." All was silent; he looked at the wall where he remembered the picture of a man with a golden helmet, near a chest of drawers. There was no picture or chest of drawers, he looked at his belt, and saw that the date was seventh April two thousand and one. Then he noticed three lights, two were at green, one at red. 'What are these for?' he thought. 'Must have pressed the wrong button.'

He wandered out and into the bathroom, dried his hair then went into the parlour, and stood in front of a radiator to dry off.

There was no sign of anyone at home, he wandered upstairs and went into a small bedroom. Exhausted, he lay down and drifted off to sleep.

He was awoken with a noise coming from the big room, people laughing. Silently, he walked along the passageway and down the stairs. People saw him and ignored him, everyone was dressed in fancy dress. He mingled for a while, helped himself to a few drinks and buffet, then asked a 'fairy' with a wand, where the owners were.

"Alice and Bob Cladmore are over there," he pointed, "near the chimney breast." "What have you come as?" the fairy asked.

"A time traveller, and it's time for me to go," said Nigel.

"Alright sweet thing, see you later," the man said in an effeminate way. Nigel just smiled and walked away.

"Hello Bob, you don't know me, but I'm a time traveller and I'm here to warn you to put a conductor on the chimney breast, because a bolt of lightning will hit this house and it will burn to the ground sometime in this year. This is not fun, it's the truth," he warned, "I've seen it burn, I hope you were not at home that night!"

"Yes, very funny," said Bob, "are you enjoying the party?"

"I'm telling you the truth, I've seen this house burn to the ground," he repeated. "I'm not part of this fancy dress party, I'm from the future. You can alter what is meant to be, if only you will listen!"

"Excuse me," said Bob, walking away to join some of his guests, with his wife in tow. "Too much drink," he whispered to his wife.

Nigel just shook his head, 'point less,' he mumbled. He waded through the party goers and onto the patio outside the front door. He put the date into his belt, seventh of April two thousand and seven, made double sure this time, and pressed the red button.

This time he kept his eyes on the belt. He saw the date slowly changing, but realised the date was going slowly forward, and stopped at August the thirtieth two thousand and one. He looked at his belt, unclipped it then laid it on the wall, this is the first time he had done this. He realised that something was wrong, the belt wasn't working properly. Then he remembered what Bill had said, that the belt wouldn't work in this zone, and it would soon disintegrate. Panic set in, he also remembered that Bill had told him that the only way back was through the gateway in the chimney breast in nineteen hundred and twelve. So he had to get back there and fast. The belt could malfunction at any time, and whoever was meant to meet him to escort him home, could well be waiting back in nineteen hundred and twelve. For the first time he noticed a time clock and it said two hours, fifty minutes to DIS, and it was clicking down! What did it all mean? Did DIS mean to disintegration he wondered. The two green lights were there and one red.

"Christ, it's going to destruct, and I'll be stranded," he muttered. The door opened and a woman stood there, it was Mrs. Cladmore, the owner of the house.

"I saw through the window, are you the house-sitter?" she enquired. Before Nigel could answer, she continued, "Please come in and I will explain your duties." With that she went inside the house. Nigel looked at the belt, the time said two hours, forty seven. He put the belt on and went through the door; she escorted him to the side room. "Sit down," she said. Before Nigel could talk she started, "As you know we are going to New York on the 10th September this year, two thousand and one, late flight, so your duties will start on the morning of the 11th September two thousand and one. We will be away for two weeks, but I'm sure you are aware of this. My son works in the North Tower of the Twin Towers of the World Trade Centre. We are going to surprise him on his birthday on the 11th, by having a breakfast in the restaurant. My husband and I are looking forward to seeing our son again; we haven't seen him for a long time."

Nigel couldn't believe his ears. "Sorry," he blurted out. "Please ma'am, listen, let me explain, there's been a mistake here. I'm not your sitter, I'm a History teacher, I'm not your house-sitter. I'm only passing by with a very important message, well more of a warning. But no doubt you won't believe it. But you must not go to New York, and most of all get your son to leave his job, because he is in grave danger! On the 11th September the Twin Towers in New York will fall, and thousands of people will die. So I beg of you, rethink your decision to go?" The shock on her face showed. "That's all I can tell you, I know it's hard to believe, but please take this warning?"

"Tell my husband what you have just told me, will you? Bob," she shouted, he came into the room. "Tell him what you have told me," she said, with a sort of menace in her voice.

Nigel told Bob, word for word, what he had said to his wife. Like her, he was shocked, "what is the reason you have to tell us this? What is your motive?"

"No motive," Nigel said as he got up to leave, and walked to the front door, "take heed, it will happen. I must go, God Bless you." He stepped outside and set the belt for the 7th April nineteen hundred and twelve, and pressed the red button.

"Haven't we seen that man before?" said Mrs. Cladmore to her husband.

"At our fancy dress party, wasn't he the one who told us the house would burn down? He's a bloody joker. I'm going to find out who's put him up to this," her husband said.

"I don't remember, it could have been, ask him?"

They opened the door and looked out, but he had disappeared. Nineteen hundred and thirty seven the belt showed, it was definitely struggling, it was malfunctioning, it wouldn't be long now. He hoped he could make it back. It was pointless trying to get to two thousand and seven, he had tried, but there was no movement at all. It could now only go one way, back in time!

Once again Nigel was surprised at it stopping at nineteen hundred and thirty seven. 'Why nineteen hundred and thirty seven?' he thought. He noticed that the house had changed somewhat, it needed painting he realised, the place was not up to scratch; the lawns were in need of a mow, and the fountain was dry! A man and woman were walking up the avenue towards the house. A short man with the features of a Jew, spectacles, little round ones on his nose and a black skull cap on his head.

"Hello kind sir," the man said, "are you the new groundsman-come-gardener?"

'Been mistaken for a chimney sweep, house sitter, now a gardener,' Nigel thought.

"No sir, I'm a messenger really. Are you Mr. and Mrs. Bactram?" He once again remembered what Brian had told him.

"Yes we are, how can we help you?"

"No, I believe I can try to help you, sir. I believe you are selling up and going home to Warsaw?"

"That's true, but how do you know that?" he enquired.

"I know lots of things," Nigel said smiling.

"Do you want to come inside and we can talk? You seem to be an interesting young man," Mr. Bactram said, indicating towards the house. "Not only that, it's a bit nippy and it's going to rain."

"No, I haven't got the time," Nigel said, thinking about the ticking belt, "I just want to warn you that this is not a good time to go back to Poland. Adolf Hitler will invade Poland within the next two years, September the first in fact, nineteen hundred and thirty nine. And he will round up the people of the Jewish faith and persecute them, as he is doing now in Germany."

Mr. and Mrs. Bactram were curious enough to listen. But then said that their mothers and fathers in Poland were getting ready to leave, and the purpose of themselves going was to help the whole family to get out of Poland, and come to live in England, but further up North. He thanked Nigel for his advice, but said that he was aware of the Jews' plight. He also said that he and his wife were studying Law at Southampton University, and would complete the course very soon.

"I'm glad you are not staying over there, it's not healthy, and it's going to get worse," Nigel said. The men shook hands, said their farewells, and Nigel made off towards the Avenue. The Bactrums went into the house. 'I may have saved them,' he hoped.

Nigel looked at his belt, the time said two hours twenty five minutes, and counting down. He once again set the belt at the 7th April nineteen hundred and twelve, although the date was still there, he re-set it to make sure it would work this time. Out of sight of the house behind a tree, he pressed the button. He kept his eyes open, and just like the time machine film he remembered seeing, flashes of trees, growing branches snapping off, green grass, then a split second later, a snow covered ground, then motor cars passing in a blur up the avenue. People flashing by, then an abrupt stop. The clock on the belt said nineteen hundred and twenty nine! "Bastard," Nigel said aloud. "What's wrong with this bloody belt?" Then he remembered what Brian the landlord had said about Mr. Bloomberg, who had lived in the house in that year and had hung himself. He had to have a word with this Mr. Bloomberg. He knocked on the now familiar big oak door.

"I've come to see Charles," he said to the maid who answered the door.

"Come in," she said sweetly, and led him in to, yet again, the family room on the right. "I'll fetch the master," she said with a half curtsy. He looked around the room, it was beautifully furnished. Within a minute the maid returned and said that he was to be taken to the big room, and Mr. Bloomberg would be there very soon. He was led past the bathroom down the hallway, and into the big room. There it still was, the big fireplace.

"Sit here sir," the maid instructed, as she went out of the room. Nigel went straight into the fireplace, set the button to April seventh two thousand and seven, and pressed the red button. Nothing happened apart from another red light came on!

"Hell," Nigel said, it was so frustrating. The clock said one hour fifty nine minutes, and one green left, and two buttons glowing red.

The door opened as Nigel stepped back into the room.

"Good evening sir," Nigel said. A portly gentleman with a big moustache came towards him.

"Nice to meet you sir, I'm Nigel Maythorn, a financial adviser. I believe you have a considerable amount of money in the Stock Market."

"And how would you know that?" enquired the gentleman.

"Oh sir, you will understand that in our business we get to know all our important players. I'm not here to ask you to invest

206

sir; on the contrary, I'm advising you to sell as fast as you can, because there is going to be a 'crash', and the market is set to fall, a fall that we have never seen before."

"Really," said the man, "I have been having doubts about the buoyancy of the market at the moment. The share value has begun to decline. It's been all this rampant speculation of late. The President doesn't seem to want to do anything about it. That American President Hoover has a lot to answer for, I can tell you," he said, stroking his chin.

"I agree," said Nigel, "and things will get a lot worse. As you know, the Dow Jones index is at 540 odd, I estimate it to drop in the next three years to 41 points."

"Incredible, bloody incredible! Let's have a brandy old chap."

Nigel had no time to refuse; it was poured out within the time it took him to sit down, then it was thrust into his hands.

Nigel continued, "Local bankers will call in loans, production will collapse, a third of the country's businesses will go down. We are in for a very black time. So that's the reason I'm here today, sir, is not to ask you to buy, but to sell up, take your profits now!"

"Thank you, but how much will this advice cost me?" he asked with a knowing smile, and taking a sip of his brandy.

"Nothing sir, absolutely nothing. Let's say for the benefit of mankind. I would hate the thought of you sir, losing all your money and hanging yourself!"

"Good God," Charles shouted, nearly choking on his drink. "That will never happen, I can assure you, I have my family to Consider. I'11 let you into a little secret; I have a mentally retarded brother called Percy who needs constant care, he's always saying he's going to top himself. Who knows, one day the blighter might," with that he burst into laughter.

Nigel laughed as well, but didn't really mean it. He was also thinking of his own demise, if he was stuck in the middle of time, and he wondered if he would ever get home! "Still," he heard himself say, "sell, before it's too late. To conclude sir, my prediction is for October the eighteenth nineteen hundred and twenty nine, and it will be called THE WALL STREET

CRASH, share prices will crash." Nigel got up to leave, finishing his drink.

"Another one?" Charles enquired.

"No thank you sir, I have very important business of my own to attend to."

"So, you haven't got the time for one more drink?"

"No sir," Nigel said, holding out his hand, "I haven't got the time." The men shook hands and they walked to the door.

"Can I give you a lift in the car? My chauffeur will take you to where-ever you want to go."

"I doubt that sir, but thanks all the same. Please heed the warnings I have given you. The market will pick up again in nineteen hundred and thirty three, for at least five years, then you can re-invest." Charles said goodbye and shut the door.

Nigel looked at the belt, one hour, two minutes, thirty seven seconds. He pressed the button again just as the door opened.

"What investment company are you with?" Charles enquired, but no-one heard him.

As Nigel opened his eyes, the whole drive was packed with cars, and army personnel were milling about. His belt clock said May nineteen sixteen. At least he was getting there, but would the belt hold out? he wondered. He was feeling desperate now, and pressed the button again, nothing happened apart from the third red light came on for a second. Fifty nine minutes left! He now took it that in that time the belt would completely stop working, or maybe it had stopped already! He was frightened to push it again.

"The meeting's starting," an officer shouted from the doorway. "Come on in and take your seats gentlemen."

Nigel went through the door with soldiers and civilian personnel, and walked up the passage way to the big room. A gigantic table went right across the room, set up with glasses of water and papers.

"Sit here sir," a waiter said as he pulled out a chair. Nigel sat down; the rest took their seats, then an officer of high rank brought the meeting to order.

"Gentlemen, I want to welcome you all to Central Command Headquarters. On the agenda today is the 'big push' that will take place in July. As we are all aware there has been stalemate since the war began two years ago, all along the Western Front. But soon that will change, by June over six hundred volunteer infantry battalions will have been raised locally, as opposed to only three hundred odd by the War Office. So the High Command have plans to push the Germans right back where they belong, Germany." A round of applause broke out.

Everyone clapped apart from Nigel. It was noticed by a few officers, but nothing was said. "The Territories have furnished fourteen divisions, and since conscription was introduced in January, over a dozen more divisions. So you see gentlemen, we are now in the position to give the 'boche' a bloody nose. The war could be over by the end of this year, nineteen sixteen!" Another round of applause. "We have the world's largest navy, and the Flying Corps are building more planes, that we use mainly for reconnaissance. We have been planning this change in our strategy for some time, and today I will put our plans to you all for your input, which we will incorporate if at all practical. But first of all, Captain Wiseman will take your names and regiment for the register. And remember gentlemen, that what takes place here today has to be top secret. There are spies around, and it is imperative that nothing is leaked out, not even to the papers. Over to Captain Wiseman."

"Thank you sir, I will go around in a clock-wise fashion, starting with you sir," he pointed to the officer sitting two away from Nigel.

"Lieutenant Colonel Nealman, Acerington Palls." Captain Wiseman wrote in his register. Nigel felt uncomfortable and started to sweat slightly, he took a sip of water and glanced at the time on his belt under the table, forty eight minutes, twenty one seconds.

Captain Wiseman looked up and said to Colonel Nealman, "That's the eleventh Battalion of East Lancashire, isn't it?"

"Yes, that's what we are now known as."

Wiseman looked at the man next to Nigel, Colonel Rigshaw, Grimsby chums. "I know your lot," Wiseman said with a slight smile. He looked at Nigel, who stood up, nobody else had.

"Gentlemen, I believe this is a big mistake, this whole campaign will cost the lives of thousands of our finest men. Fatal casualties will reach three quarters of a million. This plan is flawed; going over the top is not the best type of warfare. Men will fall in rows of hundreds as enemy machine gun fire will mow them down. The first day of July on the Somme, will go down in history as the British Army's biggest ever slaughter. I implore you not to go down this road."

Every officer's face was looking towards the high ranking officer, who was red in colour, and spluttering by now.

"Damn you man. How dare you say such things? Are you a coward? And tell me how you know about The Somme, or the date of our proposed attack? We haven't told anyone at all! Only three top officers know about it, even the Government doesn't know. You must be a spy! Who are you? What's your name?"

"I'm not a spy," Nigel blurted out. 'They shoot spies,' came to his mind. "This plan is plain stupidity, and it won't work. The war cannot end this year, you are sentencing thousands of soldiers to their deaths. This war will not end before November 1918."

"I've heard enough," shouted the officer, jumping up from his seat. "I'll deal with you after this meeting. Arrest that man," he ordered. Two burly guards were summonsed from the outside, as three officers pounced on Nigel and held him in a vice like grip on the floor. Noise erupted as the officers talked to one another. "Lock him in the side room until the end of the meeting," said the high ranking officer.

The two guards, one on either side of Nigel, escorted him out of the room, and down the passageway to the room at the front of the house. They pushed him in and locked the door, then stood outside, one either side of the door. Nigel went to the window and tried to open it, but it was firmly shut. He sat at the table and looked at his belt, thirty seven minutes, twenty three seconds. Two red bulbs glowed, one was at green, it changed from time to time to red then back to green. The belt was dying, its life ebbing away. Nigel was getting desperate, should he try again? It hadn't worked before, it seemed that every time he pressed a button a new red light would show.

He pondered his fate, now he thought that he would never get home. He went to the farthest end of the room, and could hear muffled sounds of the meeting still going on. He noticed a crack in the wooden partition that separated the rooms, and put his ear to it.

"That display gentlemen, is that of a traitor, or a coward. If he was anywhere near any enlisted men, his ideas would undermine the whole war effort. He would have soldiers raising their hands in the air at the first bullet shot! He would advocate teaching German to anyone he came across. He's the kind of person that has no allegiance to anybody but himself. Prison would be too good for him, there is only one way to deal with people like him, SHOOT THEM."

"Here here," everyone said out loud.

"He will contaminate the minds of soldiers of England." Round of applause. "If let loose. Now gentlemen, let's get down to the business of the day, the business of winning this war for King and Country! But I believe, because of the commotion we have just encountered, a drink is in order, so we can toast the King, and condemn all traitors and cowards, also for victory in the Battle of the Somme!"

Nigel walked to the window; he saw the army vehicles lined up and drivers milling around talking. One driver was looking intently at the house and for a moment Nigel thought that he looked a little like Bill, but realised that it was only wishful thinking. He had pressed the blue button to summons him, but so far, he hadn't turned up. He felt lost, and then it came to him, a plan, it was no good just waiting in the room, to be shot eventually, he had to escape! He felt in his back pocket for his wallet, and for the button, the invisible suit, he had forgotten he still had it. With one more use, one more life, and it just might save his life. Bill had once said that because Nigel hadn't been born yet, then it was impossible to die. Well maybe so, but he decided that he wasn't going to test that theory! He had to try at least to get out of this situation, and make one more attempt to get to nineteen hundred and twelve. Maybe someone would be there to meet him now?

He put the suit on, but before he put it on fully, he looked at his belt, twenty five minutes, five seconds. He held the suit just below his waist, ready to pull it over his head, and banged on the door. "I want to go to the toilet, please let me out."

He banged again when he got no answer. He went to the window and saw the reason why, the two guards were sat on the wall, both smoking a cigarette.

"Bastards," muttered Nigel. He had to wait until they returned to their posts outside the door, and the clock was ticking down. He hid behind the curtain; he didn't want to be seen as half a man, with the bottom half gone. And he dare not take the suit off, as he remembered it was the last time he could use it.

He waited, watching the men, and watching the time clicking away. At last the guards finished their smoke and stood there talking, eighteen minutes, twenty four seconds the clock said.

"Come in you rabble," Nigel muttered, then gave the window a lusty knock. He saw the men look up, and they came in the front door. He gave the door another bang. "I've got to go to the toilet," he shouted once again.

"Got to get permission first," the muffled voice shouted out.

Nigel waited, ready for the door to open, but nothing happened! Ten long minutes passed. "Let me out, for the last time, I have to go now! I'll break up the room; I'll set fire to the house, I'll shit on the floor, I have to go now, I'm warning you! This is inhumane, I'11 report you to your superiors. You can't deny me my rights to go to the toilet!" BANG BANG BANG, the door shook on its hinges.

"I'll go and ask for permission," the voice came through the door.

"Go now then; I can't wait for much longer." Nigel went to the crack in the partition, and heard the guard ask for permission.

"Of course, you bloody fool," he heard the officer say. Nigel heard the key go into the lock, and pulled the suit over his head, he had disappeared.

"Come on," the guard said, as he opened the door wide. His face was shocked as he said to the other guard standing outside, "Facking hell, there's no-one here, the bastard's escaped."

"Don't piss about Harry," the other guard said, as he also entered the room. "Look under the table, behind the cupboard, look inside! For fack's sake, we're in the shit, he's not here!"

"He must be somewhere, you heard his voice." They looked up at the ceiling, behind the curtains. Nigel made his way into the passageway; he was waiting for someone to open the front door.

"He's not here Harry; we will have to report it."

"No, you facking idiot, we have to find him, he must have got out somehow. Let's look outside first, he can't have got far. Fack this game for soldiers, I'm going to join the navy!"

Both men came into the passageway. "Have a look in the toilet," said Harry.

"How would he have got there? How could he have passed us?"

"Don't facking argue, just facking look!"

"No-one in here," said the guard.

"Outside," said Harry. They opened the big door, and looked out.

"Seen anyone come out of here, a civilian?" Harry the guard asked the driver who was standing close by, and had been looking towards the house.

"Yes, he went that way," he pointed towards the avenue. The two guards took off running towards the main gates.

Nigel made his way out of the house, on to the veranda, slipped out of the suit, and fiddled with the button. Very quickly, he tried to open it up, but its use over, it was just a button.

He threw it into a flower pot, looked at his belt, the date was already set at the seventh of April nineteen hundred and twelve. He glanced at the time left: one minute, three seconds. He glanced up and saw the driver who had directed the guards down the avenue, put his thumbs up, and a smile covered his face. The driver shouted, "You'll find out one day."

'What did that mean?' Nigel thought, but had no time to respond. He pressed the button; all the red lights came on, one flickering rapidly. He glanced up, nothing had changed, the driver was still smiling with his thumb in the air. He pressed down again, hard, and closed his eyes. He was frightened to open them, but did, and saw the belt with all lights red. Ten, nine, eight, seven, six, five, four, three, two, one, then all the lights went out! The belt was just a belt, its use spent, just like Bill had said. But a mistake had been made because it had been operational in this zone. The door of the mansion opened.

"Now that didn't take long, did it? The cap was on the cabinet in the hallway. Shall we go?"

"Yes Gerald, let's go."

A happy feeling came over Nigel as they walked down the avenue towards the gate. He had made it, just.

"Stop, stop," Gerald heard. Nigel stood there laughing. "You know I've forgotten something."

"What?" Gerald said

"I've forgotten my bloody bike," Nigel replied, walking back to the house. Gerald saw the funny side and said, "Don't go disappearing again, I don't want to see a bicycle with no-one riding it, pass me. I'll see you at the gate."

"There's no chance of that," Nigel laughed as he walked away.

Gerald was waiting at the gate as Nigel rode up.

"Thanks for everything; you must come up to see us again very soon."

"I will, I've told you that as soon as the news comes through next Monday, I'll come to see you." The men shook hands once again.

"Don't change your mind and go," said Nigel, as an after thought.

"No, I'm going to cancel right now."

Six different time zones and yet he had been away fifty five minutes as he walked into the pub.

"Anyone asked for me?" Nigel enquired.

"Nobody's been in the last hour; it's very quiet at the moment."

"I hope there's accommodation with this job, as I haven't got a place to stay? I'll be happy in the little room upstairs, or even the secret room behind the wardrobe in your room?"

"You amaze me, how do you know this? How do you know about the little room behind the wardrobe?"

"Because you've just told me," he replied laughing.

They agreed that he could live in, and he went to work that evening. Freda realized right away that he was the man for the bar job. They both worked well together, just as he had with Fanny in the 'other' world, she was almost identical.

Every time the pub door opened, Nigel thought that this would be the person who would show him the way back, but slowly hope ebbed away, as the evening wore on. Same characters, some with same names, some with slightly different ones. Nigel did his best not to answer questions about where he came from, but at times he found it difficult.

After a meal when the bar had closed, he made an excuse to retire early. In his room he lay on the bed that Freda had made up with clean sheets. A new candle was in a white, but chipped holder. What a day it had been, he had covered ninety five years, travelling through time in split seconds; seen the mansion burn down, warned people of dangers that might befall them, been accused of being a traitor and a coward, arrested, threatened to be shot! 'Time Travel' was like Bill had said, dangerous!

Now that the belt was no longer functioning, that was the end of it all. How he would get home he had no idea, he would just have to wait for his escort. In the meantime he had to make a living. He was skint, so felt very fortunate that at least he had a roof over his head, and a paid job doing something that he enjoyed.

The daylight lit up his room as he awoke from a deep sleep. He felt very refreshed as he dressed. He had asked Freda if she had some spare shirts and trousers that he could borrow until he could get some money together to buy some new ones. She obliged.

"Help yourself to my husband's old clothes," she had said, "he was never one to throw anything away. They are in the bottom two drawers in your room."

He chose the first pair of trousers he picked up, and a shirt of a grey colour. He looked at himself in the mirror, and felt his chin. "Still don't need a shave, or a hair cut," he mumbled. He wasn't aging; he was the same man as he was when he first arrived. When was it? He tried to work out how long he had been away, yet it was only the eighth of April nineteen hundred and twelve, so it was in fact just one day! Yet he had spent time on holiday with Bill, been to America, Africa, Mexico, a month on that one. Then there was the time spent with Janice, a week of walks, picnics, laughter and fun. Then the time in prison, and the hospital, it was hard to work out, but weeks, six for sure! Yet here he was on the second day! He shook his head in disbelief, and went down to the kitchen.

"Morning, breakfast is ready, I was just about to call you. Sleep well?" she enquired, with just a glance as she took the eggs out of the pan and onto a plate.

"Best sleep I've had for ages," he replied, and sat at the table.

She told him that her husband was at sea, and was coming home soon. He stopped himself saying that he already knew.

"He may be home today, he did say he was hoping to get on the White Star Line, the Titanic." 'Oh no, not that ship again,' he thought.

As he was listening to her telling him about her husband's dislike for the pub, Nigel's mind was on other things; money, he had to get some money. He then decided to take bets on the sinking, just like he had done before, but this time he would win. He could make a fortune. Tonight he'd start taking bets.

"Nice sausage," Nigel said, as he chewed on one, the grease falling on to his plate. "Nice breakfast. Now for some old fashioned hard work. Before we open I'll fix that bench out back, I saw that a leg was almost off, got to earn my keep."

She smiled as she collected the dishes, and took them to the sink.

"Like the new clothes?" He twirled around like a model would.

"Very nice," she smiled. "Yes, very nice," she repeated. She was beginning to take a liking to this strange man who had come from nowhere, into her life.

"Bar's open at noon," she said, as he walked out the back.

She ran after him and said, "Oh by the way, there was someone looking for you this morning. I didn't see him but one of my customers told me."

Nigel's heart jumped. "Who was it, what did he want?" he asked excitedly.

"He said to my customer that if he were to see you, to give you a message."

"What was the message?"

"Meeting next week, and something you had wanted, will come true."

"Yes, yes?" Nigel was almost bursting now with excitement.

"Oh yes, and the last part of the message, if I can remember…" She frowned. "Ah yes, something on the lines of, that he had cancelled."

"That's all?"

"That's all." She saw his disappointment.

"Thanks," he said, as he went to look at the bench. She returned to the kitchen.

The eighth of April passed by with Nigel working doing various jobs, and working the bar. That evening he got into conversations about the Titanic. He explained in simple terms to the pub customers, that he had no faith in this new technology, and proclaimed his belief that the ship would flounder. Bets were made, money put into the tin box, and he made out the slips of paper at the end of the betting. On the day the ship sailed, Wednesday the tenth of April, there was over hundred pounds all told.

One afternoon he went into Southampton and visited the café he had gone to in Zone Two. He didn't say anything to the lady of the café, when she told him that her husband was a seaman on the ship. He felt sorry for her forthcoming loss. He remembered the trouble he had got into. He saw the ship, saw the crew going to and fro, and said nothing, he had tried, it had been pointless. He noticed that the medieval walls of the Bargate in Southampton were there, same people, but with some differences.

The week slipped by, with Nigel and Freda becoming closer each day. He was in the bar when the news came in.

"Bloody hell, you were right, the Titanic has sunk, everyone has drowned!" the man, a regular customer, shouted to everyone as he came into the bar. There were gasps all round, and lots of disbelief.

"News has just come through, so a man I met down the road told me."

"Bloody hell, it's unbelievable."

"I told you so, didn't I? Has anything been said of how it sank?" Nigel said.

"No, just that it sank," the man replied.

"Well, it seems I win all the bets. Does anyone want to take any bets on how she sank? Because I can tell you." There were no takers. "Are you sure? Last chance?" Customers congregated around the bar. "Then I'll tell you, she hit an iceberg off the coast of Newfoundland, and over seven hundred were saved. But unfortunately fifteen hundred souls perished. I had a dream."

"Bloody hell," said the man, "you are a marvel!" All agreed. Nigel had just made a lot of new friends. Customers were more amazed as the details of the sinking were published in the newspapers. Word spread around the district, and the bar became a Mecca for people wanting to see this man who could see into the future. Nigel found himself a very popular barman indeed, and Freda showed her affections by sharing her bed after her husband had gone back to sea after a short visit. The two men, Nigel and Brian had got on well, and her husband had shown no signs of jealousy, as he got to know his wife's new barman. Nigel sensed that their love had gone, and that he had another woman somewhere in the world.

"Keep up the good work," were the last words Brian had said before he went back to his sea-faring life.

Nigel went up to the mansion when the news broke, and Gerald was so very grateful that he wanted to reward his new-found friend. Nigel declined the offer, but Gerald insisted, and said that he would put one hundred pounds in an investment company, Foreign and Colonial, in trust for Nigel Maythorn or his heirs and successors. He also forced Nigel to accept fifty pounds. They drank together many times when he had time away from the pub. Days off would be spent with Nigel telling Gerald what it was like living in the future. He explained as best he could about TV, internet, fights all over the world, wars to come, the First World War, and the Second; the stock market crash that was to happen in nineteen hundred and twenty nine. Hours of extensive talks that both men enjoyed, in-between a dram or two, before the Andersons sold the house and went to live in America. Gerald was eternally grateful to Nigel, so was Alice. It was a sad day when they said goodbye at the house, and Bertie drove them to the docks.

"Got enough petrol?" Nigel joked with Bertie, as he was about to pull away.

"Most certainly," said Bertie, "filled up this morning. Why do you ask?"

"No problem, just a thought," Nigel laughed.

"Close the gates after you," Gerald had shouted.

"Will do, keep in touch," was the parting shot. Bertha waved all the way down the avenue. Nigel had one last look at the mansion, then walked away.

He had been waiting for over a month for the 'escort', expecting on a daily basis that this elusive guide would come through the door of the pub. Bill had let him down, he was lost, left to fend for himself. Each day his disappointment wasn't as bad as the day before. He had lots of friends in the pub and Freda was a nice companion when off duty. They walked the country lanes, took trips to the city, and slowly made the pub a better place to drink for the customers.

He was rich compared with the ordinary people. Times, he discovered in nineteen hundred and twelve, were bleak indeed. Most working men brought home about one pound a week and that didn't go far with rent and rates on a family home to pay.

New clothes were a luxury requiring a windfall, and his windfall; football matches, the bets he had made including horse racing he had remembered, plus the money from Gerald, made him very wealthy in that time. He loved to see Freda's face when he presented her with a new gift, a dress or a blouse. He got his watch back from the boy, who refused to let it go, but was soon happy with the new toy that Nigel had bought for him. Nigel also paid for the pub's interior to have a face lift, and new paint jobs. He missed the mod-cons he had been so used to, but slowly adapted to life without a mobile phone, TV, modern kitchen and bathroom. The tin bath once a week was now a novelty and he made his life as comfortable as was possible.

Time slipped by and days became months, then like a flash a year had gone by! There were times when hope was no more, and he accepted his lot, at times he was a happy man, especially those afternoons spent making love to Freda in the bedroom above the bar. He organised sing-a-longs, introduced bingo at a farthing a strip with prizes of a shilling, and a jackpot of five shillings! The Fox and Hounds did a roaring trade over the time that Nigel was head barman, and he loved every minute of it.

But things were about to change as the end of nineteen hundred and thirteen approached. It started when he was behind the bar serving, when a stranger walked into the bar. Nigel found out that the gentleman was the new owner of the Mansion, Jim Giles. He had bought the property off the Andersons, and it turned out that Mr. Giles wasn't very happy living there.

"I find the place too big for me and the wife," he said. "You see, the gardens are far too big for her to cope with. She's tried; we could get a gardener, but once again, the house is much too big for us really. I just wanted a house in the country, but it's not to my wife's liking, so I may put it up for sale soon."

Nigel had remembered that Brian the landlord had given him the history of the house, and he recalled that the army had taken the place over for their headquarters during the war. That's when he had a brainwave, maybe this was his opportunity to make a lot of money!

"If you sold, how much would you want?" Nigel asked.

"I'll sell for seven hundred and fifty pounds, freehold. Why? Are you interested?" he laughed.

"When you're ready to sell, let me know," Nigel said in a serious way.

"I will," was Jim Giles's reply, as he drank up.

Nigel told Freda of his intentions of buying the mansion if it came on the market. She wasn't too happy at the thought that he would move out, and maybe leave the pub. But he assured her that it was an investment for the future, and the matter was soon forgotten by her. But Nigel started to save really hard towards the sum of seven hundred and fifty pounds, he had four hundred pounds in a suitcase under his bed. He needed to take more bets, he racked his brains to remember: football games and events of that year nineteen hundred and thirteen.

Then as nineteen hundred and fourteen came into being, the opportunity arose. In April nineteen fourteen, (he was aware of the anniversary) he had his chance. A Sunday football pub match had taken place, and the team had beaten the team from the Bull's Arms 4-1, then the 'after game' get together was in full swing.

"Gentlemen," Nigel shouted, "let's have a bit of order please. I have an announcement to make." He smiled.

"I know what's coming, he knows the winner of next Saturday's Cup Final! I'm with you, I'll take a bet!" the right back shouted.

The whole team agreed with him.

"I'll have some as well!"

"I'm in," the men shouted.

"No gentlemen, it's not the Cup Final, I'm afraid I don't know that one." There were groans all around.

"Nigel, I made twenty pounds profits last year with your tips, so whatever it is I'm in," said the goalkeeper from the Bull's Arms.

"Gentlemen please, it's not anything to do with sport. This is more serious, much more, and what I say will affect all of us, so please listen. You remember two years ago the tragedy of the Titanic, and my prediction?"

221

"I remember that," said Joe, the inside left of the pub team, "lost a bloody fortune to you, five pounds! But I'm not complaining, I have won it back over time."

"I'm glad to hear it. No, this is more of a tragedy than the Titanic, much more."

"Get on with it then, we're wasting drinking time, and my missus expects me home soon," someone shouted.

"OK…" he hesitated for effect. "WAR, gentlemen, WAR, WORLD WAR!"

Everyone went quiet for a moment.

"By August, four months from now, we will be at war with Germany and it will turn out to be a long war. It will last for four years; millions of men will die in France and Belgium. I hate to say this, but most of you here today will be affected if you volunteer for the army, and you will. My advice is to go in the navy, or emigrate to the U.S.A. Anyhow, this prediction is not meant to be a warning, but a fact. I'll take bets that the war will start on August the fourth, any bets?"

"I'll bet, but at what odds?" Bert said.

"Like the Titanic, 100-1."

"I'll bet a pound that what you have said will not come true," Joe said as he took a bag of coins and emptied them on the table.

"Same here," said other men. One man wanted to bet fifty pounds, but Nigel said that the ceiling on bets was five pounds. There was no way he wanted to fleece his friends, although he was sure he would compensate the bets with wins on other sport events.

A good afternoon was had by all. Bets and slips had been issued, and in the next few months Nigel had the amount to buy the house if it became available. By the time of the assassination of the Austrian Heir by a Serb terrorist in Sarajevo on June the twenty eighth, the men of the pub, and the football team, knew that the bets were lost once again.

"How did you know?" the question was asked many times, and the same answer, "I had a dream." He was the hero of the bar, and advice was given on many occasions as the year passed. It was always a sad time when customers would have their farewell drink at the pub before joining the army.

"Will I come back?" many men asked Nigel. He always said that they would, they believed him, and went off to war never to return, but at peace with themselves.

Nineteen fourteen past into history. Nigel bought the mansion and spent a week's holiday there, but found that he got lonely in the evenings. Freda visited once or twice, he was a little pleased when his holiday came to an end, and he was back behind the bar, or in his lover's arms again. During this time he got to be very fond of little Brian, and as he grew up Nigel became a substitute father to the boy. In early nineteen fifteen, the army approached Nigel to purchase the property, and he sold it for two thousand pounds, a tidy profit. He was about to ask Freda if she wanted a partner for the pub business, when another event took place. Joe and his friend Bert had enlisted as Nigel had predicted they would, and came on leave before going to Belgium. They looked smart as they entered the pub, and were very proud to be in the service of the King. As the joviality of the evening subsided, Joe asked Nigel why he wasn't going in the army as it said on the posters: YOUR KING AND COUNTRY NEED YOU. He pointed to the poster over the bar, above his head.

"I'm not army, more navy," Nigel had said.

"Well whatever, but you'll soon be in anyhow, because there's rumours that you will be forced to join up very soon, it's called conscription. And I've heard it's coming out next year." Joe said convincingly.

Nigel had forgotten that fact that there had been a conscription in nineteen sixteen.

"I'm too busy here, helping soldiers to forget the war, with their beer drinking," he joked, but he knew it wasn't that funny. The pub had taken a nose dive in profits since the war had started. Most of the regulars had enlisted, on some nights only the very old were in. The war was affecting everyone. There was a bad experience when a group of women enquired why He wasn't in uniform. He had felt embarrassed even though he tried to explain that he thought about going into the navy. One woman presented him with a white feather, that he displayed behind the bar, to show he wasn't worried. But inwardly he wasn't at peace with himself. As more of the customers went into the army, he felt a feeling of loneliness come over him. Some nights behind the bar, he longed for those times with the lads, who had played in the pub's football team now disbanded, with most away on active service.

The last straw in this dilemma to join, or not join, was when the news came through that two of his closet friends, Joe and Bert, had fallen in the fields of France. It has been an emotional night as he explained his intentions to join up to Freda. She knew deep down that this was the end of a chapter in her life and it would never come back.

Chapter 12

IT'S THE WAR

On the fifth of January nineteen hundred and sixteen Nigel enlisted in the Motor Transport Company, and went for training in the Highlands of Scotland. The decision to join up had been a long and hard dilemma. He had discussed it many times with Freda, as a man and wife might. Things had changed, since Freda had borne a daughter in early nineteen thirteen, she now had her hands full with Brian, five years old, and Mary two years old. It had been established earlier on that her husband was the father.

Nigel's life, it seemed, was going nowhere. Since the war had started he missed the regulars, and was saddened when the reports started coming in of the casualties and deaths: Joe, Bert, Percy, John all his good friends gone for good. He was also worried that even if he were to try to join, they would ask for a birth certificate. The Christmas before he had left was bitter sweet, Brian had come home for a spell of leave, and decided that he would stay ashore for a while longer. As he had said, "It's dangerous at sea these days." So his days of fun with Freda had come to an abrupt end.

The days of passion flew away like the days of summer. Brian started to change things to his own liking, never taking into consideration whose ideas they had been, and at times he ordered Nigel to do jobs that he had been doing for years! A decision was taken, and although Freda was against his going, he reluctantly left to 'report for duty'. No-one mentioned a birth certificate, so after a short medical, the Oath, a new shilling that belonged to the King, he was now part of a massive army. He refused infantry; no way was he going to go over the top to die in no-man's land. In his mind the motor transport would at times take him away from the front line and the fighting. His money had accumulated over the years, plus the profit from the sale of the mansion, was put into his account at Foreign and Colonial, in a Trust Fund. Now he found himself making new friends and comrades, training, marches, firing rifles, cross country running, drills. He knew what to expect, he had read numerous books on the First World War.

The ten week training passed in a flash it seemed, strangely he enjoyed it, it was a new challenge. In no time at all, the authorities could see the potential in him, and suggested that he go for officer training, for an infantry battalion. Nigel refused the offer. "No thank you sir," he said. "Driving suits me to the ground." It was soon forgotten. Nigel learned to drive buses and army staff cars, and after a crash course on the mechanics, he was in charge of a brand new staff car. He was assigned to drive Colonel Birchtree, who turned out to be a very nice fellow indeed. They even laughed together when it was just the two of them, and Nigel enjoyed his new life in the army. At night in the barracks, after a day of training, the men would all get together and talk, looking forward to doing their bit for King and Country.

"Hope it don't fooking end before we fooking get there," said Wilson Case from Yorkshire. "I heard some bastard say that the fooking war will be over by the end of this fooking year. For fook's sake, I want a bash at those fookers, they rape women and kill kids, I'll sort the fookers out," he said with venom in his voice, as he pulled back the bolt on his rifle and inspected the barrel. Nigel was getting used to this new language that only belongs to the army, and some other services.

"We'll get our chance, don't worry yourself Will. I'll help you kill some of the fuckers myself," his mate Derek remarked.

"Ten minutes to lights out you bunch of thickoes, busy day tomorrow. So get into your fuckin' pits," shouted the sergeant at the end of the barrack room. Men scrambled to bed, and so another day had come to an end.

Nigel lay on his bed, and after lights out silently masturbated over Freda. It was approaching four years since he had taken a step back in time. He rarely thought of the adventure he had had. Zone Two was becoming a distant memory tucked away in the corner of his mind. He had given up all hopes of returning to his own time, years back. The escort had never materialised, and in his mind Bill had let him down. He had been used, then discarded like the butt of a cigarette. He felt no anger or animosity, he had a positive nature, and made the best of anything that came his way. After the war he planned to find a woman and get married, but his main problem, and one that never went away, was the blatant fact that in four years he hadn't changed at all. He never shaved, his hair didn't grow! Freda had asked him on occasion when he had last had a hair cut. He told her that he had a condition that stunted hair growth. She only laughed and let the matter go. He told her that he shaved every morning, and she didn't question him. He often wondered if he would live forever, was it impossible to get killed? These thoughts often popped into his head.

Early in May nineteen hundred and sixteen, Nigel was posted to a motorised battalion stationed on the outskirts of the New Forest, Hampshire near Southampton. A wonderful posting, as he could go and visit Freda and Brian. They were very pleased to see him, and remarked how smart he looked, they enquired what it was like in France, and he told them that he hadn't been over there yet, but rumours were flying around that they may be shipping out very soon.

"Most of the men are looking forward to going," he said as he sat in the kitchen with them, drinking his favourite tankard of ale. He promised to say his goodbyes before he left. The brief time he had, he enjoyed himself playing with the children, and a kiss from Freda when Brian went out of the room, he felt guilty, but the feeling soon passed.

Picking up stores, driving officers to different meeting places, occasional cookhouse duties passed away the next few weeks.

When one morning in May he read the company notice board that made him excited! His orders were to take a high ranking officer to a meeting. The address was at Eastern Hill headquarters, The Briars, the mansion, his old stamping ground!

He picked up the officer at the appointed time, and drove up the familiar lanes. The guards at the gates saluted the car as it made its way up the tree-lined avenue to the big house. He parked the car, the officer got out and with other officers went into the meeting. After reading a magazine for half an hour, he got out of his car and looked towards the house. And at the window on the right of the big door, a feeling, a strange feeling, came over him as he caught sight of someone looking out at him!

Two guards were on the balcony smoking and talking, a few minutes after they had gone inside there was a commotion as the guards ran towards his car.

"Seen anyone come out of here, a civilian?" a guard said to him.

"Yes, he went that way," pointing to the avenue. The two guards took off, running towards the main gates. He looked over towards the house and on the veranda he saw this man throw something into a flower pot. Then he knew it was himself he was looking at! He lifted his thumb in the air, smiling broadly.

"You'll find out one day," he heard himself shout out, and he saw the man smile before he disappeared. Nigel shook his head in disbelief, and wandered over to the flower pot, and there it was, the little blue button, he picked it up and put it in his wallet, then returned to his car, and sat down on the fender.

"It's unbelievable, bloody unbelievable," he muttered. It all came back to him, he remembered vividly how his heart was pounding, as he was trying to get back to nineteen hundred and twelve, hoping that the guide would be waiting for him, that was four years ago now. And here he was four years later, and the man he had just seen on the balcony, himself, and having to go back, live for four years, then be back on this very spot where he was now, a loop in time, was the best if only way to describe this phenomenon. And maybe seeing the same man time and time again for ever.

Nigel wondered if he was crazy, when he was awoken by his thoughts. He glanced up as the two guards came back up the drive and towards the house. They stopped two feet from Nigel, and stared at him. "What?" Nigel said.

"It's him," one guard said to the other one. They grabbed hold of him.

Nigel remonstrated with them. "What the hell are you doing?" Nigel shouted.

"How did you do it? How did you get out you bastard? How did you get into uniform?" They started to take him towards the house, when the door opened and the officer came out. "What's going on here?" said Nigel's officer.

"Escaped prisoner sir," the men said, standing at attention and saluting.

"That's my bloody driver you fools, release him."

They obeyed immediately. "We must have been mistaken sir, sorry."

"I should think so," Nigel said, straightening himself up. "I saw a man run down the avenue, I told these blokes, sir. Then because they didn't capture him, they tried to arrest me, sir."

"I see that. Carry on searching!" the officer ordered, and walked towards the staff car.

"Thanks for that sir, mistaken identity I reckon."

"Bloody fools, you look nothing like the trouble maker. Back to base Maythorn."

"Yes sir," Nigel said as he started the engine. A smile came across his face. On the way back to headquarters, Nigel asked if there was any truth in the rumours that the battalion was going to France soon. The officer affirmed that there was some truth in what was being rumoured.

"In the next month, I believe, and we will be on our way, but we'll be taking over horses and buses, to some extent. I want you to know something, Lance Corporal, we have been watching you, and I know that you have turned down officer training, isn't that correct?"

"Yes sir, but I'm not a Lance Corporal, I'm just a Private."

"No, you're not Corporal," the officer said.

"Corporal Sir?"

"No, I'm joking Maythorn, you are to be made up to Acting Sergeant as from tomorrow, you deserve it with the good work you have put in. You have a knack for teaching, the hierarchy have noticed. How does that make you feel?"

"Great sir, thanks very much," Nigel said.

"It's an extra shilling a day, that's fourteen shillings a week, and more when the battalion goes to the war."

"Yes sir, thanks," he repeated.

"Right Sergeant Maythorn, no more talking, I've got to read these papers."

"Yes sir," Nigel said, he felt proud as he drove towards H.Q.

The battalion was a hive of activity during the next few weeks, as the men got ready to go to war. He took his three days' embarkation leave, and spent them with Freda. Brian was nowhere to be seen, he had got on some tramp ship heading for the Far East, and said he may be away for a year. Freda had a girl helping out in the bar full time, so she had time to spend with her secret lover, on walks and picnics in and around the countryside.

Nights of laughing and loving came to an end for both of them when it was time for Nigel to leave. They hugged one another.

"Don't ever forget me, Freda, and if I don't come back, thanks for looking after me, giving me a job when I was penniless." They kissed, and she cried as he left to go and report to the battalion, to fight a war.

It was a blur. Train, boat, Zeebrugge, there the London Omnibus stood waiting. Nigel had never driven a bus, and now he had one, his very own.

"We move off at six a.m. tomorrow morning, so get some food, and a good night's kip," an officer instructed. The men were dismissed. Nigel's first night overseas was spent in a big barn just outside of the town, with straw for bedding. Nigel didn't know it, but this was luxury living, compared to what he was to experience. Food was bread, beans, potatoes and spam.

Some of the men went to look around the town, but Nigel went to bed. He heard for the first time, the thud of explosions he knew came from the front, Ypres, and that was to be his destination in the morning.

"Well, here we fooking are at last," said Nigel's best friend, Wilson Case, or Casey, as he was called by everyone.

"I wonder if the Germans fooking know that I'm over here. I bet if they fooking did they would be shitting themselves."

Everyone laughed.

"Fuck me; I shit myself every time you're around me Casey," Derek blurted out, to more laughter. More banter flew around the barn before slowly it died out.

"Don't anyone fooking snore," Casey shouted.

"Or fart," Derek laughed out.

"Or wank" Bates, shouted.

"Lights out," said Sergeant Maythorn, "busy day tomorrow."

"Blow out the fooking lamp, Derek" ordered Casey. He did, and silence descended on fifty clean soldiers.

Six o'clock, dead on the dot, the men were woken, some from a deep sleep. After breakfast, they paraded for instructions. The drivers went to their respective buses, and the troops piled in, so they were on their way to 'Wipers' as was the British name for Ypres.

The drive for the first part of the journey was wonderful, beautiful countryside, farmers going about their business. Tree-lined avenues, that reminded him of the tree-lined avenue that led up to the mansion. Little villages, some people waved, young girls pointed and waved, as the convoy passed. Men shouted from the open tops, 'vol et vo, jig-jig'.

Men laughed out loud. There was no war here, he thought as he drove, getting used to the gears on his new bus. Men started singing songs that he knew so well: 'Long way to Tipperary'; 'Keep the home fires burning' and other war time favourites.

He had been to Ypres with his school once, in two thousand and six, so knew it well. He had heard the buglers sound the 'Last Post' at eight o'clock every night, at the Menin Gate. He had been to the trenches and walked the road with the kids, and walked around the ramparts. But that had been another time. He had read books on the place, and its destruction in war time. And now here he was going to visit again, to see first hand what it was like, it was unbelievable, but true.

The morning passed, the convoy at times slowed as traffic came away from the Front. Ambulances, horse drawn wagons laden with timber and ammunition, a few civilian carts pulled by old men, women with bedraggled children begging with arms outstretched.

"Argent pour la nourriture?"

It was very sad to see such things, most of the new recruits thought. Little did they realize that many more horrors awaited them in the not too distant future! Money was thrown, and the children fought one another for it, the men laughed.

The town of 'Pops' or Poperingue, was a stop off point where the men could have an hour or two to take a walk or eat in a café, and that's what happened. The convoy stopped, Nigel, Casey, Derek and Bates went to the café together,

on the edge of town.'ESTAMINET FRANÇOIS ' the cracked and rotting sign said. The four men ordered wine, omelette and chips.

"I'll order," said Casey, as a lovely young blond haired waitress came to the table.

"She reminds me of Brigitte Bardot," Nigel blurted out.

"Brigitte who?" said Derek.

"Never mind," Nigel said. At times he would forget where he was, not realising that some things he spoke of were from another time.

"Avay vu dan van sif vo plet? Euf, and pom du terre frede. Siv vu vulet. Voose et tre jolie. See. I told you I could speak good French," Casey bragged. They all laughed, including the girl, who showed off her beautiful white teeth.

"One, two, three, four," she said, pointing to each man.

"Yes," each one replied. She smiled an angelic smile, and walked away to a fat woman cooking the food on an open fire, in black as black could be frying pans.

"She fooking fancies me, did you see her look at me? I'll be up her like a rat up a drain, you wait and fooking see!"

"I'll be there to watch," Derek said. All the men laughed. Derek always liked to get the last word. The men tucked in to the smoky tasting food. The café was full of smoke, and it was hard to talk normally as laughter broke out from time to time.

"The 'van' is good," Bates remarked as he took a swig. Men of different ranks mixed freely, and they drank as though it might be their last. The four drivers stood out from the rest, with their new battle-dress, but generally the banter was on the joking side. A soldier came up to the table and asked if he could buy them a meal or a bottle of wine. His demeanour, Nigel realised, was of a man who was suffering from shell shock, stress of constant combat. He talked in riddles, laughed raucously. Everyone declined his invitation of a meal, but another bottle of wine was put on the table.

"Fooking nice bloke," said Casey, pouring another glass. The old woman cooking was telling her waitress to serve another lot of soldiers who had just come in the creaking door that led out to a wet street, when there was a swoosh and an almighty bang that shook the building and made dribbles of dust come down from the ceiling. Everyone ducked down, except Nigel.

"Merde," shouted the cook, as a pan of eggs clattered to the floor. She scooped them up and placed them at the side of the fire, to be served at a later time.

"Fooking hell! That was close, the Jerries know I'm here," Casey said as he came out from under the table. The waitress came to the table with a bit of paper, the bill.

"L'addition," she said, as she handed it to Nigel.

"Merci, thanks," he said.

She smiled. "Sometimes they send over a bomb to let us know that there will be no peace for us, you are very brave," she said in broken English.

"You speak good English," Nigel said.

"Thank you, for one year before the war, I was in England, Bolton."

"I know Bolton," said Casey. She smiled, but her interest was with Nigel. He paid for the whole meal, the lads were grateful, Bates only had two francs on him, he was waiting for pay day.

She took the money. "Maybe we will meet when you have leave?" she said sweetly.

"You bet," Nigel said, as the men got up to leave.

"Sarge, you pinched my woman, the woman I fooking love! The woman who was going to give me all those babies. Now I've got no-one," Said Casey. He made a sad face.

"You've got me to look after," Derek said.

"So that makes everything fooking alright does it?"

Derek put his arm around his friend, and pulled him close.

"Get off you fooking pervert," Casey said in a mocking way.

There was laughter as the men left the café. Nigel looked back, and his Brigitte was looking his way, waving.

The rain was coming down as the men hurried to where they had parked the buses. As they approached, smoke came from the area. Stretcher bearers were carting off wounded men, some shouting out for help, even as they were being helped. As they rounded a corner, they saw the carnage; horses were lying in the roadway, legs in the air, people were wandering all over the place!

"The convoy has been hit." A military policeman stopped them with a look that could kill. "Where are you lot going?"

"We're the drivers," said Derek.

"Well, some of you won't be going anywhere tonight, because some of the buses were hit," the policeman pointed out. Nigel could see that his bus was blasted in two, the rest of the boys' buses were intact. Nigel went over to a sergeant with a clipboard, and was told that because his bus was beyond repair, he was lucky to be staying here in Pops for a few days, and to report to an address in town, where he could billet for rest and recuperation, until a new bus was allocated to him. He felt happy; maybe he would see his new-found waitress again?

"Lucky bastard," Casey said. "See you soon, and leave her alone! My girl, remember!"

"See you," said Bates and Derek, as they were told to mount

234

up. They waved as the convoy pulled out of town, and headed for Ypres. He heard an officer say that Sergeant Wilson was needed at headquarters.

Nigel made his way through the town past lots of estaminets, past the house called TOC H, he remembered reading about. He made a mental note to visit the place the first opportunity he had. He found the address, and was shown to a small room in the attic, with a little bed, chair, and a small chest of drawers, with a bowl for washing, and little else. He took off his pack, and lay on his bed, and drifted away, hearing thuds and explosions that woke him up from time to time.

It was dark when he woke up; he glanced out of the window, into the streets. Lots of activity, another horse and cart convoy was passing through, on the way to the front line. He sprinkled water over his face and wandered down the rickety stairs that creaked at every step. He saw no-one in the house; he saw no sign of the old thin woman who had opened the door to him earlier. She hadn't spoken much. "Votre chambre," she had said with no warmth at all in her voice. Her expression was one of not caring, maybe the war had done this to her.

"Thank you," he had said, as he walked into the attic room. But she had already gone down the stairs. He peered over the top banister and saw her go out into the street. Now, he decided he would go back to the estaminet café François. In places the noise was very loud, as soldiers went in and out of cafés. Boisterous laughter ensued, all having a good time, and in some cases their last.

She saw him as he entered, and made a bee line for him. "You came back fast, for me maybe?" she said, and her face lit up like a sun in the morning.

"Yes for you, and for some more eggs," he laughed. She led him to a table near the window, with just two seats. A tired looking soldier was eating his supper, and a bottle of red cheap wine was being poured into a glass. "Mind if I join you?" Nigel asked.

"Sit," he said, abruptly it seemed. Nigel took off his hat, and undid his tunic.

"I'm going to die," the man blurted out, between a mouthful of food. "Ain't got long now." He looked sad. Nigel was taken aback, and at first, lost for words.

"A week maybe, then I'll be gone forever, should never have done it."

"Done what?" Nigel said at last.

"Joined up," the soldier said, as though it was expected that Nigel knew what he was talking about. "Joined up," he repeated, "made a mistake there. Bloody idiot, I am an IDIOT!" he shouted at the top of his voice. The whole café went into a hush for a moment, as everyone looked over at Nigel's table.

Nigel felt embarrassed. The fat lady muttered something to the waitress, without looking up, and she looked over at the table.

"I'm doomed, fucked, knackered, for the scrap heap, and I'm only nineteen! Fucking nineteen years old!" He looked at his food for a second, and pushed the plate away. "Wine, have some wine," he ordered, and poured some into Nigel's glass. He drank his down in one, put ten francs to one side, and handed a wad of notes to Nigel.

"Take this," he said. "I won't need it where I'm going. All my mates are gone, DEAD, and soon I'll be with them. Have the rest of the bottle." He got up to leave.

"Where are you going my friend?"

"To my death," the unknown soldier said, as he walked out of the café. Nigel shook his head in disbelief, as the waitress came with his meal.

"I put an extra egg for you," she said, with her teeth showing in a wide smile.

"Thanks. What's your name?"

"Mary, but here in Belgium, it's Marie. And you?"

"Nigel," he said, picking up a bit of bread and dipping it into the egg, "Maythorn, from Southampton, Sergeant, first class."

"Marie, Marie," the old woman shouted, "Le cliente, le cliente," and pointed to a table by the door.

"I will see you when I finish work, I finish at ten o'clock," she whispered.

"It's a date," Nigel said enthusiastically. He drank the remaining wine and was lost in thought after his meal. He had long ago forgotten his time-travelling exploits. The man who was supposed to meet him had never materialised. His hopes of getting back home had vanished long ago. He was determined to last out the war, and with his knowledge, he would avoid getting into any danger. He knew that the Battle of the Somme was coming up in a week or so's time. But he was nowhere near the Somme, and that's the way he wanted it. Driving to and fro from the port to the Front was just the way to avoid the danger that was out there, he was glad that he wasn't in the Infantry! After the war he was going to go into business, and find a wife, he had it all planned out. He was offered drinks, but declined, everyone was having a good time.

"Nous fermons, close, close," the old lady shouted out. She came to each table and joked with the men, as she helped collect the bottles and glasses, she was a different woman now it was closing time. The old dear seemed to have taken on a new personality, a nice one, at closing time, all night she had been grumpy it had seemed.

"I'll meet you in fifteen minutes outside the old church just down the street," the waitress whispered.

"I'll be there." Nigel put on his hat, did up his jacket, paid the bill, and waved as he walked out of the café.

Two streets away the bomb blew two cafés to smithereens, so sudden, same as before, a whoosh, then an almighty explosion!

He hurried to see if he could help, it was serious, casualties were lying all over the place. Men with arms and legs missing, people crying. He wandered passed the dead and dying amid smoke and debris. A soldier with blood all over his face and front lay near a broken door, covered with dust and bits of bricks. Nigel noticed that he was the soldier he had met in the café just an hour before.

"You alright?" Nigel bent down, and then got down on his knees.

He looked up, and recognised Nigel, his bloody hand

grasped Nigel's jacket. "I told you, didn't I? I told you I would die. Bloody war." His head slumped to one side, he had taken his last breath.

Nigel already knew about the havoc the First World War played on mankind, but this was something new to him, his first full acknowledgement of death before his very eyes.

Even though he hadn't really known this man, a tear formed in his eye, as he made his way to the church. She was standing near the gate, she looked different now, the coat was shabby, and her dress had seen better days.

"Sorry I'm a little late, the bomb over there," he pointed toward the smoke, "killed a soldier I knew. I had to stay with him."

"It's a shame, good men die."

"Yes, it was the man who was sitting with me in your café, remember?"

"Yes, I remember, he had told me also, that he will die, many times."

"Well, he did, he died tonight," Nigel said.

"It's the war," she replied. She took his hand and led him down the damp road. It had stopped raining, there was a smell of cordite in the air. The houses were shabby with marks of shrapnel here and there, some completely destroyed. Laughter could be heard drifting out of some houses, as men escaped the rigours of war for a few days, or in some cases, hours! Bent, shabby women cooked eggs and chips, cheap beer and wine flowed.

"Where are we going?" he asked at last.

"We are going to where I live. We can talk and I have some beer or wine for you, sergeant."

"My name's Nigel."

"Yes, and you are my boy-friend, is that true?"

"Of course I am, if you want me to be," he said, squeezing her hand.

"It is not far, I live in Rue Gasthuisstraat, number ten. I lived with my uncle and aunty, but they are gone for a while, to visit friends in Proven. I am alone for now." Her smile lit up the drab night. She stopped abruptly at a badly scarred house next door to a shop still open and selling all sorts of things; postcards, pots and pans, clothes, bon-bons, cigarettes, beer!

A miserable looking man standing at the doorway of his shop was plying for trade. "Come in sergeant, all good things to buy, knickers for the wife, cigarettes for your father, blouses for your mother, postcards, cigarettes for your father, blouses for your mother…" he repeated non stop, not talking to anyone in particular, just talking to the night.

Marie tugged at Nigel, went swiftly inside the door, and she shut out the world. With a sigh, "It's the war," she muttered.

She lit a lamp and adjusted the wick then put a glass globe over the flame. The glows showed a dirty room, a table, chairs, fireplace with the remnants of a fire.

"Take off your coat and relax, I will get the wine," she ordered, as she put a log on the fire, then went into another room. He took off his jacket and put it on the back of a chair then he sat down watching the log crackling in the fireplace.

She appeared with two glasses and a bottle of red wine. "This is a better one from my uncle's stock, he won't miss it, he has hundreds. He is so tight my uncle, but I love him just the same. He looked after me when my mother, (his sister,) and my father were killed near the railway station six months ago. They only went for a walk to see the troops arriving, and to give out leaflets for the café, when the Jerries sent over a bomb and they were killed. I hate the Germans I hate them," she repeated.

She had sat next to him, and was poking the fire as she spoke. She was very beautiful in the glow of the lamp, but there was a certain sadness in her eyes, and he saw it.

"Tell me about you, how long have you been here? How long have you been fighting the Boche?"

"Slow down, one question at a time," Nigel laughed.

"But Nigel, we must hurry, we haven't got time, we have to go, as they say, 'double fast', because this could be our last day that we live! Maybe there will be no tomorrow! One moment we are living, loving, laughing and in one moment we are dead! I have seen it oh so many times before. So for me it is 'double fast!" She smiled and took a sip of her wine.

"Have you got a boyfriend?" he asked, not quite knowing how to go with this beautiful girl.

She laughed out loud. "Me, oh yes, I have many boyfriends, I have hundreds, I have the Tommies, they are my boyfriends. They fight for me and for my mother and father, and I look after them, I comfort them while they rest, it is my duty," she said pursing her lips.

"What do you mean, comfort them?" he asked.

"I let them play with me, and I play with them, I wash them, and give them drink and food, then we sleep, and I will satisfy their needs. They are lonely boys; they have left their girlfriends, and wives back home, and I fill in the gap in their lives."

Nigel took another drink, and she refilled the glass. The fire was now catching and she threw another log onto it.

"So you are telling me that you bring home here, soldiers to comfort them, and have sex with them, hundreds of them?"

"Yes," she said, "it's the war, I have to help, this is the only way I know how."

Nigel was flabbergasted. "So I'm not really that special then, I thought I was." Disappointment showed on his face.

"But you are, you are all special, you kill the Jerries who killed my family." She cupped his face.

"And how much do you charge for this comfort?" he blurted out. Her beautiful face changed to one of anger, her smile disappeared like a magician's rabbit!

"Are you calling me a prostitute? You ungrateful bastard. I give you drink, I try to comfort you, and you asked me how much I charge! You have hurt my feelings, so now get out of my house, I will entertain you no longer! I charge nothing, NOTHING!" she screamed. "So GET OUT now."

He stood up. "Sorry, I didn't mean anything, I just thought it strange that a beautiful girl like you would be this way inclined."

"I've told you," she shouted out, "it's the war."

He took her in his arms. "Sorry, I'm sorry," he whispered. She hugged him and cried. He felt her tears on his cheeks.

"Everything will be alright, better times will come when this war is over. Here, wipe your face." He handed her his handkerchief. She took it and sniffed into it.

"Here," he gave her her glass of wine, topping it up, and she sat opposite him.

"I have never taken a franc off any Tommy for my comforts," she retorted.

"I believe you my love, but you must listen to what I have to say, then I will leave. Will you just listen to me?" he implored.

"I will listen," she said quietly, looking down at the floor.

He took her hand. "There is no doubt that you're still in shock and you are mourning the loss of your mother and father."

"Yes it's true, I miss them so much," she interjected, tears appearing in the corners of her blue eyes.

"And you feel so bad, but do you realize it's your fault?"

"My fault, why my fault?"

"Because of your love for them, love so true, love with no reservations, think," he hesitated, "think, if your love for your parents hadn't been so strong, then you wouldn't feel this way now. Love hurts, your mother and father loved you the same, and do you think that they would want to see you this way, suffering? No, they would want you to get on with your life. Comfort yourself, not others, do you realize that a lot of soldiers you have comforted have never seen a German, let alone killed one. There's some of the Tommies who will never go into the Front Line? I've never seen a German, I'm a driver, and I'll be driving from Ypres to the ports transporting troops. I'll never go to the Front Line, like the men in the dumps; hospital orderlies, boot makers, cooks, men who build roads, and lots of others. So not everyone is killing Germans, and although your concern for the comfort of the Tommies might be viewed by some to be good, I believe you are doing yourself a disservice, and your mother and father would certainly disapprove. If you want to do something for the troops, you could be a hospital orderly, or a nurse, they are crying out for women to help with the war effort. Also, there's always the risk of disease. A lot of men go with one woman after another; it's a chance you shouldn't take. And some men would take advantage of your naivety, do you understand?"

She looked up and nodded her head. "Sometimes I have wondered if I am doing the right thing, but what can I do? I must do something. I would like to be a nurse, working in the café is not good for me, but I have no money to go and train in Calais, and I need to help my uncle and aunty, who have looked after me since the Germans killed my mother and…"

"I know," Nigel broke in before she started to cry again. "Look, do you want me to help you, because I can. I don't need this money," he took the wad out of his back pocket, and handed it to her. "The soldier in the café gave it to me, but now I want you to have it. And I'm not paying you for the wine, or any comfort you may offer me, it's for your keep while you are in training to be a nurse. What do you say?"

She smiled for the first time in a while. "Thank you." She bent over and kissed him on the lips. Nigel felt his blood pressure rise!

"I will tell Claudette tomorrow, that I will finish in the café, then I will go to Calais to become a nurse."

"Good," Nigel said, "and no more comforting the Tommies?"

"No, I will see my boyfriend Henry, from before, I think he still wants me."

"Don't tell him anything about your war effort so far," Nigel advised.

"No, no, no," she said, but laughing now. "You will join me in a repas? I will cook you something special, you can drink some beer, and we laugh," she said.

He agreed, and after eating his egg and chips, he drank more beer plus wine, then left. He could have stayed with her, he could have loved her, but Nigel had certain principles. Although on this occasion it had been very hard to adhere to them. They kissed on the doorstep, and he made his way to his attic room alone. The little streets still full of soldiers wandering around aimlessly. In bed he masturbated before going to sleep. 'That's the least I can do,' he thought, for his own comfort.

His head ached; he was woken up abruptly by the old

thin lady shouting at the door. "Go war," she said sneeringly.

"What's the time?" he enquired.

"Go war," she said again, and left abruptly. He got up and sprinkled water on his face, dressed and went down the stairs, she was at the bottom with her hand out.

"Francs, ten," she demanded.

"The army will pay for the room," Nigel said.

"Francs, ten," she said with more determination. Nigel paid her; he was in no mood to argue the point. She snatched the money, put it into a black handbag and walked out of the house.

"Do I get a receipt?" Nigel asked.

"Go war," she muttered.

He went into the street, looked up at the sky, it was a rich blue, not a cloud to be seen.

"What's the time?" he asked the shop keeper standing in the doorway.

"Knickers for the wife, cigarettes for your father, blouse for your mother, postcards, beer?" He twitched as he spoke.

"No, the time please?"

"Buy watch, I show you, come." He took Nigel by his sleeve, and pulled him into the shop and pointed to a tray of watches.

"Very good watches, genuine copies sergeant, two hundred francs."

"Two hundred, that's expensive."

"It's the war," he said, "for you, one hundred and ninety francs!"

"No, cheaper."

"One eighty."

"No, much cheaper."

"This one twenty francs, for you, special price."

"Alright." He saw a white faced watch with black hands. "I'll take that one." He put the watch on his wrist. "Now, what's the time?" he asked as he wound it up.

"Look at church," the man said, and pointed to the church up the street. "You want knickers for the wife?"

"That's all thanks," Nigel said as he left the man on his shop doorstep. His attention was now directed at a group of passing soldiers out for a day's fun.

He made his way past the church and noticed that the church clock was stopped, and he made his way to the café to see if his angel was there.

As he entered he noticed that she was nowhere to be seen, a young girl took his order for a cup of coffee. Men were already sitting eating at long tables, another day in Pops had begun. He enquired as to where Marie was, and the new girl said that she had come in and the patron had sacked her on the spot because she had handed in a week's notice, because she was going to be a nurse, and that she had gone to Calais an hour before.

Nigel drank his coffee, then decided to report to the sergeant who had billeted him near where the convoy had halted the day before. The town was a hive of activity; a convoy was going through the town, not stopping, to the disappointment of the troops heading for the Front. He passed the market square, bombed out houses, when he noticed an estament 'A La Maison de Ville' with bomb damage. He wondered if the bomb had hit whilst men were trying to forget the war? Then he remembered reading a book that said that after the war the town's War Memorial stood on the very spot. And he then remembered seeing the War Memorial when he had taken his pupils on a tour to Flanders Fields, and seeing this very town in two thousand and six. Now here he was with first hand experience of what it was like in war time! If only the people could read his mind, what would they make of him? he pondered. If only they knew, that this war had more than two years to go before the carnage would end. How many more had to die?

A helpless feeling came over him as he approached the place where he had last seen the sergeant with the clipboard. There was no-one around, the sergeant had said a few days, but no instructions as to what time he had to report back, or where! He walked in the sunshine past the shops, along the street where Marie lived, and went to the house number ten, and knocked. There was no reply, so he made his way to the TOC H, Talbot House, a house of recreation, opened for all ranks to come, a time to sit in the garden at the back of the house, and in peacefulness to relax and reflect on their lives. A sign as he went in said in big letters: TO PESSIMISTS. WAY OUT, with a hand pointing to the door.

Soldiers sat reading in the various rooms, some drinking tea. Nigel went upstairs to the attic, where a short service was in progress. He sat in the back and bowed his head, but once again Nigel was thinking about the last time he had seen this attic church, of the visitors and holiday makers reading pamphlets giving out the history. Of him telling the children in his charge to be quiet in this sacred place, back then in two thousand and six.

He made his way down the stairs, and after sitting in the garden for a while, made a cup of tea. He had a talk with a man who he had seen in photographs in war books, the man who started the Toc H House, Tubby Clayton himself!

He told the churchman the story of how his bus had been blown up, and that he had been lucky to have time in Popperingue for a bit of a look around. Although he hadn't needed rest because he hadn't done anything apart from drive from the port of Zeebrugge. He told him that he came from Southampton, had worked as a barman, and bits of small talk, before Nigel thanked Tubby for his time, and left.

It was mid afternoon as he stepped out of the door.

"Nigel," Tubby shouted, "before you go, you said you were just going to wander around. Well my friend, don't go anywhere near the rail-station, the Germans are throwing stuff over, because they know something is in the wind. They know that there will be a push soon, a lot of people were killed at the station in the last day. We lost a very good friend yesterday, Sergeant Wilson, he was top sergeant here in POPS, co-ordinating troop movements and billeting personnel. He died at the station, so don't go near there."

"Thanks for the advice," Nigel said with a slight wave.

'Bloody hell, Sergeant Wilson, no wonder he wasn't there this morning! One minute here, the next minute gone!' he thought.

He had nowhere to go, so he wandered the streets, just watching troops march to war, and other troops march away from it, the striking difference in the two, one column singing on the march, 'It's a long way to Tipperary,' and others, more bawdy ones, men Laughing. Then the men who had fought, with battle fatigue written all over their faces, muddied and bloodied. He saw a sign that said BATHS, TWO FRANCS; he followed the sign down a small corridor that led to a back garden full of rubbish. Another sign, Nigel noticed, was pointing to the ground, and standing with arms folded, was the fattest woman Nigel had ever seen in his life! Her smile showed her broken black teeth, she beckoned him to come to her. "Come, come," she said, "nice time for you sergeant, you very dirty, dirty dog, need wash."

"Yes," Nigel said. "I certainly need a wash."

"Come." She almost pushed him into a room with a steamy tub of water, with a fire nearby with buckets of water boiling, and two more on the side waiting to be poured if needed.

"Get in, put clothes here," she ordered, and pointed to a bench. She helped him with his jacket, then his shirt, and pulled his boots off. He hesitated when he got to his trousers.

"Come on, get in, more clients come soon. Hurry, hurry." She undid his buttons and pulled down his pants. "Now knickers," she demanded.

"No," Nigel protested.

"Yes," she said, smiling, showing her jagged teeth once more. "Big man," she said, "get in."

He went up four steps and lowered himself into the steaming tub. An orgasm of the body came over him.

"Fifteen minutes only," she said as she walked out into the back yard.

The water was hot, he soaped himself down, and plunged in. He could hear a noise coming from next door, laughter, then all was silent for a moment, then the beautiful sound of a mouth organ playing the tune he knew. 'Keep the home fires burning' came wafting through the room.

For a moment he remembered Freda, and wondered if she was keeping her fire burning for him. A sadness descended for a moment, as he looked up at the beam in the ceiling that looked like it could break at any moment.

The fat woman came back from the back yard, and watched him for a few minutes from a rickety chair.

"Now you want woman? I can satisfy my clients very well," she said, once more with her smile, from the doorway.

"No thank you, I'm fine," he said defensively.

"Yes, you wait and see," she disappeared after walking past the tub and tapping him on the head lightly.

Two minutes passed, and Nigel was thinking of getting out and making a run for it, when a beautiful young girl with short blond hair, naked as the day she was born, came into the room, came up the steps and entered the tub.

"Hello Tommie. My name is Henrietta, it is very nice to meet you. I am nineteen, and clean, no diseases, no V.D." She smiled and thrust her hand towards him. He smiled, her breasts floated on the water like water melons. She pulled his hands to her breasts, and her hand plunged into the tub, and found Nigel's manhood.

"You like?" she said. Nigel had to admit that he did, thinking of Freda had enlarged his penis, and now he was in heaven! His hand went between her legs and found her softness, they

just smiled at one another. It was surreal. 'This is living,' he thought.

"Time up," the fat woman said, without looking. She had clean towels in her arms. "Finish off in bedroom," she said matter-of-factly.

"Come," the young girl said.

'I'd like to! Nigel thought. She took his hand, they got out of the tub, she towelled him down in a gentle way, picked up his clothes, and led him through the bathroom to the bedroom on the side, with a single bed with blankets that were wearing thin. "Now we do it," she said, laying down and spreading her legs.

"Like a fooking rat up a drain," he heard Casey say in his head, as he fulfilled his desire. She moaned, but it seemed to be very put on. He couldn't be that good, he thought. "You come, I come, you happy, I happy, yes?"

"Yes," was all Nigel could say. The woman came into the doorway and said something to the girl that he couldn't understand, and then she helped Nigel get dressed.

"You take care of yourself, don't get killed."

"I'll try not to. Do you do this all the time?" he asked as he was about to leave.

"Yes, every day but not before the soldiers came…"

"It's the war," he interrupted.

"Yes, it's the war," she mumbled, and kissed him on the cheek as he went through the bathroom to the back door. Another soldier was soaking, they nodded as he passed. Outside he paid two francs for the bath and a further three francs for the girl.

"Come again soon Tommie boy," she said, "don't get killed."

"Thanks," he said, "I won't."

He overheard the woman saying to the soldier in the tub, "Now you want woman?" as he turned the corner. The street was bustling like before as Nigel made his way down towards the church. He felt a new man, clean and satisfied, and in a way, happy. What an experience he had just had. He felt sorry for the girl, but everyone had to make a living in these dreadful times, he thought.

He wandered into a café, and ordered a beer, and chips and eggs. The same as other cafés, men drinking, messing with the waitress, telling jokes, killing time before they themselves would get killed. Time was passing; he talked with men from different regiments, was told what it was like on the front line, talk about wives at home. Girlfriends' letters were read, some men burst into song, as the wine and beer flowed. He looked at his new watch, (his old one in his pocket) and at last set the time, it was six thirty five. He was feeling tired, but ordered another three beers for his new-found friends. The beer was reciprocated, and soldiers returning to the front line spent all their money, no need for money in the line.

At eight thirty Nigel decided to call it a day, only because the café was closing. He said his goodbyes, and staggered out into the evening chill. The moon obligingly showed him the way home. It

248

had been a wonderful day, he enjoyed every moment of it. He got to his attic room with his head buzzing, and fully clothed, lay on his bed. There was no need for him to do what he did the night before, and soon he fell into a deep sleep.

"Oh, what a perfect day," he sang to himself before drifting off, a song he remembered back in his own time.

Her 'witch-like' face looking down at him startled him back to life. "Go war, go war," she sneered, "ten francs you pay for room, ten francs."

"Let me get up first," Nigel sneered back.

She left the room. As he was getting his pack together, he heard a commotion coming from downstairs. He went out and looked down. A portly woman was arguing with the witch woman, and she gave her a smack around her face and on the back of her head. The witch woman scuttled out of the door, and the portly woman came up the stairs to meet Nigel, she was really angry.

"Bloody woman," she blurted out, then explained that she had been called away to help her daughter who was expecting a baby. And each time she was called away, this woman would come to the house and charge the soldiers billeted with her money for the room, when the army paid her for the soldiers' stay.

"She is a bloody nuisance. Did she get money off you?" she asked.

"Yes, ten francs," he admitted.

"Lucky I came home sooner, many soldiers have paid her more! I can't give you the money back; you will have to get the police to arrest her. I can't do it, she is my friend's aunty, and I will not do it, but when I'm away she comes back again and again. Then I find out and hit her again! Bloody nuisance."

"It's the war," Nigel said, "everything that happens these days, it's because of this blasted war."

"Yes, it is," she agreed.

"I will be leaving now, I've been here for two nights." He signed a chit saying two nights, then she would get paid by presenting the chit to the army headquarters.

"Thank you, the bed was comfortable," he said as a parting shot, and went out into the street.

He made his way past the church, past the café where he had met Marie, and up to where he had parked his bus that had been blown sky high. He was surprised to see another convoy in its place. The sergeant, a new one, took Nigel's name and told him that a new lorry would be waiting for him in Ypres and told him to get on the bus with men from an infantry regiment, going up the line. He went up on the open top deck, and waited for the convoy to start off. He sat down at the front, and looked over to see the driver getting in the cab.

"Casey, you bastard," he shouted down.

The driver stopped and looked up, with a broad smile he said, "Fooking hell sarge, where did you fooking come from?" he laughed. "See you in Wipers," he said as he got in the driver's seat.

The men waved, and at times shouted obscenities to passing soldiers heading the other way. They shouted out names of cafés recommended, and certain bordellos to be avoided. The road was busy with all sorts of buses, columns of soldiers, horse drawn timber wagons. It took just over an hour to get to Ypres, and the town was almost demolished. The Cloth Hall, he remembered when he had taken his class to the museum there, was just about recognisable, it had been bombed, and just stood in a sort of defiance. Rubble was strewn everywhere. Orders to get off the bus and line up, as the men were to go straight to the front line, a march along the Menin Road. They would relieve a regiment on the line by midnight.

"Line up," shouted a sergeant. An officer ordered Nigel to get his men in marching order.

"I'm not in this lot, I'm a driver sir. I only got a lift here to pick up a new wagon. Mine was blown up in Pops!"

The officer dismissed him. He went to the front of the bus and saw Casey getting out of the driving seat.

"Casey, where's our officer in charge?"

"Over there," he pointed, "there's new buses waiting around the street. We have to go within the hour, to a place called Albert, near

250

the River Somme, someone told me. Fooking hell, there's no rest for the wicked. How did you get on in Pops? Nice fooking time, I bet?"

"Yes, it was great; I'll tell you about it later, got to find my vehicle."

The officer put him in the picture; the convoy would set off in two hours, for Albert. So he was told to eat then get ready for a long drive. The officer pointed out his new bus and dismissed him until three o'clock when the convoy would leave. Nigel found Casey, Derek and Bates, and they all went looking for a meal in the devastated town of Ypres.

Casey told of their billets the night before. "Fooking terrible shit hole, fooking fleas, in the battlements of old walls," he moaned. Nigel watched their faces, mouths open wide, as he recounted the story of the waitress, then the bath and the naked girl."

"Fooking hell, I missed all that, I slept with him," he pointed at Derek, "and Master Bates here."

"Don't call me Master Bates, I've told you before," he feigned anger.

"Well, you are fooking young, no-one would call you 'Mister -not at seventeen, you are a Master until you are twenty one, and your name is fooking BATES, so you're Master Bates, so fook you!"

"You'd like to," said Derek, getting the last word once again. All the men laughed.

They found a dreary café, and had the normal egg and chips, and coffee. Nigel looked at his pals, and studied each one. What great guys they were, just young men starting off in life, and having to fight. Would they all survive? he wondered.

Explosions were heard, some in the distance, some closer, and one very close, just two streets away. After a bit of banter with the waitress, the men left.

"Did you see that?" Casey enthused. "She fooking fancied me, if only I had the time, I'd be up her-"

"Like A RAT UP A DRAIN," the three men chorused. He shook his head, and raised his fist in mock anger.

"You know sarge," Derek said as they walked ahead, leaving Casey and Bates looking in a shop window, "he's never done it."

"Done what?"

"He's never been with a woman, it's all bravado, he's never had a shag in his life."

"Poor bastard," said Nigel.

The men of the regiment were having their photograph taken, so Nigel and his friends joined them at the back. He put his arm around Casey, and just at the moment the photograph was taken, a soldier stood in front of Nigel!

The convoy moved off at the appointed time, he got used to his bus quickly, and soon was enjoying the sights of the countryside. They drove non-stop, and it was dark when they arrived at a camp near the town of Albert. Nigel knew that this was very near where the Battle of the Somme would take place in just a few days. The build up of troops was massive, and thousands would be dead in just a short time, but there was nothing Nigel could do.

A meal was waiting for the men, after eating there was little to do but sit in groups and chat and by ten o'clock most of the men were asleep. Before he drifted off, he wondered who was in the attic room he had had the night before. Or if they had been conned yet by the witch face woman! He wondered how many men had used the facilities of the two franc bath, and the young girl? He could imagine men in the Talbot House, writing letters home or reading, passing a little time in peace, in a world full of war.

It was raining, not normal rain, more like pouring, a cape-day.

At least there would be no drills or physical training. There was a bombardment going on, it was constant, the smoke-filled horizon seemed like a giant wave coming close and would soon drown everyone and every thing.

Nigel had met up with his chums, and they were all huddled around talking, when an officer with a regimental Sergeant Major approached.

"Sergeant, you and your three men have just volunteered for an extra duty. We need you to go up the line with the mail, the mail unit lads have just been killed, the bloody lot of them. The hand cart is over at the letter sorting tent, so go over there and you will receive further instructions."

The four men stood at attention and saluted the officer.

"Not fair," said Bates, "why us? We're drivers."

"No driving today," Derek pointed out.

"Fook the army, they give us no rest, like Bates has said, why us? Look at all these lazy fooking bastards sitting around doing fook all, not fair."

"NOW", the Sergeant Major shouted as he went out the door.

They loaded up the hand cart with mail bags and parcels, covered it with a tarpaulin, and set off for the front line, which according to the map they had been given, was miles away.

It rained and it rained.

"We've become fooking horses," Casey moaned, but the smile was still there. Four men who had become friends, then pals, then 'brothers', pushed the mail cart through the rain, past burned out houses, dead animals, garbage of all descriptions, overturned lorries, towards the men eagerly awaiting news from loved ones at home.

They stopped in a wood, a lot of the trees had been stripped of their bark because of the constant explosions, but there was enough coverage for the headquarters to be, before the lines began, second line or support line, then the front line, through communication trenches. They unloaded the cart, because this was as far as it would go, the men would now have to carry the bags into the lines.

With more instruction, the men set off through the trenches to the front line. It was still raining; thunder and lightning streaked across the sky. The gunfire was deafening, just like the descriptions in the war books that Nigel had read over and over again, but this was the real thing! The smell you couldn't get from a book, the misery cannot be understood by reading it.

They dropped off bags at different locations, and soon after talking briefly to the men in the trenches, full of water in some places, they made their way back through the mud and filth.

The lightning wasn't in the sky, but in Nigel's head, a sensation came over him that he had never experienced, there was no pain, a flair lit up the sky and made the raindrops glisten.

He lay in a pot hole full of water; he tried to focus his eyes, and there was Casey just two feet from him, a smile on his face, covered completely with mud.

"What happened Case?" he mouthed, but no sound came out. "What happened?" he mouthed out again. Case just smiled on the edge of the hole. Nigel put his hand towards Casey's face. "You've got blood on your face my friend, just there." He touched his face, and the head rolled down into the hole and sank into the mud.

Panic set in. "What happened?" he screamed.

"We've been blown up, we're dead," shouted Bates from somewhere near, and spoke no more. There was no sign of Derek, just an arm lay, with the fingers twitching, in the smoke-filled hole.

Nigel drifted off, and came to in a tent. He lay his head over to one side, and saw other men lying on beds, and the smell of disinfectant was strong in his nostrils. He looked down and saw that his legs were gone, and he was bandaged up to his neck. Somewhere in the depths of his brain, he heard his name.

"So you became a nurse Marie, you're a good girl, you made it," he said to the nurse standing near him. "Freda, nice of you to come and see me. I love you, you know," he whispered. "Bill, where have you been? I've been waiting for years to see you again. Bill, are you going to take me home?" Nigel held his head, as the pain was acute, darkness descended over him.

"He's hallucinating" the nurse said to her colleague, "there's nothing more we can do for him, he won't last the night." She pointed, "Internal injuries. I've found his watch in his pocket, and put it on his wrist, it stopped at four minutes past twelve, that must have been the time the bomb blew him up.

Poor sod." She looked sad as she attended to other wounded soldiers.

"When will it all end? this is madness, this killing has to stop. When will mankind learn to live, love and laugh together? At the moment it's only hatred, killing! "

"C'est la guerre!" said the French soldier.

"I know it's the war, this bloody war," the nurse said.

Chapter 13

BACK HOME

A flash of light flashed through his head. He lay there covered in bricks and brick dust. He opened his eyes, his head hurt.

"Nigel, are you alright? Nigel?" her voice sounded anxious, she lifted his head to look at the bump, growing bigger before her eyes. "Bloody hell Nigel be careful, you could have hurt yourself badly." He focused his eyes.

"Get up," Jane ordered, she pulled him to the sitting position, and brushed him down.

"My legs, my legs," he shouted.

"What's wrong with your legs? Get up!" He looked down, he was intact!

"Let's get out of this chimney breast, before more bricks fall on you. Your inquisitiveness will be your downfall," she admonished.

"Jane it's you, Jane, my Jane."

"Well, who else would it be?"

He grabbed her, kissed her, hugged her. "Jane," he said over and over again. Tears ran down his face making runways through the dust.

"Nigel, what's up with you, darling? It's me, I'm here with you." She looked at him with concern, brushing more brick dust off him. He stood up, and walked into the room, and noticed the picture of the man with the golden helmet on the wall, the chest of drawers on the other side of the room.

"I'm back," he said excitedly, "I'm here." He grabbed Jane again."You won't believe it, I can tell you, you won't believe it," he repeated.

"Oh, I will, let's get out of here, it's dangerous, this place is falling apart. You were lucky that only a few bricks fell on you, one hit you here." She touched his bump.

"Ow," he said. Then having felt it himself, said, "That's nothing, worst things have happened."

He remembered a film he had once seen called A Wonderful Life, with James Stewart, and felt he was reliving the moment: James Stewart had realized that he had come back from the past, and all he thought he had lost was still there!

Nigel burst out laughing, "I made it, I made it!" He grabbed a startled Jane and danced the whole length of the room, hugging and kissing her.

She was enjoying it, but with some concern. "Nigel, what's got into you?" she laughed.

"I love you, I love you darling woman, I missed you, I missed you like crazy!"

"Missed me, what do you mean? How can you miss me? I haven't been anywhere?"

"But I have."

"When?"

"In that chimney," he pointed, "it was an adventure beyond anything I've ever had, beyond comprehension."

"Sit down here," she ordered, and they sat on the settee. "You call being hit on the head with a couple of bricks an adventure? Are you sure you're alright? Shall I take you to the Accident and Emergency at the hospital? Maybe you have injured your brain, have you got a headache?"

"No darling, I'm fine." He touched her face.

"Well, don't talk in this strange way, it's frightening me." She touched his bump again. "It's not bleeding, lucky escape. You really got me going; I was over there looking at the chest of drawers," she pointed, "when you said that you were going into

257

the chimney breast," she pointed again. "'Did you hear me Jane?' you said. I replied, telling you not to be long, that we haven't got all day, then I went back to the drawer. A second later, this almighty crash and here you are covered with bloody brick dust, and been hit on the head, poor darling. It's dangerous, let's go. I don't like this house."

"Just a second or so ago, you say?"

"Yes, just two or three minutes ago."

He looked at his watch, it said eight minutes past twelve. "It's working again," he said with a smile.

"I didn't know there was anything wrong with it in the first place. How are you feeling now, Nigel?"

"I feel great, just great, let's go," he said, "I've had enough excitement for one day. Yes, I'll say that again, enough excitement to last me for the rest of my life!"

They walked to the door that led to the passageway, when Nigel said that he would just wash the dust out of his eyes. The water cooled his face. "I'm home," he muttered, "I made it without Bill's help," he said to himself in the mirror. "A dream, was it all a dream?" But it couldn't have been, those years working behind the bar, the loving with Freda, and Fanny? He felt guilty for a moment. The army, the war, what had happened? Was it just in his mind? What about Zone Two, the parallel world? How was all this possible in just a second when Jane was with him as he lay on the floor in the chimney breast? He would have to keep all this to himself, he realized. He had lived it, he was certain of that, but who would believe him? No-one, too far-fetched, best forgotten, if that was at all possible.

He shook his head, felt the bump, it wasn't very painful, then he went into the hallway. He looked down, that was where the Andersons' luggage was, with tags that said Titanic.

She was waiting at the front door. "Feel OK love?" she enquired.

"Yes, I'm fine, I won't be a minute."

She gave a sigh, as he walked into the room that had imprisoned him once, where he had put on his invisible suit. He went to the end of the room, and looked to see if the crack in the partition was there, where he had heard the officer condemn him for being a traitor, but there was no crack. He went to the window and looked out, the guards were there, but only in his mind. Instead, he saw Jane standing on the veranda looking over the estate towards the fountain, where he had sheltered from the rain.

"Come on Nigel, I'm hungry, let's go, haven't you seen enough? There's no way that I want to live here," she shouted through the front door.

"Coming dear," he said in mock obeyance. He closed the big door and locked it.

"Well, that's that then, you're not interested?"

She didn't speak, just gave him a certain look that answered his question. They got to the car. "You're hungry you said?"

"Yes, I didn't have breakfast this morning."

"Let's go to the pub for a bar lunch," he suggested, "and I'm sure you will drive us home if I had a couple of pints, my adorable, beautiful, obligingly, non-drinking, magnificent woman."

"You haven't changed; you've always had a way with words."

"Me?" Nigel said, feigning innocence. They both laughed out loud, Nigel was truly back home.

Before he got into the car, he turned back to look at the house. 'Did I really travel back in time?' he wondered. In his mind's eye he saw Bertie in his nineteen twelve car, he recalled the very words he had spoken: "I'm Mr. Anderson's personal assistant-housekeeper." He stood at the very spot where he had parked his car, as he had waited for the officer who was in the house for the meeting in nineteen sixteen, and where he was arrested by the two guards. He remembered Mr. and Mrs. Bactram, who were going to Poland in nineteen thirty eight, and waving goodbye to the Andersons when they left for America! Vivid memories, it was no dream, he had lived it, yet his body had gone nowhere! He looked at the blue sky, streaked with jet vapours.

"A jet aircraft, it's flying to some far distant land," he shouted excitedly.

"So what dear, you say that as if you have never seen a jet before."

"It's been awhile," he blurted out. She shook her head in disbelief. He stood there looking towards the house that he had once bought, his home, even though it was only for a short time. He remembered the loneliness he had endured living in it.

"This house is dangerous my dear, I agree with you, it's not for us. It seems it's always being struck by lightning, like it was last night, next time I think it will cause a fire, who knows it could burn to the ground! Anyhow, I'm glad that we have had a look at it, it's too big for us really, it's a rich man's mansion, we would need at least three gardeners full time."

"True, and you said that you would do the gardening with your brother, remember? I didn't think you would."

"I know," Nigel laughed. "Brother, I have a brother, and a mother," he said, pulling his mobile phone from his pocket. He dialled the number, and heard his mother's voice.

"Mum, it's me Nigel, how are you? How's Dad? I'm coming to see you now, don't go anywhere."

"Mum and dad are home, I've got to see them again," he said, with grim determination in his voice.

"But you only saw them a couple of hours ago. Nigel are you sure you're alright? You're acting very strange darling, I'm concerned, I'm sure that hit on your head has affected you. I'm taking you to the hospital."

"No, I'm alright," he protested, "get in the car; we'll pop in home on our way to the pub." The wheels crunched the gravel on the drive. As they passed the dried up fountain Nigel said, "Well, that's that then, you would never have been happy living in that 'motel' anyhow, would you?"

"Motel?"

"Yes, your words, Bates Motel from the film PSYCHO." They both laughed as they drove down the avenue with the trees bending over like a tunnel, branches caressing in a green embrace. He stopped the car to open the big iron gates, the house sign THE BRIARS, was rusting and was hardly readable; time had taken its toll.

He got back into the car, drove it into the lane, got out to close the gate for the last time, and looked up the drive. The house somehow looked forlorn, the happy days it once knew, the garden parties, the hope and aspirations of the people who had lived there, gone in the web of time. Nigel got into the car, and drove down Eastern Hill towards home.

They both went in to see Nigel's mother and father, who were sitting at the kitchen table. Nigel's face lit up on seeing them again. He hugged his mother and kissed her, and shook his father's hand vigorously. They both looked surprised by his excitement.

"He's been like that since he hit his head, or put it this way; a brick fell on him in the blasted fireplace."

Nigel just stood and smiled. Jane explained how Nigel had gone in the chimney breast in the house, and the chimney had been hit by lightning in the storm the night before.

"Dangerous, but he would go into it, being inquisitive again, you know what he's like Mum."

She looked at her son, felt the bump, and put some ointment on it, after wiping away some dust he had missed.

"Don't fuss Mother," Nigel protested.

"Sit down, let's have a nice cup of tea and tell us what you think of the house, will you buy the place?" his father asked.

They sat down, and Nigel explained that the house was too big for them. But he was glad that he had taken the time to look it over, it was an experience. It had been a great house in its time and some wonderful people had lived there. It had been an army headquarters during both wars, Brian the landlord from the Fox and Hounds had told him all about the history.

"I've been up there before," said Nigel's father.

"I know Dad, you've told me."

"Yes, I believe I did, nice people I remember."

"I don't like the place," Jane blurted, "it's spooky if you ask me, I felt ill at ease, felt it was haunted. I had a feeling that there was a woman there at one time."

"What, a ghost you mean?"

"I didn't see a ghost, but it was a strange feeling. I call it Bates Motel from that film."

"PSYCHO," Nigel broke in, they all laughed.

The woman could have been Freda; she had slept there and visited him, Nigel thought. He looked at his mother and father with love; he had thought that he had lost them forever at one time. Now everything was back to normal. He asked his mother about his brother, and was told that he was away working. But she wanted to know why Nigel was asking these questions. His father pointed out that he was asking questions as though he'd been away for years, and he had only left the house hours ago!

"I've been forgetful just lately," Nigel confessed. He then thought about himself in Zone Two, Simon, how he was going through a difficult time of forgetfulness with Janice when they met up. Was it a dream? Was it the hit on the head? It had seemed so real, but years, how could he have been away for years?

They didn't go to the pub that afternoon, but had a meal, the four of them. Afterwards, they went out in the garden and sat in the sun. Nigel's father opened a bottle of wine and a few cans of beer and they talked about the forthcoming wedding, the honeymoon and babies, to Nigel's embarrassment. Mum told stories about Nigel when he was small, once again making him embarrassed. The day was warm, the sky blue, and Nigel enjoyed himself back with his loved ones. Jane mentioned the house that she wanted to buy on Moreland Road.

At last Jane said that she wanted to go home, she had a couple of hours' marking to do for her English class and she needed to get ready for their evening at the Fox, a band and karaoke after a meal with wine, she had decided.

"You have some wonderful ideas my darling," Nigel had said, "are you sure you're alright in the head?"

"Such compliments." He kissed her as she got out of the car, then waved as she went up the path to her home. As he drove home again, he passed Moreland Road, and slowed down to look at the house that Jane wanted to buy. Mike the Estate Agent was just about to get into his car in the drive. Nigel stopped and parked his car along the road, and walked back to the house.

"Hello Mike, thought you were having the weekend off?" He handed over the mansion keys.

"So did I, but I've had a really busy time today. I was here yesterday, and I left my portfolio on the table. Been looking for the damn thing all morning, then I remembered I had left it here, so I've just retrieved it," he said, showing Nigel the bundle of papers in a folder.

"What do you think then?" he enquired.

"About what?"

"The mansion, nice place, yes?"

"Nice place, but bloody dangerous, look," he pointed to the bump on his head. "Need insurance to go in there!"

"Hell, what happened?" Mike looked concerned.

"The big fireplace you know, I went inside and the bloody chimney fell on me, knocked me out, could have killed me!"

"Hell, I didn't realize, I'm so sorry, you're not going to sue, are you? The lightning that hit last night must have caused more damage than I realized, I'm very sorry."

"Don't worry I won't sue, I was lucky my fiancée was with me. It was my fault, I should have been more careful. But we will not be buying it, Jane said. She doesn't like the place at all; you know what women are like? She said it was spooky and said it was like Bates Motel." He shrugged. "But we are interested in buying another house, is this place sold?"

"No, not at the moment, the people I showed it to yesterday weren't sure, and I don't think they will raise the deposits anyhow."

"Well, that's good because I believe my Jane has her eyes on this place. Could we have a look at it?"

"Sure, you can see it right now if you want to."

They went in, and Nigel recognised it straight away. He could picture Janice in the kitchen talking to her friend.

"I believe this is for us, when do you think we could move in if we bought it?"

Mike looked at his portfolio, and calculated, then said, "Maybe late May, May twenty first. No, that's not right, it's April now, April, May. Yes, I will say that we could exchange contracts on June the first."

"That's incredible," Nigel said, as he remembered Janice. Saying that she would be moving in on the same date, in that other zone. "That would be fine; we will come to look over the place tomorrow after work, if that's OK with you, Mike. Then we will pay the deposit straight away."

"That's great; at what time do you want me to be here?"

"Five o'clock." Five o'clock was decided, and the men shook on it, and went outside.

"Nice place here," Mike said.

"You say that about all the properties you sell," Nigel said with a laugh.

"You're right," Mike smiled back, "but it is nice, you have to admit, compact, as compared to the mansion."

"That's for sure. Sorry about that place, you will have to tell your clients now I expect."

"It's my job; some places are harder to sell than others. But they all sell in the end, persistence it's called. But it's not helped by people saying that the place is haunted, puts would-be buyers off. The lady who owns the mansion is convinced she's seen a ghost! And she has told me, I can tell you now that I know you're not buying it, that in two thousand and one, six years ago, a man appeared at a fancy dress party they were having, and warned them that the house would burn down this year! Yes, that's what she said, this year some time, ridiculous! But I believe she's a bit schizo herself, it makes my job the more difficult. Then there was the other warning, but anyhow I'm boring you."

"No you're not, what else?"

"Oh, there was another occasion with a warning about going to the U.S. about her son and the Twin Towers! All rubbish, but it makes selling harder."

"I agree," Nigel said, "it sounds bloody crazy to me, very far-fetched. Anyhow, I have to go, got a date with a wonderful woman tonight, so got to get washed and brushed up." He felt his chin. "And a shave, yes, I need a shave, and a bath after the chimney debacle."

"Sorry about that," Mike said again. "What were you doing in there anyhow?"

"I saw these marks and figures on the inside of the chimney breast, couldn't make them out at first, they were covered in soot. So I touched the brickwork, and that's what happened," he pointed to his head.

"I saw those signs," Mike suddenly remembered. "It's a wonder you didn't recognised them."

"What do you mean?" Nigel asked.

"I went inside that chimney breast when I first took the house on the books, and I saw the writing, your name."

"My name?" Nigel repeated.

"Yes, your name was inscribed in the cement: NIGEL, and a date nineteen hundred and twelve!"

"Really?" Nigel gulped. "Bloody incredible, bloody amazing!"

"Maybe someone of your namesake lived there in that year. It's not unusual for people to do that kind of thing, making their mark so to speak. Anyhow, must get on, see you at five tomorrow."

Mike got in his car, and Nigel headed home.

Maybe Gerald inscribed it while repairing the chimney, in gratitude of what had happened. His family had been saved, so that only proved that it wasn't a dream, he must have travelled back in time. His thoughts were verified as he got undressed to have his bath, because the belt was still around his waist, he had got so used to wearing it he didn't notice that he still had it on. He put it in the bottom of the wardrobe, covered it up with some clothes, and forgot about it, as time went by.

At the Fox and Hounds the car park was filling up, music nights were popular. Over the years the main structure of the pub had hardly changed. Nigel noticed at times he seemed to be deep in thought, and 'miles away', as Jane put it.

He told her of his meeting with Mike the Estate Agent, how he had handed back the keys, and looked at the Moreland Road house, and of the meeting to take place on Monday at five pm.

She looked happy, he pictured Janice sitting in front of him, just like Jane was doing then. They both enjoyed the evening singing and enjoying themselves.

He stayed with her at her house, after returning home briefly to get his school clothes for the next day. It had certainly been a busy day, and at times as he lay beside her, he wondered if what he had experienced was true, or was he going insane?

He quietly got up and went to the Window and looked out across the fields lit up by a lonely moon. The sadness he had endured, the happiness he had had on holiday with Bill! The fear of prison, and the mental hospital, the thrill of Fanny, and Freda! The adoration of friends, who had thought him a genius of predictions! The laughter he had given out to all those people when he had sung songs from Elton John, the Beatles: 'I wanna hold your hand! Yea, Yea!' The talks and drinks with his friend Gerald, the comradeship of war time! A life-time in just a second, just one split second of time-travel!

But it was pointless in another respect, because he had to keep it to himself, no-one would believe a word of it, he had experienced that. The only way Gerald had believed him was the demonstration of the invisible suit. Now, he had nothing to prove his experience to anyone, even if he wanted to. He decided that he would tell no-one, but there were a few things he had to find out. He couldn't help being inquisitive, he was a teacher, and being curious was in his blood. The job he thought at one time he had lost was there, everything was the same. He squeezed Jane's hand as she went down the corridor to her first class. He opened his classroom door, and the boys were waiting.

"It's very nice to see you all again gentlemen," Nigel said, with a broad smile, and he meant it this time. "Hope you all had a nice weekend, I certainly did, put it this way, my eyes were opened, I realized that life is good, and we all must put every effort in to enjoying it. Lots of people now and in the past, have not had the facilities that we are fortunate to have to enhance our lives. Education is of the utmost importance, so gentlemen let us get down to learning. Take your books out from where we left off on

Friday, page ninety three, and read from there." He went to his desk.

"What about our homework, sir? The weekend project on time-travel," Jarvis said from the back of the class.

"Oh yes, the project, it had slipped my mind. Alright, I'11 collect your papers, but for now Jarvis, I would like to know your ideas."

"Well sir, as I said on Friday, I believe it's impossible to go back in time, and because of that sir, I didn't write anything down," there he hesitated.

"Carry on," Nigel said with authority.

"Sir, this school will be destroyed and everyone in this room will be killed when an explosion in the school boiler room will explode, no-one will survive." All the boys were very attentive at Jarvis's portrayal of disaster. "Apart from me, and my good friend James. His survival will be down to me tying him up in my shed at home, and stopping him coming to school that day."

"Thanks for that," James shouted at his friend. Everyone laughed.

"Further more, we will be at war with France within five years, then myself and James will get married in a gay ceremony in ten years' time." More laughter, including Nigel.

"Now I'll come clean, I'm not Jarvis you know, I come from the future, and I've come to warn you all! Anyone here believe me, a show of hands."

No-one put their hands up. "And there sir, I rest my case. Even if it was at all possible, no-one would believe you, just as if Jesus Christ came back and said who he was, no-one would believe him." The boys applauded.

"Well done, very good imagination Jarvis, I'm just going to check the boiler room." He made a mock exit towards the door. More laughter ensued. "James, you're not gay, are you?" More giggles.

"No sir, I'm certainly not, my boyfriend will tell you the same thing." More guffaws.

"Alright gentlemen, we have had a good laugh, but now down to work."

"Can I just give you my thoughts?" James piped up. "Yes James, your thoughts."

"The best brains," he started, "that ever lived, since time began, with going over the subject of time-travel, have never come up with anything substantial. If it was possible to go back in time, people in their millions would want to try it. You can imagine the chaos it would cause people living in the past, with millions telling everyone what would happen in time to come? Imagine millions of Jarvises telling everyone that they would die in wars to come?"

"Me?" Jarvis shouted, more laughter.

James continued. "People would run riot looting things from the past, to flog here and now. People would get lost, loved ones would be bereft! The closest we have ever been to looking at the past is in films and photographs, and that's the way it will always be. Now sir, with due respect, please don't tell us that you believe in this time-travel, or have done it, or this whole class will die laughing? That's it sir." He sat down to more applause.

"Once again, well done. You certainly have a vivid imagination, and a good imagination makes for a good mind. Enough of time-travel; I think you have made your point. We will continue with the history of World War One, a very important time in history. For the moment gentlemen, back to your books."

Nigel looked at the homework, most of it sheer rubbish, but at least it passed away the day. He was happy to be back with his class. When the bell rang, he felt closer to the boys than he ever had before, and he was sure that they would all succeed in life.

They decided that they would buy the house in Moreland Road, and put a deposit on it there and then, Jane was thrilled. That night once again, they celebrated with a meal and drinks at their favourite pub. He told her of what the boys had made of time travel and she remarked that she also believed it was a load of rubbish. Nigel agreed, smiled, then changed the subject to their forthcoming wedding planned for July the twenty third; he was a happy man.

But the thought wouldn't go away, the thoughts like waves across his brain, flashbacks, had he really time travelled?

There were a few things he had to find out, but where to start? he wondered. Jane talked about the wedding, about the friends she wanted to attend. Nigel was not listening, and at one time he was in the trenches with his pals: Derek, Casey, Bates, then with Fanny walking the lanes and countryside on those summer days long ago. He saw familiar faces in the bar, Joe and Bert.

"Are you understanding all this Nigel? You seem to be in a daze, are you with me?" she said.

"Yes dear, I'm with you, just a little tired." It sounded like a feeble excuse. They clinked glasses. "To our future my darling."

"To our future," she smiled. Nigel went to the bar to get more drinks. He said to Brian, as he poured the drinks, "Did you enjoy your day off yesterday?"

"Yes, nice day," Brian replied.

"Decided against it, not going to buy The Briars, been up there yesterday, and had a good look at the place, too big for us. Going to live in Morelands Road now."

"You're doing the right thing," Brian said matter-of-factly. "Your Jane looks happy over there." He gave her a wave, as he placed the drinks on the counter.

"She is, she's planning our wedding day. We would like our reception here, but you already know that."

"Yes, it's in the book, the twenty third of July." Nigel verified.

"Brian, there's one thing I wanted to ask you, can we stay here on our wedding day, for the one night? Do you still rent rooms?"

"Yes, there's a nice room at the back of the pub, been refurbished only a year ago, nice room, you can have that one."

"That's great, don't want the secret room, too small," Nigel said, laughing, picking up his drinks.

"Secret room, what secret room?" Brian exclaimed. "There's no secret room just the two rooms, one en-suite, shall I book that one for you?"

"Yes, book it, Mr. and Mrs. Maythorn, and put a sign on the door, Not to be Disturbed." They laughed as Nigel went back to Jane.

"Booked a room here for our wedding night, nice en-suite room above here." He pointed to the ceiling.

"Fantastic, nice one," she exclaimed.

'Maybe the bathroom was once the secret room?' he thought. Could be,' he pondered.

Before they left to go home, Brian came to their table.

"Jane, do I get your wine for the reception, or do I leave that to you?"

"Thanks Brian, will you get it in? You know what we like, red and white, a hundred bottles of each!" Nigel's eyebrows went up in mock surprise. "Only joking," she laughed.

They said their goodnights to the customers they knew, and went out into the chill of the evening. He could picture Janice riding off on her atom powered bike. The stars seemed brighter in the cloudless sky, and the moon seemed to smile down on the happy couple as they made for home.

A certain normality set in as the first week passed. Whenever Nigel had time off school he would spend it going through old newspapers at the local library, most of it on a computer. He found out that in nineteen twenty nine a hanging had taken place at the mansion, and there was the name of the deceased, a Mr. Percy Bloomberg was found by his brother Charles hanging in a shed at the back of the property. It was believed that the deceased had mental problems. It had nothing to do with the stock market crash, as it had been rumoured, Mr. Charles Bloomberg explained, as he had been warned of the crash a while before, and had taken steps to keep family investments out of harm's way. Mr. Bloomberg had said that he had sold up before the crash. His brother had had a self destructive nature. The magistrate gave his condolences to the family. There it was, in black and white, he had been warned, but nothing about where the warning had come from.

He checked on a Mr. and Mrs. Bactrum, who he hoped came back from Poland to the North of England, but after trying to find some information from the University in Southampton who had records going back, he drew a blank. But their names were in the register for that year, the same thing with the Andersons. He tried to find out what had happened to the family after they went to live in America, but once again to no avail. He enquired at the trust company by letter, if an account in Maythorn name was still active, and was informed that it was, and was now worth a considerable amount of money. The company would only discuss the details and amount if Nigel would send in proof when the money was first deposited in nineteen hundred and twelve, and that the person who had made the deposit was truly his great grandfather. He would have to have a family tree, an impossible request, and any paper work his great grandfather had left behind. Nigel asked them if a Mr. Anderson had opened the account, but was told that they could not give that information, before he had identified who he was.

He told the company that he knew that Mr. Maythorn had put the money into the fund to the amount of two thousand pounds, and that he was Mr. N. Maythorn, and could prove it.

"Yes Mr. Maythorn, but we want you to prove that the Mr. Maythorn who put money in this trust was your family. We get many people these days purporting to be related to people who died years and years ago, just to get the money. It's called fraud sir, so any documents your father or your grandfather may have kept, would do. There's nothing more we can do until that happens, sorry." At that point the phone went dead.

How would he ever explain it? It was a lost cause. But one thing, it proved that an account had been opened, so he must have been there, it couldn't have been a dream. But how? When his body had never left the floor of the breast, according to Jane. Maybe only the mind could travel through time he wondered.

On the fourteenth of April Nigel was feeling ill, his concentration at school was bad, and the Head advised him to see a doctor.

The doctor advised him to have complete rest for two weeks. He couldn't get his experiences out of his mind, he was at a stage now when he wasn't worried about proving that he had time travelled, but he had to prove it to himself. Everyone he knew

271

became concerned for him, he was always in a daze. He wasn't enjoying himself as he should, he was always deep-thinking, trying to analyse it all. Jane had, on many occasions, woken him up and told him off for not listening to what she was asking him.

His parents also noticed the change in him. He lay in bed most days trying to sleep. As he lay on his bed watching the afternoon shadows crossing his room one day, it came to him, it would prove everything!

He jumped up and phoned the Estate Agent. "Hello Mike, can you help me out here? I realize you're a busy man; it's about the deeds for the mansion."

His name had to be on the deeds, he had bought it, then sold it to the army in May nineteen fifteen, but he had never seen any deeds. He remembered Mr. Giles had said that he would let him have them, but he had never received them. They never exchanged contracts in court, Mr. Giles had said that he would see to that. It was Mr. Giles who had seen him with an officer to ask whether he would sell, he had said 'yes' and with Giles alone had agreed to the two thousand pounds he had received, once again from Giles. Giles had done all the paperwork, he remembered being grateful for Mr. Giles's helpfulness at the time.

"Can you look at the deeds of The Briars, and tell me who bought the house from the time it was built?"

"So you're still interested then, you're not going to go with the Moreland property?" Mike enquired.

"No, we still want the Moreland place, but it's Brian, you know Brian Small the landlord of the Fox and Hounds pub? Well, we have a bet, he said that he knew everyone who had bought The Briars over the years. I bet him ten pounds that he doesn't, that's all. If it's not too much trouble Mike, I'm a good customer of yours, remember?"

"That won't be a problem; it's quiet at the moment, just sitting around the office. I'll ring you back in fifteen minutes."

"Thanks Mike, I'll be waiting."

Nigel made a cup of tea, his mother and father were out shopping, so he was alone.

The phone rang in ten minutes, "Mike here, about your enquiry."

"Yes?" Nigel answered with anticipation.

"Mr. and Mrs. Anderson were the first people to own the house from nineteen hundred to nineteen hundred and twelve, then a Mr. Giles from nineteen fourteen to nineteen sixteen, he sold it to the army for three thousand pounds."

Nigel gulped. "Thanks Mike, you needn't go any further, that's all I wanted to know."

"So you won the bet then?"

"No, but I've certainly learned a lot. Thanks again, see you soon." He put the phone down, "Mr.Giles, you sneaky bastard," Nigel muttered with a smile. "Obviously I wasn't thinking straight, blinded by the profit, or in love with Freda," he mused.

The same afternoon, he phoned his doctor and made an appointment for the next day. He was starting to have headaches, and wondered if it had anything to do with the chip that Bill had said had been implanted in his head, he would ask to have a scan. He lay on his bed in the quietness of the afternoon. He heard a lonely dog bark in some back yard, crying out for attention. He felt like the dog, lonely.

The sun saying goodbye to another day, crept across the sky without compassion, taking its warmth with it. He heard the car drive in; his parents had done the shopping. He lay there, tears filled his eyes, he could see Casey's head on the top of the crater, laughing! He heard men shouting out in agony, the noise of the guns, the sad faces of men with combat fatigue!

"I'm home love," his mother shouted at the bottom of the stairs. Nigel realized that his mind wasn't functioning properly, was he going insane? He thought of little these days, apart from his time-travel. Then he understood that in the parallel world where his brother Simon lived, he was going through the same thing, mental problems!

One thing Nigel knew, he wouldn't go into hospital, apart from having the scan. After some small talk with his mother, and a phone call to Jane, he took some sleeping pills and had an early night.

The doctor made an appointment for the scan, and gave him some anti depressants, told him to rest and to come back in two weeks' time.

He drove into Southampton, parked the car, and took a stroll passed the dock gates. The café was long gone, but he pinpointed the spot where it once stood back in nineteen hundred and twelve. He looked in a few shops, then he saw a sign that caught his attention: PAST TIMES and wandered in.

An old gentleman sat in an old armchair that looked as old as he was, at least seventy years old. The bell on the door was very loud and seemed to wake up the stuffed owl that stared at Nigel with his big multicoloured eyes.

"Did I startle you?" he muttered at the owl.

The old man took it that Nigel was talking to him and replied, "No, I've had my afternoon sleep this morning."

'That's novel,' Nigel thought. The shop was chocker-block with all sorts of junk, old lamps, old pictures with adjoining cobwebs lopsided on the wall. Tables with books, mirrors, a hundred and one things from a bygone era.

"Can I help you with anything?" the old man asked.

"Yes, how long have you been here in your wonderful shop?"

The old man stood up, and with a broad smile said, "Ever since I was a boy, my father's shop, took it over when he died. Been here since I was ten years old, sixty two years ago now. Where did that time go?" he said in a reflecting tone. "Nineteen forty eight, just after the war my father opened here. He'd just come back from Germany, lost a leg, never complained, wonderful father." It was obvious that the old man liked company, and enjoyed a chat with anyone who came into the shop.

"Do you remember a café over there?" Nigel pointed to the corner of a block of flats through the dirty shop window.

"Sure I do, as a boy I used to buy my cakes in there after school. Run by a woman who owned it, she didn't have a husband, he went down on the Titanic, she told the story many times, about her husband drowning, she was always sad, poor woman. Why do you ask?"

"I remember that café," Nigel volunteered.

"No, you can't have, my friend. It burned down before you were born in nineteen forty nine, if my memory serves me well."

"No, I was mistaken," Nigel said. "I just want to browse around, if that's alright?"

"Yes do, I'm having a beer, would you join me in a glass?"

"That's great thanks, I'm Nigel," he shook the old man's hand.

"And I'm Michael J. Milford, junk man extraordinaire," he smiled. "Be my guest." He waved his arm over the table filled with things from the past. The old man left to get the beer in an adjacent back room.

Nigel rummaged through, looking at bits and pieces. He flicked through a batch of pictures on the floor, and saw one he would buy, a picture of the liner Titanic, on the day she sailed. He looked carefully, and to his shock he saw a familiar face of a policeman standing at the dock gates. And there he was, it was Bill, was it Bill? He looked closer, the picture was blurred, but it looked just like him. A man was standing close by holding a bicycle, was it himself? Then he realized that he had been on the docks with Bill in Zone Two! But not Zone One. Could it be his substitute and Bill's, in the parallel world? It was amazing.

Then he came to another lot of unframed photographs, and there it was, The Briars, the mansion with a picture of an old car and the Anderson family posing!

The date said March nineteen hundred and twelve. He couldn't believe it, there was his friend Gerald, little Bertha and Alice!

The car looked like the one he had seen Berty driving, now he was absolutely convinced he had travelled in time, there was no doubt about it. How? He didn't know.

He heard the old man shout out something that he didn't hear properly, but said 'yes' anyhow.

The old man then came out with beer on a tray, and placed it on an old marble table with a crack in it. "Found anything you fancy?" he said, sitting down in the old armchair.

"Yes, I'll take these two," Nigel said, holding the pictures at arm's length. "The Titanic picture and this one of this house."

"That's good, I'm glad you found something. I love old pictures myself. I saved old postcards from the First World War, those silk ones, they were sold in France and Belgium to soldiers, got a nice collection. You got any? Because I buy and sell here you know."

"I'm sorry, but I haven't got any cards."

"I also sell some war photos, there's a batch over there under that old horse saddle."

Nigel got up from where he was sitting drinking his beer, and moved the saddle. The old man looked on, a happy smile on his face, enjoying his new-found friend.

Nigel flicked through more than twenty photos, then he saw it: YPRES NINETEEN SIXTEEN. Troops in Transit to the SOMME June nineteen sixteen.

The men of the battalion with Batey, Derek, Casey, lined up, with the buses in the background. The fourth man in the row was obscured by a soldier in the front row, just an arm around Casey's shoulder with a white faced watch showing. Nigel shook his head, there it was, the ultimate proof. He tried to hide his excitement.

"I'11 take this one, a definite one, my friends," he said talking to himself, forgetting that the old man was there.

"Your friends!" the old man said. "Anyone would think that you were there," he laughed.

"I was, that's me," he said, pointing to the arm with the watch.

The old man laughed again, so did Nigel heartily.

"Twenty pounds."

Nigel paid willingly, and left the shop. "Thanks Mike, it was nice meeting you."

"And you, come in any time you're passing," Mike said, but inwardly knowing that they would never meet again.

Nigel was delighted with his pictures, he would make a montage of them, and they would go up in the new home in a prominent place.

In the next few days Nigel was feeling better, and the scan at the hospital had shown nothing untoward, so he ventured out on a Sunday afternoon picnic with Jane into the hills of Hampshire, that reminded him of picnics with Janice.

During the two weeks that Nigel was off work he tried to work out how and why these things had happened to him, had it all been in his mind? He came to the logical conclusion that he had to forget the past, difficult when your job is the past, history! He had to stop trying to understand. Bill, he remembered, had once said that the best minds in the world didn't understand! So with that in his head, he tried to think of other things. It worked for a short while, but he soon found himself drifting towards thoughts of his adventures.

On Monday the thirtieth of April, he went back to work, he felt better after his two weeks' rest. He saw Mrs. White cleaning one of the corridors, on his way to see the headmaster. In Zone Two she was a receptionist, he remembered.

"Hello Mrs. White, been to any good concerts lately?" he joked. "Lance Summers is appearing at Southampton Winter Gardens."

"No, too busy sky-diving," said the elderly woman joking. "Anyhow, I only listen to Elvis, never heard of that other one."

"One of the same," Nigel said, disappearing around the corner.

Mr. Smigging was puffing away on his pipe, he seemed to look a touch guilty, as he extinguished it as Nigel went into his study. "Sit down," he commanded. Nigel noticed that the desk was overflowing with books and papers.

"How do you feel? Believe you've had migraine? My wife suffered with that, bloody nuisance when you try to sleep, I recall. She had many sleepless nights, she's at rest now, God bless her," he sniffed.

"Doctor said it was exhaustion, mental exhaustion, the rest has done me the world of good, I'm feeling a lot better now."

"Well Nigel, I know you've been working hard, you're a bloody good teacher, always said so. Your knowledge of history is spot on, and your knowledge of the First World War is second to none. If I didn't know differently I would swear that you were there in the trenches, you paint such a vivid picture. You're so enthusiastic when you teach the boys. I know they love your class, Jarvis is just one of the boys who has told me, James is another one, if I remember." He paused for thought, taking his pipe and filling it with another layer of tobacco.

"You know Nigel, I'm contemplating putting you forward for the award of Teacher of the Year at the next school board meeting."

"Thank you, I'm flattered that you thought of me, sir."

"No formality Nigel, call me by my name."

"Yes Tom, sorry."

"You're a first class teacher," he reiterated, "and I'm glad that you are back at work. The boys have missed your class, yes I remember now…" He lit his pipe and sucked in the smoke as though his life depended on it. "Jarvis and the other boy," he hesitated.

"James," Nigel reminded him.

"Yes, James, as they were enthusing about the history of the war, I suggested that joining up would be the right occupation for them when they leave school. And to my surprise Jarvis said that he wanted to be a fire-fighter, and James, a bloody accountant!" he laughed and spluttered at the thought.

"Good professions Tom, worthwhile jobs I would say."

"yes, I agree," the Head remarked.

Parallel worlds, Nigel remembered in Zone Two, Jarvis and James saying the same things.

"There's only one more thing I wanted to discuss with you Nigel, and it's this business of giving the class homework on time-travel. As you well know it's not in the school's curriculum, and I don't want to waste precious school time on that subject, it's too perplexing, to use a better word, incomprehensible. The subject would baffle a young mind, so in the nicest possible way I'm asking you to desist from discussing the subject. In my opinion it's not healthy for the minds of boys. It reminds me of the question I was once asked, about the universe and how long does space go on for? 'Eternity,' I remember saying, 'for ever and ever'. I could see the boys trying to work it out! Some things are best not talked about. It's like death, it's hard for people to come to some understanding, that when one dies it's forever, twenty billion years would not cover it, it's too weird, best not to dwell on these subjects. Don't take this as a telling off Nigel, because, my friend, it's not, have I made myself clear?"

"Absolutely, Tom. It's completely forgotten. You're right, it is very complex, I'm sorry, but I did find it a fascinating subject, to go back in time, what an adventure that would be?"

"Impossible Nigel, impossible."

At that moment the 'start' bell rang for first class.

"Glad to have you back," the headmaster said, as Nigel left the smoky study.

Monday night at seven o'clock in the Fox and Hound on the thirtieth of April, he stood at the bar.

"Nice to see you looking better," Jane said to Nigel. He could visualize the exact same thing happening far away in that other world, with Janice and Simon. They ordered their food, sat at their normal table, and discussed their forthcoming wedding. Nigel glanced over to the table next to them; two men sat talking in a soft tone, after an hour they left. Nigel had a feeling that one of them was eavesdropping on Jane's and his conversation, but didn't mention it to Jane.

During the evening they discussed money they would need for the house, it would be a struggle, he had to find a spare time job to meet their commitments. He went to the bar to buy another round of drinks, and there was Brian with an old tin with a rusty rim, photos were spread on the bar as he showed them to a customer. "Nigel, did you see this?" Brian said, holding up a photo of the pub taken in nineteen twenty one. "Here's another one, nineteen thirty six, another nineteen forty five. Not changed much eh?"

Nigel looked at the photos with interest, and ordered an orange juice and a pint of bitter.

"No, this place hasn't changed much at all," he said with conviction. Brian came back with the drinks.

"Could I get a copy of this one?" He held up a photo. "I'm making up a montage of old things. I've already got a picture of The Briars at Eastern Hill, got it in a junk shop in Southampton a while back."

279

"Yes sure, help yourself." He handed over the tin, as the customer went back to his friends, plus the photo on the bar.

Nigel took the orange juice over to Jane. "Won't be a minute, looking at a few old photos." She just nodded, as she text her mother.

He returned to the bar, and looking through them he saw her, she was standing with a baby in her arms, she was radiantly beautiful."This one?" Nigel said to Brian.

"That's my great-grandmother; Freda was her name, wonderful woman, so I came to understand."

"Can I get a copy of her?"

"Of course, but what's the interest?"

"I don't know, it seems I'm drawn to her somehow, her eyes maybe."

He showed the photo to Brian, who put his glasses on and studied the photograph of his great-grandmother.

"Yes, it's those beautiful eyes," he agreed.

"Can we get a drink in this pub?" a regular joked.

"No rest for the wicked, I need to take on another barman, it's getting too busy for me," Brian moaned, as he went to serve the man.

Nigel went through the whole lot of photos, there was the baby Brian as he grew up, a picture of Freda in old age, she was always smiling.

"Good ain't they?" Brian said when he returned.

"Brilliant, I'll get these copied and let you have them back, is that alright?"

"Yes, that's fine," Brian said.

"I can help behind the bar for three nights a week, Saturday afternoons as well if you think I'm suitable," Nigel said matter-of-factly.

Brian looked surprised. "You got any bar experience?"

"Course I have, I can pull a good pint, and barmaid," he joked.

"When was this then?" Brian enquired.

"Oh, a long time ago, a very long time ago," Nigel mused.

"Start Wednesday night then Nigel, I'll give you a trial, and if you're no good there's a bike out back." Both men laughed.

He returned to his table. "Put these in your bag darling, photos I'm going to copy for my montage I told you about. And guess what, I've got a job as barman."

"Barman?" she exclaimed. "Barman, where?"

"Here, right here, I start on Wednesday night, just part-time, but the extra money will help towards our honeymoon."

"You're a darling man, will we always be together? I hope so?" she looked quizzical.

"Yes, we will be together for all our lives, I know that for a certainty."

"Are you sure?"

"Very very sure." He took her hands in his. "I love you Jane, my English teacher."

"And I love you, my History teacher."

He looked up. "See you Wednesday night at seven o'clock, Brian Mr. Boss-man."

"See you Wednesday at seven p.m. my apprentice barman," Brian said with a broad smile. Nigel could see that he was going to enjoy his job, just like Simon had told him he had. They went out into the night.

The weeks passed in a perfect summer, and on the first day of June contracts were passed on their new home in Moreland Road. Nigel decided to call the house 'HEREANDNOW which he thought was most appropriate. Jane didn't get it, but accepted the name. That morning he saw Mike the Estate Agent in court, who informed him that the mansion was still not sold, and the vendors had gone back to America.

"It's fully insured?" Nigel enquired.

"Yes, I believe so," Mike replied.

Jane and Nigel were married in a little church deep in the countryside. The reception was held at the Fox, and a day to remember was made. Nigel's brother George was best man. For years the brothers had been apart, with George working away, and Nigel at training college. Now they laughed and talked in the garden out back of the pub.

"It seems you have been away, and now you are back home," George said.

"You're right, I've been to places not many people have been. They may have been in my imagination, but they seemed so real at the time, but as you said, I'm home now." The brothers hugged each other, Nigel sang a few songs with the band, it was a wonderful day. Simon and Janice would be doing the same thing, the thought passed through his mind. That night in the room above the bar, just before he went to sleep, his thoughts were with two other wonderful human beings; Fanny and Freda. He looked at his new bride, kissed her on the top of her head as she slept blissfully, her happiness intact.

The week following was spent on honeymoon. Jane wasn't surprised when Nigel said that he wanted to spend it in France and Belgium, places she had never heard of; Poperinge, Ypres and Albert. They both loved French cuisine, the wine, and she was happy to hear her husband enthuse as he visualized them in little bistros, eating crab with French bread, drinking red wine, with the sounds of an accordion drifting through the evening like a gentle caress that lingers on one's mind, he painted a vivid picture.

Hand in hand they walked through Nigel's past, without her knowing. Although she was impressed with his local knowledge of towns and villages she had never known, and more to the point, places she had never thought that Nigel had been to. In Poperinge, Belgium, at times he seemed to be quiet, and at other times he would go into the history of the town, with a certain flair that she had never seen in him. She enjoyed the visit to Toc H, they had a cup of tea and talked to the people who ran it and welcomed everyone. The place where soldiers found rest and solace during the Great War. At times she would see the tear that appeared in the corner of his eye.

"It was the war," he said one night as they lay in their cosy room near the church, where he had met Marie.

The town had just woken up as Nigel made his way down the Rue Gasthuisstraat. He had left Jane at the hotel having a bath and getting ready for their day's outing. He had told her that he was just popping out to get a couple of bottles of wine. He stood across the street and saw number ten, the door was brightly painted now. The shop where the man stood repeating his wares was now a smart coffee shop. In his mind's eye he could see the soldiers passing by, soldiers of another time.

The door of number ten opened, and an old lady stepped out unto the pavement and looked up the street as though she was expecting to be met by someone. He glanced up the street on reflex, and as he turned back he saw her going in the coffee shop. He went across and entered. It was very neat with just six tables and a small counter at the far end. She was talking in French to the woman making the coffee. The tables were occupied apart from the one closest to the small counter. He ordered a coffee, and looked around for somewhere to sit, then asked the old lady if she minded him joining her. Her smile told him he was welcome.

"Thanks," he said, as he sat opposite her.

"I'm just waiting for my friend, she's always late," the lady volunteered, "you are a visitor to us," she smiled.

"How can you tell?"

"We are used to seeing visitors and English people coming to this town. It's been that way for years, since the Great War. This town is famous, Poperinge is popular," she laughed. "My mother," she continued, "taught me to be kind to the English, she loved the English. I'm sorry, I talk too much, she also told me that." With that she took a sip of her coffee.

"Your mother was very wise, it seems to me," he blurted out.

"Because I talk too much you mean?"

"No no," Nigel protested, "no, in telling you to love the English, good people." That broke the ice, they both laughed out loud.

"Your mother sounds as if she was a very special person."

"She was special, she brought me up all by herself, when my father was killed. And she had her nursing duties to do as well. She went through two wars, and in the second war she was with the résistance, she was killed in nineteen forty four, and she was only forty six years old. I remember it well, I was eighteen years old at the time. I'm sorry to tell you this sad story, I'm an old woman now, I'm eighty one years old, but I don't forget, ever."

"I'm sorry," he muttered, and offered the old lady another cup of coffee. She accepted gladly, she loved to talk to visitors to her town. She asked Nigel if he was in town for the day.

He explained that he was a History teacher, and was doing a bit of revision on the First World War, whilst on honeymoon, and that his wife was getting ready at the hotel.

They talked for more than half an hour, she told him that her mother had gone to nursing school in France, but only because of a soldier who had paid for her, and that the move had changed her life forever. He found out that the old lady's name was Rose, when the lady behind the counter indicated that her friend had just come into the café. The two women greeted one another like old friends do and Nigel finished his coffee.

"And your mother's name was?"

"Marie, or Mary in English," she said, with her mother's smile.

"I must go now, my wife will be wondering where I got to." Nigel shook her hand, but she pulled him towards her and kissed him on the cheek.

"I have been lucky you know, because I spent a bit of my life with her, my mother was an angel. Goodbye, and have a good life, double fast."

"Double fast," Nigel repeated, as he walked out into the morning sun. He felt elated as he went to pick up the wine, then back to the hotel. He had done some good, it wasn't a dream, he was convinced.

Jane was ready and waiting, he put the wine in the fridge, then they went on a tour of the old gaol, a museum, then a nice meal in a sort of bistro that Nigel had talked about before the honeymoon.

The train to Ypres took just over half an hour, and soon they were in the town. Near the impressive Cloth Hall in the centre of the town, he saw the very spot where the lorries and buses had been lined up. In the photo he had with him he compared the houses with the photo, and picked out the difference.

"See here," he pointed to the spot on the road, "and here," pointing at the photo. The exact spot where the men had stood, those brave men all going to war on the Somme in nineteen hundred and sixteen.

"See, that could have been Baker, Smith, Willis and here," he pointed to the four men at the back, "Bates, Derek, Casey and Maythorn."

"Maythorn!" she exclaimed. "Where?"

"There," he pointed to the obscured soldier with the arm around Casey.

She laughed. "You have a wonderful imagination darling."

"I know I have," he said, slipping the photo back into its folder.

They went on a tour of the trenches and the battlements, they ended up in the Flanders Fields museum, housed in the Cloth Hall. At night they were at the Menin Gate at eight o'clock, to hear the bugler sound the Last Post to the fallen, a moving ceremony that has been carried out since nineteen twenty two.

After a meal they went to their hotel. "Are you enjoying our Honeymoon, darling?" he asked her. Her reply was affirmative. They lay on the bed, the moon beams trying to sneak a look at the two newly weds consummating their marriage.

Afterwards she asked him outright, "Nigel, have you always been faithful to me since we've been together?"

"What a question, my little pudding." He smiled. She caught it in a beam of light from a street lamp just outside, on the opposite side of the empty street.

"Have you?" she asked again.

"I have been faithful to you since I was born. In another time, before I was born, well maybe not." He laughed, so did she, they lay in one another's arms.

"It's been an eventful day, and we're going to have a wonderful life together, just you wait and see," he assured her. "We hope to live our lives, as a dear friend once told me, 'double fast'."

"Double fast," she repeated.

"Yes, 'double fast'." They kissed, and drifted off together in sleep.

Ypres, that famous little town in Belgium, was bathed in sunshine, flowers bedecked the houses in brightly painted panniers and tubs. The newly weds said their 'goodbyes', they had enjoyed the short time in the historical town.

Albert, near the Somme battlefields, was the next place on the itinerary. Once again, tours of the trenches, but now it was too clean, the rats, lice, smell, noise, blood and death were of another time. The tourists just got a little touch of what it had been like to be there. He tried to find out where the dressing station was, the place where he remembered he lay, with legs gone, before he had arrived back in the chimney breast. But no-one remembered, so he let it go.

Soon, after a nice honeymoon, they were back home, and with Nigel back at school, and his part time job at the pub, things soon got back to normal living.

August passed and when September came, Nigel knew that something he knew about was going to happen. The weather forecast was for 'storm force' winds. On the thirteenth of September it was raining, and Nigel was at home on this Thursday evening, Jane was in the kitchen marking school papers. He went into the kitchen.

"Jane, I have to go out, won't be long, there's something I have to do." He put his overcoat on, she glanced up from her work.

"In this weather, can't it wait?"

"No, it's important, I'll be home for the film on TV, you'll be finished your work by then." He bent over and kissed her lightly on the top of her head.

The storm was venting its anger over the land, it was raining hard. He drove towards Eastern Hill and the mansion. The gates were wide open, and he drove up the avenue, strewn with leaves and fallen branches. He could see the glow ahead, and the activity around the front of the house. The fire brigade were already fighting the fire, the police were also there. He parked the car at the end of the drive, and walked towards the main entrance. He found a good viewing point under the trees that surrounded the property. He looked over at the water fountain, and through the rain, he saw a man inside the fountain, sitting watching the fire fighters doing their jobs.

"It's me over there," Nigel said to himself, in that instant he decided to go over and speak to the man, who he knew was himself! He broke cover and went towards the fountain; he could see the man clearly. He glanced at the flame coming from the roof, and looked back at the fountain, there was no-one there, he had disappeared. He looked around the fountain, and sat on the edge. The rain beat down on him. "If only I could have had a word".

It was that loop again, going back to spend that time in the past. 'There has to be an end to this,' he thought. He remembered what he had done, had had a hell of a job to get back to nineteen hundred and twelve, with stops on the way, working in the pub from nineteen twelve to nineteen sixteen, seeing himself escaping from the guards. The 'loop' again.

"Crazy, bloody crazy," he cried, under the storm's fury. Only death could end it all, there was no other way, he thought.

He made his way back to his car, and saw a few people watching the fire behind the tape the police had put up. He recognised Mike, the Estate Agent.

"Just passing," Nigel said to Mike's question, "it's a good thing I didn't buy this place after all."

"You're right, and I never did sell it. The Cladmores will be pleased; they'll be paid out with the insurance money now. I'll let them know the good news tomorrow; they are in the United States. A strange thing, but Bob Cladmore told me that a stranger at one of his parties told him that lightning would strike the house this year sometime, two thousand and seven, and that it would burn down. This man, so Bob said, had come from the future, and told him this in two thousand and one, six years ago, how weird. Mind you, I don't normally believe in that kind of thing, time-travelling, coming from the future, it's rubbish. Anyhow, that's what Bob told me."

"I agree, it does sound like a fairy tale, there are things that mankind will never understand."

"Didn't they lose a son in the tragedy of the Twin Towers in New York in two thousand and one?"

"That's right, but I've told you that story before. That's right, I remember now, at Moreland Road, the property you are in now. I remember it well. Look, they're carrying out a fireman, must be bad in there," Mike exclaimed.

"Move back a bit please," a policeman instructed.

"I have to go now, bloody soaked to the skin," Nigel said, "but one last point, just imagine if the Cladmores had listened to the stranger and heeded his warnings, the son would be alive now, they would be happy people."

"That's true, but it's not human nature to believe things beyond their comprehension, I think it's all rubbish." Mike pulled up his collar, and walked away.

"Yes, maybe you're right, goodbye Mike."

"The mansion on the hill, The Briars, is finished, burned down tonight, it's a good job we didn't buy it, it's been burgled as well, the front door had been forced, so Mike said."

"The Bates Motel burned down," she exclaimed, "when? Did you see it? You're soaked, is that where you've been? Nigel, you'll catch your death, go and get into dry clothes. Did you see the fire? Couldn't the fire brigade put it out? How did it start?"

"Hold on dear, I'll tell you all about it, let's have a bottle of wine, and I'll stoke up the fire."

The storm's venom was at its height now, and the mansion, once a dream for Nigel, was just a shell of its former glory, with ghosts of yesteryear fleeing the scene.

Over the coming month, Nigel tried to find out if his name was in the Army records, on the internet. He found out that a N. Maythorn had been in a motorised division, and had been reported missing, after being in a dressing station. So that concluded his enquiries. He was now convinced that he had gone back to the past, and that it was during the split second after he had been hit on the head by the bricks in the chimney breast and before he had hit the floor. Incredible as it sounded, that was the conclusion he settled at. His body had disappeared then re-appeared in a micro second.

He won the award at school for his History teaching. The boys loved the way he would re-enact a scene in the trenches, he painted a vivid picture. He continued to work in the pub, sang at times, loved his life with Jane his wife. As the years unfolded, he slowly forgot his amazing adventure, but at other times, it came flooding back, like when she told him that she was expecting a baby.

"It will be a boy," he had said with excitement, and it was. "William shall be his name." She had wanted to call the baby Zane, so it was agreed, Zane William Maythorn, who was born in two thousand and ten.

Father and son had a very good relationship, and it came as no surprise when Bill declared that he was going to join the police. The year was two thousand and thirty, he was twenty years old. Nigel had always called his son Bill, so did Jane after a while, only his friends called him Zane.

Nigel was also nonplussed when he heard that James and Jarvis, who had left school years back, had respectively joined the fire service, and become an accountant for a High Street Bank. Years passed by with no regard for people who wanted time to pass at a slower pace. Brian, at the Fox and Hounds had been ill for a few years, and he told Nigel that the pub would be closing soon. There was no-one left in his family to carry on.

"To think my family were publicans for over one hundred and fifty years, all Brians," he laughed feebly, "and now our time has run out. The place is falling apart, trade has fallen in recent years, it's time to go. It's been great, all the family loved the business, the Smalls never did anything else." Nigel sat at his bedside, the old man was frail. "Thanks for your help Nigel, we were a good team, put it this way, we made our customers laugh, didn't we?"

"More than once, do you remember that time that I dressed in a black suit with a gold belt, at the fancy dress ball, and you introduced me as Lance Summers? I sang, brought the house down, sounded like Elvis they said, memories eh Brian? Remember the time I was going to buy The Briars at Eastern Hill, and you warned me not to? Then the bloody place burned down! That was many years ago, now that's gone, demolished just…"

Brian spluttered, sitting up and coughing badly. When he had recovered he said, "Where did the time go?"

"If you could live your life again, would you?" Nigel asked.

"I would live every minute of it, just the same, it's been wonderful. I was lucky to have been born, and I made the most of it, I've lived, loved and laughed, and been happy."

Two days later the pub closed forever, Brian died, and Nigel never worked in a bar again. He watched the bulldozers erase a place so full of memories. 'The ghosts of the past must be restless,' Nigel mused. He had forgotten that Simon in Zone Two had told him that the pub had been pulled down, at the same time in that parallel world.

In Nigel's world things were changing, with his son in the police and married with two children, he lived from day to day, being aware that he was getting old, and his time at school was coming to an end. Thirteen Moreland Road was a happy home, Jane a perfect wife, now grandchildren to look after from time to time. His retirement from the school was a sad affair, he had enjoyed teaching the boys, his love of history had been easy to teach. Now he spent his time reading, watching documentaries, war mostly. Jane was a good companion, they would sit together at the close of the day, holding hands, with a glass of wine, reminiscing.

"I've always loved you, my English rose," he said.

"And I've always loved you, my History teacher, 'Double Fast'."

"Yes Double Fast'," he smiled, as they clinked glasses.

Chapter 14

IMPORTANT QUESTIONS,DEBATABLE ANSWERS

The big room was full of activity, computer screens flickered with operatives. Studying the data, Detective Inspector Zane Maythorn was in a world of his own, he was planning a birthday party for his eighty year old father. The Detective had been in the 'time' section of the police for ten years, he had never discussed his duties with anyone, it was all top secret. He was aware of a colleague holding a memo in his hand. "Just come through sir, says it's important."

"Thanks," he nodded; he opened the envelope and read the contents. 'UTMOST IMPORTANCE, GLITCH FOUND IN COMPUTER. CONCERNING BROTHER'S FATE, ZONE TWO. SEE COMPUTER U356 ON TIMEZONE.' Zane pushed a few buttons on his console and a picture of his brother Bill was imposed on the left hand corner. It went on to say that the computer had indicated that if something wasn't done, his father was not going to meet his mother and consequently he wouldn't be born.

Any ideas how to rectify this problem? Fate said that they would meet, but his father had somehow had a mental breakdown, and was now in hospital in two thousand and seven, Zone Two! Zane text back that he would think of something and not to worry. "After all, you're speaking to me now, so I must have come up with a solution to this problem." He then looked at the gateways to the past on another system and formulated the plan. He would use his own father to help solve the problem.

Two hours later, all was in order. He got up and went to a small room covered from wall to wall in black studded cushions, a solitary chair, with a desk and hi-tech computer that lit up like a Christmas tree. Like a space-man, he put on a helmet, and with the controls of different levers and knobs, he went back to the past on the computer.

He found himself in two thousand and seven, a doctor's surgery before he was born. His father was sitting in the surgery. Zane was invisible at the moment the doctor went out of the room. He materialised behind a plastic curtain, and instructed his father to lie down on the bed, and in a flash he implanted a small 'suggestion' capsule at the back of his head. Nigel felt no pain or sensation.

"You can sit up again," he instructed his father, then went to an outer room as the doctor walked back, perfect timing.

"You're Al Mr. Maythorn," the doctor said. Nigel left, and the same day he had ideas of looking for a house in the country near Bakefield. Although he had been thinking of a new house for the last six months, somehow the urge was stronger on the sixth of April two thousand and seven, as he was about to leave school at the end of the day. Why he drove home on a different route that day, he didn't know, but the time police knew.

The day was fine, no wind, Zane slowed his tractor and pulled into the opening of a field to allow the car his father was driving to pass, and gave instructions for the scientific operative to expose the sign for a moment with a gust of wind. Then to open up the gateway in the fireplace with a lightning bolt, that same night at the height of the storm. Zane was happy with his plan, and now it was in operation, he informed his brother that all would work out well, and he would be born. Both men laughed at the absurdity of it all over the telly computer.

A month had passed, and his plan had worked to perfection. Zane was back in his own world, and getting ready to go and see his eighty year old father. Nigel was fully aware what significance two thousand and sixty four held, now in Zone Two, he was on holiday with Bill, and enjoying the best experience he'd ever had. Yet here he was sitting in his armchair! How could anyone be in two places at once? Incredible, unbelievable, but it was true!

"Zane will be here soon dear, so go and have a shave please," Jane implored. Nigel did as requested. An hour later the son who had grown up to be a policeman, came in the door and greeted his parents.

"Had a busy day?" Nigel said from his armchair.

"Yes Dad, an unusual day, a very different one." He was the spitting image of his brother Bill, in Zone Two, Nigel had noticed the resemblance a long time ago, but kept it to himself.

"I'm going to make some eats, so you two can talk, it's not often these days that you can get together, you are always too busy doing police work, they work you too hard," his mother moaned, and she went out to the kitchen.

"They certainly do that," he said with a smile.

"You have never told me about your police work, have you?" Nigel said abruptly.

"Not allowed to Dad."

"Well son, I haven't got long for this world now."

"Don't talk like that, you've got years, you're fit, aren't you?"

"Fit, yes physically, but mentally, I'm not. I've held it for years but it's come to the time now for some questions to be answered.

"Questions? What questions do you want me to answer?"

"Come off it; don't pretend you don't know what's been bugging me all these years! Me and your mother have always brought you up to be truthful and a good person, that's the reason you joined the police. But you owe me an explanation, I've been waiting for years for you to tell me, but you never did, and now I want to have it out."

Zane felt uncomfortable, as he listened to his old father talking in this vein, because he knew what was coming.

"Ask me anything you want, but lighten up a bit Dad, it's not like you to be like this. You seem agitated and that's not good for your blood pressure."

"Let's get it out of the way son, then I can go to where ever I'm going in peace, to heaven or hell!" he laughed out loud.

"I see you two are having a good time," Jane said, entering the front room carrying plates of sandwiches. "I'm going to leave you to it, I'm going next door for an hour to see my friend, help her with some dress-making. I've poured the coffee, I'll bring it in." She placed the sandwiches on the table and went to get the coffee. "Enjoy," she said, "won't be too long." Then she left.

Nigel helped himself to the food, and placed it on a low table next to his armchair. His son did the same, opposite him.

"Start from the beginning Zane," he said, as he took a bite of his sandwich.

"What do you want to know, Dad?"

"Did I really do it or was it just in my mind? Was it a dream?" he said in a pleading way.

"Say what you mean Dad."

"OK, did I time-travel all those years ago?"

"You did, you time-travelled."

"So Zone Two does exist, Bill your brother in that zone, Janice. Simon, all real people?"

"Yes, they are all real people. You know I shouldn't be telling you this, we are bound by an oath of secrecy!"

"Maybe," Nigel pointed out, "but you used me without my permission, to set history right in Zone Two, is that correct? So I believe you owe me something."

"Yes, that's true, but can I ask you this: did you enjoy the experience? Was it worthwhile in your estimation?"

"Very worthwhile, and the people I met were wonderful." The old man's eyes glazed over, as his mind retrieved their faces in the mist of time. For a moment he was laughing with those people of long ago.

"So, you wouldn't have missed it for anything then?"

"No, nothing, it was an amazing adventure. Do you know at this time in Zone Two, it's two thousand and sixty four?"

"Yes." It runs along side out world, it's parallel."

"Well, I'm on holiday with your brother, in different

places of the world, but you also know that, don't you?"

"Yes Dad, I do."

"So, how can I be in two places at once? You did it didn't you? You planned for me to help? Bill told me everything."

"I did Dad, it was my responsibility, and I knew that you would be the right candidate. Because if my brother hadn't been born, then neither would I, that's how it works in parallel worlds, so I was only helping myself in a way. Remember at that time you weren't even married to Mother?"

"So you know about Freda and Fanny, and the girl in France?" Nigel said, looking sheepish.

"Of course I do," Zane said with a grin.

"Top secret," Nigel ordered.

"Top secret Dad."

"Why did you not meet me when I got back to Zone One? Bill told me that there would be someone there to bring me home?"

"Not many men have had the opportunity to do what you did, and I saw the one-in-a-billion chance to repay you for doing what you did, a service to mankind. I made a decision to let you enjoy yourself, and do something unique, and you did, you really did. Those afternoons in the bedroom with Freda, remember?" He looked at his father, and with big eyes, made the gesture of wanting him to agree.

"Alright, let's not dwell too much on that moment, you weren't in the room in your invisible suit I hope!" Both men laughed.

"No I wasn't, but I know, I know everything you did, you were always being watched, and because you could never die, because remember you hadn't been born yet, everything went well until you decided to join the army. The suggestion input in your head had ceased to function and had started to dissolve. But even then it seemed you were enjoying the experience, you met some good mates in the army."

"Like Casey, Derek, Bates, you mean, they were first class lads, we had some laughs," Nigel mused. "They died too young."

"They did, and it was at that moment I knew that your

295

adventure had to end. I had to bring you back, you were suffering from shock in that dressing station."

Nigel looked at his son in anticipation of what he was about to say.

"You were there in the dressing station!" Nigel said.

"I was there by your side, you thought I was Bill, you thought Marie was your nurse, but she was training in Calais."

"I also remember the nurse saying that I couldn't last the night, I was about to die."

"No father, she was referring to a soldier in the next bed."

"My legs were gone, blown off." He glanced down at his legs.

"Once again, you were intact, they had you on a table top and your legs were hanging over the edge, you were suffering from concussion. I had a white coat on, so no-one took any notice of me. I stood you up, attached you to my transport belt, and set it for England. I had picked up your jeans, tee-shirt and trainers that you had left in the drawer in your room at the pub. Then we arrived at the mansion in the big room, and into the chimney breast. I set your belt for two thousand and seven, and mine for my time, then pressed the button and you were back. You had been away for a split second, to you it seemed like years, and that's the full story. Now are you satisfied?"

"Thanks son, it's hard to grasp that you were with me as an adult, before you were born!"

"That's time-travel Dad, when you went to nineteen hundred and twelve, you lived there and you hadn't been born yet. That's the reason the Government tries to keep it a secret, it's too complex, it's mind mix up, beyond most people's comprehension. Whenever we find a hole, or gateway to the past, we block it up. That's why there's a ten foot cement seal on the site of the old mansion that stood on Eastern Hill, all top secret."

Nigel felt that most of his questions had been answered, and was now at peace. The montage was above the fireplace; The Titanic, the picture of the Fox and Hounds, the Anderson family outside the mansion, the picture of soldiers from the First World War, a photo of an old lady, Freda the landlady.

Zane pointed to the montage. "You've got your memories there Dad, people and places stopped in time."

"That's me there," he stood up and pointed to the arm around Casey's shoulder, "it's just like yesterday, so vivid up here."

He then pointed to his head. "They were my brothers, I loved them you know." His sincerity showed.

"I know you did," Zane said understandingly.

"Will you come to France with me? I want to see where they are. It will be my last trip over there; I have to say my final goodbye."

"Course I will, I will arrange for time off next month, is that ok?"

"That will be great, just me and you, your mother won't come, she has no interest in war graves, or anything to do with war, come to think of it. It will be just for a few days."

"I'll sort it out Dad, leave it to me."

"I've never told your mother of my time-travel adventure, by the way. In fact I have never told anyone, only me and you know. It's been my secret all these years, at times I wanted to tell someone. I remember once in the pub, I was behind the bar and this bloke was telling his mates about the trenches in the First World War, talking utter rubbish. I was on the verge of telling him the way it was, I held my tongue, but it was hard.

I wish I could have shared what I know with someone, but it was pointless, no-one believes. There's no chance for me now, who listens to an old man anyhow. At one time I was thinking of writing a book, then again I thought, it's been done before. There were also films, 'Time machine' was one. Anyhow I didn't bother, no point ending my life in a mental institution!" Nigel gave out a laugh, as the door opened and Jane came in.

"She's happy, the dress is finished, she wanted to pay me for my time, I said 'alright, I charge a thousand pounds an hour',

so she said that she would pay me five pounds a week. I told her that I was only joking. I'm sure she's going senile, she's such a sweety, she was so happy with my help. Had a nice chat you two? Zane, you're staying for a coffee before you go, and make sure you come to see us sooner next time."

"Yes Mum," Zane said, looking at his father. Both men smiled.

"Jane, me and Zane are going to France on holiday to visit the war graves, just for a few days next month, you don't mind do you?"

"Course not, glad I'm not included."

"Told you," Nigel said to his son.

"I wish you would forget the bloody war, it's past. You live in the past Nigel, I've told you before. You've always been obsessed with the past. I'm sure if you could go back in time, you would, and leave me here on my own."

"Never, never, I would never leave you, I couldn't be away from you for a minute, I need you to put me in my place."

"You couldn't be away from me for a minute is it? So you're cancelling your holiday to France then, are you?" She walked out of the room to make the drinks, a smile on her face.

Both men smiled at one another.

"We might get some coffee this time, she forgot it an hour ago," Zane remarked.

The month passed, and Nigel with his son by his side, stood by the graves, they were in line facing the going down of the sun, the flowers opened, smiling at the sky, there was peace and serenity all around. The soldiers of the Great War sleeping in eternity, where pain and suffering were banished. Nigel's tears kissed the ground they fell on.

"Goodbye Batesy, didn't know your name was Frank. And you Derek Pervis, and to you my good friend Casey, fooking rest in peace," he muttered.

Zane led his old dad away through the waves of hundreds of white headstones, that seemed to light up the passing day.

The same evening, to the surprise of the bistro waitress, Nigel ordered egg and chips with bread and the house wine. He raised his glass for a toast. "Here's to the best friends I ever had in my life, may God bless you all."

"Here here," Zane said.

Nigel's eightieth birthday went well. Zane, his wife, their two married children, their partners plus kids, Jane, her lady friend from next door, Nigel's accountant Mr. James and wife, Captain Jarvis, fire fighter also attended with his wife. A few neighbours from Moreland Road, all enjoyed the old teacher's celebrations.

"Speech speech," Jane shouted as she replenished her guests' glasses. Nigel turned down the music that the great grandchildren were dancing to, to their dismay.

"Unaccustomed as I am to public speaking,"(no-one got the joke) "I would like to thank everyone today for taking time out to come to wish me well on my fortieth birthday." Laughter broke out.

"Eighty," Jane shouted out, "eighty dear."

"Eighty! Am I that old?" More laughter. "Anyhow, I would like to say that I've had a good life, in a way, a charmed one. Adventure in abundance, thrills and spills along the way, ups and downs, met some wonderful people. As you know, I was a History teacher all my working life. I enjoyed history so much, at times it seemed that I lived in the past," he saw Zane give him a furtive look, "as my dear wife always told me. Regrets, as the song goes, I've had a few, but then too few to mention. One place that I miss is the Fox and Hounds pub. When I was young I used to meet my good wife there, and we did a lot of our courting there."

Jane bent her head in mock shyness. Zane hugged his mother, the guests laughed.

"I enjoyed the part time bar work I did; it was like a hobby to me. We've had wonderful times, so I want to ask you all to lift your glasses for a toast, to absent friends." A round of applause ensued, and Nigel turned up the music, to the delight of the great grandchildren, who continued dancing.

Later on after the party was over, and Jane and Nigel were alone, they sat in the front room on the settee, she had just poured the remains of the last bottle of wine into their glasses.

"Here," she said handing him a small package, "a birthday gift." "What is it?"

"Open it."

"A new wallet, how nice, just what I wanted."

"I know that, look at your old one," she produced his old wallet, it was falling to bits.

"I've had that wallet for over sixty years!" he protested.

"It looks it," she exclaimed, "that's the reason I bought you that new one."

"Thanks dear, it's nice."

"That was a good speech you made tonight, it brought back memories to me as well, our courting days at the Fox. Cast your mind back for a moment, do you remember the night on your twenty fifth birthday?"

"That was fifty five years ago, I can't remember that far back."

"You will dear, listen, I bought you a new blue shirt, you wore it on your birthday, at the Fox, and do you remember you said it was too big, and you fiddled about with the cuff? Remember now?"

"I think I do remember a blue shirt."

"Yes, and here it is." She pulled the shirt from behind her, it was under a cushion. "See, it's still brand new, you've had it in your wardrobe all these years Nigel my darling, you never throw anything away do you?"

"Yes, that's it, its coming back to me now, my blue shirt from all those years ago." He held it up and examined it, then he stood up, took his shirt off and put his blue one on. "Look, it fits like a glove."

"No dear, it fits you like a shirt. Only one thing wrong, look at the cuff." He glanced down.

"Do you remember playing with the cuff, and the button came off? Well, when I emptied your old wallet today, look what I found after all these years, that had been hidden away all that time!"

Nigel flopped down in his chair, his mind raced through time, and he remembered picking the button out of the flower pot back in nineteen sixteen, when he was a driver in the army. The 'invisible suit' button given to him by Bill in Zone Two!

"Are you alright Nigel, you've gone white?"

"It's been a hectic day darling, I'm tired out, bed time." He finished his drink. "Thanks for the gift darling, and for giving me back the gift I never used. I'll wear it now, and with all the buttons intact." But he knew he wouldn't.

"Take it off and I'll sew it on, it will only take a minute."

"No dear, I've got a place for this button on my montage."

"Why?"

"Because it belongs there," he said. She shook her head in disbelief.

He hugged her and kissed her and said, "I am the luckiest man in the world to have you. You've been a wonderful wife, I couldn't have done better, not in a hundred years."

The next day Nigel woke early and he wondered about the button, but put it to the back of his mind. After breakfast when Jane went shopping, he went to his wardrobe to see what other clothes he had that he had not worn for years. "Time for a clear out," he muttered.

He went to the chest of drawers, and underneath a pile of old clothes he found the belt. He had forgotten that he had put it there all those years ago, when they moved in. He got it out and took it to the front room, and laid it on the coffee table, the dials long dead. He looked at it carefully and noticed a small socket on the inside under a flap of leather. He wondered what the socket was for, but left it there and went into the kitchen to make a cup of coffee, he put the plug in for the kettle to boil, then it came to him, that the socket on the belt was a charge socket.

He had another look at the socket on the belt, then went to his computer and found a charge plug. It fitted in the belt perfectly, he switched on the computer and stood back in surprise as the dials on the belt lit up, all green lights! "Bloody amazing!" he said aloud.

He made his drink, and watched the belt glow, as he sat in the chair drinking. Half an hour went by, when a buzzing noise coming from the belt told him that it had charged up, that's the conclusion he arrived at; he quickly turned off the power, and took the belt back into the front room.

He placed the belt around his waist and pondered for a few

minutes, when he heard the front door open, and Jane came to the door, it opened.

"Home darling, saw Mrs. Bernard at the supermarket, she told me that her husband is ill, and is in hospital, she gives you her best regards. Sweetheart, shall we have lunch out today? Don't feel like cooking, coffee?"

"Yes dear, that's fine," Nigel said. She went into the kitchen.

'Shall I,' he thought. "Yes yes," he muttered. He set the belt to go back in time for five minutes, checked it out carefully. 'Don't want to end up in nineteen twelve again,' he thought,' just five minutes'. He pressed the button, and as before, closed his eyes.

He sat there for a minute, then he heard the front door open, and Jane come to the door. It opened, "HOME DARLING, SAW MRS.BERNARD AT THE SUPERMARKET, SHE TOLD ME HER HUSBAND IS ILL AND IN HOSPITAL, SHE GIVES YOU HER BEST REGARDS.SWEETHEART, SHALL WE HAVE LUNCH OUT TODAY? DON'T FEEL LIKE COOKING.COFFEE?"

"YES DEAR, THAT'S FINE," he said, as she went into the kitchen.

'Shall I?' he thought. "No no," he muttered now. It worked, the belt worked! He was ecstatic; he would be able to go back in time whenever he wanted to! The door opened, Jane smiled as she put the coffee on the table. "Poor Mrs. Bernard, I felt so sorry for her, she misses her husband so much. I don't know if I could be as brave as her if you were in hospital or away somewhere, I would go crazy."

"I'm not going anywhere my love, well not without you, I can assure you of that. Who would make me my coffee?"

She shook her head. "You'll never change, and I wouldn't want you to."

"You seem to be happy with our life, have you really enjoyed our life together?"

"Absolutely, every minute of it," she said determinedly.

"So you would do it all again would you?" He looked at her, anticipating her reply.

"Yes I would, if I could go back in time, I would do it all again. To be young again, to have no aches and pains as I have now, it would be wonderful. But that's impossible, so I suppose we have to make do with what we have and be grateful." She sipped her coffee.

"Would you want to go back in time, as you are now?"

"What, at eighty two years old, no way, no. If I got younger I would give it a try, but not at my age."

"Even if you lived forever, never die?"

"Live forever like this, Nigel you are now joking? If I can have another five good years with you, it will be a blessing, so no more nonsense. How did we get into this subject anyhow?"

"I don't know, just talking."

"Let's get ready darling, put on that new blue shirt I bought for you fifty five years ago, it knocks years off you, you'll be my young man again. There's another surprise for you, but wait until we go out. It's about time you went out darling, it's been a year since you went anywhere. The world's changing around you, and you're missing it. Remember our saying Double Fast eh? Double Fast?"

"Yes, Double Fast," he smiled, remembering where the saying came from.

As his wife was getting ready, he went into the garden and lit the bonfire at the bottom of the garden. Then he went in and had a wash, shaved, and put on his red shirt, he did feel young again.

"Very smart," she complimented.

"Better than the old blue one, there's a button missing," he responded. "It's going to be another good day, I can sense it." She laughed.

She drove towards the countryside, the day was warm and sunny, the fields green, and the flowers on the hedgerow seemed to dance as the car made its way towards Eastern Hill. Past the gates, now re-enforced with barbed wire, with big notice boards saying GOVERNMENT PROPERTY, DANGER KEEP OUT. TEN YEARS IMPRISONMENT FOR TRESPASSING ON THIS LAND, said another.

"Government's hiding something," Jane remarked. "That's a positive statement dear," Nigel agreed.

They drove down the lane that he had walked many times, then as they descended the hill; there it was, standing in all its new glory. Nigel was shocked, his jaw dropped.

"That's your surprise darling; I didn't say anything to you because I forgot more times than I like to admit. I intended to, but then I thought that it would make for a big surprise for you. It's opening today in five minutes, and you are to be the first customer in the door."

The car pulled into the car park, and people gathered around, greeting him and his wife.

"Extended birthday party love."

Nigel's happiness showed as he shook hands with friends he once knew.

A distinguished looking man took the microphone. "Ladies and gentlemen, thanks for coming to the grand opening today, and my family are more than happy to welcome Mr. Nigel Maythorn who I understand will be our first customer in this new establishment. So now without further ado, I would like Mr. Maythorn to cut the tape and with this key, open the door to the new Fox and Hounds public house and restaurant."

Everyone applauded as Nigel cut the tape and opened the door. He stood in the doorway and shouted to the crowd milling towards the door, "You're all barred."

Everyone broke up with laughter as they entered. Nigel was served first with the first pint of bitter.

Two pints later Jane and Nigel were sitting at the restaurant table, eating fillet steak, and drinking good wine. People passed the table and spoke to him, people he no longer remembered, but very friendly. The party was in full swing when an older man requested that he sang, like he had years ago.

Nigel obliged. "What song do you want?"

"Oh anything by Lance Summers, remember years ago you did a show of that man's songs in the old pub? I was there that night, never forgot it," the old man enthused.

Nigel sang four songs, and there were cheers all around. Back at the table Jane was radiating with happiness. "You know darling, that sounded just like Elvis, it was great."

"You going to sign me? You're an agent, aren't you?" They laughed again.

At last Nigel said, "Strange, but I have this funny feeling, it seems to have come over me just this afternoon."

"It's the drink darling," she said.

"No, it's not the drink; it's something new, something different. It's here in the back of my head, I feel free, as though a weight has been lifted off my shoulders, strange feeling, but nice."

He took a sip of wine. The afternoon was wearing thin as the sun decided to go to bed early.

The man who had been on the microphone approached the table. "Sir," he started, "my wife," he indicated to a good looking woman, "I would like to introduce you to my wife, Freda." Nigel gulped.

"Nice to meet you, I'm Freda Small."

"Nice to meet you," Nigel said, standing up and taking her hand.

"I'm the grandson of Brian Small who once ran the old place. But I guess you know that. You, I understand, worked for the family for years as Bar Manager?"

"Yes, I did, many years, wonderful man your grandfather, we were good friends. I was very sorry when he died. How's your father?"

"He's fine, but as you may know that he didn't want to carry on with the business, but I do, so here we are, a new era." He opened his arms towards the bar and restaurant. "Because of your service to the family, the drinks and food are on the house, and we have reserved the Master Suite for tonight, free for you and your good wife, with my compliments. It's available now at your convenience, if you wish to have a sleep this afternoon. The party continues tonight from seven p.m. all free."

Nigel shook the man's hand. "Thanks very much for your kindness, how wonderful."

"You're welcome," he said.

"By the way, what's your first name? It wouldn't be…"

"Brian, my name's Brian, just like my father, grandfather and great grandfather, all the way back in time. Even my long ago great great great grandmother, who ran the old pub back in the nineteen hundreds, or something like that, was called the same name as my wife, Freda."

"I know, I have a picture of her at home in my montage."

"I know, my father told me that you have her photo, and that you took an interest in our family and the business. You are almost part of the family yourself, you will always be welcome here, and drink on the house, for memory's sake."

Freda smiled throughout, saying very little, only that she was about to start a new life as a barmaid, and was hoping that Nigel would pop in from time to time for a drink and a chat. "You'll be very welcome," she said, meaning it.

Nigel couldn't help it, he hugged her, and planted a kiss on her cheek. "Thank you so much, Freda."

"Brian," someone unknown shouted, "you're wanted on the phone."

"Here we go, the business has started," Brian said, "see you later."

"Yes, thanks again," Nigel said as he sat down, to see his wife's smiling face.

"Would you believe it, I didn't know I was so popular!"

"You are my darling, you're a very special man, you really are."

"I bet you say that to all the boys," he said, as they drank their wine and laughed.

The room was fantastic, en-suite, power shower, king size bed, tea and coffee facilities, forty inch TV on the wall. Pictures of the old Fox and Hounds, through the ages, with photos of every person who owned the premises, every Brian, plus the wives.

Nigel lay on the bed, but after an hour, realised that sleep was not needed, he was too excited. So after a shower, they went down the stairs to the evening party. It was the same as it had been in the afternoon, people shaking hands, kissing. Some of the people who had been at his birthday the day before were there, including Zane and his wife. James and Jarvis offered him a drink, but Nigel declined, saying his drinks were free.

"You were the best teacher who ever taught me," Jarvis said. James agreed, Nigel thanked them.

He danced with Jane, first time in years.

"You seem to be very happy Dad; Mum told me that you have both had a wonderful time."

"I have Zane, one of the best days ever. Life in this world isn't that bad," he whispered. "l wonder if Simon and Janice are having a day like this one?"

"Most probably, it's much the same there."

"I did something today, and one day I'll tell you what I did."

"Father, I know what you did, promise me you'll never do it again!"

"Oh, you know then."

"Yes, it's my job to know. Please don't do it again, it's too dangerous, please," Zane talked with grave concern in his voice.

"I promise you my son, that I will never do it again, I promise on your mother's life."

"And I believe you Dad; I know you wouldn't say that if you didn't mean it, so it's over forever?"

"Yes, it's over forever. Now, let's have a drink on it."

He heard it for the first time in the new pub, "TIME GENTLEMEN AND LADIES PLEASE." Goodnights were said, and Nigel and Jane went up the back stairs to the suite. They lay in bed.

"It's been a brilliant day," she said.

"Wonderful, it was a wonderful surprise, I had no idea that they had built this new pub."

"It was hard to keep it from you, I told Zane not to say a word. But I know it was hard for him, because you two are so close. I'm so glad you didn't find out, it was a pleasure to see your face light up as it did. By the way, I forgot to ask you what you were doing in the garden before we left home?"

"Before we left home?"

"Yes, before we left, you were in the garden."

"Oh yes, I was burning a few old clothes that I've had for years, and a time belt."

"A time belt, what's that?" she exclaimed.

"I mean a belt I've had for a long time; it had had its use, so I burned it."

"Oh well, you know what you're doing, as long as you don't miss it, it's too late now it's burned."

"I won't miss it, it had its use, it served me well, but that time has gone for good. No good dwelling on the past, as you've told me many times."

"No darling, you're right, goodnight now."

"Goodnight, I love you," he whispered, "I'll see you in my dreams."

Back at Moreland Road, the owl had noticed the time crystal that lay in the remnants of a bonfire. The bright moon made it glisten like a precious piece of jewellery waiting to be found. The owl swooped like a landing plane, and with the crystal firmly in its claws, disappeared into the dark forest and into another world.

THE END